Pembroke Prep

Becker Gray

Table of Contents

WICKED IDOL

BECKER GRAY

CHAPTER ONE

Iris

T HE VERY FIRST thing I did as a student at Pembroke Preparatory Academy was piss off the Hellfire Club.

It had been an accident—the kind of accident that was entirely preventable, but an accident, nonetheless. I was checking my bag as I walked through the stone-paved courtyard to make sure I'd packed my camera, and then I stumbled right into a bleary-eyed teacher. Not wanting to make any extra enemies among the staff—my father was the new headmaster and had already threatened all the teachers with salary freezes along with promising to gut the athletic department—I staggered sideways and stammered out an apology.

And slammed right into the back of Keaton Constantine, sending his whipped dalgona coffee flying all over the tailored school blazers and silk school ties of his friends.

Not that I knew then that he was *the* Keaton Constantine, rugby captain, king of the school, and scion of one of the most powerful families in New York.

All I knew was that when he wheeled around, he had the fullest, firmest lips and bluest eyes I'd ever seen.

"God, I'm so sorry—" I blurted out, but he cut me off.

"Who the fuck are you?" His eyes raked over me like hot sapphires, taking in my scuffed, secondhand Mary Janes and my brand-new Pembroke uniform.

Which is when I knew I was toast. His derision was obvious in his cruel smirk.

I'd followed the regulations in the student handbook exactly and kept the pleated gray skirt at knee length and wore the sweater embroidered with the Pembroke crest over my white button-up shirt. My red hair was in two simple braids, and I hadn't worn any makeup. I didn't want to draw any attention to myself by flouting the school rules—not to mention my father would've had a fit if his daughter wasn't the paragon of student handbook adherence.

Turns out that I was drawing *more* attention to myself by wearing the uniform perfectly. The other girls had their skirts hemmed up high, fluttering well above their knees, and their shirts untucked and rumpled. Some were clearly in their boyfriend's sweater or blazer, others had skipped it all together, and all of them had artfully messy hair and influencer-level makeup.

The boys were just as bad. Untucked shirts, loosened ties, tousled hair. Some were smoking, others had girls parked on their laps.

And the boys I'd just inadvertently splattered coffee all over were the most insolently rakish of them all.

No, all I'd done with my immaculate and prudish uniform was prove how insignificant I was going to be in the Pembroke Prep social ecosystem. I'd also unofficially stamped myself as little miss uptight with my regulation-to-a-T uniform.

"I said," repeated the boy I'd run into, "*who are you?*" He took a step towards me, dark blond hair tumbling over his forehead. His skin was lightly kissed by the sun, like he'd spent the summer in the Hamptons.

"Um," I said, and then wanted to kick myself. All I wanted was to get through this year alive and get away from my parents. And in order to do that, I needed to survive everything Pembroke Prep would throw at me, including angry boys. "Iris Briggs."

"Briggs," repeated the boy. His eyebrows lifted, highlighting those deep blue eyes. "Like the new Headmaster Briggs? The same new headmaster who is talking about decreasing funding to the athletic department?"

His friends, who'd been busy scowling and disgustedly trying to swipe the coffee off their uniforms, now watched with undisguised interest.

"Perhaps she could send a message to her father for you, Keaton," someone behind him said. I looked past Keaton to see a pale, beautiful boy with glittering onyx eyes and a cruel mouth.

Danger, my mind warned. *That one is dangerous.*

Not that Keaton *wasn't* dangerous—a fact that became clearer as he took another step towards me. He worked his square jaw ever so slightly to the side, and his eyebrows were slashes of irritation over those hypnotic eyes.

And he was big—*jock* big. Tall and broad-shouldered, with muscles that tested the fitted seams of his blazer.

"Listen here, Iris Briggs," he said in a voice full of soft menace. "I'm not going to forget the coffee. And I'm not going to forget what your father is doing. And I'm not going to forget *you*."

He was so close now that he could lean down and kiss me if he wanted. Close enough that I could see the faint crease in his full lower lip.

Stop it. You don't need this kind of trouble.

Shivers raced down my spine, and chills crawled up my

neck—even as indignation fired my blood—and something went tight. Low, low in my belly.

I parted my lips—I didn't know what I was going to say, but it was probably going to be something along the lines of *fuck off, dude, it was an accident*—and his eyes dropped down to my mouth. For a minute—an instant—I could swear I saw hunger flash in his stare.

But what he was hungry for? I never found out, because a girl's voice cut into the moment and brought me back to reality.

"Don't worry, sweetheart. He's going to forget you. I'll make sure of it."

I turned around to see a slender girl with dark brown skin, a thick mass of gorgeous curls and big, arty glasses perched on her nose striding towards us. She planted her feet and folded her arms when she got to Keaton. "Fuck off," she told him. "Feeding time is over."

"Yeah, well just so you know, because of her, coffee time is over," one of the other boys said dryly, still mopping at his tie.

"I'm sorry," I said, trying not to sound irritated. But really, it wasn't like I did it on purpose. "I ran into someone else, and I—"

The girl held up a hand to stop me. "Never concede anything to these jackasses. It won't get you anywhere but under their feet."

"You never know until you try, Serafina," the onyx-eyed boy said in a silky voice.

Serafina slid her gaze to him, her eyes narrowing. "How about you try this, Rhys?" And she flipped him off as she looped her free arm through mine and marched me away from the boys.

When I dared to look back, Rhys and the others had

clustered back into a circle, muttering to each other and trying to fix their uniforms. But Keaton still stood in the middle of the courtyard, his long fingers curled around his now-empty coffee cup and his furious gaze trained right on me.

✧   ✧   ✧

A FEW MINUTES later, we were up the shallow steps and into the main heart of Pembroke, walking into the dim, wood-paneled hallway and stopping by a large window. Through it, I could make out the rolling lawn and the thick Vermont woods clustered around the brick and stone buildings that made up the boarding school. This early in September, everything was still green and sunny and warm, and students were stretched out on the lawn, making out or reading before class.

"I'm Serafina van Doren, by the way," the girl said, by way of introduction. "And you must be Iris Briggs."

"How did you—"

"Rumors have been flying about you," she said, anticipating my question. "We don't get many new students here at Pembroke. Most of us have known each other for years, grown up together and all that. It gets very stale and incestuous, so it's exciting to see a new face."

I could think of five people who weren't excited to meet me. "Who were they?" I asked, pointing my head back towards the courtyard.

"Oh, them?" She twisted her mouth. "They call themselves the Hellfire Club."

The Hellfire Club.

"That's very poetic," I commented.

"It's very ridiculous," Serafina said, rolling her eyes.

"But I'd still steer clear of them for a while. They're . . . influential." She said it in the voice of someone reluctantly admitting an indisputable truth.

"Are they dangerous?"

Serafina lifted a shoulder. "Yeah. But just avoid them and you'll be okay. They're like male lions—too lazy to chase anything unless it's threatening their territory."

I thought of Keaton's eyes—sharp and hungry in the morning sunlight. Did he think my father was invading his territory? Or worse, that *I* was?

I looked over my shoulder, suddenly terrified I'd find him at the end of the corridor, watching me.

Serafina sensed my uneasiness and touched my shoulder. "Hey, I promise they won't hurt you, okay? I won't let them. They're mostly harmless. Well, except for Lennox Lincoln-Ward, the boy with the white hair; his only goal in life is to torture Sloane."

"Sloane?"

"My roommate. She's very quiet, a little scary, but she keeps to herself mostly. I don't know why Lennox hates her so much—well, other than that he's an asshole."

I think of the boy behind Keaton, the one with the glittering eyes and sharp mouth. "What about the one you called Rhys?"

Serafina frowned. "Okay, maybe I lied about them being harmless. If the Hellfire Club were all lions, Rhys would be the lion who kills for fun. He would be Uncle Scar. Be careful around him."

"And Keaton? Should I be careful around him too?"

Serafina hesitated, then shook her head. "No. Like I said, just avoid him and he'll forget about you. Constantines are like that."

"Constantines?"

Serafina tilted her head. "You really are new, aren't you? The Constantine family is like the Kennedys—if the Kennedys made their money doing shady shit. Oh and owned half of New York City."

"Half?"

"I mean, I'm including the legal holdings as well as the less-than-legal holdings here."

Alarm spiked. "Um, are they like a *crime* family?"

"Only in the technical sense," Serafina said, waving a hand, like I was getting hung up on some insignificant detail. "They're very respectable otherwise. One of those Mayflower families, you know, like all the women wear real pearls, every summer is spent in Bishop's Landing, they go golfing in Kiawah, that kind of thing."

A *respectable* crime family? That didn't seem like a thing to me. "I'm less worried about their respectability than I am Keaton having me whacked or something."

Serafina burst into giggles. "Whacked?"

"Whacked! Offed! Rolled into a tarp and then fed to the local deer or whatever!"

She was still laughing. "I promise the Constantines don't feed people to deer. And don't worry about Keaton. He really will forget all about this morning; he's usually too busy with his girlfriend and rugby to worry about anything else. And anyway, you're with me now."

"I am?"

"You are," she confirmed, beaming at me. "I'm the queen around here. And Sloane is my lady knight. We'll make sure none of those Hellfire morons bother you."

Relief and gratitude eased something in my chest. "Thank you," I said.

"What class do you have first? I'll walk you there."

I pulled out my schedule. "AP Physics."

"Excellent! Sloane does too." We started walking down the hall towards the south wing of the school, where all the science labs and lecture rooms were. For the first time since my father took this post, I started to feel a little hopeful that this year might not be so terrible after all, even if I had inadvertently angered the son of a *respectable* crime family.

"So, what's it like being the headmaster's daughter?" Serafina asked.

As we walked to the physics lab, other students called out to her or playfully tugged on her blazer or reached out for high fives. She strode through it all like a monarch striding through a throng of courtiers, and I knew she hadn't been joking about being the queen.

I was even more grateful she'd decided to befriend me. If anyone could keep me safe from Keaton's furious stare, it would be her.

"It's mostly terrible," I said. "This is the third school of his I've gone to, and he always wants me to be the best at everything. I used to think he'd go easier on me once I turned eighteen and my perfect older sister moved out, but no. Not to mention he's not really down with my photography obsession."

I didn't elaborate any more than that. I was still upset about my birthday this summer, when I'd announced to him that I wanted to study photography in Paris and not law at an Ivy like he wanted me to. He'd wanted me to be more like Isabelle—the obedient one, the one who did everything right, including getting impeccable grades at LSE.

He'd yelled; I'd yelled back.

My mother had hidden, like she always did whenever there was conflict.

"Photography?" Serafina asked. "That's pretty fucking cool. Are you taking a class on it this year?"

Excitement—real excitement—fizzed in my veins and made me smile. "Yeah. Advanced photography seminar. First class is on Friday."

She smiled back as we got to my classroom. "I've got another lady knight in there. Aurora. She'll make sure you're taken care of."

"You really are the queen here."

"I'm a van Doren," she said, like that explained everything. "Ah, Sloane! Save a seat for Iris, would you?"

I looked across the room to see an unsmiling white girl with a very short, no-nonsense ponytail and a helix piercing high on one ear. When I came up to the table and held out my hand, she shook it without a word. But her green eyes were quick and keen as she took in everything about me, and her handshake was strong and efficient. She seemed like the kind of person who knew where every exit in the room was, along with everything that could be turned into a weapon.

"Sloane, this is Iris. We're adopting her. Also, make sure Keaton leaves her alone."

Sloane nodded and silently gestured for me to take a seat.

Serafina left with a wave and a promise to see me at lunch, and then the physics professor burst into the room, breathless and late, and just like that, my first day at Pembroke Prep had officially started.

Now, it was time to forget about Keaton Constantine. I was going to lay low and survive until Paris, when my life could truly begin, and I didn't have time to worry about spilled coffee or the rugby-playing sons of well-mannered criminals.

And I definitely didn't have the time to think about his full lips and tousled blond hair. Or his wide, powerful shoulders. Or his midnight-blue eyes.

No time at all.

I flipped open a fresh notebook, took a deep breath, and began taking notes.

Chapter Two

Keaton

BLOODY BACK-TO-SCHOOL NIGHT.

I knew for a fact the storied tradition was designed for the purpose of torturing students. The only people who looked forward to the weekend were parents who loved to come back to Pembroke Prep. Show off their money, their influence, all the while leaving behind their precious cargo for someone else to raise, someone else to teach.

Well, most parents anyway. My mother was wholly devoted to her fulltime job of being the matriarch of the Constantine family—which mostly involved hosting lavish parties, keeping my sister Elaine out of the press, and making sure my oldest brother Winston continued raking in money for the family through our various business holdings. She wasn't cold, but she wasn't warm either, and it didn't matter how many rugby games I played or how many championships I won, she was more concerned with my future than my present.

And my dad?

Dead.

Murdered five years ago, killed by the fucking Morellis—not that we could ever prove it.

13

He would have been here tonight, I thought bitterly. He never missed anything. He was a busy man, certainly, and not always an easy man to love, but he did love us, and we fucking loved him.

And now he was gone, and sometimes it felt like all my mother wanted was for us to forget our own lives and jump right into forwarding his legacy.

But not that you care.

Not that I expected Mom to show up today anyway. After all, I wasn't perfect, successful Winston, or forever-a-mess Elaine. And I wasn't Tinsley, the baby of the family, who'd decided to go to school closer to home in Bishop's Landing. I made a mental note to myself to check in on her later and make sure she was staying well away from trouble.

So, no Mom and gotta babysit Tinsley. Awesome start to the year.

Even *Rhys's* parents were here. And given that Rhys was the devil himself, I was pretty certain he had nothing but disdain for them. It wasn't a stretch; Rhys disdained everyone. If you weren't Hellfire, you were on his shit list. Top of that shit list was Serafina van Doren.

New girl's new best friend.

Stop calling her new girl. You know her name. After all you've been low-key stalking her for the past week and a half.

So sue me if I'd made it a point to know everything there was to know about Little Miss Perfect with the perfect parents. I made it my business to know. After all, I was in line to be valedictorian. If she was a threat, I needed to know that.

Also, I was a Constantine. I might not be my tightly wound oldest brother, but control was still in my blood. She was an unknown quantity and I needed to quantify her, that was all.

Oh sure, those are the only reasons.

My phone buzzed, and I scowled down at it as I headed towards the British literature stacks in the back. Clara . . . again.

Clara: *Where are you?*

Clara: *Can you run interference?*

Clara: *You okay?*

I tried not to be annoyed about my wellbeing being last. After all, Clara was Clara. And she had her own cross to bear. If Caroline Constantine's parenting motto was *rub some dirt on it*, the Blairs' motto was *Mommy and Daddy know best*. Which was why Clara pretended to date me, a Constantine, when she was really going out with a local boy and had been for the past two years. I told her that if the townie knocked her up, she was on her own though. Not because I didn't care about Clara—she was one of my oldest friends—but because Caroline Constantine would kill us both . . . after the baby was born and she'd already whisked it off to Bishop's Landing to play with bespoke silver rattles while wearing the same booties as the royal babies did or whatever.

I slid my phone back into my pocket without answering.

I couldn't be bothered with Clara or her helicopter parents right now. The last thing I wanted to do was have to explain why my mother couldn't be bothered to visit while I mustered up dry cheek-kisses and hugs to keep up the ruse that Clara and I were truly together.

The library, on the other hand, was safe. It was the first stop on back-to-school night. The headmaster always gave his address here, and Headmaster Briggs had already finished his pointless speech and then whisked the parents off to see the new swimming pool, which left my Pembroke sanctuary completely to me. Which meant I could lose myself in Keats and Longfellow as I waited for the wealthy and elite and the sycophantic to give me my campus back.

Amongst the stacks and stacks of books and the nooks and crannies, I'd learned to find solace. A little peace and quiet where no one would look for me. Sometimes, it was like they all thought I was a jock only and forgot that I was smart. And actually liked to read.

As I strolled along the smooth stone tile at the library, surrounded by the dark wood and stacks of books at the reference section, I inhaled it all. That smell of vellum and leather. It always brought a smile to my face.

Books helped me get out of my own head when my family was being waspish dicks, which was pretty much every damn day. Luckily, aside from Tinsley, I didn't have to deal with them today.

I passed one of the stacks and paused, then took a quick sniff. *What was that smell?*

It smelled like something floral. Something sweet. It smelled like *her*.

The new girl.

Fucking Iris Briggs.

I'd gotten close enough to her that first day to catch a hint of roses and vanilla in the air. It wasn't overwhelming like some girls who liked to drown themselves in the latest Dior or Lady Gaga, or God help them, eau de RiRi.

No. This was some simple essential oil type of shit. Just enough to linger and tease. Not enough to overpower. But she wasn't here.

As a matter of fact, I'd barely seen her since that first day. It was almost like she was taking all routes to purposely avoid me.

Why do you care? You have Clara.

Yes, I did have Clara. At least, that's what everyone believed. We were the golden couple, the ones people wanted to be like. I wondered how people would really feel if they found out just how fucked up Clara and I both were.

Well, they're never going to figure that out.

When I turned towards the fiction stacks, I froze. There, perched on one of the rolling ladders, was the source of the rose and vanilla. The source of my fucking sleepless nights for the past week. "What the fuck are you doing here?"

Her head snapped up and she gasped. "Jesus, you scared the shit out of me."

Why was she looking at me like that? All fresh faced with her sky-blue eyes and her dusting of freckles on display and looking so clean and fresh and fucking pure. I wanted to make her dirty.

What the fuck is wrong with you?

"I repeat. What the hell are you doing here?"

She narrowed her eyes. "It's a free country," she said slowly, as if she was trying to control her temper. "I'm reading. What are *you* doing in here?"

I scowled. Maybe no one had told her how things worked here. I asked the questions. New girl provided the answers. That's how it was supposed to go.

"Don't you know it's back-to-school night?"

The narrowed eyes turned into a full-fledged scowl. She lifted a brow. "You might remember my father is the headmaster? I don't need to be there for back-to-school night."

"Well, then, does your father know you're here?"

There, in her eyes, that quick shift of her gaze, and then the slamming shut of the book. "Look, this library is enormous. We can both find corners and avoid each other, right?"

"Oh no, if you look, the library is really only big enough for one of us."

"Well, I'm not leaving. So you can either get used to that idea or find somewhere else to hide."

"Who said I was hiding?" Why did she see so damn much?

"Come on, everyone else is with their parents, having fun, taking a break from classes, introducing their friends, introducing their teachers. You're skulking around the library with me. You already know I'm avoiding my parents. Why are *you* avoiding yours?"

I studied her. She wasn't beautiful. Not in the ordinary sense of the word. But she was striking, completely engaging. From her bright red hair to those blue eyes. The dusting of freckles on her nose. Her straight, even, white teeth to that complete doll bow of a mouth. A bottom lip plump enough to make me want to bite it.

"You know those pigtail things make you look like you're twelve."

She frowned at that. "That the best you got? I asked you a question."

I shrugged. "You're in my hiding spot. I'm not really one for the whole parental love fest." Also . . . neither was my mother.

"I didn't see your name on it. It's a library. Everyone is welcome to come and read books."

What was it about her that irritated me so much? I didn't like that she was in my space. I didn't like that she'd taken my sanctuary. I didn't like that she so casually stood here, wrecking the only peace and quiet I knew I was going to find today.

I didn't like *her*, period. "You have ten minutes to find

your book and get out."

She hopped down from the ladder, placing one of the books on the ground on her neat little stack of other books. "Oh, I think I'll stay."

"I think you didn't hear me."

She tilted her chin up. "Oh, I heard you. I just don't care. I've looked and looked, but I can't seem to find a fuck to give about your opinion."

I don't know what possessed me, but I boxed her in, causing her to back up against the books. "You are a mouthy little thing, aren't you?" I reached out a finger and toyed with a stray tendril of hair. "What I'm curious about is what would make the headmaster's daughter hide."

"I don't think you'd get it if I told you. Besides, you don't get something for nothing. I tell you, you tell me."

"That's not how this works."

"Oh my god, you're so full of yourself."

"Tell me something I don't know." Somehow, fighting with this girl made my skin tingle. I could feel it reverberating from my toes to the top of my head. She was irritating. A complete klutz. Mouthy. I didn't like that at all.

My dick was eager as ever to disagree with me. He and I were currently not on speaking terms as every time I thought about Iris, he got hard. Like a moron. "I don't think I like you very much."

She tilted her chin and smiled up at me, completely unafraid. Her gaze locked on mine, too direct, seeing more than I wanted her to. I planted both hands on either side of her head. "Tell me why you're hiding in here."

"Like I said, *you first.*"

Her tongue peeked out to lick her bottom lip, and I bit back a groan.

What the fuck was that?

I wanted to go and slide up to that flame that sparked around her, like a clueless moth, flapping to my death. And when she licked her lips again, I forgot all about why I shouldn't do this or how stupid it would be if I did.

Nope. Instead, I just leaned in and kissed her.

She tasted like strawberries. Sweet, with a little chaser of sharp tang. When she parted her lips in a gasp, I deepened the kiss. Licking into her mouth. Desperate to taste what I could before this all ended.

But still, a part of me waited. I waited for her to push me away. I waited for her to tell me to stop. *I* waited for that signal.

I *wanted* that signal. I wanted her to set that line I would not cross. But, instead, she let me kiss her.

Even better, or worse, depending on how you looked at it, she kissed me back.

I angled my head with a groan, dipping my knees slightly so I could capture her mouth better. She was so small in comparison to me.

My tongue stroked over hers, darting and playing and sliding. She further tortured me by making this meowing sound at the back of her throat. Did she know that it made me want to take up residence right fucking here and never leave?

The sound was part whimper, part moan, and all mine. It was the kind of kiss that was full of promise. Still, warning bells rang in the back of my mind because I should not be kissing this girl. I did not have time for this shit.

Hell, I didn't even *like* this girl.

Uh-huh, keep telling yourself that.

Despite myself telling my brain not to give in to the command, my hands slid to her face, and then in her hair. I fought with the braids until they started to unravel. With the silken weight of her hair flooding over my fingers, I cupped her cheeks and a whimper broke. The clash of our tongues sent a shiver with a lava chaser through my veins. I wanted to consume her. I could kiss her forever.

Before I knew what I was doing, she mewled again and arched her back, bringing her hips slightly forward, seeking . . .

I would like to be able to say that this kiss was nothing, that I didn't care, that she was only mildly fuckable, and I was bored with no one better to do. But that little motion told me that she wanted *me . . . me,* not anyone else, *me.*

It meant I could no longer walk away. I could no longer trust my thoughts and actions, because I slid my hands further into her tresses, tightening my grip, and I shook the leashes of control off, kissing her for everything I was worth, making the kiss count for everything with a girl I didn't like.

She was just someone I needed in this moment. Just call her a chaser of bad dreams, because with my lips on hers, I didn't think about the loneliness. I didn't take into account how isolated I felt most of the day. It didn't occur to me to feel unwanted, unloved, because in this moment, this girl who I barely knew, was letting me kiss her and she was kissing me back.

When she rolled her hips again, a growl broke the hushed moans.

Was that me?

It must have been, because I pressed her body into the stacks, my hands sliding down to her waist, then her ass. I picked her up, bracing her against the shelves. Squeezing her ass and holding her the way that I needed so her heat gyrated against my dick.

Fuck. Me.

I felt like the top of my head was going to blow off. Like I'd voluntarily tied myself up with a live wire and I couldn't fucking stop.

What was I doing? I had to think about Clara. This would be bad for the two of us if someone fucking saw.

But Iris wasn't Clara. And something about that made this far hotter.

A loud bang downstairs startled us apart, just enough that she tore her now-plump and bruised lips from mine, but we still shared breath. The startle wasn't enough for me to let her go though. I still held the firm cheeks of her ass in my palms, and I couldn't help another squeeze.

She wasn't like the other girls wearing thongs and skirts so short a brisk wind would tell me who had a carpet or hardwood floors. It was hotter somehow that my hands were on her ass and I was the only one who knew she was rocking bikinis. My blood ran with lava at the idea that her pussy maintenance practices were somehow still a mystery. I loved being the only one even close to knowing.

Her gaze leveled on me as she dragged in sharp pants. This close I could see just how thick and dark her lashes were. Not from any assistance of monthly trips to the esthetician, but because those were simply her lashes.

Iris was purity personified, and I wanted to be the asshole who made her dirty.

Her lips parted like she wanted to say something, but her eyes were glassy, unfocused. Likely a mirror of my own.

That line I'd been waiting for her to draw, she drew it then with a gentle push at my chest, and I eased her down, but not before rocking her once more against my steel-hard dick.

She needed to know what she'd done to me. She needed to own some of that responsibility. When her feet touched the ground, I pushed away from the devil's own temptation and stalked from the library as quickly as my legs would carry me.

CHAPTER THREE

Iris

A WEEK LATER, and I could still feel Keaton Constantine's lips against my own.

His kiss had been hungry. *Angry.* Like he was furious with me for being kissable. Maybe even for being alive.

And his hands—his hands had been everywhere. Taking apart my two braids and sifting through my hair.

Big and rough on my bottom as he lifted me up and rubbed me against him.

And that thing I'd rubbed against . . .

Being the headmaster's daughter meant that I'd missed out on a lot of the usual boarding school experiences. No fooling around after hours, no parties where I could've gotten hot and heavy with a boy. No fumbling sex in a dorm room.

But even I knew what Keaton had been pressing against me in the library. Even I knew that it would be as big and unapologetically male as the rest of him.

Keaton Constantine had been hard for *me*, the headmaster's daughter. He'd wanted more than kissing, and I think I would have given it to him. Anything he wanted, because in that moment, the entire world had shrunk to only us, and there were only lips and tongues and that maddening flicker of heat between my legs. Like someone had lit a sparkler low in my belly.

And then he'd left.

I'd pushed him away to catch my breath, and he'd turned and left me there without another word.

What the *fuck*?

"Earth to Iris," a concerned British voice said, breaking through my thoughts.

I turned to see Aurora Lincoln-Ward staring at me, a delicate eyebrow arched over an unnerving gold-colored eye.

She was Lennox's twin sister, and they were alike in several ways: an accent as a gift from their British father, pale, unearthly features, and an inborn arrogance from having a mother who was a minor Liechtensteiner princess—which made them royalty, too.

Like Lennox, she had bright gold eyes. Like a bird of prey. Or a lioness. Eyes she set off to her advantage by dying her white-blond hair a shade of inky, midnight black.

But unlike her twin, Aurora adored Sloane.

Luckily for me, she was also unlike Lennox in that she hated the Hellfire Club and every single boy in it. So when she'd learned that I'd accidentally pissed them off on my first day, Aurora had sworn me her friendship and protection, just as Sloane and Serafina had.

It was a good feeling. I'd never really had close friends before, not from school at least, and I needed them now more than ever.

I cleared my throat and shifted in my seat, feeling a little squirmy from the memory of Keaton's kiss. "Yeah?"

"I was asking you what this was all about," Aurora said, tugging at a letter sticking out of my notebook. She kept her voice down because our photography seminar had technically started, but the teacher was still at the front fiddling with her laptop and trying to get today's presentation on the screen. "Why is it written in French?"

My face heated—half excitement, half nervousness. "I applied to the Sorbonne for college, and even though I'm still waiting for a formal acceptance letter, they invited me to apply for a pre-degree program there. It starts in November and goes until July, and I'd get to work with the professors and professional photographers in Paris . . . It would mean getting a head start on the other students. Maybe even on my career."

"Sounds amazing," Aurora remarked. "Except that you'll be here at Pembroke that entire time."

"I could graduate right now if I wanted," I said, a little wistfully. "I've got the credits. But . . ."

"But?"

I sighed. "My father doesn't want me to go to Paris or study photography. He wants me to go to Harvard or somewhere like that. Go into law."

Aurora wrinkled her nose. "Good god. Why?"

I gave a cynical laugh. "Because it would be excellent for his career. If he can run a school well enough that one of his kids is an Ivy-educated lawyer on her way to the Supreme Court? If he can show off that *both* his disciplined, grounded daughters are working hard at Very Serious and Important majors? Then what school board wouldn't consider hiring him?"

"The Sorbonne is hardly an unaccredited community college," Aurora pointed out. "It's the oldest university in Europe."

"Oh, I know. But if I'm in Paris, then he can't control my life like he did my sister's, and he hates that. And photography is a joke to him."

"But—"

I didn't find out what Aurora was about to say, because at just that moment, the door to the classroom opened and Keaton Constantine insolently strolled in with his leather bag slung across his chest and his typical arrogant smirk tilting his lips.

He didn't see me at first, which meant I had time to observe how a thick lock of hair had dropped out of its classic, all-American style to drift over his forehead. I had time to see how his tailored school blazer showed off his firm chest and broad shoulders.

I had time to remember how those big hands—which were currently handing Ms. Sanderson a note—felt as they moved through my hair and as they curled around my hips.

My entire body felt like it was on fire.

He gave the classroom a bored once-over as Ms. Sanderson read the note. When his eyes lit on me, his entire body went rigid.

His blue eyes were turbulent—*incensed*—as he narrowed them at me, as if I'd somehow known he would be in this classroom today and had manipulated my entire schedule in order to be here just to annoy him.

"What. A. Bastard," Aurora muttered under her breath, catching his glare at me.

I agreed, and I wasn't having it. Not today. Not after he dropped me in the library and left me like so much forgettable trash.

I glared right back at him.

"Well, welcome to the class, Mr. Constantine," Ms. Sanderson said. "Luckily for you, last week was only an orientation, and so you haven't missed much. Take a seat anywhere, and if I can have you all put down your phones now—yes, thank you—I've got this presentation fired up now, and we can get started."

Ms. Sanderson started talking about representational interpretations versus abstraction as Keaton strode to the back of the classroom, giving me a final glower as he passed my desk.

I was about to breathe a sigh of relief when he dropped into the empty desk right behind mine and propped his shoes against the legs of my chair.

I turned while Ms. Sanderson kept lecturing, keeping my voice in a low hiss. "You know, there're other empty desks if you're so opposed to being near me."

"I'm fine right here," he said softly. Defiantly. His eyes glittered as he spoke.

I turned back around, livid. And a little bit hurt.

We didn't see each other for a week after that kiss, and *this* was how he acted when he saw me again?

Fine.

I guess I knew where things stood then.

"The partnered semester project will involve an interpretation of landscapes," Ms. Sanderson was saying at the front of the room.

I heard a faint, collective murmur of discontent ripple up around me, and Ms. Sanderson held up her hands. "I know, I know, landscapes are boring, but hear me out. The word *interpretation* is key, because I'll be asking you to step outside your comfort zone and add an element of illustration to your images. You will not only have to capture twelve stunning images of your landscape, but then you will have to use art and design to transform these images into something that tells a story. *And* you must do this all collaboratively— the photography and the design are to be a joint effort. I expect both partners to influence the project with their individual perspectives."

I looked over to Aurora, who was already looking over at me. She tilted her head and gave me a smile—the universal signal for *let's do this.*

I'd only just smiled back at her when Ms. Sanderson ruined the moment.

"We're going to pair up alphabetically," she said. "Which means—oh, that's right, Mr. Constantine has joined us. Okay, one minute..." She bent over a stack of folders on the teacher's table at the front of the room, writing on Post-It notes and tapping in notes onto her tablet, then she straightened up after two or three minutes. "All fixed!"

She started to walk up and down the rows of desks as she handed us each a folder. "You'll see your partner's name on the front of your folder. Now, the assignment gives you three weeks to prepare your prospectus, but may I suggest you start working on it now . . ."

Ms. Sanderson's voice faded away as I looked down at the folder on my desk. There, written in Ms. Sanderson's spiky, rushed handwriting, was the last name I ever wanted to see.

Keaton Constantine.

Briggs. Constantine.

Alphabetically close.

Ugh.

My stomach dropped right to the floor—and my heart along with it. I couldn't be his partner, I just couldn't. To have to see him, talk with him, *work* with him . . . In close proximity?

To have to share my photography with him, which was the *one* thing I kept for myself, the one thing that made me happy and the one thing my father couldn't control . . .

No. I couldn't do it. Not when Keaton was so cruel, so

angry. Not when he could kiss me like he did and then just walk away like it meant nothing.

I didn't turn around to see what Keaton's reaction to this was, but I didn't have to. He leaned forward and said in a low voice I could barely hear, "Guess it's a good thing I joined the class when I did. *Partner.*" He sounded utterly furious.

"You may spend this time getting acquainted with your collaborator and discussing plans for your project," Ms. Sanderson announced, reaching the front of the room and sitting at her desk, presumably to spend the next twenty minutes surreptitiously updating her resume.

I spun around immediately and gave Keaton my fiercest glare. "This might be a blow-off class for you, Mr. Rugby Captain, but this is important to me. You may rule the school, but you don't rule *me*, and especially not when it comes to this project. Got it?"

He blinked once, like I'd surprised him, and then a slow, cocky grin slid over his face.

And God help me, when he smiled like that, I could have gone up in flames.

Because when Keaton scowled, he was sexy as hell, but when he *smiled*?

It was like a fallen angel had come to claim my heart.

"You're afraid of me," he said confidently. "That's what this is."

"I'm not afr—that's ridiculous—" Who the hell did he think he was?

He nodded, stroking his jaw in mock-thoughtfulness. "You're afraid that if we work together, you won't be able to keep from kissing me again."

"*Again*?" I sputtered. "You kissed *me*! Remember?" The arrogant…insufferable…egotistical…jackass had another think coming. I wasn't kissing him again.

Aurora looked over at him, her gaze murderous. I real-ized I'd been talking a little loudly, so I lowered my voice after giving her a quick *all clear* smile. "Remember? I was minding my own business, and then you leaned in and kissed me. I had nothing to do with it."

He leaned forward over his desk, his smile fading into something darker. More intense. "Nothing to do with it? So that wasn't you licking your lips while you stared at my mouth? That wasn't you purring into my kiss as I helped you grind against my cock?"

I flushed so bright that I knew my cheeks probably matched my hair. I could feel the beads of sweat forming on my skin as my temperature reached peak embarrassment levels.

"That's what I thought," he said, sitting back. His voice held a note of satisfaction, but there was a predatory glint to his eyes that was anything but satisfied.

"Well, it's not going to happen again," I said sharply. No way was I going to be that vulnerable—that *needy*—again, and then watch him walk away. *Again.*

"Fine by me, Miss Perfect," Keaton snapped. The scowl was back in full force again, like whatever I'd said had displeased him. Which couldn't be true—I didn't have that kind of power over him. And he had a girlfriend anyway. *And* he hated me.

"So now that that's out of the way, should we get start-ed?" My voice was still sharp, and I kept my face down so he couldn't see my eyes. So he couldn't see all the stupid hope and hurt there.

"Fine then," he drawled. He gave his pen a contemptu-ous click and then flipped open his folder. "Let's get fucking started."

CHAPTER FOUR

Keaton

"**Y**OU WANT TO get drinks? Phineas is in one of his moods, and I can't handle it without a properly made martini."

I shook my head at Owen. "Can't." I held up my phone and waggled it. "Monthly penance."

Owen winced.

He was probably my closest friend in the Hellfire Club—which, might I add, was a dumb name for us, but I hadn't started it, so who was I to judge? At any rate, as my closest friend, Owen was the only one who knew how complicated the Constantines really were. And like any good friend, he kept his mouth shut and didn't say too much. But I had a feeling that later today, I'd find a bottle of Don Q Reserva Rum in my room.

No note or explanation, just one friend saying to another: God, life sucks. Here is this insanely expensive bottle of rum with which to chase that shit away.

I was a senior, so I'd earned the right to one of the coveted corner single rooms with its own shower. The rooms were passed down from seniors to those deserving. My friends and I had begged, borrowed, stolen, and forged to have these rooms. But it was well worth it to not have anyone around for the shit show that was about to take place.

After the shower, I grabbed my sports drink from my fridge, tossed myself onto my bed, and prepared for hell.

Outside the window, something caught my eye, sinking my already dour mood and making my lips turn down. There she was . . . *fucking Iris.* The reason I'd taken to two-a-day spank sessions.

Didn't matter how much I drank or worked out; I could *still* taste her. I could practically feel her under my skin. *And you want more.*

My situation wasn't entirely my fault though. She'd been there in my space with her smart mouth and her fucking freckles and I'd just . . . lost it. With irritation, I glanced down and realized I was hard. *Goddamn it.*

What the hell was it about that girl?

You better figure it out because you're going to be trapped with her for months.

Fucking hell.

Tomorrow, I would see if Ms. Sanderson would pair me with someone else. While my mother seemed to think the only thing I was good for was eventually filling a suit at one of Winston's offices, I was damn good at multimedia and design. If I wanted, I could go to college and study it. Design was nothing that would make her proud though, which meant I still hadn't made up my mind what I was going to do after I graduated. It was dumb—because I did still want to make her proud—but the idea of working for Winston . . . working for the family . . .

Ugh.

Either way, no matter what I ended up choosing, I was not going to have my opportunities tainted by some no-name girl.

I dragged my eyes away from her because all she was, was a fucking distraction. And she wasn't even that hot.

Then why are we hard?

My dick twitched as if to argue the fact. But what the hell did he know? I deliberately pulled my blinds down so I wouldn't be tempted to look out on the lawn at her, Serafina, and Sloane enjoying the sunny day.

Instead, I turned my attention to my phone, hit the speed dial, and waited. Sometimes I had to call twice because my mother forgot. This was not one of those days though, thankfully. But my mother still sounded confused. "Keaton?"

"Yes, Mother, you know, your son? Sadly, we have a standing date, same time every second Saturday of the month."

She gave me an exasperated sigh. "Of course I know we have a standing call. I have just been busy, that's all." Each word was laced with something too well-mannered to be overt irritation, but too clipped to be true politeness. "Well, are you fine?"

"Yeah, Mom. Just fine."

"Keaton, there is no reason for the attitude."

I sighed. I should have been used to this. The way she spoke to me as if I was a chart of statistics. "Classes are going well. Straight As. Top of the class. No problems. Rugby is fine. We have a pre-season match against Croft Wells Academy in a few weeks, and I was hoping you could attend."

She sighed. "I'd love to, but I've got too much on my plate with the gala. You know how it is."

I swallowed the bite of irritation. I did know how it was, and I hated it. The Constantine Foundation was one of my mother's pet projects, and every year they hosted a massive gala to raise money for whatever the charity du jour was. It took months to plan, and then all that hard work was wasted on four boozy hours in a boutique art museum.

"Well, if that's all, I'll just hop off the phone then."

A *tsk*. "I do not understand why you have to be like this. It's just busy here. One day you'll be home, working for the family like Winston is, and then you'll see."

I waited for it. The weight of disappointment. The guilt of not being like Winston—driven and ambitious and controlled.

I didn't feel it today though. After all these years, I'd finally become numb to it.

When I was younger and Dad was alive, Mom had spent more time with me—at least, that's how I'd remembered it. But as I got older, she distanced herself. Not cruelly, not coldly, nothing like that. But just like I was a scotch that hadn't finished distilling yet, a cake that hadn't finished baking. Which was her prerogative, I guess. After all, what the fuck did I care? I'd be free in a year. I could go wherever and do whatever I wanted, and nobody would give a fuck.

I was a Constantine and the world would be mine for the taking, whether I did what my family wanted or not.

For some inexplicable reason, my gaze darted to my pulled blinds, and I tugged them open because I had to know what Iris was doing. Glutton for punishment. It had to be the call with my mother. I might as well distract myself. And Little Miss Perfect was going to have to do for now.

My mother was still talking about how busy she was and how I had to understand, when she called my name. "Keaton?"

"Mom."

"I really do wish I could come to your game, you know." I could hear her trying to think of the next conciliatory thing to say. "Has there been any more interest from scouts?"

"Coach says yes. But I won't know more until the preseason games get closer."

"Are you still thinking about . . . doing it professionally?"

It had been a fight when I'd first brought up the possibility at a memorable family dinner a couple years ago. She wanted me working for Winston, *period*. Married well, *period*.

In her eyes, none of that would happen if I was travelling the world playing a sport with common people.

But despite what everyone else assumed about a Constantine kid, I didn't want to spend my days doing fuck-all nothing in a suit, handshaking and moving money around. I needed purpose. Something to do. A reason for existing. And if I didn't do design, then going pro with rugby wouldn't be the worst thing, right? Binding myself to some kind of family, artificial though it may be?

But do I really want to play rugby for the rest of my life…?

"I haven't made any decisions yet," I told her honestly.

"Good." She sounded relieved. "And your cousin Cash? Have you checked in with him?"

Cash was a lanky sophomore with great hair and no sense of self-preservation, which I deduced from his immediate attraction to Sloane Lauder—who was basically a knife in the shape of a human girl.

And for better or for worse, he was also my cousin.

"Cash is fine," I told her. "Same as last year. Not getting into any trouble." *Yet.*

"Good," Mom said. And then paused. "So . . ."

Oh god. *Here it comes.*

"Are things with Clara going well?"

"Fine."

Maybe less fine ever since you shoved your tongue in Iris's mouth.

That had been like a week ago. I hadn't done it again, so maybe I wasn't a shitty pseudo-cheater. "But I've been thinking."

She was quiet for a breath. "What do you mean?"

"Clara's a great girl, but it's not like we're getting married or anything. She's very sweet. I care about her a lot. But I don't really think that there's a point in continuing to date her."

"Keaton Constantine, what the hell?"

My brows popped. My mother rarely swore. "Wow, Mom. I didn't even know you knew that word."

"That relationship is important," Mom explained, sounding like she was struggling for patience. "It's your future."

"Mom, I'm eighteen. You can't really expect me to date the same girl for the rest of my life."

"I can, and I do. You've been raised together. *Groomed* to be together. It's not like you need to get to know her. You know exactly what kind of family she comes from. You should know that the expectation is that you two will get married."

I laughed at that. "Again, we're eighteen. We're not going to marry *anyone* any time soon. And while I care about her, I don't love her."

I could envision her pinched face. "You're being very naïve," my mother said in a brittle voice. "Constantines marry well. That's what we do. And it's your role in the family to connect us with the Blairs."

"And if I don't want to?"

Mom didn't say anything for a second. "Keaton, don't make me compel you."

"With money?" That was, after all, my parents' go-to move.

She didn't answer, but she didn't need to. I had a trust fund and a monthly allowance that would balance the budgets of most Midwestern states—but both of those could be fucked with. By her. The first wave of trust fund money would be released once I graduated—and it would be enough to see me through college until I could get my own job . . . if I didn't choose a career in rugby, that was. If I chose rugby, I'd need fuck-all from the family.

But again, I couldn't start playing pro until after graduation at the soonest.

"You're telling me that if I don't keep dating Clara, you're going to starve me out financially?"

"Don't be gauche," she said. She disliked overt money talk. "I'm just reminding you that the benefits of this family are tied to *service* to this family."

"Does it matter to you that Clara doesn't love me? Never mind how *I* feel?"

"This isn't about love, sweetheart, this is about a merger of the families. Something better and stronger. You'll see."

I ground my teeth together. My gaze went outside my window again.

To Iris.

My skin was too hot and too prickly as I remembered the slide of her tongue over mine, that sound she made at the back of her throat, the way her ass fit my hands when I lifted her against me.

And fantastic. I had to stop. *Fuck.* Why *that* girl? I didn't have time for that shit.

"Keaton? Are you listening to me?"

I dragged my attention back to my conversation. "Sorry, I was paying attention to a project I need to focus on. What did you say?"

"I told you, nurture that relationship. Please don't disappoint me. The Blairs are some of my closest friends and could be our strongest allies."

"Whatever you say. Are we done here? Can I go?"

"Keaton," Mom said, and then paused. When she spoke again, her voice was gentler. "I'm trying to raise you as your father would have wanted. I'm trying to steer this family the way your father would have wanted. That's all."

My heart stuttered at the mention of Dad, at the giant Lane-Constantine-shaped hole in all of our lives.

"Okay," I said finally.

"Okay. I love you, sweetheart."

"Yeah, love you too," I choked out and hung up the phone. I swallowed the pain as my eyes stayed fixed on Little Miss Perfect's ass.

I hadn't focused on my anger. It was *her*. *She* was near. Why would I even be thinking about breaking up with Clara? That kiss wouldn't have happened. I could have just skated through senior year with no waves made, my mom none the wiser about me and Clara. Then I'd be the hell out of here and could do what I wanted.

But Iris was the reason for this. *She* was the reason I was thinking about what life would be like if we were different, and it had to stop. Which meant, I wasn't going near her again. It just wasn't going to happen.

Okay, if that's what you want to tell yourself.

CHAPTER FIVE

Iris

"**Y**OU," A LOW voice said near my ear, "have been avoiding me."

Chills rushed down my spine as I turned my head to see Keaton standing behind me. The library was quiet and tomblike at this time of day, but I still hadn't heard him approach my table. To be fair, I hadn't really been listening—I'd thought I was safe in the very back, surrounded by the high wood shelves and out of sight from the entrance.

I'd thought wrong.

Keaton threw his big body into the chair next to me, and I was about to tell him to go away when he grabbed my chair and effortlessly dragged it around so that we were face to face. He planted his dress shoes on the outsides of my Mary Janes and his muscular thighs splayed on either side of my legs. I was trapped by his big, dumb body.

I ignored the traitorous shiver that induced in me.

"Keaton, what—"

"Listen here, Big Red," he said, leaning in and bracing his hands on the sides of my seat. I could feel the heat of his hands on my thighs through my uniform skirt. "I need this project to go well, and I can't afford to have it messed up, all right? So if you don't want to see me, that's perfectly fine. You just leave the project to me—"

"No. Way." Anger simmered in my veins as I leaned right into him. Right until I could feel his breath on my lips. "Photography is what I live for. And I am not having some rugby jock screw over the one thing I love in order to screw *me* over."

His eyebrows lifted. That one stray lock of hair he could never seem to tame brushed over his forehead as he did. "Oh, so it's all about you now? Screwing you over is all I could possibly care about?"

"What other reason could *you* have for caring about art?" I scoffed. "And *design*? Give me a break."

An expression I couldn't decipher chased itself across his face, and he broke our stare, leaning back and looking at a bookshelf while a muscle in his jaw jumped. When he met my eyes again, his gaze was cold. So very cold.

"If you care so much, then we can do this together," he said icily. "But I'm calling the shots."

"No fucking way."

"Starting now," he said, as if he hadn't heard me. "No more avoiding me. We meet every Friday night to work on this, and we meet on Saturdays too if we have to. You might be Daddy's golden girl, but the rest of us have to worry about our grades."

My jaw dropped open. The *nerve* of him—and the completely incorrect nerve! First, *Isabelle* was Daddy's golden girl, and that was a fact I could never escape, because he'd never stop reminding me of it.

Secondly, my father would never punch up my grades. Not because he cared about the ethics of it all—oh no. But because he knew how political private schools could get, and if the wrong teacher talked, his reputation would be trashed.

And thirdly: "Like *you* have to worry about GPA, Keaton Constantine, rugby captain? With your family business? With the team? Please. Your entire life is cushioned by your last name and your genetic predisposition for leg muscles. You are a walking, talking rich jock stereotype."

"And *you*," he seethed, "my uptight good-girl, are a pain in my ass. But here we are."

For a long moment, we just glared at each other, neither of us willing to surrender.

But then Keaton's eyes drifted down to my braid, which had slid over my shoulder to hang down over my chest.

His pupils dilated the tiniest amount, and then his eyes narrowed. "Why do you do that?"

"Do what?" I asked, genuinely confused by his change of mood.

"Hide your hair in that braid."

I was even more confused now. "I'm hardly hiding it. I just like it out of my face while I'm working."

"It makes it feel like a secret. Like I'm the only one who—"

With an abrupt jerk, he was off his chair and grabbing his leather satchel.

I was totally lost. "Keaton?"

He didn't look at me as he shouldered his bag. "Friday. Four o'clock in the photography lab. Be there, Iris."

And then he stalked away as fast as he had after our kiss.

WE WERE A few weeks into the semester now, and Pembroke seemed determined to punish all its students simply for existing. I had three papers to write, half a Molière play to translate, more calc problems than I could possibly ever do, and at least three AP physics problems to do a night.

Which didn't sound like a lot, admittedly, until I started doing the physics problems and realized that each problem took an hour.

Not to mention that I was still trying to build a photography portfolio for myself, and so I was spending every spare moment outside snapping pictures and then inside the darkroom developing them. I preferred the freedom of digital, but I'd need to show in my portfolio that I could do film too, so I needed plenty of analog samples to show off.

Not for the first time, I wished I lived in a dorm, where I could study and complain and gossip with friends while I worked. Sometimes I hung out in Serafina and Sloane's room, and sometimes in Aurora's, but Sloane refused to talk when she was studying, Serafina always had random visitors dropping by, and Aurora's security person had to sit in the room while I was there since I hadn't been properly vetted by the Liechtensteiner government yet.

So home it was.

Home where my father could remind me how hard Isabelle had studied, and how easily homework came to her. Home where my mother could hide from all our family conflict like it was a spider on the wall that would eventually crawl away. Home where I could sit in my bedroom and stare out the window at the boys' dormitory across the lush, green grounds.

Where I could stare at that century-old brick building and wonder what Keaton was doing inside it.

Was he with his girlfriend? With the Hellfire Club?

Was he alone?

Was he thinking of me?

Don't be stupid, Iris.

I kept hoping Friday would never come. I hoped there would be a fire or a storm or a flood. Because I didn't know if I could face him again. I didn't know if I could survive that feeling like I wanted to scratch him and kiss him and growl insults at him while he pinned me against another bookshelf.

I'd never had a crush like this, never liked a boy like this, never felt about anybody the way I felt about Keaton. Like he had crawled under my skin. I hated him.

And . . .

I thought of him constantly.

And when the books were closed and the lights were off, I thought of our kiss. Of how good it felt to have him wedged up against me, his hands in my hair and his mouth consuming mine. Of how tight my belly had been, how I'd ached and ached between my legs as he ground himself against me.

I wanted it again, and I despised myself for my weakness. What girl was stupid enough to want a boy like *him*? A boy with a girlfriend? A boy who detested her?

Not me.

FRIDAY STARTED OUT with a bang—almost literally. I was sitting in my English classroom alone, about ten minutes before the bell, when a trio of beautiful girls crashed through the classroom door and strode in like leggy soldiers. They were sleek and slim, makeup perfect, their eyes full of murder.

"Are you Iris Briggs?" the one in front asked. She had dark brown hair and pale skin, muted pink lipstick and a diamond tennis bracelet. Her features were the sort of bland but forgettably pretty that came from generations of New England money.

"Um," I said. "Yes?"

The girl leaned down, bracing her hands on my desk. "Stay the *fuck* away from my boyfriend."

"Um—"

A blonde girl stepped forward too, her lips painted scarlet and a fresh hickey visible just above her shirt collar. "Don't play dumb, Briggs. McKenna told Bella who told Carlee who finally told me that she saw you kissing Keaton in the library during the first week."

Heat rushed through me—a mix of defensiveness and unease. *You didn't do anything wrong*, I reminded myself. If they were going to be angry with anyone, they should be angry with Keaton! He was the one with the girlfriend!

"You must be Clara," I said, looking back to the brunette. "Look. If you've got a problem with Keaton kissing someone else, I suggest you take it up with Keaton. He's the one who kissed me. It's not very feminist of you to scold me instead of the boy who's actually made promises to you."

Clara scowled. "I don't care about feminism right now, Briggs. I can't afford for Keaton to be seen chasing someone else. Got it?"

"It wasn't like that—"

"I don't care what it was *like*," Clara hissed. "*Don't let it happen again.* Or I will hurt you. Understood?"

"She means we'll kick your ass," the blonde supplied. I managed to dredge up her name from Serafina's lunchtime commentary a few days ago. Samantha Morgan: notorious party girl and wild child. I was very certain she was the kind of girl who would kick the shit out of me if given the chance and enough tequila.

"If you're scared or angry or whatever this is, you need

to bring it to Keaton," I said as coldly as I could manage, glaring at all of them. Students began to file in for class, in pairs and trios, and I saw the moment Clara realized this was over. For now, at least.

"Keaton is mine," Clara said in a low, but clear voice as she straightened up. "And I plan to keep him at any cost—I can't afford not to, which makes me very, *very* dangerous to you. And I hope you remember that next time you're with him."

CHAPTER SIX

Iris

THE REST OF the day was an anxious blur. I'd already been feeling weird and twisty about working with Keaton today, and now this Clara thing . . .

What if she found out about the project? Misunderstood the time we'd be spending together? I didn't think she and Samantha would physically hurt me—surely they had more sense than to go after the headmaster's daughter—but I also wasn't certain they *wouldn't* hurt me either. I knew Serafina would say not to worry, that she and Sloane and Aurora had my back, but still.

I didn't like it.

Photography seminar was in the lab rather than the classroom today, as we practiced with the illustration and design tools in Photoshop, which meant I didn't have to talk to Keaton or listen to him or even look at him. I kept my eyes firmly on my screen, even when I felt his gaze hot on my neck, and pretended he didn't exist.

But eventually four o'clock came, and with it, time to meet him. I strode from Aurora's room where she'd been bitching about Phineas Yates—a Hellfire boy and total manwhore—and steeled myself as I walked into the lab.

Okay. Game plan.
Lady bits, listen up.

I wasn't going to let Clara's words scare me, but I also wasn't going to kiss him or even *think* about kissing him. I was going to hold my ground, and I wasn't going to let him railroad me into something stupid for this project, because I wouldn't hear back from my safety schools until December at the earliest, and I needed my high school CV to be immaculate until then, just in case the Sorbonne fell through.

Which meant this project needed to be stunning and original enough to impress an admissions team. And that was not going to happen with a ball-playing bully like Keaton mucking it up.

You can do this.
Don't piss off Clara.
Don't take his shit.
Don't get distracted by his eyes.

Pembroke's photo lab was made of two parts: the digital lab where we worked on Photoshop today and the wet lab, or darkroom. I walked into the digital lab with its long rows of tables studded with giant, gleaming Macs and found Keaton sprawled in a chair, lazily clicking through something on one of the computers.

With some horror, I realized it was *my* computer. And he was clicking through *my* images, *my* photographs. The ones I'd scanned in earlier today to play with in Photoshop.

"You really should remember to log out of a school computer when you're done," Keaton said in a bored voice. *Click click* went his finger on the mouse. Each click felt like a gunshot in the air—echoing and final.

I'd known he would have to see my work eventually, but—but not like this. Not without my permission. Not without my preparation.

As I came closer, I could make out the individual images he was scrolling through. A picture of a leaf fading from green to gold. A shot of Isabelle in the middle of Hyde Park, looking down at her phone with a frown while the wind whipped her copper-colored hair around her face. Another one of Isabelle standing by the window in her empty London flat, her hand clenched tight around her new house key.

"Who is she?" Keaton asked.

God, of course he wanted to know about her. Everyone did. She was brilliant and beautiful and always did everything right—except picking the right boys to date. She'd always been very bad at that, for how smart and pretty she was.

I wouldn't answer. I shouldn't answer.

"My sister, Isabelle," I answered, dropping my bag on the table. Some bitterness crept into my voice. "She's single if you're interested, but she is older than us. And she's in London right now for school, so you'll have to borrow your mommy's jet to go see her."

Keaton looked at me appraisingly. "You're jealous of her."

"I'm not," I said huffily, crossing my arms.

"You are," he said. "Trust me, I know when someone is jealous of a sibling they feel like they can never live up to."

"Oh, *really*."

He shrugged, not bothered by my sarcasm and also not elaborating either. "And I wasn't asking because I thought she was hot. I was asking because she clearly means something to you. You show how lonely she is, how tense she is, and you make sure the viewer feels her loneliness too. The framing of both, the empty space around her . . . it's really well done."

My lips parted as shock poured through me. The fact that he could perceive that—perceive that I did really love Isabelle despite our differences—and he actually sounded like he knew what he was talking about left me stunned. Never in a hundred years would I have thought that Keaton Constantine could assess emotion in art.

And also . . .

"Are you complimenting me, Keaton?"

"I give compliments when they're warranted, Big Red. And these images warrant them."

It was almost patronizing. *Almost.* And I wanted to be mad about it. But when our eyes met, there was nothing but honesty and reluctant admiration in his face.

He'd meant what he said.

"Here, I want to show you something," he said, getting to his feet. He'd left his bag up by the teacher's table at the front, and he paced over to it, pulling off his blazer when he did. Which was unfortunate for me, because it meant there was now nothing disguising the firm swells of muscle under his white button-down. There was nothing hiding how his broad, hewn chest led into a flat stomach or how his waist tapered into lean and narrow hips.

Nothing hiding how tight his muscle-curved ass looked in his school trousers.

He idly loosened his tie as his other hand dug in his bag and pulled some glossy pictures free. "Tell me what you think," he said, pushing them across the table. The loosened tie made it so that I could see his throat—strong and male and oh-so-lickable.

I thought about how it would feel to have my lips against his neck. To suck the skin there until he moaned, until he growled.

Then I flushed.

"Iris?" he said. "Did you hear me?"

I gratefully took the excuse to think about something that wasn't kissing him and snagged the pictures. "Yeah. Sorry, I was just thinking about the project."

Keaton braced his palm against the back of his neck. "Yeah, so. Uh. About that." He nodded at the pictures, and I suddenly understood that he was *nervous*. The fidgeting. The hesitancy in his voice.

Keaton Constantine, god of the school, was worried about showing these to me.

And with renewed interest, I looked down.

The pictures were digital illustrations, all of them. Some incorporating photography, some freehand. And all of them were bright and vibrant and *interesting*. Even the ones that weren't perfect showed an understanding of color, of movement, that I never would have expected from a sportsball boy.

I stared down at one in particular; a drawing of a man standing with his back to the observer, his bare feet sinking into the earth, the wind tugging at his suit pants and the matching jacket draped over one arm. Even though he seemed to be standing in some kind of garden, he was looking out to where the sea glimmered in the distance, like a chilly blue invitation.

I raised my eyes to Keaton, who still stood there with his hand hanging from the nape of his neck. He was tense, unreadable. Waiting for me to say something dismissive or hurtful maybe.

I didn't. I couldn't. "This is really good, Keaton."

He relaxed the tiniest amount.

"I'm sorry I assumed you wouldn't be any good at this stuff, on account of the jockitude."

"Jockitude," he repeated, the corner of his mouth curling up ever so slightly. "What a way with words you have, headmaster's daughter."

"He's someone important to you," I decided.

His smile fell off, replaced by a careful neutrality. He started unbuttoning and rolling up his shirtsleeves—a study in forced casualness. "What makes you think he's real and not just a figment of my imagination?"

I moved some of the pictures on the table so that they were side by side. "You see this one here? Another person, but the hair is more of an idea of hair and the environment around them is static. Same here. But him? This garden? There's movement in it—the wind and the churn of the sea—and you can see how it makes him feel. And the hair isn't just *blond*; it's all different shades of gold, like he's just spent the summer outside. Like you drew him from memory."

"No," Keaton said after a minute. "Not from memory. He let me sketch him that day. It was one of the first sketches I ever made, but it took me years to finish painting it in. I couldn't bear to get it wrong."

I looked over at him.

He'd come closer as we were looking at the pictures, and I could feel the heat of him burning through my thin uniform sweater and shirt. I could see his giant shadow engulfing mine.

"Tell me about him," I whispered. It must be his father—or maybe an uncle? An older brother seemed unlikely, and the man in the picture was broad and hale and blond—so not a grandfather.

"No," he said flatly.

"Is he your father?" I pressed. "Has he seen what you made for him?"

51

"I'm not talking about this with you," he said, narrowing his eyes.

"You brought these pictures here for me to look at, Keaton, surely you expected me to—"

"I brought them here for the project," he said. "That's it."

"Keaton—"

I was abruptly lifted off my feet and set on the table, my feet dangling and Keaton leaning in close to my face.

"Stop asking, Iris," he said in a dangerous voice. "It's none of your business."

My entire body thrilled at having him so close. My knees kept him at a respectable distance, but his hands were braced on the edge of the table on either side of my hips, and he was close enough to kiss me.

No. Wait.

I did not want to kiss him.

I didn't need another visit from Clara.

And he was a dick the last time we kissed.

And he looked at my work without my permission.

And now he was being a *super* dick. The manhandling of me, the plucking me off my feet and setting me where he liked, as if I were nothing more than a doll for him to play with.

I tried to ignore how hot that idea was.

I tipped my chin up defiantly. "And what will you do if I don't stop asking, hmm? Tackle me like I'm on your rugby field?"

His eyes dropped back down to my braid, and he reached up to wind the soft end of it around his finger. "Tackling might be in order, Big Red."

"You wish, asshole." I made to push him away, but the moment my hands touched his hard body, my brain cut the signal short. I couldn't think about anything other than how sexy his warm muscles felt through his shirt. About how good it felt to slide my hands up from his ridged torso to his wide chest.

He gave a dark laugh. "Change your mind about something, sweetheart?"

I glared at him. "Screw you."

But I didn't pull my hands away. Instead I ran them all the way up his shoulders to his neck, to the place where his dark hair curled ever so slightly behind his ears.

His hair was almost unbelievably soft for a boy's, and thick enough to make a shampoo model jealous.

I raked my fingernails over his scalp. His eyes closed as a shiver moved through him.

I almost couldn't help what happened next; I couldn't help parting my knees. Just a little. But enough for him to notice, even with his eyes closed.

He opened his eyes and stared at the braid still clutched in his hand, and then he stared at my mouth.

"Let me kiss you," he said urgently.

Bad idea, bad idea.

"No," I said. "I'm not in the mood for your games right now."

"I'll make it worth your while," he tempted, running a finger over the top of my knee. He didn't go any farther up, just stayed there at the hem of my skirt, flirting with the edge of the fabric. I could feel every centimeter he traced as if he was branding me with his touch. Etching it, tattooing it.

"Wh-what does that mean?" I asked, my voice trembling a little. He placed his entire hand above my knee now, his thumb curling over my inner thigh, but he didn't move it. He didn't try to reach under my skirt.

"It means I'll make you come," he said in a low voice, letting go of my braid to put his free hand on my other knee. "Has anyone ever given you an orgasm, Iris? Ever made that pretty pussy happy?"

The word *pussy* from his lips was like a punch to the chest. I couldn't breathe. I felt like everything below my navel was on fire. All the reasons why this was a bad idea fled right the hell out of my mind.

"You don't even know if it's pretty," I said nonsensically.

"Oh, it would be. And it would taste even prettier."

"Taste?" I repeated faintly. I still couldn't breathe.

His firm lips were tipped up to one side in a smirk, but his eyes were deadly serious. "I know you'd taste amazing, Iris. Let me kiss your mouth, and then I'll kiss between your legs too."

The image came unbidden—Keaton's massive shoulders tucked between my thighs while his sensual mouth explored me. While that lock of hair brushed over his forehead and he used his tongue to stroke—

"We can't," I said breathlessly. "We're in the lab, anyone could see us if they were walking by—"

I was up in his arms before I even finished talking, and then we were moving back towards the darkroom door. Within seconds, we were inside, surrounded by shelves and tables and trays and sinks. Finished photographs hung from lines all around the room like paper ghosts. Some of them were mine. *Most* of them were mine.

We were bathed in red light. Keaton's normally blue eyes were a deep, royal purple. I couldn't stop staring into them.

"Iris," he rasped. His hands cradled my ass, and my thighs were wrapped around his waist and I was burning up,

I was on fire. Every part of me ached for every part of him. "Let me kiss you now. Please."

My common sense was gone, my reason had fled.

There was only one answer.

"Yes," I murmured, already leaning forward. "*Yes.*"

CHAPTER SEVEN

Iris

THERE WAS A moment—a long, electric moment—when our lips touched, but we didn't move.

We stayed frozen, him holding me, my arms wrapped around his neck, his firm mouth just barely pressed against mine. It was like neither of us could believe what we were doing, like we were both paralyzed by the sudden, shocking *realness* of it. This was no longer a fantasy I played in my mind during a restless night, this was no longer a dirty reverie for extra-long showers. This was really happening, this was real life, this was Keaton Constantine gripping my body as he breathed against my lips.

And then the moment deepened, and the kiss became urgent. His lips slotted against mine, moving against them, all as his fingers plumped and squeezed my bottom, all as I panted and squirmed in his arms.

And then his tongue flickered at my lips, inviting me to open—and once I opened for him, it was all over. There was nothing but the hot stroke of his tongue against mine, nothing but our hands everywhere, everywhere, nothing but gasps and pants and groans.

He set me on a table, his mouth moving over my ear

and down to my neck while his hands slid under my uniform sweater and started pulling the shirt underneath free of my waistband. Once he succeeded, he slid his hands up my bare back and then back down my spine, over and over again, like touching my skin was the only thing he wanted to do for the rest of his life.

His hands were rough and warm and big, and I wanted them everywhere on me. I wanted them against my breasts, I wanted them possessive and greedy on my waist. I wanted them in my panties, in places no one's hand but mine had ever been. I wanted him to brand me with his touch and write his name onto my skin with pleasure.

I grabbed one of his wrists and pushed his hand up to cup my breast.

"You sure, Big Red?" Keaton whispered against my mouth. "Because I want it a whole lot. It might scare you how much."

"Just—please—Keaton—"

He'd already obliged. The moment I said *please,* he'd palmed my breast, squeezing gently until I moaned. He teased my nipple through the silk of my bra cup while his other hand pulled at the bottom of my sweater.

"Get this thing off," he grunted. "I need to see you."

I was too addled with lust to disagree or to remember that my smallish breasts might not be up to scratch. Or to care that Keaton had probably seen half the school population without a shirt and that I might be found lacking. All I cared about was having more, feeling more. *More, more, more.*

Together, we peeled my sweater off and tossed it on the floor. Then both of us were fumbling with the buttons on my shirt, struggling to get them open, all while we were still trying to kiss and touch each other too.

"Fuck it," Keaton growled, and he ripped the shirt open the rest of the way, sending two buttons to lonely deaths on the darkroom floor.

I shivered as he pulled back to look at me, to look at my pink silk bra and my exposed stomach.

His eyes—still that magical, eerie purple from the red light—glowed with hunger as he took me in, but when he spoke, his voice was almost soft. Almost wondering. "You have freckles even here," he whispered.

I flushed as he traced the upper swells of my tits with his fingers, and then I moaned as he replaced his fingers with his mouth, trailing kisses all over my skin. He lowered his mouth and then sucked my hard nipple through the silk.

Jolts of heat traveled from his hot mouth straight to my pussy.

"Oh my god," I moaned. "Oh my god, oh my god." As I was losing brain cells by the second, it was all I could manage.

"I'm going to look at them now, Iris," he said, and his voice was a mix of arrogance and tenderness that I didn't think I could ever get enough of.

I nodded, but he was already working the silk cups down and freeing my breasts. The cups and underwire underneath them lifted them up and pushed them out, as if they were being presented to him, and the fact that I still had my shirt on made it feel even dirtier somehow.

And the look on his face . . . like he'd just taken a shot of vodka. Like he'd just run across a bed of hot coals.

"Jesus fucking Christ," he muttered, his eyes raking over my freckled breasts and their straining, tight little peaks. "Jesus. Iris—I—"

He wasted no more time with words, and instead bent down to take the tip of one past his lips.

I'd never felt anything like his mouth there. *Never.* It was hot and wet and ticklish and sucking—it was *powerful*, it made me arch and whimper and twist my fingers in his hair.

"You like that?" he asked. He hadn't lifted his head, and so his words ghosted across my wet, needy flesh. "You like having your tits sucked on?"

I made a noise that was an awful lot like a whine, and he gave a dark laugh.

"Okay, sweetheart," he said. "I'll keep going."

He moved to my other breast, kissing around the pebbled skin, circling its peak, and then finally took it into his mouth, sucking and then fluttering his tongue over the stiffened tip. He scraped his teeth gently along it, and I jumped against him, and then moaned again.

"Yeah, that's it," he murmured—almost to himself. "Filthy girl."

It was then that I noticed he was idly palming his erection as he sucked on me, as if he couldn't help himself, and that thought was so hot, I couldn't stand it. The idea that I inspired lust in him, that I could make him hard, that I made him need to come . . .

"Come here, dirty thing," he said, helping me off the table. I made a noise of complaint that his mouth wasn't on my breasts anymore, and he laughed that dark laugh again, tugging on my braid and then spinning me around so that I was facing the table and he was standing right behind me.

"You'll like this, I promise," he said.

"H-how do you know? I've never done it before—*oh*—" My voice broke as Keaton's hand found the hem of my skirt and then slid up a thigh to cup me where I was covered in plain, white cotton. I wished I'd worn something sexier, something more adult, but Keaton's growl as he palmed me sounded anything but disappointed.

His fingertips pressed in a little, finding the place where my clit hid, and I shivered against him.

"You're right," he purred. "It doesn't matter if you've ever done this before, because you've never done it before with *me*. And I'm going to ruin you for any other boy who comes after."

He pushed with his fingers again, sending frissons of pleasure skating down my thighs and up my spine. "Keaton," I panted, pushing back against him. I could feel the clothed ridge of his erection against my bottom as I did, and he gave a grunt at the pressure. "Do it—please—just—just go—"

"Go where, Iris?" he whisper-asked, his fingers playing over the elastic edges of my panties now. "Inside these sweet panties? Right up against your skin?"

His actions echoed his words, and he slid his hand down the front of my panties now, his fingers toying with my silky curls, and then with the straining bundle of nerves at the apex of my thighs.

"I—please—" I didn't even know what I sounded like. Not like myself. Not like Iris Briggs who only had one goal: escape to Paris. I sounded like a girl who'd be happy to stay in this darkroom forever, and *not* to work on photography.

"Ohhh," Keaton said in mock-epiphany. "I think I know. You want me to—" His fingers went lower . . . and lower . . . "—go somewhere else, don't you?"

A lazy fingertip pushed past my folds and circled the slick secrets inside. I gasped, slamming my hands down on the table. No one had done this to me, not ever. It had only ever been my own hand, and I never could have guessed how different another person's touch would feel.

"You want me to go inside, Iris?" Keaton asked in a

rough, seductive voice. "You want to feel my finger inside you?"

I nodded vigorously. "Yes, I want that. Please—*oh holy shit.*"

He'd slid a finger inside of me, giving me a moment to get used to the fullness, gently grinding his palm against my clit as he did.

"How does it feel?" he asked, a hand dropping to my hip. I realized I was grinding back against his hand, riding it and chasing the friction, and he used the hand on my hip to encourage me, guiding me until I was practically fucking his touch.

"Good." I worked the word out on a long, juddering exhale. My nipples ached in the cool air, and when I looked down, I saw my skirt bunched up near my navel and Keaton's muscled forearm disappearing into my panties.

I thought I might spontaneously combust.

"Now, my dirty little Iris can take more than one finger, can't she?"

Already a single finger felt huge. "May-maybe."

"Tell me to stop if it hurts," he said soothingly, and then he started working the second finger in. Slowly, carefully, still using his other hand on my hip to urge me against his touch, against the heel of the hand still rubbing against my clit.

And then both fingers were wedged inside me.

I heard him curse to himself when they were both inside, and then he muttered something that sounded like *tight, so fucking tight.*

And it *was* tight, it was so snug. His fingers were so much bigger than mine, longer, and even better because he knew just where to press and curl and stroke. The pressure and the pleasure became the same thing, the fullness marrying with the friction. I started riding his hand even harder, needing something, chasing something.

"*Keaton.*"

"I know, sweetheart."

"*Keaton!*"

"Let it happen," he coaxed. "Let me make you come. Right here, fucking the hand I've got shoved in your innocent panties. Come around my fingers, Iris; let me feel it."

It was his words as much as his expert touch that did me in. I came like I'd never come before, seizing and contracting and shuddering from the pleasure. Wet, sweet bliss crashed over me.

"*Oh god, oh god, oh god.*"

And that was when we heard the ripple of laughter and animated conversation coming from the direction of the digital lab. Like someone was in the hallway just outside.

Or like someone had come in and now there was only a door separating us from them.

We were about to get caught.

Keaton clapped a hand over my mouth, but he didn't stop massaging the orgasm out of me, the asshole. He just kept fingering me as I whimpered against his hand, until I was slumped against his hard body, completely spent and breathless.

And finally—*finally*—my brain started functioning again.

"Shit," I said miserably against his palm. "Oh shit."

Chapter Eight

Iris

K EATON EASED HIS hand over my mouth. "Quiet, do you want to get caught?"

Meanwhile, I couldn't catch my damn breath.

What had I just done? What was I still doing? *You let Keaton Constantine fingerbang you in the darkroom.* Hell, the asshole still had his hand in my panties.

"Keaton." My voice was a whispered croak. I could not do this anymore. I had to stop.

But it feels so good.

He's the devil.

He sees you for you. Good or bad.

He's only out for himself.

No one has ever made you burn like this.

If we got caught, he would still carry on being Keaton Constantine. I would be disowned by my parents.

Silence came from outside.

We both relaxed as we realized no one was coming in to catch us.

His breath tickled the shell of my ear when he whispered. "Sorry. You okay?" He eased his fingers out of me. Gently, he smoothed my rumpled uniform skirt back down over my hips and thighs. "See? Right as rain."

I turned my head to glower at him. "Right as rain?"

He gave me a sharp nod. No harm no foul? Right as rain? In the darkroom, my solace. The place I came when I needed to get back in touch with who I was as a person.

I had let Keaton Constantine finger me. *Fingerbang me.* In the darkroom. Oh my god, I was the worst kind of teenage cliché. Hooking up with the boy I didn't like who didn't like me. A boy I could get my ass kicked for kissing. And after I'd watched my older sister Isabelle date loser after loser.

Don't be an Isabelle.

Keaton planted a kiss on my neck and my legs turned to jelly again. Damn him. I whipped around in his arms. "We have to stop this."

His dark brows furrowed as they dropped and he crossed his arms. "What?"

I licked my lips and planted my hands on the table behind me. In the red light of the darkroom his features looked more dangerous. He was all sharp angles. It made him even sexier somehow.

"You heard me. Stop. We almost got caught just now."

He rolled his eyes. "Would you relax, Briggs? Besides, if I'd gotten caught in here, no one would have said anything."

I shoved at his shoulders, but the idiot was enormous and didn't budge. "But everyone would have said something about *me*. Yeah sure, you do this kind of thing all the time. I'm the new girl. The headmaster's daughter. I can't do this. My parents will actually kill me. Not to mention, my father can think of a million ways to make both of our lives hell. I just want to have an easy year. I'm this close to freedom. Messing around with you is going to jeopardize that."

I realized my breasts were still exposed, the tips still hard and aching. His eyes dropped to them, and I felt his dick throb against me.

He licked his full bottom lip as he looked at them, and I wanted to bite it.

Jesus Christ, I was in need of a psychological evaluation. Clearly I'd inhaled too many chemicals. That's what I got for wanting to go analog for my college portfolio. I'd just switch to digital from now on. It would certainly keep my mind clearer.

"Does that matter to you, what Daddy says?" His eyes were still on my chest.

I rearranged my bra, wondering if there was such a thing as indignantly putting one's tits away. "Don't be a dick. Why can't you see that the new girl with something to prove getting caught in a compromising position with the school's golden boy isn't good for me?"

He shrugged. "Relax. A, we didn't get caught, so you can untwist your panties about that. B, no way in hell we're stopping."

I blinked up at him. Was he crazy? "What? What is wrong with you?" I started buttoning up my shirt. Well, the buttons that were left, at least. "Your rep is going to take a hit too."

I couldn't see very well, but I knew that his brow lifted. "How is this bad for me?"

"You have a girlfriend."

His brows snapped down then and he ran a hand through his blond waves. "Actually . . ."

"No. No actually. This is madness. Neither one of us can be caught in here doing this. God, what is wrong with me?" I ducked under his arm and scooped my sweater off the floor, pulling it over my head as fast as I could.

I shoved open the darkroom. Despite the earlier noises,

no one was around. Keaton's pictures were still on the teacher's table, along with our bags.

He sauntered out after me. His cocky grin plastered over his face. It was a grin that said, *I just ate out the canary.* "This wasn't anything. You don't have to make such a big deal out of it."

"Okay, maybe you're used to doing things like this. Maybe you're used to cheating on your girlfriend. I am not. And truth be told, Clara could destroy me. I'm trying to get out of here with the minimum of fuss. Why can't you see that?"

A muscle in his jaw ticked as his grin slid away. "I'm not particularly thrilled about this development either. But I do know that the more I try to stay away from you, the more I seem to find myself in a scenario where I want to know what you taste like, so instead of fighting it, I'm going with the flow."

I shook my head. "Wow, such glowing affection you have for me."

"You know what this is. And let's not pretend you like me any more than I like you."

The way he said that. As if it was obvious that he wouldn't like me. That I wouldn't like him. *Do you like him?*

Maybe. No. Hell, I didn't know. He was more than the jock he portrayed. After all, wasn't I more than the overachieving goody two shoes my parents wanted me to be? He was certainly more than the spoiled rich prick he pretended to be. He put that persona on like a suit daily. The real him was probably far more complex and complicated.

After seeing his illustrations today, I had to admit to myself that maybe the good grades he had weren't a fluke. He was smarter than I'd given him credit for, and he thought things through. And he had the soul of an artist. A really gifted eye. He also was capable of working hard. Not to mention that it seemed like he had high standards like I did when it came to his art. He needed things he was putting his name on to be right.

And despite myself, I respected him. "You know I'm right."

His brow lifted. "Do you think you can stop? I'm not particularly enthused about what's happening here either. But my dick can't seem to stay away from you, so why don't we just keep going and see where it ends?"

"Where it ends is disaster. And let's not forget the one basic tenet. I don't like you."

His panty-melting grin flashed, showing a hint of dimple. "I don't like you either. But I'm stuck with you for this project. And, obviously, we can't keep our hands off each other. So stopping isn't really in the cards."

"Yes, it is. I'm done."

"Okay. Suit yourself. But you'll be back." He stepped close, and automatically, I licked my lips, readying them for his kisses. "I'm irresistible. No one can stay away for long."

I was the problem. I had to build better walls and protect myself from whatever attacks he had against my defenses. I could do this. I stepped back. "No. Take that smile to your girlfriend. I'm out."

He stopped immediately in his tracks and held up his hands. "Okay, you say no, I stop. But I will say this. Your nipples are still hard for me. I know exactly how they feel, how they taste. They like me. You don't even have to. Not all of you has to like me, you know? But you come to me next time."

"I am not coming to you. You are the most pompous, arrogant, egotistical—"

"You realize all those mean the same thing, right?"

I wanted to hit him. I've never been violent a day in my life. I had a vicious tongue when pushed, but violent, no.

But right now, I could have kicked him in the shins and have been perfectly happy to do so.

He didn't take another step towards me. But he did lean on the table between us, planting his hands, and I could see the thick veins running through his very stellar forearms. *Jesus Christ.* "I won't touch you if you don't want me to. The question is, don't you want me to?"

"No, because we are being reckless. And you don't like me either. You can get ass anywhere in this school. Like from your girlfriend."

There was that frown again. "Don't you worry about Clara. Worry about yourself."

"I'm sorry, but I'm not a violent person. Clara seems like she is. She threatened to kick my ass. I don't even have a posse to back me up."

"What do you call Serafina and Sloane?"

"They're very nice. I call them friends. And friends don't ask friends to kick somebody else's ass on their behalf."

He shrugged. "Guys do it all the time."

I fussed with my braid, rearranging it over one shoulder. Keaton scowled at it. "Look, let's just chalk today up to an accident."

The corner of his lips tipped into a smirk. "An accident? One where I asked you if I could kiss you, and you said yes. And then you kissed me back. Then our hands were all over each other. And I was pulling down your bra and sucking on your tits. Then I turned you around against that table in there and slid my hands into your panties. You're calling that an accident?"

If my panties hadn't already been soaked, that would

have done the trick. Every muscle in my pelvic region relaxed, and then clenched, starting this pulsing motion that I couldn't stop. I wanted him.

"Look, that wasn't supposed to happen, is what I meant to say. And it won't happen again because you and me, we're just too unalike. We don't like each other; we don't even know each other."

"You want to know me? Why does it have to be like that? Why can't it just be that we like hooking up?"

"That's not who I am. I need to actually like the person that I make out with. I get it. You're a guy. You don't have to like anyone. Hell, I don't think you've liked anyone in your day-to-day life. But I need that."

A frown furrowed his brow. "You really don't like me?"

I swallowed and then lied. "Nope. You're a half-decent artist, but too rash. Too smug for your own good. Cocky. Used to being good at everything, and you think you own this place. You don't."

"Well, tell me how you really feel."

I leaned on the table. I'd opted for the same casual attitude that he had. "I can't do this. I already have all these stupid expectations. And I can feel myself in a pressure cooker. I don't need you fucking with my head too. So just back off. I'm not going to say yes anymore."

He lifted a brow then and brought his fingers to his lips and sucked.

Panties down. Panties down. They were on fire. He was licking my taste off them.

He closed his eyes and moaned, licking them clean before pulling them free. "Well, if I'm not going to have another taste, might as well enjoy the one I just had."

My mouth hung open as I watched him march out of the lab. Keaton Constantine was an asshole.

Keaton Constantine was also the sexiest guy I had ever seen in my life.

And I was a liar. I liked him. I just didn't want to.

What the fuck was I going to do?

CHAPTER NINE

Keaton

"WHY THE FUCK are you so tense, man?" Phin asked, bumping against my shoulder. "Fucking *relax.*"

"I'm plenty relaxed," I growled. *Way to be relaxed, Constantine.*

"No, you're not," Lennox drawled in his British accent. "You look like you're ready for bloody murder."

I took a drink of my lukewarm beer and made a face. I should have brought some of the good stuff from my room. Or better yet, I should have made Rhys or Lennox load me up with the high-caliber booze they always seemed to have on hand.

Bonfire party beer was *awful.*

The taste of victory, however, was very sweet, and I tried to savor it as I watched the Croft Wells bastards scowl and toss back shots of Everclear on their side of the fire. We'd handed their asses to them in the exhibition game this afternoon, and even though this aftergame party deep in the woods was supposed to be all about drinking and screwing and lighting shit on fire, there was still plenty of bad blood in the air.

Not that I minded. It felt good to win.

Then why is Phin right? Why can't you relax?

"Is Clara doing okay?" Owen asked. I couldn't tell if he was genuinely interested or if he wanted to move the conversation past an awkward moment—or if he was just bored. With Owen, it really could be all three things at once. Even though we were all rich motherfuckers, he was the most stereotypical rich motherfucker of us all, like he was trapped in an Edith Wharton novel or something.

Snooty, but also unfailingly mannered while he was judging your ass.

It was unsettling at times, like right now, when I couldn't tell if he was simply being nice or not.

"Clara's fine, she just needed to rest," I said, taking another drink to cover the half-lie. We'd made the obligatory appearance early on—her clinging to my arm and loudly praising my skill on the field—and then she'd claimed a headache and went back to the dorms, where no doubt she'd be underneath her *actual* boyfriend for the rest of the night.

As usual, our act seemed to fool everyone, but it would only keep fooling everyone if I didn't do something stupid.

Something stupid like kissing Iris in public again, for example.

Clara's your friend. You're keeping her parents off her back.
And you're keeping your parent off yours too, Constantine.
Keep playing the game.

Trouble was, the game seemed a whole hell of a lot longer now that Iris was in the mix. Something about that copper hair and those sweet blue eyes. That gorgeous mouth, which could never seem to stop sassing off to me—except when I kissed it quiet of course. Something about those fucking *freckles.*

And her taste.

I'd been jerking off to the memory of that taste for over a week. I'd even caught myself licking my lips, as if I thought it might still be lingering there.

I had to have it again.

"You're looking for her," a cold voice said. I slid my gaze over to Rhys, who was staring back at me with something almost like malice. "The new girl."

"I'm not," I replied automatically, even though I knew I had been. "I don't care if she comes."

Even though I told her about the bonfire yesterday. Even though I told her she should come.

We'd been working on the project out on the back lawn—her request, probably to avoid being in the same spots where we'd fooled around—and she'd been so buttoned up again, so remote. Quiet like she'd been the first day of school, with hardly a word to say to me that wasn't about possible landscapes or integrating illustration.

Like I didn't know about the freckles on her tits.

Like I didn't know how she tasted between her thighs.

I'd known what she was doing, and it pissed me off. She knew when we argued, we ended up kissing. She also knew that when we didn't argue—when we actually shared shit and talked—we also ended up kissing.

So she was keeping all that fire and all that sweetness locked up, far away from me and my kisses.

I'd hated it. I still hated it.

So I'd invited her tonight, hoping like a jackass that she'd also come to my game and see me play. How childish was that?

"I'm not looking for her," I repeated, after Rhys wouldn't stop staring at me. "I swear."

"Hmm."

On the other side of the fire, Samantha Morgan had

waltzed over to the Croft Wells kids, bringing the gift of a beer bong and a short skirt. The losers perked up immediately, smiling and posturing and jockeying for a position next to her.

"Samantha's going to be okay, right?" I asked.

"Emma and Romola are with her," Rhys observed. "And you know Owen won't let anything untoward happen. Not on his prissy watch."

"Making sure assholes don't do anything shitty isn't exactly prissy."

"It will feel a lot prissier after he gets on your case for making out with the new girl tonight."

"I told you, I don't care if she comes or not."

Rhys looked away. His sharp mouth was curved in a frown. "Good. Because if she comes, she'll draw attention."

Anger surged through me as I realized he was right. All the Croft Wells boys currently salivating over Samantha would shred each other bloody for a chance with Iris, with her pretty eyes and her even prettier mouth. Every part of her practically screamed delicious innocence, and there's nothing that dirty assholes loved more than innocence. I should know.

Rhys noticed my scowl at the group on the other side of the fire, and then sighed. "I didn't mean them, dumbass. I meant her *father*. The last thing you want is Headmaster Briggs associating rugby with whatever—" he gestured at Samantha, who was currently riding a Croft kid's back like a horse and doing a shot at the same time "—this is."

Fuck. He was right. Briggs had one goal, and one goal only—turn Pembroke into a fully-fledged Ivy mill. It was pretty close already; save for the kids who took eternal gap years and the ones who turned into social media influencers, most of us ended up at an Ivy or the international equivalent. But most wasn't good enough for Briggs. Most wouldn't bring in those sweet alumni dollars.

And the hard truth was as much as alumni loved the pride and the legacy of things like rugby and lacrosse and rowing, they didn't bring the wow factor the way those college acceptance stats did.

Rhys was right. We were already in Briggs' crosshairs. The last thing I needed was for him to catch Iris at a party that was practically sponsored by Gentleman Jack and Plan B.

Except then Iris appeared between the trees, and I forgot everything I needed.

Other than her.

I stepped forward, and Rhys caught my elbow. "Bad fucking idea, Constantine."

I shook him off. "I'm not going to do anything stupid."

"Define *stupid*," Rhys muttered, but he didn't try to stop me as I crossed the clearing to meet Iris.

The night was the first real night of the New England autumn—with a faint chill in the air and a restless breeze moving through the just-turning leaves above us. Which meant that Iris had bright pink cheeks as she stepped into the firelight. I wondered if her nipples were hard from the cold too.

I wondered if she'd let me warm them up for her.

She was wearing a good-girl outfit tonight—the kind of outfit that made a boy like me want to filthy her up. Thick black tights and a cute dress that looked like a sweater—long enough to be demure, but still short enough for me to easily reach under it if I wanted. Which I did.

She also had her bright hair in two braids again, and my hands flexed as I thought about taking them apart and sifting my fingers through her tresses. Rubbing my mouth against them.

God, she made me crazy. There were so many hot girls here—so many hot girls in the town not two miles away—and yet *this* girl was the one I couldn't get enough of. This tiny, mouthy, hyper-disciplined waif of a girl.

Before I could grab her and haul her off into the darkness, Serafina, Sloane, and Aurora appeared behind her, their happy expressions melting into ferocious battle faces as they saw me.

"No," Serafina said, striding past Iris to get straight to me. She put her finger against my chest. "You don't get to bother her tonight."

I held up my hands. "No bothering. I just want to talk about our project."

"*Un*. Likely," Aurora pronounced. "You've got that bothering look in your eye."

"Guys, it's okay," Iris said, stepping closer to me and pushing Serafina's finger down. "I promise. Keaton is going to be the perfect gentleman. Isn't that right, Keaton?"

There was nothing gentlemanly about my thoughts right then, or the semi that was stiffening behind my fly, but I nodded. "As gentlemanly as Owen."

Everyone except Iris groaned. Owen's brooding addiction to manners was known to more than just us in the Hellfire Club. He wouldn't be caught dead bothering a girl—he allowed girls to bother *him* and then made them tidy up before they left.

"Fine," Serafina said. "Channel Owen. And if I find out you put one cleat out of line, I'm going to let Sloane murder you."

I looked over to Sloane who was wearing a black leather jacket and the kind of boots you might wear to bury a body in.

"Deal," I said, and then I grabbed Iris's hand and tugged her away.

CHAPTER TEN

Keaton

I LED HER away from the fire and into the trees, where clusters of students lazed on Nantucket Looms blankets. There was the sound of lighters lighting up weed, the sounds of kissing and giggling, until it all faded away, and it was just me and Iris alone in the woods, with only the faint orange glow of the fire in the distance to show us where we came from. Iris yanked her hand out of mine as soon as we cleared the last of the sex-and-drugs blankets.

"Follow me into the woods said the Big Bad Wolf to Red Riding Hood," Iris said.

"Shh," I said, turning onto a little path between the trees. "You can almost hear it."

"Hear what—oh! It's a river!"

Iris ran down to the edge of the water excitedly.

River was being generous—it was a brook at best, narrow and splashy and shallow. But even I had to admit it was pretty, and even better, this part of it was surrounded by flat rocks and soft grass. Perfect for more Iris kisses.

I sat down on the grassy bank and then reached up for her. "Come here."

She narrowed her eyes at me, choosing to sit far enough

away that I couldn't reach her without lunging. "We're not making out again, Keaton."

"Okay," I said. "We can skip the kissing if you like. I don't mind getting straight to the part where I make you come."

The nearly full moon was bright enough that I could see her cheeks darken. "We said we weren't going to do that again."

"No, you said that." I lifted an eyebrow at her. "I don't recall agreeing to anything."

"You agreed that we didn't like each other."

"And then I said that it has nothing to do with this," I pointed out, moving my hand between us. "I can make your pussy feel good, and then you can get right back to hating me."

"Wow. The moonlight makes you so romantic," she said in a dry tone, turning back to look at the brook.

I was ready with a quip, I really was, but there was something about the way she looked right then, drawing her knees up to her chest and staring down at the water, that made the sarcastic words disappear.

She didn't look sad, necessarily, but she looked—I didn't know—*lonely* maybe. Or alone in her own thoughts.

I didn't like the idea of her feeling lonely. I didn't know why, because I obviously didn't give a damn how she felt unless it ended with my mouth on her tits. But somehow, I found myself moving closer to her anyway. I found myself sliding an arm around her shoulders—not to yank her into my lap like I'd wanted to earlier—but simply to hold her close. To make sure she was warm. To make sure she knew she wasn't actually alone.

I was probably a shit boyfriend, a shit friend, and a shit guy in general, but I could do this one thing. I could make someone feel like they weren't the only person on the planet.

"You're ruminative tonight, Big Red."

"*Ruminative* is an awfully big word for a boy who can run as fast as you."

Pleasure curled through my chest.

"Does that mean you've watched me run, Iris? Did you come to the game today?"

She ducked her head down, smiling a little at her knees. "Maybe."

"Maybe?" I reached over and lifted her chin. "You watched me play?"

Another flush under those freckles. "Okay, yes. I watched. You have very nice legs."

I laughed. "Is that all you took away from it, sweetheart? That rugby players wear shorts?"

"Well, and that you apparently have no fear." She shook her head in disbelief. "I really thought you were going to leave that field on a stretcher."

I shrugged like it was no big deal. Actually, I'd had to pop some Advil for a nasty bruise on my shoulder and there was a grassy scrape along one thigh that had stung like hell in the shower after the game, but my pride refused to tell her all that.

"Guess I'm just tough," I said casually.

"Uh-huh," she said, like she wasn't buying it. And she probably wasn't. She'd been able to see past my bullshit since the moment she stepped on campus.

"You didn't respond to my observation," I reminded her. "Why so pensive? Most girls would already be in my lap by now."

It was the wrong thing to say, and it earned me a fierce scowl. "Maybe I'm the only girl who happens to care that you're dating Clara."

God. This Clara thing. It was going to kill me, it really was—or at least my neglected erection. I wanted to tell Iris the truth—that Clara and I only pretended to date to keep our parents happy. That she needed the cover for dating the boy she really loved, who was too poor and too anonymous to ever win her parents' approval.

That we were riding the lie until graduation, when we'd be free. Or at least freer than before.

I opened my mouth to say it all, and then I hesitated, remembering Rhys's words from earlier. As much as I wanted this girl, as much as she dominated my thoughts, I couldn't forget who her father was. I couldn't forget that I barely knew her.

Clara had begged me to keep our real relationship terms a secret, and I'd honored that shit. Even the Hellfire Club didn't know our relationship was fake. I didn't know if Iris was the kind of girl who could keep a secret or not, and if she couldn't—if she told Serafina or Aurora—then there was no telling how many other people would hear about it. And then I would've broken my oldest friend's trust *and* screwed us both over with our parents.

Fuck.

"It's complicated with Clara," I finally said. "It's not like I can't do this, though. With you."

She frowned at me. "That's not how Clara made it sound."

Dammit, Clara. "She's worried about appearances, that's all. No one can see us here. It can be our little secret."

Iris turned back to the water, a thick red braid moving over her shoulder. "I don't want to be a secret. I'm already an embarrassment to my parents."

I scoffed. "That can't possibly be true."

She glared at me. "Want to bet?"

"You get amazing grades, you never get in trouble, you're like straight from the Good Girl Factory. There's no way they're embarrassed."

"They want me to be my older sister. They want me to go to Harvard or Brown or Dartmouth. They want me to study law. They want me to make *them* look better."

"And you don't want Harvard? You don't want to be a lawyer?"

She blew out a long breath. "I want to do what I love, and I want to do it far away from here. I want to spend hours waiting for the perfect shot of fog rolling over the Seine. I want to go into the catacombs and picnic in the Tuileries and people-watch from a cafe while I'm eating delicious pastries. I want to fall in love with a French guy and walk through the city hand in hand and go to operas and ballets. I want to start my real life and start being who I really am."

Fall in love with a French guy?

A wave of irritated possessiveness rolled through me, just at the thought of some hypothetical moron holding her hand and doing all that romantic crap with her.

She took a deep breath, looking surprised at herself. "Sorry," she mumbled. "I don't normally go off like that."

"I don't mind," I told her. *Everything but the part about the French guy, at least.*

"It's silly."

"It's not silly. But you *are* wrong about something."

Her eyebrow arched a little in defiance. "Oh really. I'm wrong about something? Care to mansplain myself to me?"

"I like it when you're saucy," I said, and I finally did what I'd wanted to do for the past ten minutes, and I scooped her into my lap.

This time, she let me.

"You're not wrong about yourself, Iris, but you are wrong that there's such a thing as *real life*. This, right now, is real life, and you have the power to make it the way you want. Are you always going to be what everyone else wants you to be?"

She tucked her head against my chest as I finished.

"Or are you going to do what might actually make you happy?" I asked her, more gently than I thought I was capable of—maybe it was because I was also asking myself at the same time.

Am I going to keep trying to please everyone else?

Even if it keeps me away from what I really want?

She tilted her head to look up at me. "And what do you think would make me happy, Keaton?" she asked. Her voice was soft, a little husky. Her pupils were huge pools of obsidian ringed in cobalt.

Fuck. I needed this. I needed *her*.

"I can make you happy," I growled, tugging the hair ties off those terrible, wonderful braids. Terrible because they kept all that pretty, Titian hair locked away from me. Wonderful because they gave me moments like this, the moments when I got to free it and feel it tumbling cool and silky over my fingers. It was like the first pour from a good bottle of scotch. It was like the first firm stroke of my hand when I needed to get off. It was the promise of something decadent, with so much more decadence to come.

"Can you?" she whispered, sliding her hands up my chest. Through the thin fabric of my long-sleeved Baracuta tee, I could feel the warmth of her hands as they moved over my pectoral muscles to my collarbone and then to my neck. She stroked her fingers over a spot behind my ear, and I nearly had a heart attack.

I wanted her to do it forever.

I wanted to flip her over onto her back and nibble on her fingers until she begged me to make her come.

"I can make you very happy," I informed her in a growl, moving her so that she properly straddled my lap and then working my hands into that mass of glorious hair.

"You shouldn't," she said, still whispering. "*We* shouldn't do this."

"We're not doing anything."

"You're going to—" Her voice went shy and husky all at once. "You're going to stick your hand in my panties and make me come again."

"I promise not to make you come with my hands." I said absolutely nothing about my tongue.

"We still shouldn't—"

"Clara doesn't have anything to do with us."

"*Us* has to do with us. We don't even like each other!"

My hands were still in her hair. "I like you plenty right now, Iris Briggs. Let me kiss you."

Her lips parted, and I could see the hesitation and need warring on her face. She wanted it.

She just didn't *want* to want it.

But then she shifted a little in my lap, lining up the hard ridge of my need against her center, and a heavy shudder moved through her body as she moved away again. "Just a kiss," she murmured, drugged by the friction she'd felt between our lower halves. "Just one. Or two."

I needed no other encouragement. I pulled her closer and took her mouth with my own.

It was everything I remembered.

It was as hot and sweet and wild; it was vicious and delicious. She tasted clean and sweet, like strawberries, and her lips were so soft, the kind of soft that wet dreams were made of. When she let my tongue past her lips to stroke against hers, heat surged down to my groin. I was so close to losing it and we hadn't even *done* anything yet.

We'd kissed.

We'd *kissed*, and now I was trying not to come.

What was this girl doing to me?

There was too much of her I needed to touch—I needed her mouth and I needed the soft hollow of her neck and I needed my hands in her hair and I also needed them shaped to the curves of her tits.

I needed them on her hips, pressing her harder against me, and I needed them up her dress, where I could make her moan and whimper for me again.

"Keaton," she murmured, dipping her face to suck at my neck. I tilted my head, offering more skin for her mouth, as I slid my hands down to her hips and guided her firmly against my lap. Now, with her dress pushed up and her legs wrapped around me, the soft warmth between her legs was once again pressed directly against my denim-covered erection.

"Oh my god," she whispered, rocking against it and shivering. "Oh my god. We shouldn't . . ."

"Just for a while longer," I said in between searing kisses. "Just a few more moments."

She nodded her head, a small noise whimpering in the back of her throat as she screwed her hips against mine. "We'll stop. Very soon."

"That's right," I told her. "As soon as you want. *Fuck*, Iris, that feels so good."

I moved my hands from her hips to her ass and helped her. Helped her grind down on me, watching her face as she did. Copper hair tumbled everywhere, and the moonlight caught along the tips of her long eyelashes. I seriously never thought about shit in this way, but she looked like a princess. Like a princess about to come from riding my lap.

"Feel good, baby?" I rasped, working her harder over me. My cock *ached* like a motherfucker, and my thighs were tight from trying to hold back the orgasm that wanted to hit like a tsunami. But I wouldn't come until she did. No matter how good it felt to have her soft pussy grinding over me. No matter how sexy it was to feel her thighs around my hips.

No matter how fuckable she looked right now, with her lips parted and her eyes wide.

"Keaton," she whispered, and then shuddered over me, rocking and rocking, her head dropping down to roll on my shoulder.

I held her tight, loving every fucking minute of it: her shivers and her pants, how eagerly she kept rubbing herself against me, as if she was chasing every last second of her orgasm.

The only thing I wished was that I could feel it for myself—that I had my fingers inside her, or my dick—

Shit.

Even just thinking about being inside had my cock leaking precum inside my boxers. While she was still coming down from her release, I rolled us back and over—fast enough to make her gasp, but careful enough to make sure she was comfortable—so that she was on her back and I was over her.

"I want to see you," I said desperately, getting to my knees and pushing her dress back up to her hips. "I want to see where you came for me."

Her eyelashes fluttered—gleaming silver from the moonlight—and a slow, lazy smile curved her lips. She was all satiation now, all loose limbs and dozy eyes, while I was strung as tight as a piano wire.

"Okay, Keaton," she said, all the pleasure I'd just given her still thick in her voice. She parted her thighs even more in invitation. "You can look."

I was already moving my hands up her thighs, sliding my palms over the synthetic material of her tights. They were thick as far as tights went, but as worked up as I was, they were no match for me. I tore a hole right between her legs, ripping it open enough to get a good look at the pink cotton panties underneath.

I hooked them to the side, and for the first time, I got to see her. I got to see where she was wet and soft, just for me.

"Babe." My voice was rough.

She grabbed my shirt and pulled me down to kiss her again, her hips undulating lazily underneath me.

"You want more?" I whispered against her lips. "You want me to give you another one?"

She nodded, still kissing me, and then sighing as I moved a thigh between her legs for her to move against. By this point, my dick could have hammered nails, and I had to bite my lip to keep from grunting every time she accidentally brushed against it. I'd never gone so long without getting off, and I couldn't even say why exactly, other than that I would tear off my own arm before I stopped right now. I had to make her feel good again.

"What about you?" she asked between kisses. Her hand slid down, down, and then her fingers skated over me. Showers of sparks chased her touch—down my belly, deep in my groin, all along the aching length.

I covered her hand with mine. "You want to make this feel better?" I breathed. "I can show you how."

Her heavenly blue eyes were wide on mine as I guided her into rubbing me, as I decided I needed to pop open the button of my fly—

Honk.

Honk honk.

Hooooonk.

"Shit."

Her face screwed up in confusion. "Are those cars?"

Honk honk honk.

"Yeah. Shit. Here, let me help you up—" I rolled to my feet and took her hands, hauling her easily to standing and then tugging her dress down. Her hair was tousled and her lips were swollen and her tights were torn—but the tights were hidden by her dress and the rest could be chalked up to drinking.

And not, you know, having her pussy seen to by the rugby captain.

"The honks mean we're being busted," I said, taking her hand and tugging her away from the river and towards the bonfire. "We need to get back to the school."

"Okay," she said, looking pale and worried, and I stopped.

"You've never been to a party getting busted before?"

She shook her head.

"You'll be fine," I reassured her. "You haven't been drinking and we don't have any alcohol on us. If someone stops us, the worst that will happen is they tell us to go home."

"If you say so," she muttered as we started walking again, but she didn't sound convinced. All around us were scrambling students, some of them dumping out liquor or weed, others trying to cram it in their pockets and then make a run for it through the trees, taking the long way back to the school.

Me, I preferred the direct route. I figured if it were the cops or school admin, either way, they'd already have their hands full with Samantha Morgan and the Croft Wells kids. We'd just waltz past all the mess and then right back onto the school grounds.

Except there was one thing I wasn't counting on when I reached the bonfire clearing.

One *person.*

I dropped Iris's hand.

"Daddy," she whispered. It could have been horror, or it could have been relief, I didn't know her well enough to say.

You don't know her at all.

"Did you tell him about the party?" I asked, looking over at her. Headmaster Briggs was striding towards us, thunder in his face, and all I could think was that Rhys was right.

She'll draw attention.

The last thing you want is Headmaster Briggs associating rugby with whatever this is.

Shit. Had I just fucked over the entire team—and myself—by fucking around with the headmaster's daughter?

Iris's face was difficult to read. She seemed hurt or indignant or both. "Of course I didn't," she hissed. "Do you think I would have . . . *you know* . . . if I knew he was coming?"

"I don't know, Big Red. How badly would you like to see me in trouble?"

Her mouth gaped. "*What?*"

"Were you bait?"

She closed her mouth then, and her eyes narrowed. "I hate you."

"So you say. And so here we are." I nodded at Headmaster Briggs, who'd finally reached us, his cheeks florid with rage.

I knew I should have run then. And I could have; in the

dim, flickering light, he probably hadn't gotten a good look at my face and would have thought me just another fleeing teenager. But as suspicious of Iris as I was, as pissed as I was about what this might mean for the team, I couldn't leave her there. I didn't know why.

Something about her made me stupid as hell, I guess.

I drew myself up to my full height, fully expecting the headmaster to start laying into me.

Instead, it was as if he didn't even see me at all. He only had furious eyes for his daughter. "You," he said coldly to her. "Home with me. *Now.*"

She didn't look at me. But she didn't have to look at me for me to sense that something normally bright and vibrant inside of her had gone dim. And it was her father's fault.

She stepped forward, and they both turned and walked away, leaving me in no trouble at all.

And yet still feeling guiltier than ever.

Chapter Eleven

Iris

THERE WAS A very specific format to a Milo Briggs lecture.

It was always guaran-goddamn-teed to start with stern disappointment sewn in with some mild derision.

Add a little dash of expectation, some confusion as to how you could have possibly disappointed when you were a Briggs, and then, finally, some love.

There was always love intertwined, which should have made it hurt less, but somehow always managed to make it worse. Because at the end of the day no matter what, I knew my parents wanted the best for me.

The problem was they never actually listened to me or asked me what *I* wanted. They just had their plans laid out, *their* expectations. And I was expected to comply. To follow along, to do as I was told. To follow the rules. And all I wanted to do was to break the rules.

Total lie.

I didn't want to break the rules. That was ridiculous. Who *wanted* to break rules? I liked rules. Rules guided things. I just liked the rules that made sense. If a rule seemed dumb to me or arbitrary, then I was less inclined to follow it.

The number one important thing to me was my freedom. I just wanted to be out of here. And it was almost within my reach. Unfortunately, my father had other plans for me.

"I cannot believe you, Iris. Out cavorting with god knows who, drinking and doing god knows what."

He had a point about the god knows what part. I knew that this was the portion of the lecture where I was supposed to inject the, "I'm sorry, Daddy."

Instead I said, "What is it you can't believe?"

I blinked. Then blinked again. Wondering if somehow I'd become a ventriloquist dummy. That was not what I intended to say.

His brows furrowed. Likely because I had never ever said anything like that to him before. "Iris, I know a move to a new school in your senior year was not . . . ideal."

"Not ideal?" He was kidding right? He'd gotten the new post right after Isabelle had gone to school in London. "You uprooted my whole high-school experience. You didn't even ask. And when I asked if I could stay with Aunt Helen, you said no. 'A family has to stay together,' you said."

He sighed. Clearly flummoxed as to where this new-found mouthiness was coming from. The truth was I was always mouthy. Just, I didn't usually say things out loud. But for some reason, the comebacks, the sly comments, the quick wit, they all came out when I was talking to Keaton. It was easy to forget to control myself with him. Usually because he was making me so mad.

Also for other *reasons.*

But for my parents, I bit my tongue. I knew how important it was to present the right image. But it was like being with Keaton had loosened something in me, and that half of a fuck I had left had dwindled to nearly nothing. Now, it was open season and I couldn't stop the words from tripping and dancing and twirling out of my mouth.

"Iris Briggs. I am your father. I mean, to find you at a party? I am disappointed. Fine, you're young. I know you need to have some social experiences. But you, with those kids from Croft Wells? From the Hellfire Club? What in the world is wrong with you?"

"Aren't you always the one that says, 'Make new friends, get to know the school culture. Immerse yourself fully.'" I tapped my chin. "That was you, right? Or should I go round up Mom and see if she remembers who said those words? It was either her or you. Or hey, maybe it was Isabelle. But ah wait, that's right. Isabelle is not here to check with you, because you let my sister go off to London."

"She's off to study economics."

That was the crux of it. Unlike my sister, I was being impractical. They didn't want me studying photography. And that chafed me raw.

"Look, Iris. Your mother and I, we love you."

"And I love you. I just, I feel trapped, Daddy."

"And that is not what we want for you. It's your senior year and we didn't want to just leave you behind with your aunt. We are a family."

That seed of discontentment that had planted itself in my belly, rooted, and had started to sprout little leaves, blossomed into a blood-red flower, covered in thorns. I knew they loved me. And I loved them. I just didn't want what they wanted for me. And they were unwilling to listen.

"Daddy, I don't understand what the problem is. I have straight As. I work hard, I've been making friends. Getting to know people."

"But you're distracted. I can tell. Back-to-school night, where were you? Your mother and I were counting on you. You know the rule. You know your role. Whatever the new school is, you make everyone feel welcome and that you are excited to be a student there. We did not have that this time."

I muttered under my breath, "I'm sorry, a student needed me."

"What student? Was something wrong?"

I swallowed down the pang of jealousy at his immediate concern for some fictitious student. My jealousy was only salved by the knowledge that the student was Keaton Constantine. And my father would not be too worried about him.

"I took care of it. But that's what I was doing. So sorry I couldn't be by your side."

He shook his head. "Iris, we need you to get things together. Honestly, your mother said it's like you're not even interested in the college application process."

More like I wasn't interested in the applications they wanted me to be interested in. "Oh that. I filled out some of the forms you gave me." I had done my essays. Or rather, I'd taken a series of essays through school and from working on past school newspapers as well as my blog and repurposed several of them to fit the questions being asked. "What about my applications?"

"What about them is you don't seem interested. Is there anywhere that you're dying to go? We could make calls. You're not campaigning for yourself, Iris."

"I've applied to my dream school and several safeties," I hedged, hoping he wouldn't ask for more details. "Well, I'll see where I get in and then I'll make a decision."

He softened then. We were about to get to the I-love-you portion of the lecture. "I need you to buckle down and show me you want this."

I did want this. I wanted my parents' approval. Just not

at the expense of myself.

"Iris, we need you to get back to your focus. You have opportunities awaiting you. Can you show me that you care? Can you show me that you're not distracted? That you're not going to let some boys and wild parties get the better of your senior year? Screwing around is not what you do."

My brow furrowed. "Daddy, I went to *one* party. I didn't even drink. I hung out with kids from the school. I didn't even talk to the kids from the other school. I did everything that I was supposed to do and then some. But the first time I go to a party, you're mad?"

"I'm not mad. I'm disappointed. If you'd just told us. . ."

"Oh my god, so I'm that kid. The one who narcs on her friends. Besides, what is so wrong with a party?"

"You forget I was young once."

"Oh no. I don't forget. You keep telling me. But you keep acting seriously uncool."

He sat back, crossed his arms. "All right, fine, you can go to your room now. But finish the rest of your applications, would you?"

I couldn't give a shit about Harvard—where he wanted me to go. Columbia didn't interest me, although NYU did, and I'd applied there as a safety. My mother's alma mater of Brown held zero appeal. But of course, she had already made all the calls to the director of admissions and the alumni board. Dad had gone to Dartmouth. And so that's where he was campaigning for.

Neither one of them wanted Yale.

God forbid.

So Harvard was the compromise. *Obvi.*

I shook my head. Neither one of them had asked me where *I* wanted to go. What dream would make me fly, soar.

The good news was I was eighteen. My college fund was fully funded. And I could get a loan for living expenses. I had it all figured out. And they couldn't stop me.

With my father's disappointed eyes watching me warily, I stood and grabbed my backpack off the floor. "If we're done, Daddy?"

"Yeah, we're done. Just try to stay out of trouble, Iris. I've never had to say that to you before, but maybe without your sister here as an example, you need to hear it. But I really don't want that to be our relationship now."

I refrained from rolling my eyes for fear that one of them would get so far lodged I wouldn't be able to get it back. Izzy, perfect Izzy, brilliant and scarlet-haired and beautiful. A hard act to follow.

There was a small part of me that wanted to be like her. I wished I could just toe the line. But I didn't want to. I wanted to be in Paris. I wanted to have freedom.

Problem was Dad wasn't wrong about me being distracted. Keaton Constantine had me twisted. God, I'd been making out with him, at a party. Lying down. He'd been grinding on me with his hand up my dress and that delicious pressure right at the juncture of my thighs.

I had been flying. Feeling like my skin was on fire and I was vibrating all at once. It felt so good. But god, he was so evil. Swear to god if he somehow still managed to tank this project for me, I was going to kill him. Not to mention that fucking *bait* comment!

I was super going to kill him.

Funny how my usual Keaton Constantine feelings included thoughts of murder. I thought about it frequently. I wondered if I could hit him hard enough to make him pass out, if I could throttle him. I wondered what would happen if I took my dad's car and just ran him over.

And then on the other hand, I wondered how far this thing between us—the whispered hushed secrets and soul baring—was going to go. And, of course, there was the desperate forbidden deliciousness, the need to be near him even when I knew I hated him.

You don't hate him.

I shoved that thought aside. What the fuck? I absolutely *did* hate him. I hated everything about him. The kind of guy he was, that smug alpha asshole. I hated alpha guys. Loathed them. I didn't necessarily want a beta guy either. But I hated that cocksure I-know-everything-and-you-know-nothing kind of attitude. It made me want to punch things.

That attitude roiled against my need for independence, and so I stayed away from guys like that. But somehow, I couldn't stay away from Keaton. It didn't matter how much I hated him.

You don't hate him.

God, I did. *Please, God, let me still hate him.*

The problem was I knew that was right. I didn't hate him.

Being lectured now, that sucked. And the first person I wanted to talk to was him. Not to Sera, not Sloane. Not even Rachel from back home. I wanted Keaton.

From a few of the things he'd said about his parents, I got the impression he would understand. That he would feel me and my annoyance so hard. And the disappointment, and the need to be my own person. The need to break free. I knew he would get it.

Then why are we still pretending we hate him?

My boots shuffled on the old wood floors of the headmaster's residence as I passed dark window after dark window on my way down the hall. The house was situated behind the dorms and surrounded by trees, as if the encroaching forest wanted to swallow it whole, and it seemed as ancient as the forest too, with its stained glass windows and dark wood paneling and tiny fireplaces in every room. Whereas the Pembroke campus was all New England charm, the headmaster's house had more of a *Turn of the Screw* vibe—a little creepy, a lot creaky, and very cool.

Except, of course, if you were trying to get down the noisy Victorian-era staircase for a midnight snack. Then all the creakiness and creepiness were suddenly a lot less amusing.

I got to my room and quietly closed the door—even though slamming it would've felt really good right about now—and took a look around. It looked the same as it did before I went to the party. Before I once again fell into the logic-abyss that seemed to be Keaton Constantine. Before I let Keaton give me an orgasm—*again*.

Frustrated, I tossed my bag on my bed and then sat at my desk.

I knew I had the other applications to the other schools that were on my parents' hit list. The problem was I had zero motivation to apply to those, not even to add to my pile of safeties. Instead, there was the one that I wanted, and the even earlier escape it was promising through the pre-degree program.

What if you don't get in? What if they reject you?

The seeds of doubt were right there in my gut along with the seeds of discontent. The doubt had this gray smoky flavor to it. Hard to pinpoint, hard to make dissipate.

I pushed aside the Harvard, Brown, and Dartmouth applications, and I pulled out my letter for the Sorbonne program instead. And then I cracked open my laptop to the tab I'd had open on my browser since I'd gotten the letter.

The online application for the program was already

done. Complete, ready. All I had to do was hit *submit*. But for over a week I'd been unable to do it. Unable to just pull the fucking trigger.

My father's lecture reverberated in my head.

Get your act together, that lecture said. *Be what we need you to be.*

Keaton's words came rushing back to me too.

Are you always going to be what everyone else wants you to be? Or are you going to do what might actually make you happy?

I didn't even need to think about it anymore. I knew what I wanted. I clicked *submit*.

The Sorbonne. Photography. An early escape. The last thing on earth my parents would ever approve of.

But it was the first thing I'd done in months that felt entirely like me.

CHAPTER TWELVE

Keaton

"YOU CAN'T STAY angry with me forever," I said, watching Iris stare determinedly out my car window. Outside the car, there were trees and trees and trees, heavy with leaves that were newly flushed with fall. You'd think we were still in Vermont with all this foliage, but no, we were driving through Yonkers, which meant we'd been in the car for four hours.

Four *long* hours.

Four hours of Iris pretending I barely existed, four hours of her answering all my questions with one-word answers. Four hours of her glaring at me when I nudged her knee or brushed against her hand.

Actually, the entire past week and a half had been strained between us, which was not great timing because it had finally come time to take the pictures that would eventually turn into our project, and we needed to cooperate now more than ever.

We'd both managed to agree that we wanted to get away from Vermont to get our images at least. Everyone else was doing trees and mountains and lakes, and I'd turned to her during our last session and said, "I want to do the city."

Because fuck that trite bucolic crap. Any idiot with a cell phone could take a picture of some trees, dial up the contrast, and then write a douchey exhibit label for it. But Iris and I weren't idiots. We were better than the obvious answer. And what was less obvious for a landscape than a city?

Iris had immediately seen the appeal, dropping her cold shoulder act to look at me with a thoughtful expression. "Skyscrapers instead of woods. Streets instead of rivers. I can see that."

"We could contrast it with what a typical landscape is expected to be," I'd said, tapping my pencil against the table we were sitting at. "I could integrate some illustrated landscape shit between buildings or on top of them. On the sides. Rooftop farms, you know, like a solarpunk feel . . ."

Iris had shaken her head. "Too futuristic."

"It's conceptual," I'd defended.

"It's season three *Westworld*. It's Wakanda. It's *Zootopia*. It's been done."

"Yeah, it has. Because it's fucking cool."

She'd narrowed her eyes at me. She'd been pissed since that night in the woods when I'd dry-fucked her to orgasm and then called her "bait" ten minutes after, and it seemed like she took a particular, resentful delight in saying, "It's *fan art*, Keaton. Is that really what you want your semester project to be? Fan art?"

"Fan art is badass stuff. Don't be such a fucking snob."

Her eyebrow had arched. And then she'd continued on like I hadn't spoken at all. "We'll do a fake double exposure. One of the city, one of the landscape it would have been if it had never been developed."

I'd considered it a moment. It wasn't a terrible idea, and as much as I'd like to get her to admit that my idea was cooler, I couldn't deny that her vision was probably more reflective.

And *reflective* was the kind of shit that got top marks and written up in the local papers, which I wasn't about to say no to.

So Iris's idea it was.

And now here we were, using my family's car and driver to get us to the city, planning on staying at the Constantine penthouse while we worked since my mom was currently in Bishop's Landing and we'd have it all to ourselves. I'd pitched staying at my place to Iris as a way for her to save money on splitting a hotel room and as the option that made the most logical sense—but I'd be lying if I said I hadn't thought about her swimming naked in my family's rooftop pool. Showering in *my* shower. Sleeping in *my* bed.

I'd be lying if I said I hadn't thought of all those things constantly.

God, I wanted her again. I wanted to kiss her so badly that sometimes I caught myself licking my own teeth. I wanted my fingers back in her panties so terribly that I had to curl them into fists to keep from grabbing her.

I wanted to nudge those thighs apart and show her everything I could do, everything I could make her feel.

I just wanted *her*.

The good news was that we had a pretty good track record when it came to fooling around when she was pissed at me. And with that comforting thought, I crossed my arms and leaned back in my seat, giving her my smirkiest smirk.

She very pointedly didn't look at me, but I knew she could feel my stare heating against her face. She frowned out the window.

"So does your dad know that you're spending a weekend in the city?" I asked. "With me?"

She sighed. "No, of course not."

"It's for school, Big Red. I figured he'd understand."

She cut a look at me that very clearly said, *I know you are trying to irritate me and it's working.*

Unfortunately for her, I knew the secret. And the secret was that a provoked Iris was a horny Iris.

Not exactly incentive to stop.

"And I'm sure your father wouldn't have minded that you'd be staying at my place," I teased. I let a hand trace an idle circle on her knee, just below the hem of her uniform skirt.

She shivered a little, but she didn't stop me.

"And he wouldn't have minded knowing you'd be in my bed. Wearing something cute. Needing kissed good night."

"Keaton," she scolded. Her eyes were on the driver's partition in front of us.

I circled her knee again, a bit higher this time, flirting with the bottom of her skirt. "He can't hear or see us."

"It's still not right," she protested. Although her objection wasn't very convincing when she was also parting her legs the tiniest bit, like she couldn't help but want me between them.

"Tell me where your parents think you are," I persuaded, letting my fingers drift higher. I was caressing the soft skin of her inner thigh now. It wouldn't be much longer until I felt cotton.

God, I was hard just thinking about it. Hard thinking about *plain, cotton panties.*

I was good and fucked for this girl, and she had no fucking clue.

"They think I'm with Serafina," she finally admitted, and when I rewarded her with a graze of my fingertips right over her cotton-covered core, she instinctively arched against my touch. "On—on a campus visit to Columbia."

She was breathless now. I stroked her again and grinned evilly as she mewled and shivered, now shamelessly spreading her legs.

"There. That wasn't so hard now, was it?"

"You're cheating."

I plucked teasingly at the edge of the cotton, so close to her heat. "I had to, Briggs. You weren't playing fair."

"You weren't playing fair when you accused me of being bait."

"*Aha*," I crowed softly. "I knew you were upset about that."

"Of course I was—" Her voice broke off as I slid a finger between her panties and her skin and caressed her there.

"I'm sorry I said it," I told her. "I shouldn't have."

The pad of my index finger found her clit and I started working it in small, light strokes.

"It's okay," she said, her eyes fluttering closed. "I forgive you."

"Huh. That was easy."

She opened her eyes to look at me again. It wasn't a glare this time, or even one of her suspicious sidelong glances. This time, she looked at me like she wanted to spend the rest of her life with her mouth on mine.

"You make me forget why things should be hard," she said, and then her hand slipped down to cover my own.

Together we pushed my finger inside her sheath. I hissed when I felt how wet she was. "Jesus Christ, Iris."

"I want to see you," she whispered, her eyes dipping down to where my cock was currently trying to drill a hole through my pants. "I still haven't seen you."

I was ready to do it, ready to give her whatever she wanted, if only it meant I could keep my finger inside her, when I looked out the windows and realized we were on Park Avenue, and almost in front of my building.

I pulled my fingers free and sucked them clean, wishing I could take a video of her watching me as I did it. Because with her eyes like this—dark and glazed with desire—with her full pink lips parted and her cheeks flushed under all those freckles—she was the sexiest thing in the entire goddamn world.

"We're going to finish this," I promised her in a growl as the car rolled to a stop.

She made no move to close her thighs, and her hand made a naughty movement downward, like she was going to finish it by herself if she had to.

I caught her wrist. "Uh-uh, sweetheart. As much as I need to watch you get yourself off, it's not going to be where I can't savor it."

"And why can't you savor it right now?" she asked, squirming and squirming with her uniform skirt pushed high up on her thighs. My erection surged, and for a moment, I nearly said *fuck it*, and gave in. Fingering her while I jerked off suddenly felt as necessary as breathing.

Think of the pool, Constantine. Think of her all adorable and whimpering in your bed.

With superhuman strength, I clawed back my control and smoothed her skirt back over her thighs as the doorman opened my door.

"Because we're here."

✧　✧　✧

"WOW," IRIS SAID, spinning in yet another circle. "Wow *wow* wow."

"It's a good thing you want to go to Paris, Big Red, because you seem to only know one word in English."

She flipped me off, but kept spinning, eventually spinning her way out to the rooftop terrace, which had a northern panoramic view of the city, including the Chrysler Building and the Empire State Building. It also had a private heated pool and lots of big outdoor couches and beds at the side—perfect for kissing and petting while the city lights glowed around us. It might get chilly, though, so I'd need to grab a blanket to wrap Iris in . . .

I followed her onto the terrace, shaking my head at myself.

Since when had I become that guy? Blankets-so-a-girl-wouldn't-get-cold guy?

I wasn't an asshole—at least, I wasn't a *super*-asshole—and I was always good to the girls I was with. I just couldn't remember the last time it had occurred to me to be chivalrous. To make sure the girl I was with didn't just leave with a satisfied body, but a happy heart too.

Iris stopped spinning and smiled at me, the wind ruffling her bright hair all around her face. Her blue eyes were the same color as the autumn sky, and a dimple was denting her cheek, and she was so gorgeous, so sexy, that I couldn't stand not to be touching her for a single moment longer.

"I need to thank your mom for letting us stay here," she was saying as I was striding towards her, my hands already itching to grab her and haul her close. "I'll have to thank her at Parents' Weekend next week."

I seized her by the arm and drew her into me. "You'll have to settle for a note, Big Red. She never comes to Parents' Weekend."

"Never?" She looked surprised as I slid a hand into her perfect hair and then tightened the tiniest bit. Her eyelids fluttered in pleasure as I did it again.

It made me want to growl in satisfaction. I knew she

liked me bossy, I knew she liked me a little rough, but god, to see it out here in broad daylight and without me warming her up for it first . . .

I needed to taste her again.

Now.

I tugged her head to the side to open up her neck to me. "Never," I confirmed for her as I started kissing along her jaw and throat. "She usually can't be bothered. My other siblings take up most of her time."

"But why?" she asked, sounding confused. "You do all the right things. The grades, the rugby. The girlfriend . . ."

And at the mention of Clara, I felt her stiffen under my kisses and start to pull away.

Shit.

"Every time," Iris said, almost to herself. "Every fucking time. I say I'm not going to let you get to me, I'm going to keep my distance because you have a girlfriend, and yet—"

I couldn't let her pull away. I couldn't let her go another minute without knowing that I was fucking obsessed with her and nothing else mattered but us.

Sorry, Clara.

"She's not really my girlfriend," I confessed.

It felt strange to say it aloud, finally, after all this time— I felt both heavier and lighter all at once.

"We aren't dating, we aren't in love, we don't fuck. We are nothing, Iris. She and I are a lie."

I still had my hand in Iris's hair, and I guided her face to look up at mine. She blinked at me with so much wariness and hope and uncertainty in her autumn-sky eyes.

"But why would you pretend to date someone for this long?" she asked.

I let out a long breath. "My mother. She's close with Clara's parents. They've always seen us as a destined pair, I guess, since a Blair and a Constantine marriage would be good for both families."

Iris wrinkled her nose. It was unbearably cute. "Can't you just tell them that you're not interested in each other?"

"We've tried. But then Clara had to go and fall in love with a boy her parents would hate, and then us dating became a convenient cover for her. I became her alibi when she needed to sneak off to see her real boyfriend, and she became a way to keep my mother happy with me. Well, maybe not happy so much as 'less disappointed,' but you get the idea."

She stared up at me, searching my gaze. "So . . . you're not really dating Clara? She isn't really going to kill me for kissing you?"

"She might be pissed that you're blowing her cover, but that's all."

She pulled her bottom lip between her teeth.

My cock responded like she'd shoved her hand in my pants, and I dropped my forehead to hers, closing my eyes. "Let me kiss you again," I said. Begged. "Let me taste you."

"Is that . . . is that all you want to do?" she asked. Her voice was strange. Not hesitant exactly, but more like—more like shy. Like she wanted to ask for something but didn't know how.

I opened my eyes. "Babe, you can't expect me to answer that honestly."

"Why not?"

Why not? Because I had an entire folder in my brain full of fantasies and scenarios so filthy they'd send her running. Because *all I want to do* had a very easy and short answer.

Everything.

I wanted to do everything with her.

I wanted time to stop and the world to freeze, and then

I wanted to fuck her in every position I knew of and some that hadn't even been invented yet. I wanted to finger her in public, I wanted to eat her out while she looked at the stars. I wanted to come all over those freckled tits.

I wanted to make her climax so many times that she'd be as obsessed with me as I was with her.

"Keaton," she said, sliding her hands up to my face. "Tell me what you're thinking."

I leaned down and nipped her lower lip. "No way."

She did the thing again, where she ran her fingers through the place where my hair curled behind my ears. It sent hot, shivering thrills all over me. "Then show me," she whispered. "Show me everything you want to do to me."

I pulled back. The breeze ruffled between us as I studied her face.

"You sure?"

She blushed. "Yes."

I palmed her hips, pulling her lower half tight against mine. My thick erection dug into the softness of her belly. I wanted to fuck her. I wanted to go through an entire box of condoms with her.

But I also needed her to be sure.

"You know me," I told her. "I'm not the hearts-and-flowers type. I'll make it good for you, but I can't promise it will be sweet."

She pushed back against me, licking her lips. "Keaton," she said, her fingers brushing the hair behind my ears.

"Yeah?"

"Shut up."

I laughed as I kissed her again, sliding my hands around to cup her bottom and then lift her into my arms. She wrapped her legs around my waist, and I carried her back inside the penthouse, kissing her the whole way.

CHAPTER THIRTEEN

Keaton

"YOU'RE A GIANT," she told me between kisses.

My chest swelled a little. Working out meant I slayed on the field, yes, but being able to sweep Iris off to my bed like this was pure magic. I'd endure Coach's brutal conditioning every single day for the rest of my life if it meant being able to kiss her while I carried her off to be fucked.

"You're just tiny," I said, but I couldn't hide the smugness in my tone.

"More like you're just full of yourself," she teased back, but she didn't sound upset.

I bit her jaw as we walked past the kitchen island. "You're about to be full of myself too."

She groaned, and I stopped walking, because I needed to touch her again, I needed to taste her again. *Right now.*

I set her on the counter, my hands already diving under her skirt to pull off her panties. I worked them off her hips and legs, stuffing them in my pocket. Like hell was she getting those back.

"Hold up your skirt and spread your legs," I told her as I got to my knees. I was just tall enough that when I knelt, her pussy was right where I wanted it. And so, when she finally did as I asked and pulled up her skirt, I was presented with a view that would keep my right hand busy for years.

I'd been able to glimpse her before, in the moonlight, but it was nothing like this. Nothing like being able to see her in broad daylight. Nothing like seeing where she was pink and slick and ready for me. Nothing like being able to see her silky, scarlet curls. Yes, it was a stereotype that guys love redheaded pussy, and yes, it was still hot as hell, stereotype or not.

I didn't warm her up. I didn't kiss my way up her thigh. I didn't give her chaste, closed-mouth kisses against her seam. Instead, I dove in like a starving man and clamped my hands over her hips to keep her still as I stroked into her with my tongue.

"Fuck, babe," I murmured into her, barely able to stop devouring her in order to get the words out. "You taste so good." Even better than I remembered. Even better than I'd dreamed.

She was so sweet here, so very *Iris*—and it was a taste I was worried I'd never get enough of, given the rock-hard state of my dick.

She tried to arch as my tongue flicked over her clit, but I wouldn't let her. I held her fast and started going in earnest—fluttering, caressing, sucking—full on burying my face into her. My nose was in her curls and my lips were wet with her, and when I chanced a look up at her, she was already looking down at me with a look that fired my blood right up.

She was looking at me like I was some kind of king.

Like I was some kind of idol.

"Keaton," she whispered.

"Keep still and keep that skirt up," I ordered, going in

again, abandoning myself to every dirty kiss and lick I'd fantasized about giving this pretty ginger pussy. She was so soft and so warm here.

She was heaven, and I was going to give her heaven in return.

I carefully worked a single finger inside, keeping my mouth at the swollen bud above her opening, feeling her thighs tense around my head. She was getting close, her body practically thrumming as she got wetter and tighter— and wetter and tighter still.

Fuck. I'd jerked off to the thought of this so many times, it was nearly impossible to keep myself from reaching down and freeing my cock, like a perverted Pavlovian response to having my mouth between her legs.

Soon, I promised my aching erection. *So soon.*

But Iris first.

I used my free hand to hold her hip even tighter—and just in time, too, because as her climax broke against my mouth, she sank her fingers into my hair and rocked against me, trembling so hard I wondered if she'd tremble right off the edge of the counter. I wondered if I'd have to catch her and then lay her down right there on my kitchen floor and sink into her slick warmth.

Because if she literally fell off the counter because I made her come so hard, there was no way I was making it all the way to my bed. No fucking way.

Luckily for us both, I managed to keep her braced up on her perch while I finished the job, making sure to kiss her pussy through every last flutter and squeeze. And then when she was all done, I withdrew my finger and stood, scooping her into my arms without a word.

"Keaton," she sighed dreamily, resting her head against my shoulder.

"You're always so sweet after you come for me."

"Is that why you do it?" she asked, her tone half drowsy, half teasing. "So I'll be nice?"

I smirked down at her. "I like it when you're mouthy too, you know."

"Oh, is that so?"

We were in my room now, and thank God, because I was so hard I could feel my heartbeat in my dick. Need for her had bunched itself into a hot ball at the base of my spine, and the pressure was painful, threatening to snap my resolve.

"You know it is," I told her as I set her on my bed and then crawled over her. The light was slowly fading into the lavender light of evening, and my big shadow dwarfed her small frame on the bed. "Whenever we fight, I end up begging to put my mouth on you."

She gave me a doubtful look. "I'd say you're more *bossy* than *begging*."

"I don't know what you're talking about. Now, take off your shirt."

She rolled her eyes at me but smiled to herself all the same as she pulled off her sweater and then started unbuttoning the white shirt underneath. I mirrored her as I rose up to my knees, opening my shirt and then tearing it off. I kicked off my shoes and pants, wearing nothing but boxer briefs as I palmed my erection and looked down at the living wet dream in my bed.

She was in nothing but her bra and her skirt now, and when she parted her legs, it was obvious there was nothing underneath. Nothing between my hot gaze and her waiting pussy.

"Bra off," I said hoarsely. "I want to be able to suck on your tits."

The smile on her face turned into an expression so hungry I nearly came in my boxer briefs. "Oh, really," she said softly. She reached behind her back, and in a few seconds, I could see her perfect breasts—pert and freckled and tipped with nipples already straining to be sucked on. "I think I want that too."

She gathered her skirt up in her fingers, pulling the hem all the way up past her naked pussy.

"I think I want everything," she whispered.

Looking at her made me feel like I'd been kicked in the chest. Those sweet tits, her soft stomach, that place between her legs that I could still taste on my lips . . .

Those bright blue eyes, looking up at me with hunger and trust, and still glazed with satisfaction from the orgasm I just gave her . . .

And her hair, all flame-colored satin, tousled over my pillow as it should fucking be. Her hair should be spilled over my pillow every night for the next eight months. For the next million months.

I could barely fucking stand it, how good and right it was to have her like this.

Once I could breathe again, I reached over to my end table and pulled a condom from the drawer, tearing the packet open with my teeth.

"You've done this before, Big Red?" I asked as I tugged my boxer briefs down and rolled the condom over my thick length.

I figured she probably hadn't; she'd had *virgin* written all over her from the start. And normally I didn't care about that kind of caveman shit—sex was sex, didn't matter if it was the first time or the ninetieth—but it did matter that we went at the right pace.

Her eyes were hot on my dick as I worked the latex

down. A flush was working its way up from her chest to her neck. "No," she murmured. "This is—you're my first."

It shouldn't matter, I told myself again. It *didn't* matter.

But that she was trusting me with this—trusting me to make it good for her—it made something behind my ribs go tight and sharp.

"I promise you won't regret it," I swore, leaning back over her. I kissed her thoroughly as I reached down to sweep the head of my cock through her seam, rubbing her up and down with my tip until she started moving underneath me and chasing it.

I kissed her neck and then a soft breast as I finally nudged myself inside—just the tiniest amount. Just the tip.

I held my breath. Christ she was tight. And warm. And so slippery wet. She stiffened underneath me, pulling in a breath, and I bent to take a taut nipple into my mouth, sucking and working it until she relaxed again.

And then I pushed in.

Not much—just an inch—but it was enough to send her hands flying to my shoulders. Her eyes were round when I looked down at her, and her lower lip was caught between her teeth.

I froze. "Does it hurt too much?" I asked. It was almost hurting *me*—she was that tight and warm inside. My balls were already drawing up to my body, eager to release into her, and I had to clench everything in my stomach and thighs and ass to keep from blowing my load right then and there.

She shook her head after a minute. "No. No, it feels better now." She ran her eyes down my chest and abdomen, her stare going dark with lust as she looked down at where my cock was wedged into her. "Just go slow if you can," she said in a husky voice.

"Anything," I promised her. "Anything you need." Although going slow felt like a Herculean task right now. Everything in my body was screaming to thrust, to rut, to pump into her until I exploded.

I reached down to gently massage her clit as I pushed in a little bit more, my entire body trembling with the restraint.

"God," she breathed. "It's—it's so much. Are you all the way in yet?"

I almost laughed, and the noise came out pained. Nearly animal-like. "No, babe. Not even halfway."

"*How?*"

I bent down to suck on the firm berry of a nipple. "Because I'm big and you're tiny. Now, *shhh*. Let me make you feel good."

It was the hardest thing I'd ever done, working my way into her virgin slickness without losing control. There was no word for how that velvet grip felt around my dick, for how slick and hot she was, for the way her silken walls caressed me. I gritted my teeth, I clenched my jaw—I even closed my eyes so I wouldn't see all that fiery hair or those sweet, cinnamon freckles—and then somehow, miraculously, I made it all the way to the root without hurting her or embarrassing myself.

Once I was sunk to the hilt, I managed—with some deep breathing and counting backwards—to get a hold of myself enough that I could open my eyes and look down at her. When I did, I nearly regretted it, because she was so fucking beautiful like this, all flushed and flutter-eyed, her lips parted and her nipples still hard and begging for my mouth again.

I braced myself on one hand and started circling her needy clit with my thumb, not moving my hips at all. I just rubbed and circled with her impaled on me, and then bit by bit, little by little, she started to move. She started to fuck herself on my erection, chasing the pleasure, circling her hips and rocking against the pressure on her swollen bud.

"Oh god," she whispered, her hands pushing back into my hair and pulling tight. I hissed in response, only barely able to keep from coming then. "Oh god, Keaton—it's like—it feels so—"

What it felt like I never did learn, because she shattered beneath me with a long, delicious cry that had my hips churning between her thighs before I even realized what was happening. Her body went tight and quivery around me, squeezing me, milking me, and it was as if her body was trying to pull the orgasm right out of my cock, like it was yanking it clean out of my soul.

I fell over her, sliding my arms beneath her slender frame and giving her my weight as I gave in. All these weeks of wanting her, of needing her, of jerking off constantly because she made me crazed with lust—it all came out now, ripping through my body with the force of a storm. I buried my face in her hair and pumped the condom full of my orgasm, rocked to the core by each and every jolting pulse. Slain by every jagged surge of pleasure as I emptied my need into her body.

Wrecked with how beautiful she was, even now—sweaty and tousled and looking exactly like a girl who'd just been thoroughly fucked.

When the orgasm finally slowed and then abated, we shared a long, lazy kiss. And when I pulled away to take care of the condom, she murmured, "You did it, you know."

"Did what?"

She smiled a smile that could shame the sun. "You made it good for me."

My chest went all tight again, for reasons I didn't understand—or didn't want to understand. "Yeah?"

Then that smile turned incendiary, and she reached for me as I walked back from the small wastebasket by my desk. She licked her lips in a way that had me getting hard all over again. "Now, let me see if I can think of something to make good for you."

"Iris," I groaned, already climbing back on the bed, because—what, I'm going to say no?

"*Shh,*" she teased, getting up and crawling down my body. "Let me make you feel good."

And then her slender fingers were on me, and *good* was nowhere even close to how I felt.

CHAPTER FOURTEEN

Iris

"**D**O YOU THINK we've got enough?"

Keaton was scrolling through my camera as we stood on a sidewalk in Chinatown, combing through all the pictures we'd taken today. We'd snapped expansive views from the observation deck at 30 Rock; we'd captured the bustle and rush of Grand Central Terminal. We'd found Grove Court—the almost eerily out-of-time nook of ivy-covered, white-shuttered brick—and we'd gotten shots of the Brooklyn Bridge from every possible angle. We'd used up all that delicious autumn light, and now evening was creeping in, along with a stiff, chilly breeze.

"I think we've got everything we need," he said, lingering over a picture I'd taken from the observation deck this morning. I'd taken it right as the sun was breaking through a fluff of thick clouds, and it managed to catch the way its newly released rays broke over the skyline like gilded waves upon a jagged, glassy shore.

"This looks like something out of a movie," he said, grinning up at me. "You're brilliant, babe. I'm fucking an actual genius."

I grinned back, but the grin was short-lived.

The words *brilliant* and *genius* went down like compliments should—smooth and sweet.

But I had no idea how to parse my response to the last part. When he said the word *fucking* like that, rough and proud and suggestive all at once, I wanted to tackle him to the sidewalk and rip his pants off. But I also couldn't help the sharp stab in my chest at hearing it.

Was fucking all this was to him?

What else did you expect, Iris? Did you expect him to tell you he was in love with you?

No. *No.*

No, of course not. That would be both stupid and ridiculous, and I was neither. I knew sex didn't equal love. Even an idiot could see that Keaton Constantine wasn't the loving type—and I definitely wasn't in love with him, anyway. I mean, hell, hadn't I only just decided I didn't hate him? Of course I wasn't in love with him.

It's just . . . looking at him right now with that *grin* and that lock of hair falling over his forehead . . . feeling the tenderness between my legs and the flutter of my pulse at his nearness—I couldn't say that the idea of love sounded that awfully stupid. He was sexy and secretly talented, he was cocky and bossy and also the kind of guy that would do anything to help a friend.

Would it be so terrible? To fall in love with him?

It would if he didn't love you back.

Because that—it would break me.

Of that I had no doubt.

✦   ✦   ✦

"I STILL CAN'T believe this is your *home*," I said as we walked back inside the Constantine penthouse. When we'd woken up this morning after having sex two more times last night,

I'd demanded a tour—which he'd given and which also ended with us having sex on a rug in front of a fireplace faced with some fancy green marble imported from Italy.

It wasn't that I hadn't been in expensive houses before—attending boarding school and having boarding-school friends invariably meant staying over at places that were infinitely nicer than a headmaster's residence—but the Constantine penthouse was still far beyond anything I'd ever seen.

The huge windows looking out onto the city, and the soaring ceilings, and the glass and steel staircases that looked like works of art . . . it all screamed *money*. And not just any kind of money, but like, *big* money. Russian oligarch money. Own-multiple-private-islands money.

Keaton Constantine wasn't just the king of Pembroke.

When it came his time, he was going to be king of the world.

And it didn't do anything to make me feel better about where things stood between us. Why would a king want a freckled new girl with parental baggage? Of course he wouldn't.

And you don't want him either, remember? You're bound for Paris—the sex stuff is just a fun stop along the way.

"I can't believe I still haven't gotten to see you naked in my pool," Keaton said as he came up behind me and pulled me into his arms. He was hard again, and the rigid heft of his erection pressed into my backside like a luscious promise.

I should have been too tender to think about sex again, but when he nipped at my earlobe and slid a hand down to cup my pussy over my dress, my entire body went hot and shivery. The sore place between my legs ached for more.

I pushed into his touch, and he made a noise deep in his chest, like a growl. "You ready for more, baby?"

"How about," I said, looking at the darkened sky outside, "we try out your pool?"

His grip didn't loosen on me, like he was torn between fucking me bent over a nearby sofa or finally getting his Iris pool fantasy.

With a heavy breath, he finally released me.

"No clothes, Iris," he said huskily. "I want you bare."

God, when he used that voice . . . I quivered. It frightened me how much control he had over my body, over my reactions, just by being *him*. It frightened me to think he might have that kind of control over my heart—that he could set it to racing with happiness or thudding with anxious pain. I couldn't let that happen.

I wouldn't.

Resolved, I stepped away from him and cast a coy glance over my shoulder as I started walking towards the terrace, lit only by the glow of the city and the underwater lights set deep in the pool. I pulled off my dress as I walked. And then my bra. And then my panties. Until I was in nothing but goosebumps and the little ankle boots I'd worn around the city today.

Keaton prowled after me as I went, his eyes glittering in the shadows and his hands clenching into fists, as if to keep himself from grabbing me. I bent at the waist to unzip the little zippers on the boots, giving him a show, and when I stood back up with bare feet and glanced back at him, he looked downright *dangerous*.

"Careful, Iris," he warned.

I arched an eyebrow. "I thought you wanted me naked."

"I can't remember a single thought I've ever had," he said darkly, "when you bend over like that."

I gave him my naughtiest smile and then dove into the pool without another word. The water was warm—so much warmer than the fall air outside—and when I broke the surface, I could see little wisps of steam hovering over the pool like fog. Above me, stars twinkled, and all around the terrace, the city twinkled back.

The illicit feel of the water sliding over my pebbled nipples and past the exposed secrets between my legs hit me harder than liquor. And even more intoxicating were Keaton's eyes, glowing in the near-darkness as he sat on the edge of the pool. While I'd jumped in, he'd kicked off his shoes and socks too, rolling up his pant legs so he could sit with his feet in the water.

"You're not coming in here with me?" I asked, swimming up to him.

He leaned back on his hands, his eyes raking over my naked form. His voice was all hunger and stormy greed when he said, "No, Iris. I'm going to watch you swim for me."

I could see where his cock strained against his pants, but he made no move to touch it; he did nothing that would interrupt this visual feast for himself.

The intensity of his gaze was—heady.

Flattering.

So very easy to confuse with something more than lust.

I flipped over onto my back and kicked my way to the far edge of the pool, knowing he'd enjoy seeing my wet stomach and breasts as I did. When I got to the wall—which was made of thick glass and gave me a dizzying view down to the street far below—I asked him, "Do you make all the girls swim naked in your pool?"

"Just the bratty ones," he replied. His voice was low and soft—so soft I could barely hear him over the lap of the water and the whipping breeze. I turned to face him.

"So I'm not just the latest in a long line of naked pool

nymphs?"

The corner of his mouth curved up. "Jealous, Iris?"

Yes, I wanted to say. The idea of another girl doing this with him, doing anything with him—it sent scalding knives of jealousy stabbing into my chest. And I hated it. I hated being jealous. It wasn't as if I hadn't crawled into his bed with my eyes wide open.

Okay, so I didn't so much *crawl* as I was scooped up and carried to his bed, but the point stands.

I knew what kind of guy he was. I knew I couldn't expect much.

Then why do you care so much about the other girls?

"Not jealous at all," I lied, pushing off the wall and swimming back to him. His eyes slid over me appreciatively as I cut through the water, his tongue slipping out to lick his lower lip. Like he was thinking about tasting me.

"You can rest easy," he said as I swam up to his feet. "You're the first girl I've ever brought here."

"Really?" I hated how happy that made me. I hated how happy I sounded about it.

Keaton nodded, and his expression had changed—less hunger, more inscrutability. I had no idea what he was thinking right now. "This place is full of memories for me. Some of them happy, and some of them not so happy. But even when it comes to the unhappy memories . . . I never wanted to bring someone inside my home unless they were worth it, if that makes sense. If I didn't feel like they could understand those memories. And me."

I could feel my cheeks glow with pleasure. He was saying that I was worth it. That he thought I understood him. Maybe even that he cared—

Don't get carried away.

I refused to fish for compliments, no matter how badly I

wanted to, so I just wrapped my fingers around his ankles under the water. I was about to ask a follow-up question— not about me but his house and how long he'd lived here— when he said, "What about you, Briggs? Brought any boys back to the headmaster? Snuck someone into your twin bed and kissed them there?"

I gave a humorless laugh. "And reveal to my father that I do anything other than zealously prepare for college? No, I'm smarter than that."

"He wants you to go to an Ivy that badly, huh?"

Keaton didn't sound incredulous or disbelieving. He sounded like he understood. It truly was par for the course in our world.

The only difference between me and the other Pembroke students is that I had to get into my chosen school on merit alone, because I didn't have the guarantee of a legacy or money that could be conveniently endowed.

"Yes," I said. "It's all he wants from me."

"And you want to go to Paris instead," he stated. "And fall in love with a French guy."

He frowned rather adorably at that last part, and my heart gave a leap, before I pushed it firmly back down where it belonged. The frown wasn't because he was sad I might go somewhere else, and it wasn't because he was truly jealous. It was just caveman possessiveness, and while it was kind of hot, I was too smart to mistake it for anything more.

But I still found myself confessing, as if to reassure him. "The French guy is optional. The real reason I want to go to Paris is so I can attend the Sorbonne. To study photography."

I let go of his ankles, feeling suddenly awkward. I tried to swim away, but before I could, he reached down and snatched my wrist, pulling me between his legs so he could look at my face.

"So that's the real reason for Paris," he said softly. "Not for some European guy or for petit fours at a cafe, but to follow your heart."

When he said it like that, I felt a little embarrassed. Embarrassed that I had such an earnest, pie-in-the-sky dream. Embarrassed that I was that easy to read.

"I mean, the petit fours and the European guy are still *part* of it," I joked weakly.

His gaze was so intense right now, so penetrating, and I wondered if this was what his opponents saw on the rugby field. This stare that allowed me no secrets, no quarter. This stare that said *you, and everything you hold dear, is about to be mine.*

It made fresh goosebumps prickle all over my skin. It made heat pool low, low in my belly.

"Don't hide from me, Iris," he said finally.

"I'm not—"

Abruptly, I was hauled from the water—first by my wrists and then by his large hands firmly under my arms— and then with no effort at all, he lifted me in his arms as he got to his feet. Once again, I realized how massive he was, how powerfully built, and my toes curled with lust as I realized he was using all that power to sweep me off somewhere to have his way with me.

"Joking about what you really want is hiding," he said as he carried me inside. "We've been real with each other from the start. We're not going to stop now."

CHAPTER FIFTEEN

Iris

W E WERE CLOSE to his bedroom, but he walked right past the door to the adjoining door, which opened up into a spacious bathroom with a freestanding marble bathtub and a glassed-in shower the size of a small principality. He set me carefully on my feet, and then tugged off his shirt—slowly enough for me to appreciate the flex and play of the muscles banding his lean abdomen and broad chest.

"Well, Briggs?" he asked, starting in on his jeans. I had no idea why it was so sexy to watch him as he popped open the button of his fly and tugged down the zipper, but it was. I felt like I was being hypnotized by the subtle flex of the muscles in his forearm. By the vein tracing along the back of his hand. By the slow revelation of his lower abs, with their dark trail of hair leading deeper into his jeans.

"Briggs," he prompted, sounding amused. "I'm up here."

"Sorry," I breathed, not sorry at all. He had me naked and dripping in his bathroom—what else did he expect?

"I want to know if you're going to be real with me," he said, kicking off his jeans. "No hiding. Just *us.*"

He walked forward, his erection yet another display of

shameless male power. It was big and thick and dark, framed between his narrow hips and those giant, rugby-playing thighs.

"No hiding," I said. "What does that mean?"

"It means no pretending like you do for the world. You want something? Own it."

A smile pulled at my mouth. "I want you."

His eyes hooded, and without breaking eye contact with me, he reached out and slid something off the bathroom counter. A condom.

"Is that so, Big Red? What else do you want?"

I could feel the flush starting on my chest, I could feel how my nipples drew even harder. "I want you inside me again."

He tore the packet open with his teeth, and within seconds, his proud erection was sheathed in clear latex. He gave himself an idle stroke as he stalked towards me, backing me towards the shower. "Inside your pussy, Iris? Fucking that sweet, tight place so deep that you're standing on your tiptoes while you beg to come?"

Guh.

Was it possible to have a heart attack from being too turned on?

"Yes," I whispered, stepping backwards into the shower. "That's what I want."

He reached past me. With a few deft movements, he had the water turned on, warm and already starting to fill the shower with steam, and then he spun me to face the wall.

"Hands here," he murmured, guiding my hands to the wall so that I was braced against it. The water fell hot and pleasant against our sides as he pressed his giant foot to mine and nudged it to the side so my legs were spread. He stepped between them with a satisfied noise that had my core fluttering in response.

"You still sore?" he asked as one big hand found my breast and kneaded it.

"A little," I admitted.

His other hand slid around my hip to circle my clit. "Tell me if it hurts," he whispered, and rubbed me so exquisitely that I couldn't even remember what hurting felt like. He waited until I was arching against his touch and panting into the steam before he notched the plump head of his cock at my entrance. And slowly—so slowly that I could feel every thick inch of him as he pushed in—he slid home with a muttered *Jesus.*

"It's so deep like this," I moaned, pressing my forehead to the shower wall. There was a tiny bit of soreness and sting with the intrusion, but it was nothing compared to the building knot of pleasure currently cinching between my legs. And when he answered me by thrusting again and doing what he promised—pushing me up to my tiptoes—I needed the wall more than ever.

"Fuck," I whimpered, and then whimpered again when he reached down and gave my clit what it needed.

He bent his head and bit my neck as he began pumping between my legs and giving me all the desire that had been coiling inside him since we first left the penthouse this morning. Every dark promise he'd made, every sultry look he'd given me—he was settling up now, demanding payment from my body. And not just with his pleasure, but my own too. Because the minute I broke apart around him, he followed, surging heavy into my body with a delicious growl, and before I had time to catch my breath, he was on his knees, stripping off the condom and sealing his mouth between my legs.

He ate me like that—him on his knees behind me—my hands still braced against the wall, and he spared no amount of filth. He licked where he shouldn't. He fucked my entrance with his tongue. His fingers worked me as he reached down with his free hand and jerked off.

And after we both came a second time—me against his mouth and him with hot ropes of seed between my feet—and I slumped to the shower floor next to him, he asked me again.

"What else do you want?"

I only had one answer, and it was the same one from yesterday.

"Everything."

✧   ✧   ✧

I *WAS* SORE the next day, but it was the kind of soreness that felt good. Like the sting after a giggling belly flop into a pool. Like the ache of a muscle well used.

And the way Keaton looked at me as his car pulled away from the Park Avenue curb and we started back towards Pembroke—god, that *look*. He looked at me like he was a conqueror and I was the fresh, green country he was about to claim.

But I also couldn't help the doubt that slithered through my thoughts. Of course we'd have a weekend of secrets and orgasms in the magic tower of his penthouse, but now that we were coming back to real life? To the world of gossip and grades and bonfire parties and my status as the headmaster's daughter?

What then?

I looked over at Keaton, who pulled my feet into his lap the moment the car started and was now stroking up my

bare legs with greedy fingertips. "Are we—do you want to—"
I cleared my throat, feeling awkward and needy and
repugnantly anxious. "Are we going to do this again
sometime?"

His hands went still on my legs, and when he looked
over at me, that lock of hair was hanging over his forehead,
like he was a cartoon fairy-tale prince made real. "Tell me
what you mean by *this*, Iris. A trip to New York? Staying at
my place?"

I was already shaking my head, even though I wouldn't
say no to either opportunity if they arose again. "I mean us
spending time together, Keaton. The hanging out. The
fooling around. When we get to Pembroke, are we going to
pretend this weekend never happened?"

Now all of him was completely still. Tense. I couldn't
read his expression when he said, "Is that what you want? To
stop?"

An instinctive pain welled up inside me at the very
thought of stopping. And then a wave of fear followed that
pain. If I was this far gone for him after only a weekend,
what would happen after weeks of this at school? Months?
I'd be broken over him. He'd break me, and then I'd just be
the stupid girl who fell for the king of the school. The girl
that fell for the rugby idol and his arrogant smirk.

No better than a fool.

"I don't know," I whispered, looking away. "I don't
know what I want."

He didn't seem to like that answer at all. My seatbelt
was unbuckled and I was in his lap before I could blink. He
yanked me to his chest with one burly arm while his other
hand slid up my skirt. Not to toy with me or tease, but to
cup me. Hard. And with his hand molded possessively over
me, he said in a fierce, rough voice, "Don't keep me from

this. Don't keep *us* from this."

I couldn't help how I reacted to his touch. Just like in the library that very first time, his breathtaking arrogance only fired me—and my half-glaring, half-aroused response only stoked his need higher. He curled his hand over me even tighter, sending quivering heat to the place that needed his touch the most.

Focus, Iris!

"What about Clara?" I demanded, scowling at him.

He looked confused. "What about her?"

"We can't be having sex while everyone thinks you're with her!"

Keaton's brow wrinkled. It made him look unfairly cute. "Why not? She's got nothing to do with us."

My stomach knifed. "So you're just going to continue dating her," I said dully. "While you fuck me on the side."

"Iris," Keaton said, the arm around my waist now moving up my back. He buried his fingers in the wavy mass of my hair. "You're making this sound worse than it is. She and I don't fuck, we don't fool around, we don't even kiss, and you know why? Because I only kiss the girls I want."

I blinked at him.

I didn't want this ugly doubt nestled inside me. I didn't want what we'd shared this weekend to end up poisoned and ruined. I wanted to believe him. I wanted to imagine that the next few months or longer would be full of the same heady, thrilling fun we'd had this weekend.

A long minute passed while I thought. "Are you saying you don't want her?" I asked shyly. A little miserably.

Blue eyes searched my own as his hand tightened in my hair. "I want *you*," Keaton swore. "Your body. Your mouth. Your sass when we argue." He pressed his hips up underneath my bottom so I could feel exactly how much and how hard he wanted. "You're the one who's tied me up in fucking knots for weeks, and you're the one I can't stop thinking about, can't stop jerking off to, can't stop touching. Clara and I are playing a part. But you and me?" He let out a low, rough exhale. "We're the real fucking deal, Briggs."

As declarations went, it wasn't exactly Jane Austen-worthy. He didn't love me. He wasn't even willing to give up his fake relationship for me. He wanted to fuck me in secret, and that wasn't exactly a happily ever after.

But there was no mistaking the earnest ferociousness in his gaze, nor the colossal erection underneath me. And I wanted to believe him, I wanted to believe that he could chastely play his part with Clara and save all his desire for me.

God, how I wanted to believe it.

I pressed my hand to his sharp, sculpted jaw and pressed my forehead to his.

"You better mean that, Keaton," I whispered. "No wanting her. No touching her. No kissing her. You have to promise."

"I promise," he said seriously. "You and I together? We're real. Clara and me? We're fake as fake can be. You'll see for yourself when we get back."

I hoped so.

And I threw myself into that hope like a thrill seeker throwing themselves off a sea cliff into the waves, praying the whole time they didn't die on hidden rocks below, but also laughing with sheer adrenaline the whole way down.

I kissed him, and he kissed me back, his fingers finally nudging beneath my panties while he ducked his head to suck on my neck. And then I was lost to him the entire way back to school.

CHAPTER SIXTEEN

Keaton

NEARLY A WEEK later, I woke up thinking of Iris, just as I had every damn morning since I met her.

With a groan, I rolled over and grabbed my phone to send her a quick text.

Keaton: *I woke up thinking of you.*

Iris: ☺ *I woke up thinking about you too.*

That warmth in my chest spread out to my extremities. God, is this what it felt like? To really care about someone and have them care about you back? It had been so long for me. Maybe never. With Iris, I felt like myself. Like I belonged somewhere. This girl owned me, and she had no idea.

I was already making plans. There were plenty of design schools in Paris. I was a little late to get a portfolio together but given the money I'd have access to after graduation, I could make anything happen. I knew how important Paris was to her. I had no set plans, so I could try Paris. I loved the city. And any city with Iris in it was one I could stay in for a while.

Keaton: *Meet me by the Giant Oak? We'll have a picnic away from the prying eyes.*

Iris: *Keaton Constantine, well, aren't you romantic?*

Keaton: *I plan to try to feel you up in the great outdoors.*

Iris: *LOL, you're ridiculous.*

I wasn't sure why she thought I was joking, but if I would get to see her and make her smile, I would take it.

Keaton: *I'm only half kidding. But I can't wait to see you smile.*

She sent a photo of her looking sleepy and bed rumpled with a huge smile on her face.

Keaton: *Day made.*

I pushed out of bed, still bleary-eyed, grabbed some clothes and a towel, and headed towards the bathroom when my phone buzzed again. Like the completely pussy-whipped jackass that I was, I ran to grab it. Because what if she sent me another kind of photo entirely?

Sure, you tell yourself that. Mostly, knowing she could have texted you just makes you smile.

Yeah, it did. And it was alarming. When I picked it up with a shit-eating grin on my face, I paused when I saw who it was. My mother.

Mom Monster: *I've decided to come to campus after all today for Parents' Weekend. I'll meet you for lunch with Clara and her parents.*

What the fuck?

Could I get away with pretending I hadn't seen it?

Mom Monster: *Also, I can see you've read this. So acknowledge.*

Fuck read receipts. There's nothing more passive-aggressive to my mother than reading a message and not replying immediately.

Keaton: *Sorry, Mom. Busy.*

Lies.

Mom Monster: *I'm here. It is Parents' Weekend, so I know there's no games or practices, and there's nothing else on your agenda. I'll see you at 12:30.*

Fuck. I didn't even bother with texting. Instead I picked up the phone and called Clara. "What the hell?"

She groaned. "You got the text too."

"Yeah, what the fuck? I had plans today."

She paused for a moment. "With the new girl?"

"She's none of your business," I said—politely but also firmly. I knew she'd been on Iris's case and that was stopping right now. "And make sure she stays that way. No more threats, okay?"

"Okay, okay. Sorry. I was just trying to keep up the front, you know? And she didn't even seem like your type."

"And who is? You?"

"Harsh much?"

I groaned and ran a hand through my hair. "Sorry. You're not the enemy, *they* are."

"Tell me about it. I was supposed to see Charlie. He got into Duke. So as luck would have it, we'll be at school together next year." She sounded so happy. That kind of elation was unusual for her. But she was always that happy when she talked about him.

"Congrats. I am happy for you."

There was another beat of silence. "Did you just express emotion and empathetic joy for another person?"

"Don't get too excited."

"Wow, new girl—sorry—Iris is good for you then. You seem almost happy too."

"Well, I'm not happy about today. What are we going to do?"

"I don't think we have any choice. We have to go."

"But I don't want to."

She sighed, "Keaton, all you have wanted all this time is for your mother to pay attention to you. To show up for you. She's doing that. I'm sure Iris will understand."

That was just the thing. Iris *would* understand. But I didn't. I didn't want to go. But I couldn't deny that little ball of light at the idea that my mother had come. For Parents' Weekend. And I hadn't even asked.

"Yeah, okay, that's a good point."

"Look, I know our parents aren't really the ones to give us hope and shit. But maybe this is good. I mean my parents always come, so I'm just praying that with your mother there they're not going to harangue me about my choice to go to Duke—if I get in, obviously—and not Harvard."

"Duke's at least still a good school though."

"Yeah, but it's not prestigious enough for Mommy."

"Well, good thing you have your own trust fund and you don't have to listen to her."

"Thank God for little miracles."

"Look, I'll see you at 12:30, yeah?"

I hung up with Clara while trying to figure out what the hell I was going to say to Iris. But in the end, all I could do was tell her the truth. She picked up on the first ring. "Hey. Are you about to get in the shower thinking about me?"

The smile pulled at my lips, and I couldn't help it. "I had been thinking about that shower in New York."

"Me too. So how does this work? Why isn't this video? It's a lot better if I can see you touching yourself."

I coughed a laugh. I had created a monster. "Actually, there's a change of plan today. I'm really sorry." I wasn't used to apologizing. Usually people apologized to me. While I withheld emotion one way or another.

"Oh, what's up?"

"My mother showed up."

There was a beat of silence. "Your mother?"

"Yeah, I know. Shocking right?"

"Hell yeah. But that's actually a big deal."

I sighed. "Yeah, that's what Clara said."

This time there was a longer pause. "Clara?"

Fuck. Should not have said that. "Yeah, my mom is insisting on lunch with her family. So I called her to find out if we could weasel out."

"Oh."

That one word carried the weight of so many sentences. So many orations. A whole goddamn Julius Caesar speech. Just with an *oh*.

"You know it's not like that."

"No, I know. I just still hate that you get to spend the afternoon with her. And not with me."

"Trust me, I'd rather be spending it with you." And that was the truth. I wanted to spend every moment with her. We luckily had the excuse of our project for another month. But I wanted to spend all the time in the world with her.

I wasn't going to tell her that yet though. She was dead set on Paris, and I didn't want to change her plans. I also didn't want to scare her off. But she, Iris Briggs, and I were endgame. And I wanted to ease her into the idea of that.

"I'm sorry, Iris."

"It's okay. I'm not insecure or jealous. Okay, a little jealous, but I get it. Did she have plans with—what is that guy's name again? Charlie?"

"Yeah. So she's in the same boat as us."

"Charlie and I should form a support group."

"We probably could go out together if you wanted to."

"I think it's going to be a minute before Clara and I are, like, you know, *friends*-friends."

"Yeah, I get that. But I'm really sorry. I'll make this up to you tomorrow. Okay? That's just about enough time for my mother to get bored of me."

"Okay. Look, it's fine, honestly. I get it. I have some reading I want to catch up on. And there's a lot of stuff I need to do to edit the photos, picking out the best ones, seeing which ones work for the illustrated double exposure."

"I wanted to do that with you."

"We will. I'm just going to do the preliminary sifting. The dregs of the work. You'd hate that stuff. It's boring."

She had a point there. But still, I didn't want to make her do it all by herself. "Are you sure?"

"Oh my god, Keaton. It's fine. I'll see you tomorrow. Hell, if you're up tonight, call me. I might even sneak out of my room."

I clutched a hand to my chest as I gasped. "Oh my god, Iris Briggs, what have I done to you?"

"You have just encouraged my inner bad girl to come out and play."

"I am so here for that. Okay, I'll see you tomorrow. I love you," I said then hung up.

For a moment after I hung up, the words hung in the air, practically still echoing against the walls.

What.

The.

Fuck.

The words had just tumbled out of my mouth, unexpectedly. As if I had meant to say them all along. What was she thinking? What did I just do?

My mother sent a text.

Mom Monster: *Do not be late.*

Mom Monster: *I'm serious.*

Jesus Christ. I had to go. Excellent.

I'd deal with Iris and the three little words later.

✧　✧　✧

LUNCH WAS NOT nearly as terrible as I thought it would be. My mother was in a mellow mood. Actually, a pretty good one.

There was laughing, there was talking. Mom touched my arm and said she was proud of me—as she chattered about my grades and rugby season and how it was going to be amazing and how I not only had scouts looking at me, but from the UK and New Zealand teams. Which was true. But how did she know all of that?

She's a Constantine, I reminded myself. There was no way she wasn't keeping tabs on me here at school.

It was strange how I was almost warmed by it, even if it meant she'd delegated taking an interest in me to someone else. But it still showed she cared.

The Blairs seemed dutifully impressed, and then conversation segued off into the usual Bishop's Landing gossip and travel talk, which was always the same. Someone sleeping with someone else, so-and-so getting ready for their trip to the Seychelles, the Morellis are sniffing around some development opportunities on our side of the city, etc.

My mother was shockingly pleasant the entire time. Even her normally cool eyes were warm, and her smile—only rarely bestowed—was out in full force as she charmed the Blairs. As she charmed *me*.

This was the mother I had seen only glimpses of in the past five years, this was the mother I remembered from before Dad's death. This was what it felt like to be fully her son, someone who had value in the here and now, and not just as Winston's clone someday. Maybe…maybe I'd been too hard on her?

If she was making an effort now, then shouldn't I as well?

We took her car back to campus after lunch, and as I watched the red and gold trees flash by the window as the driver sped down the highway, my mother cleared her throat. I looked across to where she sat next to me, calmly studying her pale pink nails.

"How are you and Clara doing together? Have you thought any more about carrying this relationship into college? Beyond?"

All the happiness, all the light that I'd been feeling earlier began to dim. A bitter taste crawled up my throat. "That is not going to happen."

My mother pinned me with a cool look. "We need it to happen. The Blairs are thinking about expanding their portfolios with investments in WC Tech—but it's the kind of deal that only happens with an ironclad family tie in place, which is why we don't need any broken hearts complicating things."

"That's not what this is. I'm not breaking Clara's heart."

The look got even cooler. "Can't you see your family needs you? All I'm asking is that you try to make things last with Clara."

Clara. Right. That was the only reason she'd come. *For the Blairs and their money.* I was such a fucking idiot. I'd thought she'd come for me. For once. I thought she'd turned up for me.

"I don't love her," I said finally. "And she doesn't love me."

"Love is not the only thing that makes a marriage," my mother responded, pushing her fingertips against her temple as if she was getting a headache. "Take it from me. Your father and I—we had a strong partnership. A good partnership. And we did love each other. But when that love grew . . . complicated . . . what kept us together was the family and what the family needed. I've made sacrifices too—more than plenty—to make sure that there is a legacy for you and your brothers and sisters to carry on. Because that's what being a Constantine means; that's what it looks like to grow up and succeed in a world hell-bent on tearing you down."

I stared back at her. "I want to help, but I'm not Winston, Mom. I can't be blood on the family altar."

She wrinkled her nose. "Don't be dramatic. All I'm asking is for you to think about your father's legacy. What he died for—what he was killed for. We can't let that sacrifice go to waste."

✧   ✧   ✧

BY THE TIME we parked in visitors' parking, I was in a hell of a mood.

I wanted to tell Mom everything about me and Clara and Charlie and Iris so then it would all be out in the open, and I could just be with the girl I loved. But I also wanted to make my mother proud and honor my father's legacy.

I wanted my own life.

But I also didn't want to fuck over my brothers and sisters.

I climbed out of the car and then helped Mom out, watching as she straightened her dress and smoothed her hair. The sun accentuated the tiny lines by her eyes and mouth, and caught the thin strands of silver threading through the blond, making them gleam.

She was still beautiful, Caroline Constantine, but it struck me then that she was getting older. That she might be tired from steering a family that walked a razor-thin line between prosperity and utter destruction. That she might truly and genuinely need my help—not because she was controlling or cold, but because the work of running the Constantine family was too big for one person alone.

"Do you remember how your father loved the sea?" Mom asked as we walked towards the stone stairs where Clara and her parents waited for us. Her voice was no longer cool, but wistful, and a little bit sad.

"Yeah."

"Every time he'd get to Bishop's Landing, it wouldn't matter how late it was or if we had guests waiting—he'd go right through that back door into the gardens and stare at the ocean. As if he wasn't really home until he saw it."

I remembered. It's why I'd sketched him that day, wanting to capture an image that was so indelible to my childhood. The image of Lane Constantine looking out onto the water, wind ruffling his hair, his shoulders and back relaxing as the business of the day or week melted from his body. He was no longer a billionaire, a mogul, and emperor ruling over an empire of both legal and less-than-legal realms, but a husband about to go kiss his wife on the cheek.

He was a father about to hug all his children and ruffle their hair and ask about their day at school.

He was a man at home.

My throat closes at the memory; my eyes burn at the thought of him.

Fuck, I miss him.

My mother continued. "Your father loved the sea because it meant he was home. But that home won't be there for the next generation of Constantines unless we safeguard it. I know I can count on you." Her voice started to break when she added, "You're such an amazing son. He would have been so proud to see you now."

These words—words that I'd wanted to hear for years. My throat clenched even harder.

"Mom?"

"I love you, Keaton," she said, eyes shining. She blinked fast, swallowing it. "He loved you. Anything I've asked of you hasn't been about control . . . it's been about love."

"I—" I stared at her.

It had been so long since I could really remember feeling her love, so long since I'd felt the glow of being her son all for myself, instead of feeling jealous and resentful that my brothers and sisters soaked up all her attention.

I couldn't marry Clara. I couldn't even date her in college. But to keep pretending for now, until I could make my mom understand? Until Clara was ready to come clean about Charlie?

What could it hurt?

It will hurt Iris.

But my mother would be gone soon, and then Clara and I would resume our usual pattern of staying out of each other's way, and Iris and I could get back to us.

"I can keep trying with Clara for now."

She touched my shoulder. "Thank you, Keaton. This means the world."

Subconsciously, I glanced around for Iris, searching the crowds for her smile. Just seeing her smile would stop this ugly churn of doubt and flattered desperation inside me.

You told Iris you love her, and now you're agreeing to pretend to love someone else. You're really ready to see her right now?

Okay. No, not really.

And I knew she would be making herself scarce anyway. This was Parents' Weekend. Her parents would be busy playing host to all the visitors. And this time she wouldn't be needed to help, since most parents would be wanting to talk to the headmaster about grades and behavior—nothing she could help with or was even allowed to hear. She was all alone today.

But I was glad she wasn't around to see what I was going to do.

This is a bad idea. You don't want *to do this.*

No, I didn't. But neither could I relinquish the feeling of my mother's love and pride in me so easily.

But Iris. . .

But this was just for today . . . just for the year. Until Clara went to Duke with Charlie, until I got my first stage of trust fund money. Why shouldn't I get to enjoy this version of my mother for a while longer? Why shouldn't I get to feel what it was like to be Winston and always do the right thing?

When we approached Clara and her parents on the stairs, Clara gave me a smile. And her mother clapped her hands. "Let's get a picture of the happy couple together."

Automatically, my arms wrapped around Clara's waist, and I pulled her against me in a pose we had practiced a million times.

My gaze flickered up. For once I had Mom's approval. Her attention.

And that felt so very, very close to being cared about. Like she finally gave a shit that I was her son.

I turned and gave Clara a tight smile.

She frowned and lifted a dark brow. "You okay?"

"Yeah. I'm fine," I whispered. The fear and pride and the need to please my mom mixed together inside me, like a whirlpool of toxic chaos. All I'd ever wanted was to be a real part of this family, to prove I had value, and now I had my in. My chance.

With every muscle tense and every nerve thrumming like I was going into battle, I leaned in and kissed Clara. Not just a regular kiss. But the kind of kiss that left no argument about our relationship.

We always touched strategically at school. Holding hands, sitting in laps, even chaste brushes of lips when it was warranted. But I'd never kissed her like this. It was always just quick pecks before, but this—this was a real kiss. This was the kind of kiss I'd given Iris.

My lips molded over Clara's lips, the pressure possessive and claiming. Heat seared over the back of my neck and between my shoulder blades, stinging and hot, like I was being watched. Like I was being judged.

It was shame, maybe. Or guilt.

The cost of doing business with my mother.

I eased back, and Clara blinked. Slightly dazed, she lifted a brow but then her gaze skittered over to my mother and back to me, and she understood. She gave me a slight nod. And then ran a finger delicately under her bottom lip as if to fix her lipstick. That prickly heat feeling didn't stop. It was all too familiar.

Why was that?

And then I knew. My gaze searched the crowd. And I found her.

Iris.

Under the tree watching me.

I'd chosen my mom. My family. Over the girl I'd fallen for.

And now she knew.

Chapter Seventeen

Iris

IN THE WEEK since New York, in the stolen moments in the library and in his dormitory bedroom—and yes, the darkroom again—I hadn't dared hope. I wouldn't let myself.

It was much too ridiculous to fall in love with Keaton. It was even more ridiculous still to expect him to fall in love with me.

How many girls must he have screwed here at Pembroke? How many girls were still lining up to be screwed by him, by this ridiculously handsome idol of the school? I'd be a fool to take the moments we had together—urgent, sweet moments when he murmured the most wonderful filth in my ear—and turn them into some kind of romance.

But I *was* a fool.

Because between that first night in New York and now, I'd somehow done the unthinkably dumb thing, and I'd fallen in love with him.

And no amount of guarding my heart—no amount of reminding myself that *we're the real fucking deal* was just boy-speak for liking me and my body, and not some kind of code for love—could smother the daydreams and the fantasies. Him and me, hands laced as we walked through

Paris. Him and me years from now, with rings and tuxes and a white dress—

No, I couldn't hope. And every time hope dared to sprout, like a tender green shoot of spring, I crushed it and buried it. And I'd keep crushing it and burying it until the end of time. I could do that. I was a smart girl. I had no interest in going to Paris with a broken heart.

But then—this morning on the phone—

I love you.

His words sank into my skin like hooks, they burned themselves onto the curves of my heart.

He loved me.

And for two glorious hours, I walked on air.

THE GIANT OAK was set on a small rise near the edge of the forest, and it was an excellent spot for making out due to its size and the deep hollow between two of its big roots. It was easy to nestle in there on the forest-facing side of the tree and out of sight of the school and kiss until the cold drove you back indoors.

It was also an excellent spot for surveying the grounds— the gentle rise that hosted the oak gave an excellent vantage over the lawn, quad, and buildings—and I sat there with my back against the trunk, watching parents and students mill around the buildings as small, stunned smiles chased themselves across my face.

He said he loved me.

I'd come to the oak because if I couldn't be with Keaton, then I needed to be somewhere that reminded me of him, as if running my fingers through the cool grass where we were supposed to be kissing right now would make up for the fact that we weren't touching at all, that he was currently with Clara instead of me.

I was jealous of that, of course, jealous of any time she got to spend with him, jealous that it was her that got to be part of the family—but the jealousy was soothed by the memory of his words.

I love you.

He loved me.

As if summoned by my thoughts alone, Keaton appeared, unfolding from a gleaming Bentley like the muscular king he was and then was joined by a slender blonde woman with a regal bearing that screamed *generational wealth.* Whatever she was saying to Keaton as they walked was upsetting, I surmised, because the set of Keaton's shoulders slumped and he was nodding his head at the ground, as if he was looking into his own grave.

As if he was remembering something painfully and indelibly sad.

I leaned forward as they talked, wishing I could be down there with Keaton, touching the place behind his ear like he liked me to do. I hated that his mother was making him feel this way; I hated that parents had this power over us. That they could take good days and turn them wretched just with a few words.

The minute Keaton was free, I would go to him and I would kiss him until he smiled again. I would kiss him until he murmured those sweet words to me, and I finally got to murmur them back.

I love you.

Together, Keaton and his mother arrived at the shallow stone stairs that led up to the cluster of brick and stone buildings making up the Pembroke campus. My stomach tightened when I realized people were waiting for them on the steps—Clara Blair and two adults who were presumably her parents.

What happened next felt like it happened in slow motion. Like time had frozen and each millisecond stretched to the length of a year.

Keaton's arms went around Clara in an affectionate embrace.

And after a beat, maybe two, he tilted his face down towards hers.

My fingers were numb. My lips were numb. Even my heart beat numbly.

No, I thought to myself. *No.*

His hand cupped the back of her head, her brunette hair spilling out below his grip in glossy waves, and then he brought his lips down to hers. It wasn't a pretend kiss. It wasn't a kiss meant to placate a parental audience. It was a kiss like he meant it. A kiss like he wanted her. A kiss that said *we're the real fucking deal.*

And it wasn't meant for me.

It couldn't have lasted more than a few seconds, but when Keaton finally broke away from Clara, I felt like I'd aged a year. Five years. I felt like I'd been standing there watching him kiss Clara for as long as the Giant Oak had been sitting there on its little hill.

And when Keaton's eyes—somehow, impossibly—lifted and found mine, I felt more than old.

I felt broken.

I turned and fled, my feet pounding over the grass as I ran all the way back to the headmaster's residence, and not once did I look back—not because I was afraid he'd be chasing me.

But because I knew he wasn't.

✧　✧　✧

HE'D LIED.

That was the first real thought that pushed its way forward after god only knew how many minutes I spent sobbing into my bed.

He'd lied about everything. About him and Clara being pretend, about them not kissing, about all of it, and I'd been stupid enough to believe him. So desperate to hear what I wanted to hear that I refused to look the truth solidly in the eye and see what any idiot could have seen.

Keaton Constantine was using me. He was doing what guys like him had always done—he'd come, he'd fucked, he'd conquered, using any means necessary, and it was so *obvious* in retrospect, that I wanted to bang my head against the wall. How many times had I thought the king of the school couldn't possibly want the new girl? How many times had I marveled that this arrogant Adonis desired *me* of all people?

How many times since this morning alone had I giggled in wonder to myself that this muscle-carved idol might love me?

Why hadn't I listened to my gut?

Why hadn't I known that he would do what all idols invariably did, and fall?

He'd never loved me. He'd loved fucking me maybe, but that was the extent of it, and if I'd ever believed otherwise, well, I only had myself to blame.

I rolled over to my side, still crying. Tears soaked the duvet beneath my face, and my stomach was starting to hurt from all the heaving sobs. When would I stop crying? When would I stop seeing Keaton's hand in her hair, his mouth firm and dominating over hers?

In my jeans pocket, my phone buzzed against my bottom. Sniffling, I pulled it out to see Keaton's name on the screen.

No.

No.

I declined the call, and then put my phone on my end table.

It immediately buzzed again. And again. Followed by short buzzes—text messages. Text messages that I absolutely refused to read. I couldn't stand to listen to any more lies, any more excuses. He would tell me it meant nothing, that it was all for show, but I knew what I saw. I knew what a passionate kiss from him looked like.

And maybe I had been stupid. Maybe I had been the world's biggest idiot.

But I would break my own fingers before I let Keaton sweet-talk me back into stupidity again.

I turned off my phone.

In the silence that followed, my tears returned in full force. I stared across the room at the sweater dress flung over my desk chair—the same one I'd dry-fucked Keaton while wearing—and I stared at my camera, which had had Keaton's strong fingers curled around it in New York.

I flopped to my back so I didn't have to see all the reminders of him. And suddenly, I felt so *lonely*, so utterly and miserably bereft that I couldn't stand it any longer.

I couldn't just cry in my bed all day, reliving that horrible kiss with its horrible implications; I needed to leave, I needed to do something, see somebody—

It hit me nearly as hard as seeing the kiss had.

I needed to see my friends.

I needed to cry in Sera's bed while she and Aurora promised to hold him down while Sloane skinned him alive. I needed ice cream and trashy TV and a fresh, dry pillow to wet with my tears.

Without wasting a single second, I threw my laptop and phone into my bag—so that if my dad stopped by my room, he'd assume I went somewhere to study—and I made my way to the girls' dorms, sniffling the entire way.

Chapter Eighteen

Iris

SALTY TEARS TRACKED down my face. No matter how hard I wished, they wouldn't stop. The well of emotion had come rolling through me, crashing through me like someone who'd stood a little too close to shore, and unfortunately as I tried to stand back up, another wave came to knock me down and choked me, sending salt water up my nose.

Serafina rubbed my back. "Jesus, Iris, I'm so sorry. He is such a dick cunt."

"What the fuck is a dick cunt?" Aurora asked, brows furrowed.

Sera shrugged. "I don't know. It sounds bad though."

Sloane pursed her lips. "I know a thing called a Colombian necktie; you want me to do it to him?"

I lifted my gaze to hers. "What the hell is a Colombian necktie?"

She shrugged. "Well, first I'd slit his throat, right? And then, you pull his tongue out through it. Sounds fitting for a lying cheat bag."

I could only blink at Sloane. "What in the world?"

Aurora shook her head. "No, no, no, no. That's too on

the nose. We have to make him pay slowly, over a period of time. Make him rue the day. We need to make every single thing about his existence hurt. Make it excruciating."

I stared at her. Her unusual golden eyes flickered with glee and merriment.

"Jesus Christ, you're crazy, do you know that? Actually, you know what?" I pointed at both her and Sloane. "Both of you are batshit. We're not necktying anyone. And I'm not here for the revenge, but what I will tell you is I'm going to stop fucking crying. My mistake was in thinking that I wasn't the cool girl, that I was the lucky one. But no—*he* was the lucky one."

Sera gave me a brisk nod. "Hell yes. *He* is the lucky one in this scenario and *he* fucked up. You are not going to sit here and cry for him. You are a badass. You're Iris Briggs. Your whole future is ahead of you. You're going to be this huge photographer one day, and he's going to beg to come to your exhibits. And all of us will be there, and we will laugh as he is turned away at the door."

I did like the sound of that. "Keep talking."

Sera and the others grinned. Aurora handed me a glass with a dubious-colored mixture inside it. "What's this?"

She grinned. "Well, I won't say where I learned the skill—" her eyes slid over to Sloane "—but I happen to be a decent lock picker. I broke into Keaton's room and stole his expensive bottle of rum. It's a fifteen-hundred-dollar bottle, so you're going to drink it."

My mouth hung open. Not that she'd broken into his room, or stolen his bottle of rum, but the fact that it cost fifteen hundred dollars, Jesus. "I don't—I don't really drink."

"Well, we will drink in your honor this very expensive rum, but also, you're going to have one. He popped your cherry and fucked you over. You can't just let it go without finishing his rum."

A flush crept up my neck, and Sera blinked at me.

"*Wow*," Aurora said, stunned. "I was just guessing, but *really*? You had sex with him?"

"Iris, you didn't!" Sera exclaimed before I could answer. "And you didn't tell me?"

I swallowed. "I did. But I didn't want to tell you, because I knew I was being an idiot over him."

I was that clichéd girl who believed that the gorgeous, rich golden boy could have fallen in love with her, that we were more alike than we were *different*. That he understood me, and that he wanted my dreams for me as much as I did. But I had been duped. That wasn't on Keaton. That was on me.

Aurora gave me a sympathetic look. "You wouldn't be the first one."

"Jesus Christ." Sera rubbed my back. "Okay firstly, I'm never forgiving you for not telling me immediately. Secondly, who you sleep with is your business—well, also mine, but mostly yours. No one gets to judge you for who you take to bed. You are a modern-times girl. You can sleep with whomever you want, whenever you want. Hell, you can still give him a repeat revenge bone. That's up to you. No one gets to judge you for that, least of all yourself. You slept with him because you are Iris Briggs and you wanted to. Don't beat yourself up for it."

"I know. It's just . . . it was my first time, and it was a textbook first time, you know?"

Sloane coughed a laugh. "You mean awkward fumbling?"

I shook my head. "No, it was that perfect kind of thing. He wasn't at all awkward. He was gentle. But there was also something that said he couldn't hold back. A feeling that told me I made him lose control. He hadn't wanted to hurt me. And it had been amazing. You know, beautiful and perfect, and you get to have an orgasm for the first time kind of thing."

Aurora lifted a brow. "Really? The first time?"

"Yeah." I glanced around. "Is that normal?"

Sera shrugged. "I don't know what normal is, but look, take the experience for what it was. An experience. Even if it was with Keaton Constantine. It was positive, and that's what you needed at the time. Now, is that going to preclude us from kicking his ass? *Hell no.* There are still months left of school, and we can make his life a living hell until then."

I shook my head. "As much fun as Colombian neckties and a slow steady plan of revenge sound, my best revenge is getting the fuck out of Dodge. I don't need to be here. In fact . . ." I reached over to my bag and pulled out my laptop, pulling up the webpage I visited nightly like it was some kind of virtual shrine.

Aurora leaned over and looked, a shot glass of amber rum balanced easily in her hand. "Your Sorbonne thing," she said, understanding.

"What Sorbonne thing?" Sera demanded.

"She wants to go to this pre-degree program in Paris," Aurora explained for me. "She's got the credits to get her diploma now if she wants, so she could go."

"They provide housing and a student stipend too," I said quietly. "Because my college fund is strictly for a degree-seeking program, it's the only way I can go without asking for my father's money. Which he'd never give me."

"So you want to leave here," Sera said, sounding unimpressed.

I looked up at her, suddenly feeling like I'd like that

rum very much right now.

"I can't stay here. Not with him."

Sloane and Aurora seemed to agree with me. But Sera pressed her lips together. She did "disdainful mother" very well. "I don't know, Iris. Look, I'm here for you. And I just think Keaton deserves to pay. He really does. But do I think you should run? No. I think he needs to face what he did. I think he owes you an apology. Now, either he does that voluntarily or we make him give you one, but something needs to happen."

I shook my head. "Nope. I just want out. I want to be gone from here. Dad's moved schools almost every two years, you know? And after Isabelle left, I think they needed a change—their entire lives had revolved around her and once she was gone, the place we were at didn't feel like home anymore. So we came here for them, but no one consulted me on how I felt, what I needed. So this time, I'm going to do what I need to do for *me*. I want to go."

Sera winced. "That sucks. Just when you're getting settled."

"Tell me about it. But you three can visit me in Paris anytime. You should come."

Sera bit her nail delicately. "Look, it's not like you're going to make any changes right now. You still have to, at least, see if you're accepted. Not to mention telling your parents, convincing your father to let you graduate early, and booking your trip."

I did need to make some kind of plan. I couldn't just up and get on the plane tomorrow. I had to wait, be patient. Who knew how much longer until I heard if I was accepted? "Okay, you have a point. I need a better plan than *fuck this shit, I'm leaving.*"

She snorted a laugh. "Yes, *you* definitely need a *plan.*"

I looked at my nails. "I'm not that bad, am I?"

My friends nodded. "Um, yeah, you're very much a planner. We dig it though. Team Iris all the way."

The four of us picked up our shot glasses, clinked them, and tossed them back. I coughed at the burn at the back of my throat. Jesus fucking Christ. But the liquid did go down smooth after the initial shock of it. And it warmed everything on the way down.

The other three didn't even seem to notice. Sera peered at her glass. "Ooh, that's nice. I never thought I could rob Keaton blind with a rum drink. I thought he was one of those pompous assholes who swirls their scotch like they were important. But he has taste. And a rum, no less. If he wasn't such a douche asshole, I might like him."

Aurora peered at her glass too. "You know what, fuck this, let me find a chaser."

She walked over to Sera's mini fridge, yanked it open, and saw a bottle of Pom juice. She got a pitcher on top of the fridge and then poured some of the Pom juice she found into it, added the rum, swirled it around, and then poured little shots of it. That went down much smoother. A little too smooth, if you ask me.

As we were on our third shots, I glanced around the room at the girls sitting around me. I hadn't thought this year would yield anything normal. But despite Keaton lying to me, using me, and breaking my heart, completely degrading it, I'd made some good friends here. The kind of friends that I probably needed in my life. Ones that wouldn't let me get away with being boring old Iris. Ones that pushed me to be different, to try different things, to experience life.

I smiled at them. "So who's going to join me in Paris next summer?"

All three of them raised their glasses, downed them, then slammed the glasses back down onto Sera's dark wood coffee table. Sera clapped. "Me, for sure. Whether you decide to go now, or you leave at the end of June, best know that come July, I will be with you. And there will be shopping to be had."

I grinned. "All that Parisian shopping will need a bigger, fancier place. You realize I'm going to live in a shoebox, right?"

She scoffed. "No, no, no. When I come visit, we're going to rent a giant fucking Airbnb, and it's going to be fabulous. Then we're going to get rid of all the boring things that you took with you because you were being frugal about money. We're going to sell all those things and buy something fun and exciting."

"Hear, hear," Sloane said.

"I second that. Actually, make that 'third that.'"

I laughed. "Guys, shopping isn't really my thing."

Sera bumped her shoulder into mine. "That's because you've never done it right. Now, if you did wait, I would just come with you. I'd go see my mom for plans, and we'd set up a place and meet cute French boys."

Aurora butted in. "Oh, you are not doing that without me."

"Me neither. We're here for that."

I laughed. "But Sera, you guys—what about your parents?"

Sera waved her hand. "If I come see you and wait around for two weeks, then I join them in St. Kitts, it's the same thing. They go for a month every year. I was going to go with them for two weeks and then I'd come and see you. No big deal. I'll just pop in."

"Either way, you're coming to Paris?"

"You better believe it."

"Who needs Keaton Constantine anyway, right?"

She nodded. "Absolutely. Because remember, you are the hot girl, and he is a pencil-dick-ass face."

I bit my bottom lip, my body clenching as I remembered his dick. "Yeah, except it wasn't exactly a pencil dick."

All three of them stared at me. But then Sera howled. "Oh my god, you have been withholding. Tell us *everything*."

I snorted a laugh. Even though my belly knotted, a little girl talk was what the doctor ordered.

A little girl talk was healing. It didn't matter that I'd fallen for Keaton's bullshit. It didn't matter that he'd broken my heart. What mattered was, I didn't need him. What mattered was, I was strong all on my own. As Sera and the others said, *I* was the *it* girl. He was just someone who'd been lucky enough to bask in my presence for a short time, not the other way around.

As far as I was concerned, Keaton Constantine didn't exist.

And right as I decided that, I heard a chime from my still-open laptop.

An email.

Curious, I woke up the screen and looked—and then promptly forgot how to breathe.

It was from the program coordinator at the Sorbonne.

I've been accepted to the pre-degree program.

I still couldn't breathe.

The director also wanted me to know that starting this week, all the program students would have access to the student housing near the campus, in order to give them plenty of time to get adjusted to the city before the seminars and work started in earnest.

I stared at the screen for a long time, wondering if the rum had gotten to me. But no—this wasn't the rum. This was real life.

And I was in.

I was going to Paris.

CHAPTER NINETEEN

Keaton

I WAS A colossal fuckup.

I could hear Clara behind me as I tore away from her and stalked up the stairs. "Keaton, what are you doing? *Keaton?*"

I wanted to run after Iris. But she was gone, and anyway, what would I say if I caught her? *It's exactly what it looked like? Don't worry, baby, I thought about my mom the entire time?*

Jesus Christ. It sounded pathetic and creepy even in my head.

Clara caught up to me, touching my elbow. "Hey, what's wrong with you? That kiss, what was that for?"

I ran my hands through my hair. My gut churned, and I felt like I was going to vomit.

I felt ill.

You are a colossal fuckup.

"I'm sorry. I shouldn't have kissed you."

She crossed her arms over her chest. "Yeah, clearly. But that's not what I'm talking about. Why did you kiss me in front of *everyone* else? What's gotten into you?"

I mean, what the hell was I supposed to say? "You know

the deal. I was faking it for the cameras, basically."

Her sigh said it all. She was exhausted. Just like I was. Tired of the lies. Tired of the bullshit. "We've been faking it for so long. Some of it is automatic . . . but that was not an automatic kiss. We have never put on that good of a show."

I couldn't breathe. It almost felt like I was going to pass out. Back and forth, back and forth, I paced.

"Fuck. Fuck. Fuck."

Clara put up her hands and approached me warily like you would a wounded animal. "Okay. Okay, calm down. Relax. What's going on?"

"My mother, she said she needed me, she wanted me to make our relationship look good. She wants your father to invest in Winston's new company eventually and—"

I couldn't fucking breathe. The words wouldn't come out. I had hurt Iris to please my mother. Iris—the one person who had always been there for me. The one person who told me the truth, the person I would rather see smile than anything else. I had hurt her deliberately. I was the worst kind of human being.

Clara's voice went low. "Okay. Okay, relax. This has gone on too long."

I frowned at her. "What?"

"*This. You. Me.* It's gone on too long. It served a purpose for a while, but it doesn't serve that purpose anymore. I'm going to tell my parents that we're done. And I'm going to tell them it's my fault. And that I have a boyfriend who does not have a penny to his name, but a scholarship to Duke, and I want to be with him."

My jaw unhinged. "Why would you do that?"

"Well, for starters, so none of this blows back on you and your family, since they do, in fact, want my parents for something."

"I've never really known you to be altruistic, Clara."

She shrugged. "I'm sick of it—the lies. And I can see the way you look at her. I might not like Little Miss Perfect, but I do like you. You're like family. And if I can help, I will." She turned to leave, but my mother rounded the corner and found us just in time.

"Keaton, what is going on?"

Clara's parents came around too. *Oh, fantastic.* Everyone was here to witness the show.

Clara cleared her throat. "Mom, Dad, listen, there's something you need to know. Keaton and I aren't—" She faltered, as if suddenly realizing the storm she was about to cause.

She looked at me with wide eyes, and I picked up where she left off, touching my hand to her elbow to let her know she had my support. "Actually, Mr. and Mrs. Blair, the truth is, Clara and I haven't been truly dating for a long time."

My mother's hand went to her throat, but she didn't speak.

Clara, however, was not going to let me go down alone. She patted her mother on the arm. "Mom, what Keaton is trying to say is, we were thrown together so often, and the expectation seemed to be that we were going to be together. So we pretended we were. And since both of you were quite happy, it gave us some freedom to do what we wanted on our own. You never seemed to question anything I did if I said I was with Keaton."

The furrowed brow and lines around my mother's mouth said it all. She turned to Clara's parents with an apologetic smile. "I think this is some kind of misunderstanding. Young people these days, their relationships always go up and down, you know how it is."

She kept talking, but Clara's words were the only ones

her parents were listening to. "Look, I thought you wouldn't approve," she was saying, "but I have an actual boyfriend. And he doesn't have a dime to his name."

It was her mother's turn to touch her pearls in shock. "Clara, what are you saying?"

"What I'm saying is that I'm completely in love with someone else. His name is Charlie Jones. A completely common name for a completely common guy. Except to me, he's not common at all. He's extraordinary. And he treats me exactly how I should be treated. I love him. And he loves me. I'm not going to Harvard next year. I'm going to Duke."

Her father raised a hand. "Now, wait just a minute young lady, you are not—"

She shook her head. "We *lied*, Dad. Don't you see? It was never real, and it can never be real because we're both in love with different people. Keaton too."

The parents all swiveled their heads to me in tandem.

"It's true, I'm in love with someone else," I admitted. "Her name is Iris Briggs. Her father is the headmaster. I really care about her, and I want to be with her. I'm not going to fake this anymore."

Clara's father and mother looked back to their daughter. Her mother whispered softly, "So you've been *pretending* to date Keaton?"

"Yeah. Sorry."

Her mother shook her head. "But why?"

"Because I knew you wouldn't approve of Charlie."

Her mother pursed her lips. "Clara Blair, I'll have you know that despite your father's fancy old-money name, he was penniless when I married him. And I didn't give a fuck back then. I'm horrified you thought we would be like that."

Clara opened her mouth then closed it again, and then

tried one more time to get words out, but to no avail. Her father shook his head. "Your mother is right. I had been living on the generosity of family and scholarships, but her parents accepted me without any conditions. There is no reason for us to not like anyone you date. Especially if they're actually a good person. We'd like to meet your actual boyfriend—Charlie. Not that Keaton isn't a fine boy. But if you don't love each other, what's the point?"

My mother made one last attempt to salvage this. "Listen, they're young, they're impulsive . . . maybe we should talk about—"

Mr. Blair shook his head. "Caro, if the kids don't want to date, what's the purpose?"

My mother pinked, but when she spoke, she had steel in her voice. "And who is this Iris Briggs girl?"

"I told you, she's the headmaster's daughter."

Clara's father frowned. "Yes, I met her. Smart girl."

I grinned at that. "Yeah, she is."

I could tell that just the fact that Clara's parents even knew of Iris upped her status in my mother's eyes immediately. "Yes, you know, Keaton, I'd love to meet her."

I couldn't be sure if she was saying that to save face or not. I decided to take it as a genuine offer. "I'd like that too . . . but I have to be able to trust that you can accept her for who she is, and not condemn her for who she isn't. I love you, Mom, but I can't be what you need anymore, and I won't make Iris be either. I'm done. And I need to go and find her and tell her exactly that."

Clara stepped up to me and gave me a big hug. "I'm not in love with you, but I do love you very much." She planted a kiss on my cheek and then gently let me go. "Go get your girlfriend back."

The heat spread through me at the uncomfortable emotional display. "Thanks, Clara."

"Anytime."

I left them all behind to find my girlfriend.

That is if she is, in fact, still your girlfriend.

One problem at a time.

✧   ✧   ✧

SHE WASN'T ANSWERING my calls. She wasn't answering my texts.

After checking the Giant Oak to make sure she hadn't doubled back, I swung by my room, even though I knew the chances of her waiting for me there were extremely slim.

That only left one place—her house—and I didn't want to crash in unannounced, so I'd tried calling and texting, but to no avail. I debated waiting, waiting until she responded . . . but what if she never responded? What if she never gave me a chance to apologize and make it right?

What if I've really lost her forever?

Panic choked me, and I knew I had to see her, I had to see those sweet blue eyes and hold her warm, slender hand while I told her everything, while I explained to her that Clara and I were done and I'd never hurt Iris like that again—*ever*.

When I reached the headmaster's residence, I was panting and out of breath. My hands were shaking, not from exhaustion, but from worry. I banged at the door, but nobody answered.

God, she could be anywhere. I banged again. "Iris. Please God, Iris, open the door."

When the door did open, it wasn't Iris, it was her mother. "Oh, Mrs. Briggs, I'm so sorry to disturb you. I didn't mean to barge in, but I'm looking for Iris. I need to talk to her. There was a complete misunderstanding and—" I dragged in my breath, trying to calm myself down. "I'm so sorry. I, um, if I can only talk to her, if you can tell me where she is, I would really appreciate it."

Mrs. Briggs didn't seem *un*sympathetic to my desperation, but neither did she move out of the doorway to let me in. "I'm afraid Iris isn't in. She's gone to visit her friends in the dormitory."

Shit.

I knew my chances of getting Iris back probably diminished with every minute she spent with Sera and them. They weren't exactly the biggest fans of the Hellfire Club—or me.

"Do you know when she'll be back?" I asked, past caring how reckless and despondent I sounded.

Iris's mother gave me a kind look. "I'm not sure when, but I will certainly tell her you stopped by . . .?"

And I realized that Iris's mother didn't even know my name. Because I'd never introduced myself—I'd never even tried. Because instead of being the kind of boyfriend that met his girlfriend's mom, I'd been the kind to make her hide while he pretended to date someone else.

Jesus, no wonder she wasn't answering my calls or texts. No wonder she wanted nothing to do with me.

"Thank you, Mrs. Briggs," I said, trying to keep my voice steady. "I'd appreciate that." And then I turned and left.

✧   ✧   ✧

AS MUCH AS I wanted to go to the girls' dormitory and haul Iris back to my room like a caveman, I knew there was no way I'd get past Sera or Aurora—or God help me, Sloane, who seemed like the kind of person who knew how to kill a man as painfully as possible.

So waiting it was, three impatient hours of it, checking my phone obsessively and drinking straight from a bottle of gin since I couldn't find my good rum. When enough time had passed that I thought I could reasonably go back to the headmaster's residence to check if she was home, I left my dorm and stepped out into the path that led to the headmaster's house.

Where I slammed straight into Serafina. "Jesus fucking Christ."

When I saw who it was, I righted myself and then helped her up. "Were you with Iris? Do you know where she is now?"

Serafina pursed her lips, and then narrowed her gaze to slits. Her eyes slid over me with nothing but venom. "You mean that poor girl that you humiliated in front of the whole school? She's around here somewhere, wishing to god that she had never met you."

I swallowed hard. "I fucked up. I know that."

"Do you? Because I'm pretty sure *guys like you* think the world owes you something. You thought that you didn't have to play by the rules, and you hurt her. But she deserved better than that."

"I know. I know I fucked up. And I need to fix it. Tell me, where can I find her?"

She shrugged. "I'm not sure. She was with us, but then she left, maybe to find her parents or something. I really don't know."

"I'm not a complete douchebag, Serafina."

"Then how about you prove it? Show me, don't tell me. Better yet, show Iris."

"You're right," I said, and Sera squinted up at me from behind her big, trendy glasses.

"Are you fucking with me right now, Constantine?" she

demanded.

"No, I—" I sighed down at the tiny van Doren heiress. "I need to show her I'll never hurt her again, and I plan to. I will."

Something in my voice must have softened her, because she let out a sigh of her own. "You won't be able to see her tonight anyway. She's packing."

I thought I was done feeling panic; I thought there was no way I could feel any more misery. I was wrong.

"Packing?" I repeated hoarsely.

Sera gave me a look that was one part sympathy to three parts loyal friend. "I don't know if I should tell you . . ."

"Please," I croaked. "I have to know. Is she leaving Pembroke? For a while? For good? If she's leaving, I don't know what I'll do—I *love* her, Sera. I love her so much that it feels like I can't breathe sometimes. And if she's gone . . ."

The heiress considered me. "I've never seen you like this," she said.

"Like what?"

"Like a wreck. A messy, dumb wreck." Her mouth twisted to the side as she thought for a moment, and then she let out another sigh. "Iris was accepted to a pre-degree program at the Sorbonne. It starts next month, but the student housing is opening up this week. Which means she's leaving. Very soon."

My brain fizzed and popped, filling with static. None of this made sense. "But she can't leave tomorrow. She has classes. We have a project. She can't go anywhere until she graduates. She can't just *leave!*"

"She can," Sera said, a bit archly. "And she is. She's got more than enough credits to graduate early, and she talked with her dad about it after she got the acceptance email. They fought about it, but she threatened to go over his head to the board if he didn't let her go. She just texted to say he agreed to arrange her academic exit, and she'll be leaving for Paris tomorrow."

I cursed under my breath. Jesus Christ. I really fucked this up. "Tomorrow."

Sera's archness disappeared, and she gave me an understanding look. "Look, Iris has always known that she wanted something different, and she's been hoping for this Sorbonne thing since before she met you. This would have happened whether or not you broke her heart."

Knowing Serafina was right didn't make me feel any better. There was a difference between Iris chasing her dreams and Iris being chased away *to* her dreams because I'd hurt her.

"I can't let her leave like this," I said, staring up at the sky. It was early evening now, a perfect autumn twilight, cool and vibrant. I wished it were storming or gray, something to reflect my miserable mood. "If she leaves with the way things are . . . then it's over for us. Really over."

"I don't disagree," Sera said, not sounding like she cared very much. But then she added, "I guess . . . I guess, if I found out when her flight left, I could let you know. And you could show up at the airport and see if she'll talk to you there."

I had to resist the urge to pick her up and swing her around. "Really?"

She held up a finger. "On one condition. You stop going full stalker tonight, and let her enjoy this last night with her parents, okay? She deserves to say all the goodbyes she wants without you knocking down her door and blowing up her phone. If you can manage that, then I'll call you tomorrow morning with her flight info."

I did pick her up and swing her around that time. I

couldn't help it, and surprisingly, she had a smile on her lips when I put her down.

"I'm still not rooting for you," she said, but the smile remained.

"That's okay," I told her. "I don't think I deserve to root for myself at this point."

CHAPTER TWENTY

Keaton

THE NEXT MORNING, I was sitting in my parked car and trying not to scream with impatience when Serafina finally called.

"Which airport did she go to?" I asked, already starting the car and moving out of the lot.

"You're lucky I'm doing this," she said. "You don't deserve it."

There was a time when I would have argued with her. When I would have thought I deserved anything I wanted. No longer.

"You're right," I said. "I don't." There was no traffic up here—there never was—and I pushed the accelerator down to the floor as I sped down the narrow highway through the trees. "Please don't play coy with me, van Doren. I can't take it today. Where's she flying out of?"

"Firstly, Keaton Constantine," Serafina said, "I am never fucking *coy*. Secondly, I don't particularly care what you can or cannot take today, especially since you were the one who royally screwed up your chances with Iris to begin with."

I had nothing left to lose, and surprisingly, it barely bothered me at all to be brutally, humiliatingly honest. "If you tell me where she went, I'm going to grovel until she either forgives me or airport security drags me away."

Even from the other end of the call, I could tell Serafina liked that visual very much. "She does deserve a good grovel," she mused. "And the additional vengeance of watching you yanked off to a room for a body cavity search. Hmm."

I was getting close to the interstate now—I needed to know which way to go. "Sera."

"*Fine*," Serafina sighed. "She's flying out of Burlington. And you should hurry if you want to catch her before liftoff." She also gave me the airline, and when it was supposed to depart.

"Thanks, van Doren."

"You better grovel harder than fucking Darcy—"

I'd already thrown the phone on the passenger seat and sped up the car before she finished talking.

✧　✧　✧

AT FIRST, IT looked like no one was getting a Darcy-level grovel. When I got to the airport, it was to the knowledge that Iris's plane had just finished boarding, and she was about to be in the fucking air and lost to me.

But I didn't grind Croft Wells into the rugby field every season because I gave up easy. I stalked up to the airline desk, pulled out my wallet, and played to win.

Which I did.

Twice.

Firstly, I was able to catch a connecting flight to JFK, even though it was leaving in less than an hour, which would get me to JFK in plenty of time for Iris's transatlantic flight.

Secondly, I was able to buy out the entire first class

section of the flight from New York to Paris, and I upgraded Iris's seat. It took an obscene amount of money—thank God for my insane allowance—an even obscener amount of scowling, demanding, and coldly threatening since it involved rescheduling several other passengers, but I've found there's very little that stands in the way of a guy's will when enough money is lubricating the way.

And just like with sex, I made sure there was plenty of lubrication.

The flight to JFK was short and uneventful, but I was still a mess the entire time. What would I say? What *could* I say? I hadn't just broken her heart—I'd broken her heart enough to send her running across the ocean without so much as a goodbye. That wasn't something I could fix with a simple apology. It wasn't even something I could fix with a grovel alone.

I was going to have to show her that I would put her first. Starting right now.

I waited to board the plane until the very last. Partly because I needed time to bribe a few flight attendants, and partly because I didn't want her to see me and then bolt. To that end, I lingered in the first-class bar until we were ready to push back from the gate, not wanting her to see me until it was too late.

Yes, it was a bastard move to wait until the doors were almost sealed to board the flight and finally take my seat, but what could I say? I was playing to win, after all.

When I finally stepped into the first-class cabin and saw her, I felt like I'd been tackled right down to the grass. The air left my body, my muscles flared—sparks and heat sizzled along every nerve.

She was fucking perfect. A vision of red hair and sweet features, long limbs folded in a graceful symmetry as she tucked her knees to her chest.

But it was her sadness that hit me like a fullback slamming me to the cold, wet ground. It was the drawn look to her face, the paleness behind those cinnamon-colored freckles. The red rims around her bright blue eyes.

I'd done that.

I'd done it by being selfish, by choosing the status quo. By choosing a family that wanted me only for how I could be of service over the girl who was willing to risk her heart and her pride just to be in my arms.

How could I have been so stupid?

I waited as a flight attendant brought a fizzing flute of champagne to her, presented on a silver platter. Iris took it wordlessly—and then froze when she saw what was under the flute.

A giant glossy picture of the sun over the New York skyline, breaking free from the clouds. The one she'd taken during our perfect weekend together.

Slowly, hesitantly, she picked it up and stared at it. And then her eyes gradually lifted, and she saw me standing at the far end of the aisle.

"Iris," I said softly, stepping forward as the flight attendant took her obvious cue and left.

Iris shook her head, her grip tightening on the picture. "What is this, Keaton? Why are you here?"

I reached Iris's seat and knelt down on both knees so I could look up into her beautiful face. "That is a reminder of how brilliant you are. Of how much you deserve to follow your dreams in Paris. And I'm here to tell you that I'm sorry. I know *sorry* is a word that doesn't mean much, and I know it especially doesn't mean much coming from me, but you still deserve to hear it."

With a shaking hand, she put her champagne flute on

the small table next to her seat. She didn't meet my gaze. "Are you sorry you kissed her? Or only sorry that I saw it?"

"I'm sorry I kissed her. I'm sorry that I pretended to date her at all instead of deciding to come clean to my mom. I'm sorry that I chose her approval over your happiness. I thought all I wanted in the world was for her to be proud of me, but I was wrong, Iris, so wrong. If I'm not by your side, then nothing else matters."

She finally looked at me again, doubt pooling in her eyes. "That kiss—it wasn't a kiss born of duty. You kissed her like you kiss me. Like you meant it."

I knew I was supposed to be contrite, but the idea of wanting Clara made me snort. "I've never wanted her, Iris. I wanted more than anything to prove to my mother that I could help, and that I was part of the family, and that's why I kissed her the way I did. Not because I want her or because I'm in love with her, but because I was desperate to show my mom I could be a team player."

The flight attendant came by as the announcement came over the PA: it was time to sit down and buckle up. I sat in the seat across the aisle from Iris, hating the distance between us. I reached for her hand.

"It wasn't about Clara. It wasn't even about you. It was about me being too chickenshit to own that I want my own path. I want *you*, even if that means finally accepting that my family may never want me."

She took my hand and allowed me to wind my fingers through hers. She studied them with a small frown on her lips. "Does this have something to do with the dad you won't talk about?"

I shouldn't have been surprised that she remembered our conversation in the photography lab. But it was still like a small, icy arrow to the gut to hear it spoken out loud.

My family's pain. *My* pain.

"Yeah," I finally said, feeling that icy arrow burrow deeper. "His name was Lane."

Iris looked up to me, her expression transforming into one of sad horror. "Was?"

I took a deep breath. I had no practice talking about this; hell, even my mother barely talked about this with me. Nothing beyond the occasional muttered invective against the Morellis, or the slightly more common: *If he were still here* . . .

"He died five years ago. Murdered, we think, although no one ever got locked up for it. He was . . ." How could I even explain it? How could I even make it make sense? "He was the perfect patriarch, you know? Never flinched at what he had to do to keep the Constantine name and legacy as one that commanded respect. And then Winston stepped right up after his death, no questions asked, no hesitation. He was the perfect son, and I could never be as perfect as him, no matter how hard I tried. And I tried so hard, Iris. The grades, the rugby, the right friends . . ."

"And Clara," Iris supplied softly, her eyes searching mine.

"Yes. And Clara." I heaved a breath, knowing how it sounded. "This all seems so stupid when I say it out loud. Like something I should say to a therapist or some shit."

She squeezed my hand, and my heart lifted a little, buoyed with the slightest wave of hope. Beneath our feet, the plane vibrated and hummed with impending liftoff.

"You're wrong," Iris said. "I mean, not about the therapist—you should probably definitely go talk to one sometime about your dad and your family—but about it sounding stupid." She made a rueful face. "I completely understand about Winston. Isabelle has been the standard my parents have held me to my entire life. She's the perfect daughter. And all I ever wanted was for someone to see me exactly how I am . . ."

She looked down at the photograph in her lap.

". . . to see me for *who* I am," she finished quietly.

"I see you, Iris. I'm only sorry that I didn't see how much I needed you before it was too late."

We were in the sky now, soaring high above the same skyline that gleamed up from the picture in her lap.

She pulled her hand free, staring out her window. "I don't know . . ."

Another arrow lodged in me—this time in my chest. But I had expected this. "You don't have to know right now, baby. But I thought maybe—just maybe—you could give me the chance to show you how much I see you. How much I love you."

"In Paris?" Her brow furrowed. "But you'll have to go back the minute you land. School—"

"I can miss a few days."

"But your grades! And the project—"

"Fuck the project."

"But—rugby—"

"Is not as important as you. Not as important as you pursuing your passions and me helping you do everything you want. And it's only a practice or two. Everything will be fine."

Now that we were safely in the air, I got out of my seat and knelt by hers again.

"Please, Iris. You don't have to decide to take me back now. In fact, you can tell me to fuck off at any point. But let me show you how much I love you. Let me stay with you in Paris for a while. Let me join you there after graduation so we can be together for good."

She drew in a long breath. When it came out, it was shivery and hesitant. "I'm scared," she whispered. "I want you more than anything, and I love you—"

Hearing her say it was like swallowing pure sunshine. I was up and had her in my arms and then sat back down with her in my lap before she could say another word.

"You love me?" I asked, pulling a ponytail holder from the end of her long, messy braid and freeing her hair. "Because I love you, Iris. So fucking much. And I think I have since the first day of school."

She pulled her plump lower lip between her teeth. "Really?"

"Really."

"I'm scared, Keaton. I'm so scared. What if you hurt me again?"

I held her tight to my chest. "I will never hurt you again," I swore fiercely. "I promise, Iris. You're it for me. You're *it*. There's nothing else."

She tilted her face up to mine. "Nothing else?"

"And no one else. There's only you."

"Then I guess, maybe . . ." She paused, chewing on her lip again.

I felt like it was my heart between her teeth instead of her lip while I waited for her answer, but I waited patiently. It had to be her choice. Her forgiveness.

"Then I guess we can try," she finally said in a soft voice. "I'll try with you, Keaton. Try loving you and letting you love me."

"Thank fucking God," I said, letting out a ragged breath of existential relief. And I couldn't help it then—I had to kiss her. I yanked her even closer and sealed my mouth over hers.

She came alive in my arms, like Sleeping Beauty after

her kiss. She dug her fingers into my hair and kissed me back, rubbing her sweet little ass over my lap as she did.

"It's a good thing there's no one else in first class right now," she breathed.

"I made sure of that."

I also made sure the flight attendants wouldn't come up to our cabin unless we called.

"You bought out first class just so you could do this?" Iris asked against my mouth.

With one hand, I grabbed the soft, folded blanket for her seat and wrapped it around her waist, and with my other, I sought out the sweet, secret place between her thighs. Within seconds, I had her panties pushed to the side and had her riding my fingers like a champ.

"No," I answered her. "I bought out first class so I could do *this*."

And then there were no more questions at all, just kisses and hot, sweet pleasure as we flew over the dark ocean on our way to the start of Iris's new life.

Our new life.

Epilogue

Iris

That summer . . .

OH MY GOD. Sunlight streamed into my student apartment, turning everything in my room into a wash of white. I squinted and tried to shut my eyes. Had I forgotten to draw the blinds?

Keaton kissed the back of my neck. "Rise and shine, sunshine."

"Mmm, I want to sleep some more."

"No more sleeping. I have fun ways to wake you."

I grumbled. I loved Keaton's wake-up kisses, especially when they were over my clit, but I was just so tired. We'd been up so late for Bastille Day last night. The fact that the man even thought about waking me up right now proved that he was the devil.

The past several months of living in Paris had been like a whirlwind of a dream. We still had a month before I began actual classes for the fall semester, and before Keaton left for England and preseason rugby training. He was still planning on going for a degree in art or design, but after he'd played pro rugby for a few years. Not like he needed the sportsball money, since Keaton Constantine could stand on his feet without it just fine, but simply because he wanted to.

And luckily, this time, he was standing on his feet including me by his side.

There were some people that were just charming, and Keaton was one of them. I asked him the other day what he was more happy about, the rugby deal, or maybe one day opening his own multimedia or design company. He had said both. And then he'd said neither. Then he'd kissed me on the nose and told me that the thing he was most happy about, was having *me*. And that for once, he felt on top of the world. That he could do anything.

He kept kissing me. "*Uhh*, Keaton, I'm tired. I went to bed at two."

"I know. Come on, up you get."

I rolled over reluctantly, but still I rolled over because well, it was Keaton. And the man was magic with his tongue. "Okay fine, convince me."

He laughed, a low rumbling chuckle that made my pussy clench. Okay, he clearly knew definitive ways to do that because now I really was interested.

"Why are you laughing?"

"Because of you, love. Yes, I absolutely would love to wake you up with my mouth on your pussy. But this time, that's not why I'm trying to wake you."

I groaned, irritated. "Then what is so worth getting up for? What time is it?"

He laughed. "It's nine. You've had at least seven hours of sleep."

I was going to kill him. "I hate you."

"No, you love me. But come on, get your lazy ass out of bed."

"Fine. I'm getting my lazy ass out of bed. Why in the world would you wake me up?"

He shook something that sounded like a paper bag, and my nose twitched. He shook it again, and this time my whole body moved towards the sound and the decadent smell of sugar. "Mmm, is that from La Maison Pichard?"

"It sure is."

"Give me."

"Tsk, tsk, is that how you ask for things that you want?"

"No, please give me." I reached my hand up blindly, unwilling to open both eyes.

"You have to try harder than that."

"I'll be your best friend."

"Already are. Try again."

"I will blow you like crazy. Just bring your dick over here."

His voice went husky. "God, are you serious? You would blow me for pastries?"

I nodded blindly. I would do anything for a bag of treats from La Maison Pichard. It was across town. It was a very tiny bakery, but they had my favorite pain au chocolat and they made these to-die-for beignets that they dusted in crack cocaine. Not that I had ever even seen crack cocaine, but I heard it was addictive, so that was what it must be. "There is no way you went all the way to La Maison. But I need them. I will do anything."

He unsnapped his top button, the popping sound making both my eyes open, and I had to blink rapidly to diffuse the light. "Oh really, you'll take the blow job?"

He grinned down at me and rubbed a thumb over my cheek. "I'll always take your mouth on me. Anywhere you want to put it. But if you're offering a blow job, I'm taking it."

Feeling mischievous, I reached for him, slid my hand inside his jeans. When had he gotten dressed? I found him, steely hard and thick and long, and I moaned. What was that thing that made me always want him? That made my core wet and needy, made me desperate for him? I wish I could explain it. I wish I could bottle it. When I pulled him out of his jeans, he groaned. "Jesus fucking Christ, I was kidding. Your hands, they feel so good." He groaned low, moaning.

Feeling excited, I leaned forward—bringing his cock to my lips—lifted my tongue, and licked the head.

He cursed with a little grunt. "Fuck. Fuck. Fuck. Jesus Christ, take it. Take it now."

I snatched the bag out of his hands and continued to lick him. I sucked him in, all the way to the back of my throat. And then there was a knock on our bedroom door.

"Are you two in there boning? It's the last time I bring you pastries from La Maison."

I released him with a loud pop and gasped. "You didn't tell me there were people here."

Keaton held up his hands as his dick bobbed furiously in front of my face. "To be fair, you didn't give me a chance, before you started offering blow jobs, and you know me. I'm completely horned off for you."

"Crap." Then I stopped. Realized something. "Sera, is that you?"

"The one and only, bitch. I mean, how quick can you make that blow job? Because there's shopping to be done."

I glanced right back at Keaton's cock as he was trying to take deep breaths and will it down. "Give me five minutes."

Keaton's brows lifted. "Five? Give me some credit."

I reached for his balls and then licked my lips, and did it again. When his hands fisted in my hair, he groaned. "Okay, fine five. Five minutes."

I pulled back. "Less."

"Woman, you're going to kill me."

"Probably."

Four and a half minutes later, Keaton was laid out on the bed, panting and laughing so hard that I worried for his sanity. I grabbed my bag of goodies, yanked it open, snatched a beignet, then shoved it into my mouth, with no jam or anything—just the powdered sugary goodness, and I moaned.

On the outside of the door, Sera hollered again. "Bitch, you said a blow job, not a full-on sex session. You don't have time for that. Shopping awaits. Come on."

Keaton coughed. "Hey, I do take longer than that in bed."

Sera laughed. "Yeah, *sure* you do. Now come on, Iris. Get a move on, Briggs."

I giggled and scooted out of his reach, but I forgot how fast Keaton was. His hand grabbed my wrist gently and pinned me down. He kissed the powdered sugar off my lips. "I love you, Iris."

I grinned at him. "I love you too, Keaton. Now, if you don't mind, I'm going to go hug my best friend and eat my weight in beignets and pain au chocolat."

He groaned. "Didn't you tell me you were going to be my best friend?"

I shrugged. "That's when you were withholding pastries from me. I would have said anything. Hell, I already *did* do anything to get them."

He groaned. "You know payback is a bitch, right? When I get my hands on you, I'm going to tan that beautiful ass."

"You're welcome to try."

I grabbed a T-shirt and a pair of boxers from the dresser drawer, not caring about dusting the sugar everywhere, or that I probably smelled like orgasms. And then I ran to the door and tugged it open. Sera immediately glanced away. "Lord, make sure the man is dressed. I don't need to see all that." She paused. "Unless the rumors are true and he really is hung like a—"

From inside the bedroom, Keaton cut her off, "Oh, but you'd be lucky to see it."

Sera came right back with a, "I've seen better."

Keaton just snorted a laugh. "I know exactly who it is you see in bed and you wish."

The two of them had learned to bicker properly. "Come on, the gang is all here. We were waiting for you to wake up."

I laughed with sheer, surprised happiness when she dragged me out towards the living room and found our friends. My friends, Keaton's friends. "Holy shit, what are you all doing here?"

There were hugs and kisses all around, and then Keaton came back out from the bedroom, wrapping his arms around my waist. "Happy birthday, love. Your parents will be here tonight, but I figured you would want to celebrate with our friends."

My parents still hadn't gotten used to the idea of Keaton, but they were warming up. And my mother had said that as long as I loved him, she could love him. But if he broke my heart again, she was going to slaughter him.

I turned in his arms, snuggling in the warmth. "I love you so much."

"I know. I love you too."

I looped my arms around his neck and pressed my body to him, and everyone in the room made gagging noises and groaned. But I didn't care. I had Keaton who I'd always wanted, and my freedom. And I had my freedom *my* way.

"So what do you say? A day in Paris with our friends?"

"I couldn't ask for anything more."

CALLOUS PRINCE

BECKER GRAY

CHAPTER ONE

Sloane

I CHANGED MY mind the minute I saw the ballroom.

"No," I said, coming to a halt. "No, I think I'd rather not."

"Come on," Serafina van Doren wheedled. "We've been planning this for weeks. *Pleeeease.*"

"No, *you've* been planning this for weeks," I corrected. "*I've* been dreading this."

Through the doors, the entire student population of Pembroke Preparatory Academy was arrayed in a glittering panoply of wealth and privilege—silk gowns, elaborate masks, jewelry borrowed from Mommy or Grandmama—the works.

The ballroom itself had also been spared no expense. There were flickering candelabras everywhere, and garlands of greenery threaded through with autumn leaves and berries. Entire trees with leaves the color of flames had been brought in, along with green-leafed vines hung with hefty pumpkins. The cumulative effect was to make the ballroom feel like an enchanted autumn forest—perfect for this year's Halloween masquerade theme.

Fairyland.

The annual Pembroke Halloween Masquerade was one of the events that Serafina lived for—and one that I'd managed to successfully avoid for the last three years. I wasn't really all that much for dressing up. Or being on display. Or being around people in general, actually.

I much preferred to hang back, to watch from the shadows unobserved, to escape notice. It would be essential if I wanted to follow in my father's clandestine footsteps, but that wasn't the only reason I did it.

The other reason I hid in the shadows would certainly be here tonight, watching the ballroom with disdain pulling at his beautiful, sullen mouth, candlelight flickering off his white hair and his eerily golden eyes.

He was the same reason I was regretting letting Serafina talk me into this. *Last chance*, my ass. What did I care that this was my senior year and my last chance to go to the masquerade? All I wanted was to be free of Pembroke—I certainly wasn't going to be pining after a dumb costume party when I was carving through the world's chaos and mayhem at INTERPOL.

"Look, you're already dressed for it," Sera coaxed. "Why not come in and at least give your costume a chance to be seen?"

I rarely felt self-conscious, but seeing the ballroom packed with silk and velvet and lace made me balk. "No one wants to see this costume," I muttered.

"Uh-uh. I think it's crazy hot," Aurora declared. She plucked at the half cape I wore over one shoulder. "You look like a 16th century fairy assassin. Who *fucks*."

Fairy assassin who fucks had indeed been the theme of the costume—Serafina's theme, not mine. All I'd asked for was a costume with pants and boots. And maybe a sword.

Serafina had come back with skin-tight black pants and

knee-high black boots, an ornately handled rapier for my hip, and a velvet capelet which matched the light jade of my eyes and set off my lingering summer tan. And of course, the tight black corset that went over the white Renaissance-era blouse. "Sera, do you want to explain to me why I was your unfortunate guinea pig and not Tannith?"

Sera planted a kiss on my cheek. "Because, my love, Tannith is currently in Los Angeles for the fellowship, and she needed to focus."

"Like you couldn't have flown her in for this."

She grinned. "I could have. But you were the far more fun project."

Before we'd come here tonight, she'd dressed me, slicked my short bob back, and fastened a mask over my face that matched my cape. "There," she'd said proudly. "You look like you just finished fucking some gorgeous but dissolute prince and now you're creeping through the palace to kill his father. Tannith would absolutely *die* if she saw this."

Tannith was our resident bookworm—well, *usually* our resident bookworm. She was currently doing a fellowship in Los Angeles and had been gone all semester. We missed her an awful lot, and I especially missed her right now, when I needed an anchor in the storm that was Sera and Aurora in full Party Mode.

But in the end, I'd liked the idea of the fairy assassin who fucks enough that I'd let Sera and Aurora pack me in the van Doren limo and drag me all the way to the ballroom doors before my doubts crashed in again.

"I don't know," I said in the here and now. "I think I'll just head back. You two don't need me—"

"Is this about my brother?" Aurora asked. She let go of my cape so she could touch my elbow, and underneath her pearl-studded mask, I could see her golden eyes go soft with concern. The same golden eyes that belonged to her twin brother.

Lennox.

Lennox Lincoln-Ward. A literal, actual prince. The most beautiful boy I'd ever seen.

And also the worst. The meanest and the most heartless. Callous beyond belief.

Aurora's voice suddenly went bright and helpful. "I could kill him for you, you know."

I gave a small laugh. "I think that's my line."

Sera crossed her arms, studying the ballroom. She had that look on her face—the one I thought of as the Queen look. Like she'd just ridden up to a battlefield on her steed and was about to order the cannons to fire. Her thick curls were pinned in an elaborate updo and set with flashing red gems, and her scarlet gown brought out the jewel tones in her medium-brown skin. Aurora and Lennox might have been actual royalty, but Sera was every inch Pembroke's real monarch tonight.

"He doesn't get to do this," Sera said, eyes on the ostentatious revelry in front of her. "He doesn't get to keep you away from things you want to do."

I opened my mouth to protest that I didn't actually want to do this, but then I closed it again as her words truly sank into my mind. She was right, as a queen usually was. It was stupid to let Lennox chase me away from anything. Despite the fact that he was Liechtensteiner royalty and part of the Hellfire Club—and despite his persistent hatred and low-key torture of me—this was my damn school too. I deserved to be at this silly ball just as much as he did, and I was done with this pointless game of ours. The Fairy Assassin Who Fucks was going to dance, drink, and laugh like she never had before, just to spite him.

For three years, Lennox Lincoln-Ward had tried to make my life a living hell.

And tonight, that ended for good.

✦   ✦   ✦

AN HOUR LATER, I was less sure.

I'd thought it would be as simple as ignoring Lennox; I thought I'd barely notice he was here.

But I hadn't taken two things into account.

Firstly—there was no such thing as me *ignoring* Lennox, and there hadn't been since the first week of freshman year when he started persecuting me for no reason at all.

His mere presence made me flare with awareness and trepidation; simply knowing he was in the room made my skin tighten and my pulse race. Tonight was no exception, and as I tried to laugh with my friends, as I accepted a few dances from boys I barely knew, I could feel his eyes on me, burning into my skin. Whenever I looked his way, he was already looking somewhere else, but I *knew* he was watching me. Hating me. It made me tense, electric. Like I was about to spar with my martial arts instructor—certain I was going to lose but eager to prove myself all the same.

Secondly—I had not adequately prepared myself for how Lennox would look tonight. It honestly hadn't occurred to me that he could be any more devastatingly beautiful than he was in everyday life, but here he was, putting everyone else to shame. His starkly blond hair tumbled white and silky around a circlet of golden stars set into his hair, and the crown only further set off the sharp gold of his eyes. The white mask he wore left his forehead, jaw, and mouth bare, and rather than disguise the near-inhuman elegance of his pale features, the mask only served to highlight them.

The jaw so gorgeously sharp that it looked rendered by an artist. A mouth so painfully sensual, even when pulled into its usual sulky pout.

And his costume . . .

While most of the Pembroke guys had used the masquerade as an excuse to show off their latest bespoke suits and imported Italian shoes, Lennox had taken the fairyland theme to heart and come fully as a fairy prince. He was barefoot and wearing tight leather pants, with a Renaissance-style white shirt and a doublet made of gold silk and velvet. Both the doublet and the shirt were open—and the shirt was all the way unlaced, exposing a shocking amount of smooth, firm skin. The hollow of his collarbone, the lean but solid muscles of his chest—they were all on display.

He really looked like he had just strolled out of a fairy forest. He looked wicked and unearthly.

He looked perfect.

It wasn't fair.

It wasn't fair that he hated me, when I'd done nothing to deserve it. It wasn't fair that he looked handsome and delicious while I looked—well, less like an assassin who fucks and more like a girl who was uncomfortable wearing dresses and lipstick.

After I finished dancing with a boy from my AP Physics class, I went for a drink of water. There was stronger stuff on hand if I wanted it, not to mention all sorts of artisanal punches that were all fairyland-themed, but I wanted to keep my head and stay hydrated. A hydrated body is a strong body, and a flexible one too, and I needed my body to be both.

I took my water behind a tree and watched the dancers from underneath its arching branches. I watched *him*, dancing with a girl a year or two younger than us. Whatever she said made him laugh; it made a smile carve itself across his normally-sulky mouth.

And as always, whenever he smiled, there was an answering slice across my heart.

"I've seen lions less aware of wounded gazelles than Lennox is of you tonight," a silky voice said from behind me.

I turned to see the devil himself, Rhys Huntington, standing just behind my shoulder, pale, dark-haired, and dressed all in black: a black suit that probably cost as much as a regular person's car, black and silver vest underneath, black silk tie stuck through with a ruby-studded tie pin.

"Lennox doesn't even know I'm alive," I responded evenly, knowing it was a lie but also too wary to engage Rhys further. "And I thought tonight's theme was fairyland—not vampire coven."

Rhys stepped forward, a tilt to his sharp-edged mouth. We were shoulder to shoulder now. "I'm a dark fairy. From the Unseelie Court. Don't you know your fairy stories?"

The honest answer was no. As the only daughter of an INTERPOL bureau chief, my childhood had often been stranger than any fairy tale, and anyway, my father wasn't much for fantasy. He was all about what could be seen and touched and uncovered—all about this world and those who would sin against it. I suppose I took after him in that way.

If only there wasn't a certain sinner that fascinated me so much . . .

"Anyway," Rhys pronounced, still in that silky voice, "if you don't think Lennox is looking at you tonight, just watch this."

Within the blink of an eye, my water was set on a table and I was whisked out onto the dance floor. *In Rhys's arms.* Staring up at those near-black eyes glittering from behind his dark mask.

"What are we doing?" I asked him, easily catching the rhythm of the waltz as he turned me across the floor. I was a decent dancer. It wasn't so different than martial arts, after all: posture, form, balance. And Rhys was a surprisingly graceful partner for being someone whom I'd always assumed was pure evil.

Whenever we turned, my cape swung out behind me, and whenever we stepped, Rhys's firm hand on my back made sure to keep my hips close to his. For anyone watching, the dance might have looked . . . romantic.

"I would've thought it was obvious what we're doing, Sloane Lauder," Rhys said softly. "I'm proving a point about Lennox."

My father had trained me better, he really had, but when it came to Lennox, I never could seem to control myself. I swiveled my head and looked to where I'd seen him last.

And was hit with a golden gaze so malevolent I could practically feel its heat all the way out here in the middle of the dance floor.

"He *is* watching," I said, more to myself than to the tall devil spinning me around.

"He's always watching you."

"He hates me, you know."

Rhys smiled a cipher-like smile. "Maybe."

"I don't think he likes seeing me have fun."

The cipher-like smile grew bigger. "If he hates dancing, then he'll definitely hate this."

And right there, right in the middle of the ballroom floor with couples waltzing around us and candles flickering everywhere, Rhys Huntington kissed me.

Kissed me!

I could have fended him off if I wanted. No one could touch me when I didn't want to be touched, thanks to my father and years of martial arts. But I found . . . I found I didn't want to.

Not at first, at least.

His kiss was silky, just like his voice, and his mouth was surprisingly warm for someone with a heart chiseled from ice. And while it didn't necessarily set my heart to racing the same way a mere glance from Lennox did, and while it didn't make me hot and restless the way the mere thought of Lennox's mouth made me, the kiss wasn't *un*pleasant. It was almost nice, in fact. Like the sensation of kissing without all the fervor and heat that usually accompanied the act. Like the *idea* of kissing without all the complicated feelings coming to mess it up.

Rhys's fingers curled around my cape as he pulled me closer and deepened the kiss, his tongue slipping between my lips to caress mine. It was instinct as much as anything that had me tilting my face up to offer Rhys more—and that's when I heard it.

The clatter and crash of a candelabra falling over, and the gasps and shrieks that followed. I broke away from Rhys's kiss to see Lennox disappearing through the far doors, his stride quick and furious.

From the way people were staring and whispering, it was clear he was the one who knocked over the candelabra.

As if he'd flung it to the ground in anger before storming away.

"Well, then," Rhys said with satisfaction, his eyes also on Lennox's retreating form. "I was right."

Chapter Two

Lennox

R *AGE. IT WAS* the only way to explain what was happening to my body. My skin was clammy and hot. And all I wanted to do was hit something. It was like my skin hummed and my blood was trying to force its way out by exploding it.

I was going to kill him. Bloody Rhys.

I knew the Hellfire Club wasn't a knitting circle or an etiquette class. We mostly did whatever the fuck we wanted—hell, the whole purpose of the club was so the wealthy and the powerful could increase their wealth and power so that they could continue to do whatever the fuck they wanted after they left Pembroke. This kind of power-brokering, good old boys club shit didn't exactly make for a milieu of politeness and courtesy. We were sharks chosen by the sharks who came before us, and when we graduated, we would wade into an ocean where we were already kings.

So no, we were no knitting circle, but there were still a few fucking *codes*.

You didn't fuck with other Hellfire members, and you certainly didn't fuck with their toys.

I knew better than to totally lose my shit at the masquerade ball though. I'd been raised better than that. There were appropriate times and places for caving to anger, and the ball wasn't it. Besides, there was no way any adult in there would have let me kick Rhys's arse the way I'd wanted to. Also, I wanted to give him more time to sober up. Because when I put him into the ground, I wanted him to remember it. I wanted him to feel it. I wanted to burn him down.

Some fucking mate he was.

She was mine. She had *always* been mine. And Rhys, arsehole that he was, thought he could just stroll in and take her from me? No. Ever since I laid eyes on hers, we'd had our unwritten rule. She was *mine* to torment. Mine to *torture.*

After what her father had done to mine, it was the payback I needed. She was nobody else's to even look at. And all things being even, Rhys didn't even want her, I was certain of it. He just found her interesting for some fucking reason.

All around me, limousines dropped off the children of the world's wealthiest at the Everwood Country Club, this year's location for the Halloween Masquerade Ball. Nestled along a lake, surrounded by the jaw-dropping fall foliage, the country club was the perfect location. The employees had set lights into the water along the property to carry on the fairyland theme.

Knowing I'd be drinking, I'd opted for the safer option of the limo. Some of the other lads had caught a ride with Owen.

I wanted to leave, just say fuck it all and head back to campus, but Keaton was riding with me, so I had to wait. I was in the middle of texting him when I saw Owen and Rhys coming my way.

Owen, as to be expected, was in cold control. If he'd

been in the mood to display any emotions, he'd likely be disapproving of my antics inside the ballroom. Owen was our living and breathing Ice King. He didn't fucking get it. He had no feelings. Or he'd been smart and learned a long time ago to lock that shit away.

Just seeing Rhys's face again made me want to raze every car on the jammed country club drive. He gave me nothing. He was always a cool and contained sociopath. "What the fuck, Rhys?"

He gave me his barely-there smile, those cruel eyes crinkling at the corners, telling me that he'd been looking forward to this. "What the fuck what?"

"That kiss, that fucking show—what the hell is wrong with you?"

He grinned then, and it was so strange to see a full-on smile on his face, I almost didn't know what to do.

You kick his arse, that's what you do.

I re-focused myself. "You're such a piece of shit. You don't even want her."

"But I *do* want her. She's interesting to me."

Owen could see where this was going, and his lips pressed into a harsh line as he stepped between us. "Lads, get your shit under control. This isn't the place to do this. Teachers are milling about. You two tossers want to take a hunk out of each other's hides, you do it where it can't be seen. And where you won't get blood on my tux."

"Careful, Mr. Robot, somebody will begin to think you care."

He lifted a dark brow. "Hardly, I'm just calculating the odds of who to bet on in this fight. I'm inclined to put my money on Rhys, because he's not whining like a bitch."

"Fuck you. And for the record, I have exactly zero fucks to give about teachers." What, like they were going to expel me? I was fucking royalty.

You are also the son of royalty. This is what's expected of you.

I knew what I needed to do, but unfortunately, I couldn't stamp down the fury.

Rhys was laughing now. What the hell was he saying?

"I have to tell you, Lennox, I'm amused by your response. I thought you *hated* her."

"I do. The point is, she is *mine*."

Rhys's eyes went wide. "She's yours?" Mirth laced each of his words.

"Yes, that's right. Mine to torture. Mine to ignore. Mine to pull along on a string like a puppet. *Mine*," I ground out. Her father had ruined my life. Systematically. Everything was gone because of her family. And so, if I was going to take my revenge, it was going to be through her. And Rhys wasn't going to ruin her before I got there.

"Did you tell her that? Does she know she's—" he made air quotes. "*Yours?*"

I lunged for him again, and this time, Owen put a hand on my chest, more than capable of stopping me. We were about the same height, but I was leaner. He had a good twenty pounds of muscle over me, but I was meaner. I spun out from him, elbowed him in the chest for good measure so he'd back off, and Rhys just taunted me, "If you want her, you are more than welcome to try and take her from me. But I'm not going to just give her to you. I think I'll play with her for a while. You know, she's surprisingly a good kisser. Soft lips. The way her tongue tentatively seeks yours out as if she can't believe her luck. God. I always find that a major turn on. These quiet girls, they're the best ones in bed. It's going to be fun finding out with Sloane."

I lunged at him again. This time, Owen had an arm

around my waist, and out of the corner of my eye, I saw Keaton running towards us too. Fuck. Not Keaton. He was building up for the pro rugby season. *Shit.*

"Guys, what's going on? You don't want to do this out in full view."

Rhys grinned. "Hey, I'm a lover, not a fighter. I prefer to destroy people without my hands, but if it comes down to it, I will use them."

It was true. Rhys never needed to lift a finger. The guy was always working out though. Fucking *Muay Thai* or whatever it was that he did all the time. He had his trainer personally come to the school. Who the hell did that? But despite being probably more than capable of using his fists, Rhys was mean as a snake. He preferred to destroy you with words.

So beat him at his own game.

"You can let me go. I'm not going to fucking hit him." Lies. All lies.

Keaton laughed. "I love you, man, but I don't believe you."

"Rhys, you know what, you can have your fun with Sloane. It's all right. I get it. You're bored, but you'll get tired of her too."

He grinned. "I don't know if I will. You know, she's fascinating. Smart as a whip. Slightly deadly. And she's unusual. God, those lips. I mean, it must kill you that you've never tapped that at all, because wow, the girl can kiss."

It felt like there was a dragon in my chest trying to claw its way out.

Be smart. Use his one weakness against him.

I forced myself to still then. "You know what, you're right. You can get whoever you want. And yes, I'm losing my shit. I don't like someone stealing my toys. But you do have a point. We're all free agents here, except for Keaton, and that's by choice. But we should think outside the box, explore opportunities we've never considered before. You know, Sera was looking damn fine tonight. Well fit. Gorgeous, really. But that red dress, her mask, the hood, she looked like something from Venice. I think I'll find out just what she had on under those skirts, yeah?"

I found out in those two seconds exactly what happens when you poke a dragon. I'd miscalculated. And unfortunately, I was the only one being held back by our friends.

Rhys was quicker than a flash. It was almost like the motherfucker flew into the air, and he was on me. His first hit grazed just off my jaw because I turned to go with it.

When the rest of my mates realized they were holding the wrong arsehole, they tried to go for him, but he was quicker.

I'm not proud of it, but I did give him a good sucker punch to the kidney. But Rhys really was the devil. He didn't cry out. He didn't moan. But he did hiss and turn on me, his hands knotted into tight fists, but this time, Keaton had him. He'd hooked Rhys's arm and wrapped it around his back. Owen planted himself in front of him, like a statue made of ice. Both of them were muttering something in low tones.

Now free, I stood at my full height and grinned. "Yeah, everyone knows how hot Sera is. Now I'm going to find out just what she tastes like."

Rhys snarled at me. "If you put your fucking hands on her, I will *kill* you."

Being the arsehole that I was, I grinned back. "Oh, but I thought Sloane was the most interesting person to you. I guess not. I think I'll go find Sera now and see what she's up to." Then I deliberately turned and stalked away.

It was a calculated risk. He could have lunged for me. We were too evenly built, so it would have been one hell of a fight. But I was confident that Keaton and Owen had him. So I continued on my way, and I didn't turn back.

I'd considered Rhys a friend, but he'd stepped over the line, and I was going to make him pay for it.

CHAPTER THREE

Sloane

"T HANK YOU," THE junior said gratefully. She looked around the empty classroom, as if to confirm again that we were alone. "You're sure it's gone?"

I uncrossed my arms and gave her a sympathetic but utilitarian nod. "He had it in his photo library, and he'd emailed it to himself, but he hadn't sent it to anyone else yet. Both the phone and the email have been scrubbed, along with his cloud storage."

The junior slumped in relief. "Thank god," she murmured. "Thank god."

Her asshole ex had threatened to send a nude picture of her to everyone at the school once he found out she was dating a new boyfriend. I took care of it last night, using some stealth and a few sturdy lockpicking tools.

"I'm so glad I came to you," she said. "Do I . . . like . . . owe you anything?"

I shook my head. "Free of charge."

She squinted at me. "Are you like Pembroke's revenge porn vigilante or something?"

The corners of my mouth pulled up. I liked the idea of being a resident vigilante, but really I just had a keen sense of justice, and—much like Liam Neeson—a very particular set of skills. Over the last two or three years, I'd become something of a Veronica Mars here at school, helping students out when the administration couldn't. It was unbelievable the amount of boys who thought sending a girl's nudes around was a totally justified thing to do, but I also had my share of "is he or she cheating?" cases and a fair amount of theft. It kept me from getting bored, kept me sharp and proficient at moving through the shadows, and also it was just fun. Satisfying.

Some students had sports, some had parties—I had this.

"I'm just happy I could help," I told her.

"Me too," she said. "Thank you again."

I nodded and made for the door.

"Hey, do you know anybody at Croft Wells who does what you do?" she asked.

Croft Wells was another coed prep school only an hour away, and Pembroke's eternal rival. Despite that, there were still a healthy amount of cross-school friendships and even dating. "I don't," I said. "Why?"

The junior sighed. "My cousin says there's been some girls attacked at parties over there, and they don't know if it's like one guy or a bunch of guys or what. The police and campus admin have been no help. Seems like the kind of thing you'd be good at."

I frowned at that. "When was the last assault?"

She shook her head. "They stopped in the spring. Maybe the attacker got bored?"

Or he found a new hunting ground.

But I didn't tell the junior that. "Probably he got bored," I said reassuringly, and then I stepped through the door and made my way to class, vowing to keep an eye on things here at Pembroke.

I had no way to get to Croft Wells, but I'd be good and goddamned before I let an asshole get away with that here at Pembroke.

✦   ✦   ✦

"RHYS IS LOOKING at you," Sera announced a few hours later.

Even in the clanking, chattering din of Pembroke's giant, vaulted dining hall, I could hear something strained in her voice. I glanced up from my dog-eared copy of *The Book of Five Rings* and gave her a quelling look. "Stop it. You know I don't care."

"You certainly seemed like you cared at the masquerade a couple days ago," she pointed out.

"It was just a kiss," I said, going back to my Musashi. "It wasn't a big deal."

"For 'not a big deal', my brother went totally off his trolley," Aurora said cheerfully. "And Rhys is still looking, by the way."

For the millionth time, I wished Tannith were here instead of spending the semester in Los Angeles. Because normally we absconded to the library together to read during lunch, and so it never mattered what Rhys Huntington was or was not doing.

To satisfy my friends—and *not* because I cared that a certain gold-eyed prince might also be sitting there—I looked over at the Hellfire Club's table across the hall. They sat at the far end of the wood-ceilinged, portrait-bedecked space, right under the largest stained glass window in the room. A cluster of gorgeous, insolent boys, sprawled in their chairs like so many bored lions. The bright autumn sunlight through the glass lit their table with shafts of blazing orange and glowing ruby—as if hellfire truly burned in the air around them.

Fitting, since next to Lennox sat the devil himself, grinning at me from across the room like we shared some kind of secret. I ducked my head as soon as I realized we'd met eyes, but it was too late, of course. Rhys had obviously been waiting for just this moment.

"Rhys is standing up," Sera said, her voice still strange. "He's walking over here."

"Oh, Lennox looks quite tetchy now," Aurora said, sounding pleased. She took typical sisterly delight in anything that annoyed her twin. "Yes, very tetchy indeed."

I couldn't help it; I lifted my head again, my eyes sliding right past Rhys's approaching form to Lennox again. Even at this distance, I could see the hatred sizzling in his eyes and the angry tilt to his mouth. The same look he'd leveled my way since that first day in freshman seminar.

I'd long since stopped trying to understand why Lennox Lincoln-Ward hated me—although I used to think about it constantly, used to wonder if I could fix whatever it was. Or at least change it so that he'd *stop*. It couldn't be that I'd offended him before the first day of freshman year, because until then I'd gone to school in D.C. And it couldn't have been anything I'd done that morning, because when I initially walked into the seminar, he'd looked up at me and offered me a careless grin—like he wanted to know what my lip gloss tasted like but he was too lazy to try to find out.

It wasn't until he heard my name that he'd swiveled his head to stare at me—lips parted in shock, eyes bright with fury—and then abruptly scooped up his bag and stormed out of the room.

And after that, the true torment began.

Lube in my book bag, caricatures drawn of me in bathrooms, classroom projects replaced with a single, thoroughly dead rose. The rumors he started about me—some silly, some ridiculous, some vicious as hell—and his cruel laughter following me everywhere I went.

And his *presence.*

The presence of him was its own torture.

He didn't stalk me, I wouldn't go that far, but he haunted me, he encircled me and bedeviled me, made it so that every corner of Pembroke was suffused and pervaded with him. He would be in doorways I needed to go through, blocking my escape, or sitting at my desk before class started, eating an apple and staring at me with glittering eyes. He'd be at my chair in the library when I'd come back from grabbing a book, his three-thousand-dollar Italian shoes kicked up on the table, or jogging behind me as I did my morning run on the track, never approaching me or coming closer, but keeping pace with me perfectly no matter how much I sped up or slowed down.

Being raised by my father meant that I was more capable of defending myself than anyone knew, and it also meant I wasn't in the habit of taking anyone's shit. For every time I found my books and tablet slicked in lube, I discreetly and efficiently picked the lock to his room and replaced his hair gel with KY and his toothpaste with Astroglide (for variety). I wasn't a fan of bathroom vandalism, but I did help myself to some classified student records early on, and then occasionally amused myself by distributing his cell phone number to giggling freshmen eager to kiss a real-life prince.

And when he blocked a doorway, when he sat at my desk, when he ran behind me every morning with a gray hood drawn over his striking blond hair—I never let him see the fear that sizzled over my skin. I couldn't.

Because if he saw the fear, then he might see how it

mingled with other feelings. How the adrenaline made my blood spark and made something deep in my core go all twisty and hot.

He could never know.

I could survive his hatred maybe, but his pity?

His smug superiority once he learned that under my defiance crawled something much, much more embarrassing than fear?

I didn't even think I could *attempt* to endure that. I would have to move and change my name. I would have to change all distinguishable identifiers. I would have to dye my hair and wear colored contacts and take the helix piercing out of my upper ear. And I really liked that piercing.

No, he could never know.

Which actually made it very convenient that Rhys was coming over to our table just now. Although he'd been as bad to me as Lennox had over the years—I suspected the most creatively depraved of the bathroom graffiti was the work of Rhys's degenerate mind—I really hadn't minded kissing him at the masquerade. And I minded even less that it made me appear indifferent to Lennox, that it made it *very clear* I did not think about Lennox in any kind of kissing capacity ever—that I did not sometimes let my hand wander over my body at the thought of Lennox's mouth or his lean body or his elegant, long-fingered hands which looked like they'd feel so very good shoved into my panties.

Rhys was an opportunity to protect myself, and I'd learned early on from my father never to waste those.

My father.

I had wondered before . . .

Well, there *had* been a scandal with Lennox and Aurora's father, years ago—a massive Ponzi scheme and substantial prison time after. INTERPOL had been the investigating agency, and it had been the US and several European bureaus working together to make the arrest. I'd asked my father about it once, not long after Lennox's torment had begun, but he told me he had only consulted on the case once and barely looked at it after. So I knew his vendetta couldn't be about my father.

Maybe Lennox merely hated anyone or anything to do with INTERPOL? But Aurora had mentioned more than once that both she and Lennox were very happy about their father being in prison and hoped he'd stay there, so it made no sense to hate me over a father whom they were quite satisfied to have rotting in prison.

It couldn't be that. So what was it?

"Ladies," Rhys was saying as he sauntered over. "How beautiful you all look today."

"We're not interested," Sera replied shortly. "Fuck off."

The evil grin faded, replaced by a look so cold that even I fought the urge to shiver.

Sera, for her part, just continued glaring up at him.

"I'm not here for you," Rhys said in a silky voice.

"Then god is real," said Sera.

Rhys's face didn't change, but his eyes did, growing even blacker. "If I want you, I'll have you."

Sera looked away, her expression cool. "I'd like to see you try."

And then—most frightening of all—Rhys smiled. "Maybe one day, van Doren. But only after you beg, and who knows? Maybe then it will be too late."

Sera rolled her eyes and got up to leave. Rhys stepped forward, towering over my slender friend, and for a moment, I thought he might stop her from leaving. But then, with that eerie smile again, he stepped aside, and with a huff, Sera stalked away from the table with a muttered *see you later* to me and Aurora.

Rhys took her seat with a prompt grace which suggested he'd been planning on driving her off all along. "Now, Sloane," he said, as if we were picking up on a conversation we'd started before. "What time should I have you picked up next Saturday for the gala?"

Aurora nearly spit out her drink. "You're going to the Huntington Gala together?"

"No," I said, narrowing my eyes at Rhys. "I've never been invited to the gala, remember, Aurora?" While my father made decent money in his work—decent enough to send me here—he didn't make *gala* money, and I hadn't exactly grown up with the gala set. The annual Huntington bash was one of the events that everybody knew about and only a chosen, insanely wealthy few could attend. And I had never been one of them.

Which I truly hadn't minded—Tannith was as unconnected and socially obscure as me, and so we usually spent the evening in the near-empty common room watching a weird mix of BBC literary adaptions (her choice) and bloody action movies (mine). And I hated getting dressed up anyway.

Plus, the Huntington mansion was outside of Boston, which meant that attending the gala was a weekend-long commitment with the long-ass drive factored in. No thanks.

"Consider this your invitation then," Rhys said, undaunted. "And of course, you're welcome to come down early with me on Friday. Spend the night, see my childhood room."

Even out of the corner of my eye, I could see Aurora's jaw drop.

"Okay, this is getting weird. I'm out," I said, standing

up and slinging my bag over my chest. "I'll see you later, Aurora. Bye, Rhys."

Rhys was up and next to me in an instant.

"Let me walk you to your next class," he said smoothly, taking my hand in his.

Just like his kiss at the masquerade, it didn't feel unpleasant at all. It was nice, actually. I normally didn't mind that karate and exercise kept my curves more flat than interesting, and I had no interest in changing how I dressed—usually a short ponytail and boots to go with my school uniform. But I couldn't deny that I was hardly luring boys to my side this way and getting to hold hands with someone was a nice change. Even more so when he pulled me out into the almost empty corridor connecting the dining hall to the main lecture building and pressed his warm lips to mine.

"Come to my family's gala," he murmured, pulling back to look down at me. Those black eyes were inscrutable. I had no idea what he was thinking and no reason to trust that it might be good.

"Wouldn't you rather go with someone else?" I asked. "*Anyone* else?" I wasn't a knockout like Sera or royalty like Aurora. I wasn't rich like Clara Blair and her friends. The most interesting things about me—what my father did for a living and all the things he'd taught me—weren't apparent on the surface.

In short, there was no reason to believe that Rhys wasn't playing some kind of stupid Hellfire joke on me right now. But then he said the one thing that made me believe him.

"I'm never going to fall in love with you, Sloane Lauder. But right now, you're the most interesting girl at this school to me. And I like interesting things." He gave me an assessing look, like he could see my bra and panties underneath my school blazer and skirt. "I like interesting things quite a lot."

With another penetrating but mysterious look, he walked away, calling over his shoulder, "Five p.m. next Friday, Sloane. We're going to my house."

I didn't answer him. Mostly because he was already prowling away, but also because the answer that leapt to my lips wasn't an immediate *no*. As much as I thought I'd hate the idea of going to something like the Huntington Gala . . . it *was* really flattering to be asked.

Maybe it wouldn't be the worst thing if I went.

With a glance down at my phone, I saw I had some time before my next class, and I decided to take the long way to the science building. I'd only made it a handful of steps down the stone-flagged corridor when the hair prickled on the back of my neck.

I spun around just in time to stop Lennox from grabbing my arm, my training flaring up instinctively. I blocked his grab and was about to seize his wrist and twist it when he did something I had no preparation for.

He hauled me tight against him with his free arm around my back, so tight that I could feel the angry heave of his chest and the firm wall of his abdomen, and at the press of his body against mine, all my instincts left me. Well, all except the dumbest one, which pleaded for me to rub against him like a cat and purr until he petted me.

"No need to fly into a fit, darling," Lennox said, his British accent curling around me like the tendrils of a lovely but lethal frost. "We can be civilized about this."

"Civilized about wha—*Lennox!*" He was dragging me into a nearby storage closet, throwing open the door with one hand as he easily pulled me inside. The only way I could have broken free was by hurting him—a finger rake to his eagle-gold eyes, a knee to the groin, maybe some broken fingers—and I found . . . well, I found that I didn't really want to do that. Not until I had no other choice, at least.

"Let. Me. Go," I demanded the minute the door was closed.

He flicked on a light, still keeping me close, and then looked down at me. We were surrounded by boxes of paper towels and industrial-sized rolls of toilet paper, but even in here, he looked like a prince; arrogant and majestic. The dim light from the single light bulb caressed his sharp cheekbones and pout-shaped mouth.

"Lennox," I bit out. "I'm not asking. Let me go."

He looked a little surprised at himself when he admitted, "But I don't want to."

I glared up at him. "You realize I can make you, right? And it won't be pleasant."

"I don't doubt it," he said honestly. "But I don't think you want to make me. I think you like being right here." A cruel smirk twisted the corner of his mouth. "I *definitely* like you being right here."

He tugged me even closer—and I could feel more than his chest and stomach now, I could feel his . . . oh wow.

Wow, wow, wow.

He might technically be a prince, but there was one place where he was *all* king.

No! Focus, Sloane!

I twisted away and this time he let me, dropping his arm and leaning back against a wall of shelves as I took a deep breath and steadied myself. Karate prepares you for chokeholds and grips, for locks and strikes, but it definitely does not prepare you for the feeling of a hot, hard cock attached to an even hotter and harder prince, and I needed a second. Maybe two.

Finally, I could think with a mostly clear head again. "What do you want, Lennox?"

"I wanted to warn you about Rhys."

There were so many things about that statement that didn't make sense. But the only thing I could articulate was, "You needed to warn me in a *closet?*"

He frowned. "Well, obviously, we can't be seen talking like this. Think of my reputation, darling."

"I'm not your darling," I said irritably. I wasn't darling; I was deadly, and also it was very unfair how sexy the word *darling* sounded with his accent.

"My apologies," Lennox said with a slicing grin. "What would you rather I call you? Poppet? Dove? My sweet, heartless huntress?"

"I'd rather you call me nothing," I said emphatically, even though I didn't *entirely* hate the way any of those endearments sounded on his lips.

Lennox kept smiling. "My nothing, my sweet nothing. Oh, I like the sound of that. It's quite Shakespearean."

I refused to indulge him a moment longer. "Okay, well, if that's all—"

The frown returned. "That's not all. I haven't warned you about Rhys yet."

"A warning is unnecessary," I told him. "I know exactly what kind of guy Rhys is."

Lennox took a step forward. In the small expanse of the closet, it brought him within touching distance again. I tried to ignore the thrill my body gave at that.

"I don't think you know at all," he said, and for once, his voice wasn't dripping with scorn or crackling with hate. He sounded completely serious. "Rhys is practically sociopathic. He's a monster. If he asked you to the Huntington Gala, it's not because he wants to go on picnics and skip through the bloody park with you."

Irritation surged within me.

Finally! Here was my fighting instinct!

I stepped right up to Lennox and lifted my face defiantly to his. "He's already told me all of this."

Surprise moved across Lennox's aristocratic features. "He has?"

"Yes. He's been nothing but honest with me. *And* you know what else?"

Lennox's face was tilted down towards mine now, his soft blond hair tumbling over his forehead. "What else?"

"He can talk to me outside of closets. He's really romantic like that."

A muscle jumped in Lennox's jaw.

And then in an instant, his hands were on me again, dragging me against his body as he pressed his lips to my ear. "How would you, my cold, heartless sweetheart, know anything about romance?"

His words whispered warmth over my skin and sent shivers skating down my spine.

I meant to push his hands away, I meant to wedge my elbows between us and drag them over the nerves in his forearms. I meant to shove my head into his, and then finish him off with a swift strike to the sternum.

I meant to do all of those things. But instead, I melted into him. I melted into the hard, arrogant heat of him, I melted into those sinful lips against my skin. And even though he whispered hatred and poison with those lips, my body responded like he was whispering the tenderest, naughtiest secrets instead.

"You wouldn't know, would you? Because you, my sweet, frigid *darling*, are the lowest order of virgin. You are locked up so tight that no one's ever been inside, and no one's ever even been close, have they? Is that because you won't let them or because nobody wants you—"

Of its own accord, my right hand reached up and cracked across his perfect cheek, slapping him as hard as I could. And for a single moment after that, neither of us moved. Me with my hand still stinging in midair, and him with his cheek and jaw growing red, his gold eyes blazing down at me like he wanted to light me on fire with his fury alone.

But he didn't light me on fire. He didn't even speak.

Instead, he slashed his lips over mine and took my mouth in a searing kiss.

A kiss that went from mere hungry lips to hot, searching tongues sliding against each other in seconds.

My slap hadn't affected his erection in the least. If anything, he was even harder than before, his thick column digging into my belly as he hauled me closer and closer with impatient hands, and then finally—with a growl I'd remember for the rest of my life—he shoved me up against the door.

"Wrap those legs around my waist," he grunted between wild, angry kisses. "I know you're strong enough."

"Fuck off," I retorted. But I did it anyway, because I needed—oh *God*—yes. I needed this. I needed my legs around his waist and my skirt up around my hips and his big erection right against my center. It felt *so good*.

"Bleeding Christ," Lennox muttered, tearing his mouth from mine to look down at where he rocked against me. "Even through your knickers, I can feel how hot you are."

My head dropped back against the door as he moved his hips again, dragging his clothed erection against me, dry-fucking me. I'd never done this—I'd barely even kissed a boy before—and it felt so much better than anything I'd ever done on my own; it felt so good I thought I might die right there among the paper towels.

My panties were damp, and my nipples were beaded so tight in my bra that they ached. And every time Lennox moved, there was an answering surge from deep inside my center, an urgent clenching, like my body was trying to . . .

"Are you about to come for me?" Lennox breathed, dipping his head to bite at my neck. "Are you about to make me miserable? Hmm? Show me what I'm missing?"

I couldn't answer. I couldn't even think. My hands were in the thick silk of his hair and my lips burned without his on mine and I was so close . . .

"Can I touch it?" he asked, sliding a hand under my ass far enough that his fingertips could press against my cotton-covered seam. "Let me touch it, please, my darling—"

Nothing sounded better than his fingers on my bare skin, *nothing*, and the minute I moaned out a *yes,* his clever fingers were pushing my panties aside and searching me out, finding where I was wet and hot. Finding the place where I opened and then lingering there, pushing at my center but not quite going inside.

It was torment not having his fingers inside me, it was pure misery, and I squirmed in his arms, trying to seek out more of him.

He gave a low chuckle against my lips. "Want something, do we?"

"Screw you," I said, still squirming. Fuck, I was so close, so very close, and I knew if he touched the inside of me, if he filled me with his fingers . . .

"Then perhaps I shall remove my hand, if it doesn't matter to you either way—"

I scratched at his shoulders and back, I writhed like a wild thing, I leaned forward and bit his collarbone through his uniform shirt. "Lennox . . ."

He pulled back to look at me, his lips swollen, his hair a mess, his pupils blown so wide the gold was almost all black.

"You—" he said, but then he stopped. As if he didn't know what he wanted to say next . . .or knew but didn't want me to hear it.

It didn't matter. He could have scalded my ears with insults, he could have mocked me, debased me, recounted every horrible thing he'd ever done to me, and my body still wouldn't have cared. It was under his spell completely and utterly, it was drugged by his warm lips and rough, impatient hands, and it was poised to dissolve. And then finally, *finally*, I felt the breach of his finger.

We both froze, staring at each other.

Lennox Lincoln-Ward, prince and bully, was fingering me. And it felt better than anything in the entire world.

"This is mine," he murmured.

My eyes fluttered as he went deeper, as he resumed grinding against me with that arrogant cock. "But you hate me," I managed to whisper.

I could hear the dark promise in his voice when he said, "That's exactly why it's mine."

And I came.

To the sound of his possessive, cruel words, I came—so hard that I had to bite his blazer to keep from screaming.

Shudders moved through me, detonating around his long finger and behind my clit, and I was feral in his arms, trying to fuck his finger, trying to rub my clit against his erection, trying to hold on for dear life as my inner thighs and lower belly were seized by delicious, animal bliss.

It took so long for the climax to finish that I was gasping for breath after, that I was nearly weak with holding myself against him. I slumped back against the door, my pussy still sporadically jolting with pleasure, and looked at Lennox.

He had a wild look in his eyes—a look so unlike his usual calculated cruelty that I was almost scared.

"Don't go to the gala with Rhys," he said in a voice just as wild as his expression.

His finger was still inside me, and it was so hard not to start fucking his hand again. "Why not?" I asked. I barely recognized my own voice. It was as far from disciplined and reserved as could be—I sounded sexed-up and lazy and . . . happy?

He slid another finger inside me, and I moaned, rolling my hips. "Because this is mine now."

"I don't think so." Rich words coming from the girl currently fucking herself on his fingers.

"You made a mistake, my darling, letting me feel it, because I'm not about to let it—or you—go. And I'm certainly not going to let Rhys anywhere near this."

"You have literally zero say in who gets near me," I countered, but again, my words were lazy and husky with pleasure. Not exactly ringing with authority. "Plus I kind of want to go to the gala now."

"Then go with me."

I stopped moving and stared at him. He stared back, that wildness still in his eyes, his body taut as a wire against me.

"You've got to be joking," I said.

"I'm not."

"You hate me."

"Yes."

"You don't even want to be seen talking in public with me."

"Correct," he said.

"But now you want to go to the gala with me as your

date?"

He blinked slowly, his long eyelashes framing those impossible eyes. I had the sense that even he didn't know why he wanted to go to the gala with me, but for a moment—for a stupid, dumb, terrible moment—I thought . . .

No. I wasn't foolish enough to think that he liked me. I wasn't deranged enough to think that he suffered from the same sickness I had when it came to him. But I at least thought he'd tell me that he wanted to get under my skirt again, that he wanted to kiss me again.

Instead, what he said was: "Rhys doesn't get to touch you."

Somehow *this* was what shook me down to reality.

Not the best orgasm of my life surrounded by paper towels and toilet paper.

Not him admitting—twice—that he hated me.

Not even him asking me to the gala.

But this.

This reminder that no matter how much he enjoyed mauling me in the supply closet, no matter how desperate he'd been to touch me, I was nothing more than prey to him. Prey that he'd already marked as his own and wouldn't deign to share with Rhys.

And I, Sloane Lauder—daughter without a mother, daughter of a father who chased criminals all around the world, a black belt and a badass—was not prey. Not even for beautiful boys with fingers like magic and lips like sin.

I moved out of his arms, which made his fingers slide free. My core clenched at the emptiness, but I ignored it. "I'm going with him."

He frowned down at his hand, as if unhappy that it was no longer up my skirt. Then he looked back to me. "You're going with me, Sloane. That's the end of it."

I laughed a little, astounded at his conceit. "Do I look insane to you? I'm not picking you over him. At least he's the devil I know."

"That's because he *is* the devil," Lennox replied. "I am only a monster."

I pushed him back enough so that I could smooth my clothes and then turn to open the door. He slammed a hand up to stop me, pressing against me to whisper in my ear.

"You can't hide from me, Sloane. You've belonged to me since the day I saw you."

The first two fingers of his hand were still glistening with me, and the reminder of how they felt inside my panties was enough to make my knees weak. I somehow managed to say, "Belonged to you for *what*, Prince Lennox?"

"To toy with," he said against my ear. And then he ran his nose along the curve of my neck. "To break."

I reached back behind me and wrapped my fingers around his unsatisfied length.

He shuddered.

I squeezed.

And then his hand fell from the door as he reached for me again.

"I don't break so easy." I warned him with a final squeeze hard enough to make him growl. And then I opened the door and left him there with the paper towels.

CHAPTER FOUR

Sloane

I T WAS OFFICIAL. I was living in the twilight zone. Not only had Rhys Huntington kissed me twice now—in full view of everyone—but Lennox had just destroyed me in a supply closet with nothing more than his filthy mouth and his long fingers. For the first time in my entire life, I had a boy striving for my attention.

Two boys, in fact.

And how do you actually feel about that?

Oh, Rhys was attractive. I wasn't blind. He was *very* pretty to look at. But there was something cold and distant about him. Something told me ice wouldn't melt in his mouth. But he was a very good kisser.

Although, I wondered just how irritated Serafina was about the whole thing.

She hated Rhys. No doubt. But I was an expert at watching people. And there was something about her that was fascinated by him. It could well have been that she wanted to dissect him like a frog, but it couldn't be denied that there was a part of her that perked to attention every time he was nearby. Or, maybe she just liked fighting with him.

Then why were you kissing him?

That was a good question. Maybe because for once, it was nice to feel pretty. Desirable. Ninety-nine point nine percent of the time, I'd tamped down any and all of my femininity. I wasn't a beauty queen like Sera, or hell, even Iris. I was pretty, but I didn't have that knockout body. I was built lean and athletic. Twiggy, actually. And I learned early on that it's better to have personality and skills than it was to have beauty.

Or at least, that's what you've told yourself.

Whatever. The point was, Rhys Huntington had taken to kissing me. And I still wasn't entirely sure how I felt about it.

I liked being kissed. Kisses, for all intents and purposes, were *awesome*. And every time he kissed me, something warm blossomed in my chest. It was pleasant. And he was a very, very good kisser. I just—I don't know.

Rhys kissing me was nothing like what happened with Lennox in the supply closet. At. All. That was wild, and fiery. And hot. Like I was being burned alive from the inside out.

The way Iris talked about her and Keaton made it seem like there were firecrackers all around her, but also this sense of tenderness. Lennox certainly hadn't been tender. God, Iris would know what to do. I missed her terribly. But she was in Paris, having left school early to go live her best arty life. Keaton went to see her every other weekend. That's what happened when your family had a private jet.

The fact that she'd gone off to Paris, leaving us mere mortals behind, made me wish it was summer and we could go and visit her already. But we'd gotten good with the online video chats. I checked my watch. Sera, Aurora, and I would wait up until one or two in the morning to talk to her.

She and Keaton were doing the long-distance thing, and then he was going to see her for the holidays. Then it would again be back to long distance until the summer. God, they were so in love. It was crazy. But Rhys and I, we *weren't* that. And maybe I was just fascinated by him. Or fascinated by the fact he'd taken notice of me. Because the question was, why had he taken notice of me? Why now?

I'd known Rhys since freshman year. He wasn't exactly nice. He could be excessively cruel. Not usually to me though. It was usually the people who dicked with him. If you dicked with him, god help you. He was savage. Unrelenting. And he'd make your life a living hell. I'd mostly just kept out of his way because I already had Lennox obsessed with breaking me—I didn't need anything worse than perverted bathroom graffiti from Rhys.

The sudden interest . . . there was something behind it, and I couldn't quite figure it out.

Maybe he was just bored.

Then why did you let him kiss you?

Maybe I was bored too.

Or you can't have who you really want?

I swallowed that down. Lennox's kisses were . . . different. I could still feel the tingle of his lips sliding over mine. The way he'd gripped the back of my neck, holding me in place as he completely devoured my mouth. Lennox's kisses were dangerous. Designed to fog the brain and then make it impossible to think. I had a sharp mind. I liked my mind. And PS, why was Lennox even kissing me? He was very clear on his hatred of me.

And I hated him.

Liar.

Okay fine. Maybe I didn't hate him exactly, but god, I

loathed the way he treated me. He was cruel in the way only the powerful can be in that off-hand manner, giving out insults in mini barbs. I could hold my own. The things he said to me didn't hurt. But that kiss, at the supply closet today, *that* one hurt. I knew he was only kissing me, touching me, because Rhys had. I didn't want to be some dick measuring competition for them. I just wanted someone to notice me. Why was that super hard?

My cellphone rang as I made it to my room. I was alone, so I plopped on the bed and tossed my bag as I fished the phone out of my back pocket. "Hey, Dad."

"Sloane, how was class today?"

"How do you know I went to class and I wasn't out ditching?"

"You're my daughter. You don't ditch. You like rules."

"That I do. It's alarming you know me so well. Shouldn't you factor in at any point that I am a teenager?"

"You are a teenager, but you are cut from the same cloth as I am. You like rules. You like following them. If you ditch, there would be a damn good reason."

I hated that he was right. Maybe a part of me wanted to ditch. Cut class. It was a rite of passage. Why hadn't I done it more?

I shoved that thought aside. "What's up, Dad?"

"What, I can't just call my daughter?"

"It's not Sunday. You always call on Sundays, 10 a.m."

He sighed. "You know, I do miss you at other times other than Sundays at ten."

I winced. I hadn't meant to hurt him. "I'm sorry. It's just unusual, I guess. Is everything okay?"

There was a beat of silence. "Yes, everything is fine. I'm healthy, before you start worrying about that."

My mother had died of cancer when I was eight. And

with Dad's job, he couldn't drag me around all the time, so he'd sent me to boarding school. But he'd taken to reassuring me of his health all the time. Probably so I didn't worry. Unfortunately, that just made me worry more. "You're sure you're okay?"

"Definitely okay—a little tired, maybe, since this Constantine case has blown up. I suppose Colston hasn't been doing anything suspicious lately?"

"Like what? Trying to fence stolen Bronze Age burial goods in rural Vermont?"

"Ha," Dad said dryly. "Very funny, and you know what I mean. The Constantines act like they're above anything criminal, but we all know that's hardly the case. They're just better at hiding it is all, and I've got authorities from three different bureaus breathing down my neck about what they've imported in the last year alone."

Colston's mother apparently had a yen for collecting antiques—the kind of antiques that were illegally extracted from war zones or unethically lifted from dig sites before they could be catalogued—that sort of thing. Dad had asked more than once if I'd ever seen Colston doing anything untoward, but Colston was a floppy-haired sophomore who liked boobs and extra tacos on taco Tuesday, so obviously not. He was as clean as a whistle. A whistle who loved cafeteria food and boobs.

"Hey, I wanted to ask," Dad continued, "you're close to that Lincoln-Ward kid, right?"

I frowned. "Lennox? We're not friends, but I know him, I guess."

"Right, right. Listen, can you do me a favor and keep an eye on him?"

"An eye? For you?" I was honestly baffled. Lennox wasn't a *good* person, but it wasn't like he was collecting stolen antiques like Colston's mom. "Why?"

My dad cleared his throat. "You remember his father? The investigation that put him in prison?"

Uneasiness dripped down my neck like cold water. "Yes. You said you consulted on it once."

Another throat clearing. "I wasn't—well, I wasn't *entirely* forthright about that. I did work on the case quite a bit, in fact. I was the arresting agent on the scene."

I took a moment to respond, because I wasn't sure *how* to respond. Dad and I never lied to each other. Not ever. Lying was what art thieves and con men and fences did— not family. "Why didn't you tell me?"

It could explain why Lennox disliked me so much . . . although that didn't really make sense either. Not if he'd told Aurora that he *wanted* his dad in prison. Why hate the daughter of the man who put him there then?

"It's not a stage of my career I'm proud of," Dad said slowly. "It's a little difficult to look back at the things I did then, much less talk about them."

"Things you did during the investigation?" I asked, the uneasiness growing into horror. "Like unethical things?"

"Oh god, no, no, not that," Dad said. "Nothing illegal or immoral. I just didn't handle the . . . political . . . aspects of the case very well."

"Political? Like intra-bureau politics?"

"Among other things," Dad murmured. "But nevertheless, the older Lincoln-Ward keeps coming back to haunt me, like a bad penny. A bad, *conniving* penny. He's making noise about an appeal now, of all things, and we're still trying to figure out where he's hid the rest of his money to get the victims the restitution they deserve. And it's possible that he squirreled that money away for his kids somehow. Which maybe they're aware of, maybe they aren't. Which is why if you could keep an eye on him . . . see if he's doing anything other than the norm . . ."

He trailed off. I was staring at my ceiling, seeing nothing, my chest tight.

"You want me to . . . what? Tail him?"

"Of course not, honey," Dad said, his tone the epitome of reason and sanity, as if *I* were the unreasonable one right now. "You know, it merely would be great if you can get information from his laptop. Or something."

I frowned, the unease making my stomach cramp. Illegality shouldn't bother me; I knew that on an abstract, intellectual level. Sometimes there was a greater need and all. But it was like the lying . . . I didn't think we were supposed to do that. I didn't think we *did* do that.

"At school, he must leave it around sometimes," Dad prompted.

I frowned even deeper at that. On the one hand, my father, my idol, basically, was asking me to take part in a job to actually assist him at work. He knew how much I wanted to be like him. How much I wanted to work in intelligence one day. So this was the opportunity of a lifetime. On the other hand, it made me feel squicky.

Oh, Lennox was cruel. And worse, he was deliberate in his cruelness. He'd tortured me for years. But there was something about *this* that made me feel like I shouldn't.

"Sloane," my father prompted. "Can you do it?"

I'd been silent for too long. "Yeah, but Dad. I mean, Lennox is just a kid. He's eighteen like me, so there's a great possibility that he's not involved with his father. We're too young for that."

"Like you're too young to be creeping around campus solving certain problems for your peers?"

"Uh . . ."

Dad laughed a little. "Yes, I know about that. And no, you're not in trouble. I know you do what you do in order to help the people you know need it. Which is why I'm asking this of you—I know you're capable and lots of people need your help right now. Not just me, but all the victims Lincoln-Ward swindled. If he succeeds in moving the last of his money around, we may never be able to return it to the people it was stolen from."

I sighed. He was right.

Truth was, I didn't *know* Lennox that well. I mean, I did, but it was more on an emotional visceral level. Something like *this*, I couldn't say whether he would or wouldn't do it. I had no idea.

"Listen, Sloane, I know you've been wanting to intern at INTERPOL before you go to Georgetown. I think we can work that out. This is a small opportunity for you to prove yourself."

Way to twist the knife, Dad. "Fine. I'll do it. Just information from his laptop, right?"

"Yeah, that's it. Nothing else. Obviously, I don't want you to take any unnecessary risks."

"I won't," I mumble, a knot forming in my gut.

"We want information only. Strictly for surveillance. Do not get any more involved than that. You can do that, right?"

I swallowed. "It'll be easy, Dad. He leaves his laptop everywhere." Actually, I didn't know if that was true. I'd seen him and the Hellfire boys sitting around it watching dumb videos on the lawn a few times, but that was only when the weather was nice, which November in Vermont rarely was. But sometimes in the classroom he left it lying around, so I just had to find my window. Enough to do a recon. "I can get it done. When do you need it by?"

"Within the next week or two."

"Consider it done."

He was silent for a beat. "I knew I could count on you."

As he hung up, the words *I love you* were at the tip of my tongue. But I knew they'd only be met with a *me too*. So I hung up as well.

Just how the hell are you going to get this done?

I could do it. I could do anything. Even if it meant getting a little closer to Lennox Lincoln-Ward than I wanted to.

Chapter Five

Lennox

I *DON'T BREAK so easily . . .*

Sloane's words echoed through my mind as anger and lust hit me in the gut. It had been three days since the cupboard, three days since I'd dry-shagged her with her uniform skirt pushed up around her hips. Three days since I informed her that she was going to the gala with me, damn it all.

Because she was *mine*. And she had been since I was fourteen, she just hadn't known it yet.

Mine to torture. Mine to break.

I *deserved* her.

"Daddy wants a call," an airy voice said from behind me in my room.

I turned from my desk to see my sister throwing herself into my chair, as if she belonged here and not in her own bloody dorm. As if my bloody door hadn't been locked.

I scowled. "How did you get in here?"

Aurora kicked her feet in the air before grinning at me. Normally her hair was as unnaturally blonde as mine, but for some unknowable sister reason, she'd dyed it black last summer. Now whenever she smiled with her gold eyes and midnight hair, she looked like she was about to carve out a boy's heart. With a dull knife. While it was still beating in his chest.

"Sloane's been teaching me a few tricks."

My body gave an automatic stir at the mention of her name. "Of course. Probably learned it from her father."

Aurora leaned her head back and closed her eyes. "You have to stop blaming her for what her father did. I have."

"Her father *ruined* us. Ruined our mother. Ruined everything."

My sister made a face, her eyes still closed. "No, Len, *our* father ruined everything. Remember?"

I didn't answer her. I didn't need to, because I did remember.

As children, we only knew our British billionaire father worked in the city doing something with money. *Like a banker, but an artist too*, he'd told us once. *I paint entire worlds with money. I paint a new life for people.*

Of course he was an artist; that made sense to us. He was creative and playful and charming—the kind of father who would come home late from a trip and wake us up to eat all the treats he'd brought for us. The kind of father who'd play hide and seek, who'd make silly faces at the table, who'd give us ice lollies whenever we scraped our knees.

We worshipped him; even our mother worshipped him. He was often late, often absent when he shouldn't have been, often caught in small lies that had seemed harmless at the time. But he was so charming, so funny and so full of smiles, it was impossible to stay angry with him, and our mother never could.

Until the day it all came crashing down.

Aurora and I were thirteen—me at school in England, her at a Swiss boarding school—when it happened: a yearslong international investigation came to an end, definitively proving my father was the mastermind behind a sprawling Ponzi scheme that totaled billions and billions. Proving my father was a swindler and a liar who had defrauded thousands of investors.

A *painter of money* indeed.

If that had been the worst of it, we would have already been devastated. Gutted and humiliated. But the day they came to arrest my father, he wasn't at home, he wasn't at his city office—he was in a hotel in Monte Carlo.

With a woman who was *not* our mother. A woman he'd apparently been with many, many times before.

The paps caught it all. Their embraces on the balcony before, their flushed faces as they were both led out of the hotel in handcuffs after.

And so our family shame was complete. Our father was not only a deceiver but a cheater; he'd thrown money onto the flames of his greed and thrown the dignity of a princess back in her face. The tabs loved it—the con artistry and the philandering—and so did the more serious news outlets, and within days, both Aurora and I were pulled from our schools for our own safety. Our father had defrauded too many people—too many wealthy people—and we were the targets they could reach, the scapegoats for our father's sins. Even with the security the Liechtensteiner government gave us being the grandchildren of the Queen, we were still in danger.

Of course all joint accounts of my parents were seized— our home in England too. Luckily mother had her own royal trust accounts and we had our untouchable trust funds which we were able to access when we'd turned eighteen. But we'd had to move back to Liechtenstein; we'd had to find new and more secure schools to attend.

We were lucky—I knew that. How many families have princesses for mothers? Queens for grandmothers? The retreat of the Lincoln-Wards was a retreat into shame and humiliation, yes, but it wasn't a retreat into abject poverty. Aside from the pride and the hole our father had ripped through the world, we would survive. Comfortably, if not happily.

But I could never forget that *everything* we lost—and how publicly we lost it—could be laid at the feet of one man alone.

Nathan Lauder.

Former FBI agent. Head of the National Central Bureau for INTERPOL in the States. It was Nathan who'd taken the first fraud claims against my father, and it was Nathan who'd spearheaded the entire investigation.

For that, I would have forgiven him. His job was to stop criminals, and my father was a criminal, after all. A criminal who I knew roundly deserved every day in prison he got. No, it wasn't the arrest or the conviction that infuriated me, that made me crave revenge.

It was that Nathan *chose* not to bring my father in quietly, privately. Nathan *chose* someplace tawdry and public.

He'd not only ruined us, but he'd made it a spectacle, made it so garishly and vulgarly visible.

And I'd hated him for it.

After the arrest, I had a lot of time in a new home, in a different country, to think about how much I hated Nathan Lauder. I had a lot of time to research him—to cajole, beg, and command my grandmother's security people to research him too.

Which was when I first heard the name Sloane.

Sloane Lauder. His daughter, my age.

There were no pictures of her online—Nathan was too

careful for that—no other information at all actually, save for her name listed in a single obituary. Her mother—his wife—had died when she was young. No siblings, no extended family. They lived in D.C.

I used to fantasize about growing up and finding her. I'd humiliate her the way Nathan had humiliated *us* and see how much he liked it then. Having his precious daughter dragged through the tabloid mud, having all of his family's dirty linens flapping in the very, very public breeze.

But of course that hadn't been necessary, had it? Because I'd come to Pembroke, and whom should I find?

Sloane herself. *Here.*

Now.

Gracefully lethal. Green-eyed and quiet.

She held herself with a discipline that fascinated and enraged me—actually everything about her fascinated and enraged me.

And nothing enraged me more than her soft, lush mouth.

She had a pout that was made for kissing, licking, and sex—not for getting up at 6 a.m. and running five miles, only to turn around and train for hours in the gym the moment classes ended. Not for the careful, expressionlessness she always kept on her face, like she was already training to be a spy. Not for the way she never gave anything away, ever, even when I pushed and pushed and pushed . . .

Except for the cupboard.

Fuck me, the cupboard. I'd finally felt that plush mouth for myself, felt it warm and drugging against my lips. And her soft, tight cunt . . .

"Len," Aurora said impatiently, "are you going to call Daddy with me or not?"

I leaned back in my chair, thinking about it for exactly

one second. "No."

"You're so eager to hate Sloane, yet you hate Daddy too. Don't you remember anything from Mass? We're supposed to forgive people."

"Like how you're forgiving Phineas, for example?"

She shot upright, glaring at me. "Low blow, Lennox, even for you."

I held up my hands. "I don't even know what he *did* last summer, Sister Dearest. Only that he seems to be coping with it by shagging half the school, and you're coping with it by making his life a living hell. *And* I don't actually give a shit, I'm just pointing out that it's rather hypocritical of you to want me to forgive people when you're constantly planning Phineas's untimely death."

"Fine," she bit out, standing up and striding to the door. "I'll call Daddy alone then."

"Tatty byes, Aurora."

She turned the handle and then paused. "You know he wants to help make things right, Len. He's trying to be better."

I let out a long breath.

I was a bastard, yes, and a bully definitely, but I did love my sister. It gave me no pleasure to say the words I said next. Not to the girl who'd once chased Daddy through the gardens right alongside me, who'd eaten sweets on his knee next to me while he told us all about Germany or Italy or Japan or wherever else he'd been.

"He's lying, Aurora," I said, studying her face. "You know that, right? He's trying to charm you. Swindle you back into loving him."

She smiled sadly, as if she knew that just as well as I did.

"Better than trying to swindle us out of our trust funds at least," she said, and then she cracked open the door and left.

The trust funds. The two protected assets the government didn't seize, because our father had made our grandparents the trustees, and therefore he couldn't touch them. He'd been clever enough to do that at least, although he hadn't been clever enough not to get caught.

But because he couldn't touch them, because they'd been preserved, I had no doubt he had his eye on them. Especially if he won his latest round of appeals and had his sentence reduced. Wouldn't he love to be released and immediately have access to millions of pounds sterling?

I don't think so.

I turned back to my laptop and clicked open the email I'd been about to read before Aurora barged in. It was from the lawyer who managed our trust funds—a lawyer I could trust. A lawyer who was conveniently—at least for me—intimidated by my mother's family and the crown which came with it.

I scanned the email before opening up a fresh word processor file, writing a letter I'd been drafting in my head for over a year. I rubbed at my chest as I wrote it, feeling something strange. It certainly wasn't happiness, but maybe it was something close.

Satisfaction. Gratification, maybe.

Well, why wouldn't I be gratified? Together, the lawyer and I had devised a very clever path through the warren of trust stipulations. We had figured out a way to move substantial chunks of money through various systems until it was allocated where I saw fit.

Investments into my own future, as it were.

Never let it be said that a prince would be a pauper, I thought as I closed out the email and then shut the laptop. *Father, you taught me better than you can ever know.*

CHAPTER SIX

Sloane

LENNOX, IT TURNED out, was a lot less freewheeling with his laptop than I thought he'd be. Or perhaps he was just more interested in me since I'd shamelessly come all over his fingers a few days before. Because now there was no leaving his things unattended in the library, there was no milling around the classroom during free time and leaving his laptop at his desk. Now he was right next to me, always sticking close, always sliding in with little verbal jabs and slices, cutting me into pieces with his cold smiles. Wherever I was, Lennox somehow found a reason to be also, and so there was no way to do what Dad had asked and search out what he wanted.

And then Thursday morning came, and just like every other morning, Lennox was on the outdoor track with me, following me through the early morning fog as I started my laps. I could hear his footfalls behind me—soft and graceful, like a cat's—I could hear his breathing, steady and even. No huffing and puffing for this prince, no way. He was all cool and arrogant control all the time. When he played, when he worked out. Even when he tormented me.

I'd only ever seen him lose control when he—

My cheeks flushed as I remembered the closet. He'd been wild to kiss me. Wild to touch me between my legs.

Wild to *keep* me.

At that thought, I sped up—not sure if I was running faster because I was angry or creeped out or turned on . . . or some fucked up combination of all three.

Predictably, he sped up behind me, as if reluctant to let any more space between us.

Rhys doesn't get to touch you.

You've belonged to me since the day I saw you.

To toy with. To break.

Fuck it, I *was* angry. He'd treated me like trash since day one, and now when another boy was taking notice of me for the first time ever, he suddenly had a problem?

He got to be first in line to treat me like trash, was that it?

It had been infuriating before, when it only affected me. But now his abrupt possessiveness was keeping me from helping my father, which by extension was keeping me from my dream of following in my father's footsteps. It had to stop.

I wouldn't be his plaything. I *couldn't*. There was too much at stake.

Anger flooded me, and determination too, and I spun around to face him, my hands coming up automatically in a guard position, as if I were about to spar.

Lennox's reflexes were irritatingly sharp, because he was already stopped by the time I'd turned, his mouth in a flat line and one eyebrow raised. Only the quick thrum of his pulse above the collar of his too-expensive workout shirt betrayed that he'd been exerting himself. "My god, Lauder, are we about to start a fracas right here on the track? Am I going to regret forcing my poor security fellow to stay at the track entrance?"

I lowered my fists, finally realizing they were raised. Too much karate or too much time with Dad, I guess, because I knew Lennox wouldn't try to hurt me, not like this. Punches and strikes weren't his way. He preferred to hurt me more . . . *creatively.*

"What do you want?" I asked him, tense and coiled all over with fury and frustration. "Why do you come out here every morning? Why won't you leave me alone?"

Fog drifted around him as he took a step closer. "You already know what I want."

"No! I don't! And you know what? I don't think you know what you want either!"

His golden eyes flashed. "I know exactly what I want. For you to stay away from Rhys."

"It's none of your business, Prince Lennox. Just like my morning run is none of your business."

His expression sharpened and so did his voice. "Haven't you figured it out yet, my sweet nothing? You belong to me, and I'm not in the habit of letting my things go unattended. Especially when they are so . . ." His eyes dropped to where my fists were still balled at my sides. ". . . willful."

"The closet changes nothing," I said.

"About that and nothing else, you are right, darling." He stepped closer again, and this time, we were close enough to touch. Close enough that I had to tilt my head back to look into his sharp, sculpted face, close enough that I could see how the gold and amber spun together in his eerie eyes. "The closet didn't change anything, because you were already mine. Before I tasted you. Before I felt your cunt against my hand. You were mine before all of that."

Jesus, he wasn't a prince, he was a pirate. He'd spotted me on the horizon and decided to wreck me before I'd ever even known his name.

"Get some therapy, your highness. I'm not *anyone's*."

Another flash of those eyes and he reached for me, like he was going to pull me close, and I dodged him easily. He reached again, this time half lunging at me, and he was quick, so fucking quick, that he nearly had his arms around me.

But I don't spend every free second training for nothing. I let him get close—let his arms start to circle me—and then with a hook of my foot around the back of his and with my shoulder pushed into his chest, I had him flat on his back. I went down with him, and by the time he'd stopped falling, I was straddling his hips with my forearm to his throat. We'd gone down in the practice field in the middle of the track, and I could feel the cool, wet grass through my knees.

The fog around us was thick enough that we couldn't be seen, but I still checked around us with quick flicks of my eyes. I trusted that Lennox really had made his security guy stay off the track, but still. The last thing I needed was an angry Liechtensteiner guard shouting at me in German and turning this into an international incident.

Convinced we were alone and out of sight—*thank you, fog*—I turned my attention back to the beautiful, heartless boy underneath me.

"Leave. Me. Alone," I said between clenched teeth.

"No," he replied, as coolly as if he were sitting bored on a throne somewhere. "I won't."

I pressed harder with my forearm. Not enough to choke him, but enough so that he knew that I could if I wanted to. "I mean it, Lennox. No more following me. No more shitty remarks. No more lube in my bag or caring about who I kiss. Keep my name out of your mouth and my face out of your thoughts. Got it?"

Lennox almost seemed amused. "I've gotten to you rather terribly, haven't I?" Satisfaction curled through his voice.

I leaned forward. "No. You haven't."

But leaning forward was a mistake, because now I could see, in utter and perfect detail, the tempting lines of his mouth. The sharply masculine peaks of his upper lip, the firm but plush bow of the lower. And below me, where I straddled his hips, I could feel the effect this position was having on him. The silky material of his athletic shorts hid nothing of his desire, and my running pants were no better. They'd be damp soon, if they weren't already.

Unconsciously, without meaning to, I rocked forward over him, rubbing my sex against his erection like a needy kitten. The corner of his mouth sharpened—an almost smirk—even as his hips lifted to give me more.

"See?" he said.

"You're not—I don't—you haven't gotten to me." But the lie was in my body, in how I tried to fuck him through our clothes, even as my forearm kept him pinned to the ground underneath me. The lie was in my voice, which was breathy and husky and transparently aroused.

"Oh, but I have," he said, his mouth still in that bitter smile. I felt his hands curl over my hips—something that would have been a threat if we'd been truly fighting, but of course, this wasn't a fight, not really. I . . . I didn't know what this was, exactly, but I did know that whatever it was meant he could touch my hips like he was now.

And slide his hand across the flat plane of my stomach and find the hem of my tank top.

And tug down the waistband of my pants and push his fingers into my panties and between my legs.

My eyes fluttered closed as he found me, stroked me.

There was no hiding that he *got to me* now, there was no hiding how much my body reacted to his presence. I was wet enough to be slippery, wet enough that even he seemed surprised—although that surprise faded quickly into a dark satisfaction.

"Good," he whispered. "I refuse to be the only one."

I kept my forearm on his throat as he slid up to my clit. He knew *just* how to touch, *just* how to rub. Fast then slow. Circles then up and down. I hated thinking about all the practice he'd had, I hated knowing scores and scores of girls had come before me . . . but I didn't hate it so much I'd make him stop. Not at all.

I was a simple girl, after all. A direct girl. A good spy would use any means at her disposal to meet her goal, after all, and if my goal was to have a toe-curling orgasm on the practice field inside the school track while straddling the school's resident bully . . .

Except that a good spy would also not be fooling around with her mark.

Outside.

When his security detail could be anywhere.

"When you come, my sweet nothing, consider this: if you aren't mine, then why is it that I find this pretty pussy wet for me every time I touch it?"

"Shut up," I told him, riding his touch, feeling everything between my knees and my navel grow taut and trembling. "You're ruining it."

"Oh," he said softly, smiling again. "I don't think I am. And if you come for me like this, just imagine all the other ways I could do it . . ."

I didn't have to imagine much. His mouth, cruel and soft all at once, the kind of mouth that promised vicious and punishing pleasure. And that thick erection was underneath me again, huge and hard . . .

My orgasm came at me like a freight train, running me over, laying me flat. I cried out and bucked against Lennox's hand, coming and coming and unable to stop, unable to think, unable to do anything but *feel*. That powerful but elegant hand in my panties, the firm bulge of him beneath me. The cold grass wet against my knees and the fog clinging to my throat and chest as I arched against the feeling.

And then it faded—the tight waves in my sex and my belly slowly growing looser, more languid—until I was just a girl slumped over a boy in the grass, with his hand in her pants and her forearm on his throat.

No.

Not just a girl, not just a boy.

I was Sloane Lauder, and this was Lennox Lincoln-Ward.

What the *fuck* was wrong with me?

Without a word, I scrambled off Lennox, retreating back several steps as panic clawed at my throat. People thought I felt nothing, that I was a robot or some kind of stoic, but nothing could have been further from the truth. I felt *everything*, every single thing, which was why I needed my father's lessons and karate so much. I'd needed to learn control, to learn patience and discipline, and it was only the years of training, years of practicing calm, cool control, that helped me find my breath again.

I looked down at Lennox, who was now up on his elbows in the grass staring at me like there was going to be a test later. The fact that I was leaving him high and dry for the second time this week didn't escape me. How could it, when the evidence was so proudly—and urgently—tenting the front of his shorts?

"Come back here, Sloane," he said, his accent curling around the words like the fog curled around my ankles. "Come back here and finish what you started."

"No," I said. But it came out shaky and uncertain. He stared at me a moment, his chest moving up and down, his pulse pounding in his throat.

"Suit yourself," he said, as if he didn't care at all, and then he slid his fingers in his mouth—the same fingers that had been in my panties just moments earlier—sucking them, licking them, getting them wet. And without a single beat of hesitation, he pushed his hand past the waistband of his shorts and took a hold of himself, giving his length a short, rough stroke with his wet hand.

A sound left me then, a *guh* noise, like I'd just been punched in the stomach during sparring practice. Even though his dick and his fist were covered by the material of his shorts, seeing him lick his hand—the hand that tasted like *me*—and then stroke himself was painfully hot. A conflagration of crude and arrogant sexiness that should have been straight up illegal.

A jolt of fresh need sparked between my thighs, and I almost wanted to join him, to kneel beside him and wrap my hand over his hand and help him.

A bell tolled through the fog, as familiar as it was solemn. Seven a.m. Classes would start in 90 minutes. More importantly, various teams would be out for their morning practices momentarily, and we'd no longer be alone on the field.

To my great disappointment (and shame at the aforementioned disappointment), Lennox realized this too and stopped that wonderful stroking motion.

He pulled his hand free and rolled to his feet with enviable grace, although there was nothing graceful about the prominent column of his cock still pushing against the front of his shorts. "We're not done," he promised. "Saturday. The gala. We're finishing this."

"I told you," I said, shaking my head, as if I could shake off the strange slick of regret spilling through my chest. "I'm going with Rhys."

"Maybe. But you won't be leaving with him," he said enigmatically, and then turned towards campus and stalked off into the fog. Within a handful of steps, he was no longer visible, and I was left alone, damp from the grass and trembling at my lack of control.

CHAPTER SEVEN
Sloane

THIS COULDN'T GO on.

This . . . this *hold* that Lennox had on me, it had to stop. How had I let an argument turn into a closet fingerbang? How had I let defending myself turn into a *second* fingerbang?

On the *practice field* no less?

No, I was better than this. I was better than having pants-feelings for my gold-eyed tormentor. I was better than letting my father down because I couldn't *keep control*.

"You seem, uh, intense today," Colston remarked from the bag next to mine.

I grunted in acknowledgement, giving the bag several jab-knee combinations.

"Well, more intense than usual," Colston amended. "You okay? Are you having trouble with one of your . . . you know . . . *cases*?"

He whispered the last part as if my helping people around the school was some kind of state secret. It was kind of cute, actually.

I delivered two more combos—hard and quick enough to send the bag swinging—and then turned to face the sophomore. Like his cousin, Keaton, Colston was blond and tall and broad-shouldered, although unlike Keaton, he hadn't yet filled in all that height with muscle yet. He would though; he had the kind of frame that promised power and strength. But I knew he felt self-conscious about his still-wiry body. Enough that he joined me in the gym every chance he got.

At least, that was *one* of the reasons he joined me in the gym.

The other reason was fairly apparent in the way his eyes kept flicking down to my damp sports bra and sweat-slick stomach.

"I'm fine," I said, tilting my chin up in the universal *eyes up, buddy* move.

He flushed and locked eyes with me, swallowing with what looked like embarrassment. Poor kid. He really was a sweetheart.

"You don't seem fine," he said, and I had to admire his balls. Not many people dared to disagree with me. "Can I help?"

I shook my head automatically. I didn't accept help for anything; it wasn't in my nature. And I could hardly explain the problem to Colston. Either of the problems, really— neither how I accidentally kept dry-humping Lennox Lincoln-Ward, nor how my father needed me to scrape up illegal dirt on Lennox.

A prickle of guilt needled through my chest as I remembered how my father was also investigating Colston's family.

Antiquities fraud was antiquities fraud—if his relatives had done it, then that was that and they deserved to be investigated. But looking at this cute puppy of a sophomore, with all that messy hair and those hopeful eyes, I just . . .

Well, I didn't feel awesome about it. That was all.

"If I can help with anything, let me know," he said softly.

I didn't love lying, but if I was going to be a good spy, I'd need to embrace it, so I forced myself to nod and say, "I will."

He smiled—a slightly crooked smile with a megawatt dimple in each cheek. He really was going to be a heartbreaker soon. "And if all else fails, go full WWJBD, am I right?" He clapped my shoulder and then left the bags, grabbing his water bottle and trotting off to the locker room to change out.

WWJBD?

What would Jason Bourne do if he had to look at Lennox's laptop?

I stared at the bag for a moment, stunned at my own ineptitude.

I'd been going about this all wrong, searching for windows of opportunity the way a civilian would. Looking for the easiest solutions, the most obvious ones.

But Jason Bourne didn't search for windows of opportunity—he *made* his own windows.

Or crashed through them dramatically, but whatever. That didn't materially change my point.

The point was Jason Bourne would find a way to Lennox's laptop no matter what. And I would too.

✧   ✧   ✧

SEVEN HOURS LATER, and I was really, really realizing why Jason Bourne only did the shit he did in the movies and not in real life.

I was a dab hand at picking locks—a skill Aurora had taken up with ease when I taught her—but I knew going into his room through the door was a no-go, no matter how late and seemingly asleep the dorm was. Lennox had a twin arrangement to what Aurora had in the girls' dorm: his security team slept on the same floor, and one member was always awake, patrolling the building. Additionally, there were cameras watching the hallways—monitored more or less consistently by the team—and the last thing I wanted was for there to be any record of me doing anything near Lennox's room.

So the interior of the building was out. But the exterior . . .

Pembroke was an old school, and while an old school meant constant renovations and unreliable air conditioning, it also made for *very* climbable exteriors. Sills and lintels and gables and string courses and entablatures and trellises. *Trellises.* I mean, what level of trust do you have in your students if you cover the outside of their dorm with trellises? That's just asking for people to sneak out.

Or *in*, in my case.

I knew the way from my previous lube and toothpaste missions, so I had a plan. I glanced behind me to make sure the campus lawn was still completely and utterly empty, and then I made my careful way up and over to the window I wanted, using the trellis and the occasional lintel to climb it. It was cold enough that my hands already hurt, even inside my thin leather gloves. My breath puffed out in thick, white clouds every time I exhaled.

Dad would hate that I'm doing this.

He would hate it because not only was it dangerous, but because it was legally dicey.

And by legally dicey, I meant *very, very illegal.*

But part of me suspected he knew I'd have to bend some rules in order to get what he wanted, and I figured he wanted the info more than he wanted me to have a rigid code of ethics.

And it was okay that my code of ethics wasn't that rigid, right? I mean, I wouldn't call it flaccid—I had some hard limits around what I considered right and wrong—but a little laptop spelunking didn't bother me. And neither did a little window-peeping.

When I got to my destination, I raised myself high enough on the trellis that I could peer inside. And what I saw there satisfied me. I'd made a pit stop at Rhys's window on the hunch that the Hellfire Club would be in there, doing whatever it was they did when they weren't making the rest of the school miserable. They were probably deflowering virgins or drinking the tears of the damned or something equally monstrous—although when I finally got a good look inside, it appeared that they were all arranged around Rhys's TV, watching an episode of a reality show about drag queens. Keaton Constantine was arguing with Phineas Yates about who actually won the lip-synching competition, and the argument erupted in some kind of wrestling/fisticuffs scenario that had equal parts laughter and yelling. I was about to scan the room more thoroughly when Rhys—who was sprawled on his bed like a Roman emperor—slowly swiveled his head toward the window. As if he sensed my presence.

Shit.

I ducked lower on the trellis, knowing full well I hadn't made any noise, but also knowing full well that if Rhys actually came to check the window, I'd be hosed.

WWJBD?

Jason Bourne would probably fling himself into the bushes below and then sprint off to find a car chase to get involved in, honestly, but I didn't have ankles of steel. Or a car.

Instead, I trellis-scrambled—quietly—over to the corner of the building and edged around it, praying Rhys hadn't decided to come look out his window. Which, given the lack of yelling/cat-calling/devilish laughter, he hadn't. Thank god.

Only a few more bays down, and I found myself safely on Lennox's windowsill, perched like a pigeon. Well, okay. A pigeon if it had a boot collection that would put the *Matrix* franchise to shame. I paused for a moment and took stock of what I'd seen in Rhys's room. I'd seen *all* the boys there, right? Including Lennox? Surely, I had. Surely, he was in there, arguing about wigs and lip-synching with everyone else.

Which meant I was all clear to do what I needed to do next.

Like all the rooms in this building, Lennox's had a casement window, which usually meant a vertical latch, but in the case of this old window, there wasn't a proper latch at all, just a hook and eye lock painted over so many times that the hook was too fat to properly rest in the eye anyway. I pulled a slender jab saw from my boot and slid it into the frame. With an embarrassingly little amount of effort, I had the hook undone and half the window swinging open.

I was, as they say in the movies, *in*.

The room was dark and silent, just like I'd anticipated. Excellent. I lowered my feet carefully to the floor, and then once I was off the sill, I swung the window mostly closed behind me, clamping off the flow of chilly air. The last thing I wanted was for Lennox to come back to his room and find it strangely cold.

I used the moonlight to navigate over to his desk where his laptop sat on a surface cluttered with finance magazines and newspapers printed in German. I slid into the desk chair and opened it up, not surprised to see that it was password protected, but not happy about it either.

I had something for this, a little toy I'd lifted from Dad last year: a smartphone loaded with just one program. I could plug it into almost any device running standard software and bypass a one-step password lock. It wouldn't work on anything truly protected—nothing governmental or corporate—but for personal devices and school devices, it worked like a charm. Perfect for tonight.

But suddenly, I wasn't wild about using it on Lennox's things. For the very dumb and illogical reason that using it made this whole "spying on a classmate" thing feel wrong somehow, when it didn't really before. Which made zero sense at any level, because I'd already broken into the room and planned to invade Lennox's privacy, so what was a little electronic help along the way?

And anyway, this was basically nothing I hadn't done before; I'd broken into countless classmates' phones to hunt for pictures that didn't belong to them, and I'd broken into many a dorm room to hunt for stolen jewelry, tablets, and things.

The only thing that was different this time was Lennox.

Was how I felt about him.

But if I really wanted to be an INTERPOL agent one day, I couldn't afford to be squeamish about these things, right? Even if my mark had given me the world's best orgasm on a dewy practice field that morning?

WWJBD, Sloane.

With a sigh at my flexible morals, I plugged in the smartphone and ran the program, watching the screen flash and scroll, poking idly at the newspapers on Lennox's desk. I'd taken some minimal German in middle school, and *mein Deutsch war sehr schlect*, but I could make out that the newspapers focused on business and finance, just like the magazines. Not exactly light reading.

Why would a boy in high school need to know so much about finance?

Hmm.

Maybe my father was right. Maybe Lennox *was* into something shady like his dad—going into the family business as it were.

The phone flashed a final time—unlocking the laptop screen and also showing me his password too. *Non ducor, duco.*

I am not led, I lead.

I snorted.

Lennox was a prince through and through, I guess. Or just a gigantic asshole.

I navigated over to the internet browser and opened up his email account. It was all in German, and I had to rely on my shaky language skills to skim through his folders and most of the subject lines. But even with my bad German, I could see that most of the emails in his account were from a lawyer. And several words didn't exactly need a linguistic expert to parse into meaning: bank in German was *bank*, money was *geld*, funds was *fonds*.

I replaced the password-cracker phone with a tiny external hard drive, screenshotted any email that looked suspicious, and then dropped them onto the drive.

I didn't feel disappointed that the boy I've fooled around with twice might be into some suspicious shit, I definitely wasn't feeling that *at all*.

But if I had been—if there was a tiny part of me that had fallen under his cold, delicious spell—it would have sucked. It would have felt like my stomach was crawling with bugs, it would have felt like the worst kind of reminder that Lennox was a bullying, selfish douchebag.

Ugh.

I combed through the rest of his inbox, catching everything I could, hyperaware of the clock in the corner of the screen. While I fully believed that Rhys was an actual vampire who never slept, Lennox always looked well enough rested when he joined me for my balls-early runs, which meant he probably got a decent amount of sleep. Which meant he could be heading back here at any moment. And as much as parts of my anatomy buzzed and sparked at the thought of another confrontation-that-might-lead-to-funtimes, I categorically did not want him to find me. Especially now that I knew Dad was right, and Lennox was moving his money around.

I'd finally worked my way up to the last email at the top—the most recent one—which came with several official-looking attachments.

Attachments that looked a lot like bank transfer notices.

More disappointment bug-crawled in my gut, and I found myself hesitating when it came to documenting it and saving it to the external drive. The rest of the emails were smoking guns, but this was the bullet, and if I showed this to Dad . . .

Wait, what was I thinking? This was what Dad wanted—what *I* wanted. If Lennox had moved money someplace he shouldn't have, then that wasn't on me, that was on *him*.

I squared my shoulders and made images of everything—but stopped at the last moment, catching a few words in the email itself. Words that normally didn't come with shady bank transfers. *Familie. Haus. Universität.*

Kinder.

Nicholas.

Family. House. University. Children.

Nicholas.

Who was Nicholas? Had my father mentioned a Nicholas in his call?

My fingers paused over the keyboard, and I tried to think. Was this truly something that needed more dissection? Or was I just grasping at anything that might make Lennox seem like—well, like not his father?

Fuck.

Fuck, I didn't know.

With a muttered oath, I made screenshots and moved them over, and then I quickly deleted all the images, emptied the trash, and cleared the history of everything ever.

Time for the rest of the desk.

The middle drawer and top two drawers were painfully organized—pens, pencils, paperclips. A rubber stamp embossed with his Pembroke address and a stamp with his Liechtensteiner address. They were like the drawers of an accountant and not a horny teenage boy. The bottom drawers were all meticulously alphabetized files.

They were labelled by school subject and year, but as I went through them one by one, I saw that some labels were clearly decoys. *Hon. Global Lit. – 10ᵗʰ Grade,* for example, held more financial-looking documents in German. *Philosophy of the Greek Golden Age* was a series of letters from a British solicitor. And *Hon. Biology – 11ᵗʰ Grade* had no biology homework at all, only a single letter. Written by him to someone named Nicholas.

Nicholas.

It was tucked away inside a cream envelope that was already stamped but clearly unsealed and unsent. Like Lennox had written this letter, gotten all ready to mail it, and then balked.

The letter was short, and—*sigh*—in German again, so I

could only catch a few words here and there. There was one word I could read very clearly though, and it cropped up a few times in the letter. *Vater.*

Father.

And the way Lennox had signed it—*Alles Liebe*, which meant something like *all the love to you* or *I wish all good things for you.* A very informal way to end a letter, and even though this Nicholas had been mentioned in the emails from Lennox's lawyer, it made me doubt that the letter was anything sinister or criminal. It sounded . . . affectionate.

My phone hovered above the letter. I should take a picture and give it to my father along with everything else. I should trust my instinct that this was an important secret.

But—I couldn't. I couldn't make myself take the picture.

Instead, I folded the letter back into the envelope and decided to take it with me. That way I could still have it, but I could give it a closer look before I gave it to Dad. It was a very un-Bourneish thing to do, but also it didn't feel right to do anything else. I wasn't ready to throw Lennox under the bus until I knew for certain he belonged there.

That was the thing about flexible morals—you couldn't bend them too much, or they'd break altogether, and I wasn't ready for mine to break just yet.

I quietly closed the drawer and stood up.

Which was when I heard it.

Soft. Angry. A little urgent.

"*Sloane.*"

There was no way to describe the panic pounding through me. Pure, uncut panic, like a fist to the kidney, like a knee to the solar plexus.

I froze and kept my breathing as slow and shallow as possible. Dad had a saying from his field agent days—*you're not made till you're made*—and maybe I still had a chance to escape. Although how had I not heard him come inside? I hadn't been *that* absorbed in his emails, and surely the light from the hallway would have alerted me, even if he'd moved without a sound—

There was another soft noise, an *unf*, followed by something short and murmur-y. It was definitely Lennox, but he didn't sound anything like he normally did—all sharp edges and bitterness. He didn't sound like someone who'd just walked into his dorm and found his enemy going through his things.

Slowly—as slowly as I could manage—I turned to face the rest of the room.

It was dark enough in the far corner that I didn't see him at first, I only heard him. The rustle of blankets as someone restlessly tossed underneath. The short, irregular breaths.

Fuck. I was a terrible damn spy, because Lennox had been in his room *the entire time*. In his bed, in full view of the rest of the room, and I should have checked, I should have taken the time to really look. But instead I'd relied on a split-second glimpse through Rhys's window and the silence when I'd come in from outside, and now I was screwed.

Although . . . maybe . . .

I took a step forward. A slow, quiet one. With the laptop shut, my eyes were adjusting to the lack of light, and I could begin to make out the shape of the bed and the shape of the prince on top of it.

Another step closer, and his head tossed on the pillow, turning towards me and towards the moonlight coming in through the window. His eyes were closed, his lips parted. Even from here I could see the flush dusting his cheekbones.

He was asleep.

He was asleep.

Jesus Christ. The relief that thudded through me was so powerful that my knees practically buckled.

I hadn't been made. I hadn't been caught. I could still leave right now with everything I needed and with him none the wiser.

But I didn't leave, which was more proof that I was a terrible damn spy. I was the *worst* damn spy, in fact, because instead of leaving, I crept closer to his sleeping form.

I knew I shouldn't, I knew it was a terrible idea, but I couldn't stop myself. I felt pulled toward him, like a princess in a fairy tale drawn toward something clearly sinister but beautiful for all that.

He was my enchanted rose, my cursed spinning wheel, my shiny, poisonous apple.

All I wanted was to take a bite, even though it might kill me.

He was still mostly in shadow, but the moonlight revealed enough. His sharp mouth was softer now, parted as he breathed, and his thick hair was sticking in every direction in a mess of platinum silk. His sheet and blankets had pulled down to his stomach and his top half was bare. Lean muscles moved under his skin as he tossed and turned, his eyelashes fluttering on his flushed cheeks.

He mumbled my name again, in a throaty, choked voice. "*Sloane.*"

I held my breath, freezing again, but his eyes didn't open. He didn't say anything else. His chest still rose and fell with deep but slightly fitful breaths.

He was dreaming of me.

That sent a hard, hot thrum down every nerve I had, as if someone had shot lightning down my spinal cord. My fingers tingled, my face tingled. Everything prickled and sparkled with—I didn't know actually. Pleasure? Fear? Nervousness?

All three?

He stirred again, the blankets pulling so low on his waist that I could see his navel, and in the moonlight, the line of slightly darker gold that led from his navel down to where his hand . . .

Jesus, Mary and Joseph. He's jerking off. In his sleep.

Those long, elegant fingers were wrapped around himself, and I could see now that every twist and turn I'd attributed to mere restless sleep was actually something much filthier. His hips rolled, his back arched. His stomach rippled and tightened, and I could see at the bottom of the bed how his bare feet flexed and then slid under the covers as he fucked his own fist in his sleep. As he dreamed of me.

My body responded precisely as it had every time Lennox's cock—or fingers—or mouth—or mere proximity—had entered my awareness, and a hot, edgy knot began tying itself somewhere between my legs. Goosebumps erupted everywhere on my skin, and my mouth started watering. If my body called the shots, I'd already be kicking off my boots and jumping into his bed vagina-first.

But luckily I had more control than that. Enough control to realize that Lennox could never, ever know that I saw this. This was so much more private than a laptop and some emails. This was something I knew he would never forgive me for seeing. This was naked want—no walls, no weapons.

Just desire.

And I felt exactly the same. If only I could join him, skin to skin, mouth to mouth, fingers moving together . . .

"Beautiful," he murmured sleepily, and the word felt like sparks all over my skin. "So fucking beautiful."

Beautiful. Not hot. Not even *pretty.*

Oh my god. Oh my god. Was I sure he was dreaming of *me* still? But then he said something that obliterated all my doubts—and also reminded me that this wasn't a fairy prince at all, but Lennox Lincoln-Ward instead. "Suck me," he whispered as he twisted and moved his hand down his length. "Oh my god, suck me. Feels so good. So bloody good."

The accented words disappeared into sleepy mumbles as he continued to writhe and arch, one long leg getting tangled out of the covers as he rolled to his side and pressed his cock against a pillow. *That* seemed to be even better for him, and his breaths came in short bursts as his hips surged against the soft material. Because of the way the covers were rucked up, I could see the hollow at the side of his ass. I could see how the lean but powerful muscles bunched and flexed as he rocked his dick forward.

And because of how big that wonderful dick was, I could see the thick, flushed crown of it surging forward every time he moved.

"Yes," he mumbled again. "Fuck. Waited forever."

Me too, I thought, half-miserably. *Me too.*

The sparks across my skin were roaring bonfires now. The heat between my legs could melt whatever they tiled space shuttles with. I wanted to watch the rest. I wanted to see what happened when that thick erection finally throbbed and pulsed out its release. I wanted to see Lennox's face as the pleasure of it moved through him.

I wanted it all.

And I could have nothing.

All of this was wrong as hell, and I had to leave before I did something irrevocably stupid, something that couldn't be undone.

And so with a hard swallow and a wince as my entire

core protested this new plan of action, I crept quietly to the window. And there I made my escape, climbing back out into the cold and dropping into the quiet, foggy night.

CHAPTER EIGHT
Sloane

I HADN'T SLEPT. The small external drive I'd used to copy Lennox's files and the letter I'd stolen had burned a hole in my pocket.

I tossed again and punched my pillow.

You don't have feelings or emotions. Control this. Get over it.

The problem was, there was no way I was ever going to get over watching Lennox Lincoln-Ward wrap that big hand of his around his, let's be honest, *enormous* dick and stroke. I will never forget the way my name sounded on his lips. I will never forget how he whispered, *'You're so beautiful.'* I will never forget the way he groaned as he begged imaginary me to suck it.

The other thing I would also never forget was how my entire body flushed like I'd been lit on fire from the inside as I was standing there holding a letter I shouldn't have been holding, and unfortunately having a bird's eye view of his hand on his dick.

You are so beautiful.

But that wasn't true. Lennox didn't think I was beautiful. And also, I was pretty sure of the fact that I just wasn't beautiful. I was pleasant-looking enough, sure. I had interesting features. Almost too delicate, too fine. But I had a body like a boy. What the hell was beautiful about me?

Serafina was standardly gorgeous by all meters. Starting with her medium-brown skin tone with nary a blemish in sight for all the years I'd known her, add to that ridiculously high cheekbones, enormous almond-shaped eyes, to that mass of curls I would die for. And her body. . . . . Jesus. It was like the body of a runway model. She was tall and athletic, but curved in places where I could only *dream* about curves.

When we'd first met as freshmen, she was slightly colt-ish, had more gangly arms and legs than anything. But now, she had turned into this complete and total knockout. She also possessed this unwavering confidence. I was her friend, so I knew that most of that was a complete lack of interest in what other people's opinions of her were. She knew who she was, and she didn't care what people had to say about her. But also, it was as if she didn't even see her own beauty. Like she somehow woke up every day and overlooked it.

She'd put on the adornments. . . . . Earrings. Makeup. And all that other shit. She didn't even need lashes. How is that fair? But she didn't revel in it. She could take or leave makeup. Take or leave the pretty trappings of patriarchal beauty. She didn't need it and she didn't care. She did it for her when she felt like it and because she liked it. And that's why I love her.

Then, of course, there was Aurora, the princess with the golden hair and the golden eyes. Well, black hair now since last summer. She practically screamed 'I'm a fairy princess, everyone should take care of me.'

That wasn't fair either, because Aurora was kind and generous. But if crossed, dear God help you. Which, of course, I respected. She had that inner core strength thing going for her. Her main motto was, 'do no harm, but take no shit', and that's why we were friends. But when your two best friends are complete stunners, it can get real complex.

My bedside clock said six-thirty, and I knew I didn't have to be up for another hour. But tonight was the gala, so I assumed Serafina and Aurora were going to kidnap me and make me try on dresses. I had tried to explain to Serafina about this gorgeous Howie pantsuit that I had, but she just stared at me. She said she had just the dress. She had yet to show me this dress, so I was slightly concerned. But I knew Sera, if she had made the decision, I was going to end up complying one way or another. With a groan, I sat up slowly, mindful not to wake her. She was still snoring heavily. Careful not to make noise, I pulled open the drawer by my bedside and took out my little locked box. I put in the code and then opened it gently. I took the external hard drive out then headed over to my desk to open my computer, plugged it in, and opened up an email to my father. I typed quickly. *"I've put on the encrypted server the files you requested."* Then I hit send, making sure all the files had, in fact, moved over to the encrypted server he'd set up for us to be able to send any sensitive documents. It was done.

No, it's not.

There was one thing I hadn't sent over. I could take a picture with my phone and easily send it, but something held me back. The *letter*, I wasn't sure what it was yet.

Are you really going to keep this from your father?

No. Of course I was going to share it. Just not right now. I, at the very least, wanted to know more about what it was, or what I was dealing with before just blindly handing it over, because maybe it had nothing to do with any of us.

And also maybe you shouldn't have done it.

That was at the core of it. Up until I had heard Lennox whisper how beautiful he thought I was, I'd had some reservations about what I was doing. But my father's request had far outweighed those. However, after Lennox's whispered words, after knowing that I wasn't the only one who surreptitiously watched the other sometimes, after knowing that all his cruelty was directed at me because he felt something he didn't want to feel, that knowledge had changed how I felt about myself for taking that information.

I felt sick. Like there was some invisible line I had crossed, and I couldn't go back. Which is ridiculous though, because there are many lines I would cross for my family. But there are also ones that I wouldn't. I had my integrity. The ends had to justify the means, and I believed in justice.

Is this justice?

Lennox's father was the worst kind of greedy asshole. He'd stolen billions from unsuspecting people. The question was, was Lennox like that? Did he know what his father had done? Was he in some way an accomplice? My father would figure it out. My part was done.

Except for the letter.

I scrubbed a hand on my face, gathered the drive and put it back in my lock box, and then back in my top drawer. I would think about this another time. I'd done enough damage for the day, hadn't I?

I tried to climb onto the bed, hoping now that I'd handed the information over, I could at least get another hour of sleep. But suddenly, Serafina dragged the covers off and sat up. "Oh no, you don't. You're not going back to bed. We have a long day ahead of us."

I groaned. "Yeah, I have a couple of projects I want to get a head start on. And then I should answer some emails, and I have some errands to run before we drive down."

Serafina just gawked at me. "No. You're not doing any of that."

I frowned. "What? I do have errands to run. I have a lot of stuff I need to do before the gala tonight."

She shook her head. "You are going to take care of those errands tomorrow. The only thing you're doing right now is trying to get ready for the gala."

I frowned. "Sera, you know that that's not until seven o'clock tonight. And even with the drive, there's no way I need *that* much time. I promise, I'll get ready around two or three? Quick shower—I'll even work on putting on some good eyeliner."

I wasn't bad with makeup, when I bothered to try. I wasn't some YouTube influencer, but when I put on makeup, I liked to think I looked presentable. Well mostly, I could do some mascara and some lashes. I never had figured out contouring or any of that nonsense. But basic concealer, powder and the eyes, I could do that.

Serafina just shook her head. "My god, how can I love one person so much, and still watch her be a daft cow—as Aurora would put it. This isn't just a 'hey, we're getting ready to go out with the team, half makeup' kind of situation. You need to be scrubbed and exfoliated from head to toe."

I laughed. "No, I don't. I promise. I mean, I'm going to shower."

Sera just rolled her eyes and went to her closet, yanking it open. When she reached in to grab a zipper bag, I frowned. "What's that?"

"*This*, Sloane, is your dress." She marched over wearing her cut-off tee that said, 'my brain is bigger than your brain' right across her boobs, and what looked like boys' boxers.

She laid the dress on my bed and then proceeded to unzip. The gorgeous teal fabric had me gasping. "Oh, the color is so pretty."

"I know, right? The moment I saw it, I thought of you. It's going to bring out the green in your eyes."

Even I could see the dress was perfect for me. A corset-y bit to make the most of my athletic curves, a slinky skirt to flatter my long legs. But the best part was, it had a slit. Two actually. So I'd be able to walk in it, and it wouldn't hinder my movements. I lifted my head and grinned up at her. "Oh, I love you, I think."

She laughed. "Uh, I know I'm loveable."

"You are loveable, but really, do we have to do the whole beautifying thing?"

She nodded. "Aurora is going to be here any minute. We're going to start the basics here and then we're headed to the spa."

I blinked once. Then again. "A what?"

She laughed. "Honey, I love you. You're a complete and total badass, but the fact that these girly places freak you the fuck out, we *have* to get that fixed. The manis and pedis are in order. A facial, an all-over body scrub. We're getting the works, babe."

"I don't need it. I don't need a scrub."

She ignored my protests and continued rattling off the treatments I was going to get.

"But I don't want treatments. I just—honestly, I don't really need that. Plus, I can't really afford any of that. I'm sure it's very expensive."

Serafina whirled on me and lifted a brow, then crossed her arms over her shirt. "Are you serious right now?"

"Look, I know you've gone through a lot of trouble, and I appreciate it. I do. But I don't need this. I—"

"It's a gift. You're my bestie, I'd rather have your company than not, and Tannith isn't here for me to spoil, so I have a lot of spoiling built up right now. So, you're coming whether you like it or not. Besides, my mother owns that spa. So treatments are free anyway."

I sighed. "Jesus Christ, there's no way I'm getting out of this, is there?"

She laughed. "No, there's no way. Besides, you're going to have Rhys and Lennox eating out of the palm of your hand."

"I don't want anyone eating out of my hand. Besides, you feed a stray once and they'll never leave you alone." I slid her a glance. "What about you? Will a certain Harvard sophomore be in attendance tonight? I know he's been sniffing around." Bryce Kessler was the oldest son of Jeffry Kessler, the actor. He'd graduated two years ago and had always had a thing for Sera. She, on the other hand, had always kept him at arm's length.

"I'm not worried if he shows or not."

"Oh c'mon. I know you've been talking to him on the phone sometimes."

Sera always played things close to the vest when it came down to her personal feelings. "Sure, we talk. But he's not my boyfriend or anything. Hell, I'm not sure I'll ever let him take me on a date. I like to assess the whole field before making a choice. Dating is a game of chess and not checkers. Best not to move too quickly. Besides, Rhys hates him. So son of an actor or not, no way he's welcome."

The way she said Rhys's name made me flush. "Serafina, you're okay with me going with him, right?"

She blinked wide eyes at me. "Yeah, I'm totally fine with it."

"Are you sure? Because I know you and Rhys have a—"

How the hell should I even classify their thing? It was intense loathing, followed by an 'I will kill you in your sleep' vibe.

"Honey, I know you're not super into him. And also, I just don't care. He can date whoever he wants."

"We're not dating."

"You're kissing and making out on occasion, that spells *dating* to me." She waved her hand, dismissing the topic. "Honestly, I'm good. I love you. And if you think Rhys can make you happy, then fine."

"Oh, my god, Rhys does *not* make me happy. And let's be really clear, I don't think he'd make me happy. For some reason, I'm interesting to him at the moment, and I'm not sure why. He's probably just bored with nothing else to do, spotted me and decided I'd be the apple of his eye for the time being. In my case, I figured he'd make a good practice boyfriend, so here we are."

Serafina lifted her brows. "What?"

"I mean look, I know Rhys isn't really interested in me. Why he is trying to hang out with me, I'm not sure. But he is . . . well, he is a very good kisser. I sort of feel a little warm and tingly when he kisses me, although not that fireworks-exploding kind of shit like with—"

I cut myself off before I said too much.

She lifted a brow. "Like with who?"

"Wow, look at this dress, isn't that—"

She shook her head. "Don't you dare try to change the subject. Like with who?"

I swallowed hard. "Like with Lennox."

Her eyes went wide. "I knew it. Did you ask Rhys to kiss you to make him jealous?"

I frowned at that. "No, I wouldn't do that. I don't want to play games."

She sighed. "Yeah, I know. That's not you. You're really direct and straightforward. But I knew there was something going on with you two."

"There's nothing going on with *us two*."

She folded her arms again, settling on her chest. "Oh yeah? Then tell me what happened when I saw him dragging you to a supply closet the other day?"

I opened my mouth to say something but decided otherwise. Then I opened it a second time, but then closed it again. I made another attempt trying to find just the right words, but it never came. Then on my fourth attempt, I just sighed. "You saw that?"

"Yes. Spill girl, spill."

"It wasn't—I don't even know how it happened. He dragged me in there and told me Rhys was the bad guy and I couldn't date him. And then he asked me to go to the gala with him instead."

Serafina laughed. "Oh my god. You are the cutest innocent badass vixen ever."

"I don't even know what that means."

"It just means that you're not even trying, and you have these guys falling all over themselves for you. Please, teach me your ways."

I gave her the once over. "You and I both know full well, all you have to do is give somebody the time of the day, and he's at your feet. *You* have this quality that just says, 'I'm badass and sexy'. *I* don't have that quality. I just have the badass and scary vibe which I cultivate, and I'm good with, but that's just it."

"I think you need to see yourself differently. And we're going to do that today. Because I don't think you see yourself clearly enough."

I opened my mouth to argue, but Serafina held up a

hand. "Nope. I have spoken."

I laughed. "I'm going to regret this whole day, aren't I?"

She grinned. "Yes, you are. But also you're going to look like a total bombshell. You're going to see *you* properly for the first time. I promise."

Maybe it was because she said it, or maybe it was that fierce glint in her eyes. Maybe it was just because I wanted to. But for some reason, I believed every word out of Serafina's mouth.

CHAPTER NINE

Lennox

T HE PROBLEM WITH benefit galas was, by and large, unless you snuck off with your mates, there was nothing to drink. No one cared that at eighteen, in UK, or anywhere else in Europe for that matter, I'd be able to drink. No, I was relegated to soda water. Or Cokes. Or ginger beer. And right now, I needed a fucking drink or I was going to lose my mind.

Where the hell was she? I kept looking for flickers of her slicked-back hair, glimpses of her bright green eyes. I could almost guarantee she'd be wearing some kind of pantsuit, or maybe something fitted and tight. *You never did know with Sloane.*

She was always a little edgy, in an understated way, but she liked to be comfortable and she liked to be able to move. It was always strange talking to her, like she was looking for the exits. I knew for a fact she'd grown up—while not as wealthy as most of us—entirely comfortable. So why did she always feel the need to be so guarded? So afraid?

Why do you care?

I didn't.

I was in luck. Some geezer had left behind his scotch as

he'd gone to dance. I could easily liberate him from this.

I grabbed the glass of the untouched drink and smiled to myself. "Sometimes it's just too easy."

On the dance floor, I caught sight of Serafina and my twin totally enjoying themselves. Aurora was in a short frilly-looking pink tulle dress of some sort.

And Serafina . . . Oh god, Serafina, she was in some white and mint-colored ensemble. It was sleek. Elegant. Maybe I *should* turn my attention towards her.

Serafina had the benefit of being a girl who didn't hate me, *and* it would piss off Rhys.

Although, I'd never really imagined that Serafina would give me the time of day. She was always nice enough. Had no real problems with me. But she didn't seek me out or look at me like most of the other girls at school did.

The last thing you need is to chase a woman who clearly doesn't want you.

Maybe she would. I knew what I looked like. More than half of the girls at school had indicated they'd love to try it on. Not her though. And come to think of it, I'd never seen her with a boyfriend. Maybe she wasn't into guys.

I could always just ask around to see what she's like.

Or, you could wait for a woman you actually want.

My gaze raked over Serafina once again. She was absolutely stunning. And I'd be lucky to have her in my bed. Hell, I was half hard just thinking about it. The problem was, she didn't make my skin itch. She didn't make me want to crawl out of my own skin. She didn't make me want to roar or howl at the moon, or whatever the hell that was. She didn't make me crazy. That was all *Sloane*.

Where the hell *was* she? The three of them were attached at the hips—even more so after Tannith went to Los Angeles and Iris went to Paris. So, if Sera and my twin were together without her, someone must have dragged Sloane off somewhere.

And I knew who that someone was.

I watched as Aurora gently tapped Serafina's arm with her hand. And then Sera turned towards the stairs. A wide grin spread across her face, making her appear even more stunning and regal. I turned to see what she was looking at, and I gasped. At the top of the stairs was Rhys in an excellent Oswald Boateng suit. On his arm was the girl I'd been waiting for practically my whole damn life. She was with him, and it made me want to kill someone.

My gaze homed in on her. She was wearing a teal-green dress. The top part looked like some kind of a cap sleeve corset or something. I don't really understand how the dress worked, but it somehow made Sloane look like she had curves. *Full ones.* It took whatever boobs she did have and encased them in some silk and shoved them up under her chin. I wanted to lick them.

Easy does it. You can't go sporting the goods at a gala.

The rest of the dress hugged her figure expertly, flaring slightly at her hips. It had slits that went all the way up to her thighs, allowing her freedom of movement. Her hair was down instead of pulled back in her characteristic short ponytail. It hung free and loose with a little more body than usual. Slightly curled. Her hair came to her chin, more to one side of her face. She looked stunning. Pity she was being escorted by a shit-eating, smirk-faced Rhys.

Suddenly, Owen appeared at my side. "You good? You're not going to do anything daft, are you?"

I drained the rest of the scotch. It went down smooth, warming up my belly when it hit. "I feel fine."

"Are you sure about that?"

"I mean, my desire to kill him is only . . . I'd say at an

eight instead of a ten from the other day. So count that as progress, mate."

Owen chuckled low. "You two have got to figure it out, bro. Are you really going to lose your shit over a girl?"

"What would you know about it?" I grumbled. Owen never lost control. Girls flocked to him and then he dismissed them when he was done.

But interestingly, Owen's grip tightened around his glass, and something hungry and possessive flared in his eyes.

"I'm learning something about it," he muttered darkly, taking a drink.

I stared at him. "Is there something you'd like to tell me?"

"Nothing to tell. I'm Owen Montgomery, and I'll get what I want eventually. She won't say no to me."

"Who is *she*? Does she go to Pembroke?"

Owen actually bared his teeth. "None of your fucking business, twat."

"Goddamn but you are really twisted up over this girl," I said. "I never thought I'd see our Ice King brought so low as to have human feelings."

"They're not *feelings*," he bit out. "And I'm not twisted up. I know exactly what I want, and I have no doubt she'll give it to me. Unlike you, I don't let a random girl fuck with my plans. Or my friendships."

Owen really should know better. Sloane wasn't just *any* girl. She was mine. And the fact that Rhys was getting that pleasure right now pissed me off. Beyond Sloane being mine, he could say or do something to really damage her. At least I knew when to stop. I had drawn some lines I would not cross.

It was a delicate balance, and I didn't think Rhys had that line.

Owen's voice was a low whisper. "Look, just let her go. If you didn't do anything about wanting her all this time, don't be cheesed off that he's doing something about it. And don't let it fuck with your friendship. Definitely don't let it fuck with Hellfire."

"What would you do? If Rhys was planning to stick his tongue in your mystery girl's mouth?"

Owen didn't answer, but he didn't need to. The cold, murderous flare in his eyes was answer enough. Whoever this mystery girl was, Owen wasn't about to let her go.

"If he hurts Sloane," I said, "I will rip his fucking cock off and peel it. Mate or no mate, Hellfire or no Hellfire."

Owen whistled low. "Wow, thanks for the visual. I really needed that."

Across the room, I watched as Rhys led Sloane to the dance floor, and I caught myself grinding my teeth. *That fucking arsehole.*

I sat the glass back down on the bar top and then glanced around the crowd looking for Sera. She had moved from her last position. When I found her in the corner talking to Aurora, I stalked over. "Ladies." Aurora gave me a quick glance over and a small smile. But I knew only one girl would have the desired effect. "Serafina, what do you say we dance?"

She lifted a brow. "Well, can you dance, Lennox?"

I clasped my hand to my chest as if horrified she would ask such a question. "I will have you know that royalty are taught to dance at a very young age. I shall not embarrass you."

She shrugged. "Sure, why not? Let's see what moves you have."

I led her to the dance floor, making sure we were standing three feet away from Rhys and Sloane, and then I twirled

Serafina in my arms. She giggled. Her laugh was light but throaty and it made me smile. I mean, hell, what was I doing chasing a girl I wasn't sure I liked when I had one I knew I liked right in front of me? She was beautiful. Brilliant. Ridiculously wealthy. And she had the kind of name nobody could sniff at. She was a god damn *van Doren*. I should want to date her. And she did have very nice lips.

As we danced, I tried to picture myself kissing her. And I imagined her staring at me with longing in her dark eyes, but then she lifted a brow asking me what the fuck I was doing.

I had to bite back a laugh as I pulled her close.

"A little close, aren't you, Lincoln-Ward?"

"It is a dance, after all, van Doren."

She pulled back with a smirk. "I don't think you and I have ever been this close."

I glanced over her shoulder at Rhys, who was holding Sloane far too close. Wanker looked like he was trying to kiss her.

"Well, to dance, you have to get close. It's like the Zayn song; *I just want to get closer.*"

She laughed this time. A deeper and throatier one. And I was momentarily stunned. God, she really should laugh more, but I wasn't going to be the insensitive arsehole who would suggest that.

As we danced, she proved a fantastic partner. She not only knew how to dance, but also she took gentle leads well. It was effortless. So simple.

But my gaze over her shoulder was trained on Rhys and Sloane, and then that motherfucker kissed her. His eyes locked with mine as he leaned in and kissed Sloane nice and slow. Like she deserved to be kissed.

My throat constricted. I knew the one thing that would

have set him off. The one thing that would have him releasing what was mine. I flicked my gaze to Sera's and she lifted a brow. "What are you looking at me like that for?"

"Is there a reason why you and I have never gone out?"

She laughed. "There are several reasons why. Are you looking for just one? I could do a whole dissertation."

"Ouch, I'm not that bad."

"No. You're not that bad. I don't know. It wasn't meant to be, I guess."

"Maybe we should change that." I leaned in close, and she snapped her head back.

"If you put your tongue anywhere near me, I will bite it off."

My jaw unhinged. "You don't want me to kiss you? I thought we were having fun."

"Yes, we're having fun. And I'm not going to lie; you are very pretty to look at. The hair, the eyes, and you have very sexy lips. But I prefer to be kissed by people who *want* to kiss me. I'm nobody's substitute. I wouldn't stand for it. And frankly I'm disappointed you think I would . . . or should. Is that what you think, fuck face?"

Fuck. "I—I'm sorry. That was shitty. I'm a wanker."

She shook her head. "Oh my god, you're such a loser. If you want her, go and get her. Don't let Rhys fuck with her head. I know she's brilliant and amazing, but he doesn't. I'm pretty sure if you actually stepped up and weren't a dickhead to her, she might actually like you."

My gaze flickered to the happy kissing couple on the dance floor and a gnawing hunger churned my gut. "You know what? You're right. I'm fucking done with this."

She patted my arm. "Well then go do something about it. I'm tired of watching that shit show too." I gave her arm a quick squeeze before I released her and marched over to

Rhys and Sloane.

When I reached them, I tapped on Rhys's shoulder. He lifted his hand and snarled at me. "Fuck off."

"I'm cutting in, mate."

Sloane's brows knitted together. "What in the world are you doing?"

"What I should have done a long time ago."

Rhys rolled his shoulders. "If you want to tussle again, we can do that. I'm not letting her go. Why should I just give her to you?"

"She's not yours, Rhys. She never fucking was."

I took Sloane's hand. She tried to fight me on it. "What the fuck do you think you're doing? Everyone is *staring*."

"I'm sorry. I'm going to apologize for this now. You can kick my arse for the next part later."

"Kick your ass for what?"

With the palm of my hand, I shoved Rhys away from her, and then I bent down, picked her up and tossed her over my shoulder. "You and I are going to talk. Rhys isn't bloody invited."

With the whole gala staring at us, and with Sloane slumped over my back doing her level best to fight her way free, I marched out of that ballroom.

Chapter Ten

Sloane

To say the Huntington mansion was large would be like saying being gutted with a fish hook stings a little. The mansion had a footprint bigger than most national museums, with grounds that stretched for acres and acres, sloping all the way down to a cold and crashing sea.

And I was currently being hauled like a Viking captive across *all of it*.

Well, maybe not all of it, but close enough. Lennox carried me, struggling and twisting atop his shoulder, out of the ballroom, and through another arched room strung with fall foliage and thousands of twinkling lights. It was also filled with people talking, mingling, drinking, and not one of them stopped to help me, even though I was clearly being hauled off against my will. No one hardly even *looked* at me, and when they did, their eyes would slide over to the famous white of Lennox's hair and they'd give me an apologetic sort of look. As if to say: *I couldn't possibly stop a prince, you understand, don't you?*

Rich people were absolute garbage.

Except then, I realized—belatedly and only as we walked through a set of massive doors and onto a breeze-buffeted portico outside—that I'd been smiling.

Smiling!

Fuck, no wonder no one had helped. I must have seemed positively gleeful to be perched atop the tuxedoed prince's shoulder.

"Lennox, put me down," I said, as authoritatively as I could. "Or take me back to the portico."

His arm was banded around the back of my thighs, and it tightened, as if even the idea of letting me go pissed him off. "If I put you down, then I'm tearing your dress off right here on the steps, darling."

He made the word *darling* sound like the angriest and filthiest word in the English language. "And it's not a portico," he added, "it's a loggia."

"And you're not a prince, you're a *prick*. Put me down."

"No."

"I mean it, Lennox."

"Or what? You'll hurt me? We both know if you truly wanted to be off my shoulder, you would be in a heartbeat." He was taking the shallow steps two at a time down to the moonlit lawn, away from the house and towards the sprawling hedge maze that stood between the mansion and the sea. "But you don't want to be off my shoulder, do you?"

"I do," I said, but it came out weak even to my ears. He was right; if I'd really wanted out of his hold, I would have been out by now. I knew at least seven different ways to get down from here—four of them wouldn't even require any strength or particular skill at all, only speed.

So why was I still here? Why was I barely able to keep that smile off my face? Why did I want him to make good on his threat and rip my dress right off me?

Lennox's shoes crunched on the crushed gravel of the path as we walked away from the house.

"You're not going to throw me into the ocean, are you?"

His voice dripped with scorn when he answered. "Don't be ridiculous."

"Don't be ridic—you have me over your shoulder like a caveman! Or a Viking! Or a Viking caveman!"

"And what do you think Vikings did with their beautiful captives, Sloane? Do you think they threw them into the ocean?"

There was that word again. *Beautiful.* Something hot and dangerous bloomed in my chest to match the hot and dangerous thing already pulsing between my legs.

"Well, historically, yes," I managed to say, "some were probably sacrificed—"

"I'm not throwing you into the ocean," he interrupted coolly. "Although I have half a fucking mind to. I told you that you belonged to me, and I meant that shit." We were entering the maze now, Lennox's strides long and sure like he'd walked this path many times before. "Clearly you need to be reminded."

Familiar ire itched at me. "I already told you. I'm not yours." I kicked my legs to prove my point, which earned me a hard, fast slap on the bottom.

I should have shrieked. I should have pulled his hair or scratched his eyes out. Instead, I moaned.

Moaned.

I was becoming seriously unhinged over this boy.

At the sound of my moan, Lennox's entire body stiffened under me. "How interesting," he said after a minute, his voice sneering and soft and fascinated. "I don't even need to have my fingers inside you to hear that noise."

Embarrassment flooded me everywhere. I *hated* that my desire for him could become a weapon in his hands. I *hated* that I didn't hate him . . . or that I didn't only hate him.

"Fuck you," I breathed. "Fuck you so much."

"Believe me, darling, I've thought about nothing else since the day we met," he said coldly. "Breaking you and fucking you. My twin obsessions."

"I could break you first."

"You could try. But we both know that the minute I touch your pussy, you sheathe those kitten claws for me, don't you? We both know I can make you come so good that it doesn't matter how much you hate me, you'll keep coming back."

I knew it was reckless when I opened my mouth, but I didn't care. I wanted to piss him off. I wanted him to be as angry as I was. "Maybe that's why I'm here tonight with Rhys. Maybe any Hellfire Club boy with long fingers will do, and I want to get my fix elsewhere."

Fury rippled through him, palpable and hot, and then he started walking even faster, muttering under his breath in his delicious accent. I could only catch a few words—*owed, mine, come*—but it was enough. Enough for me to know that whatever came next would be our biggest clash yet. Enough for me to know that he was serious as hell about me being his to torment and break, and he would stop at nothing when it came to wrecking me.

I WAS FREEZING by the time we got to the center of the Huntington maze. My dress was a gossamer-thin silk with barely any sleeves and two high slits up the front, which meant I was covered with goosebumps head to toe.

It also meant I felt the warmth of the fires before I saw them—dancing flames throwing light against the dark hedge walls. We were in the very heart of the maze now, approaching a stone structure that faintly resembled an ancient Greek temple—or at least, the idea of a Greek temple according to some Victorian-era Huntington who'd had too much money and not enough firsthand exposure to ancient architecture. Four braziers burned brightly at each of the corners, and the open spaces between columns were hung with curtains. Some were opaque, some were sheer, and they were all billowing gently in the breeze, parting just enough for me to make out a sunken fire in the middle surrounded by cushions and pillows and blankets. It was a space clearly meant for leisure and relaxing.

Or sex. Because everything about it—from the fires to the silk curtains to the cushions—screamed *do immoral deeds here!*

Which was exactly what I suspected Lennox had in mind.

Lennox mounted the stone steps into the open-air room and finally set me on my feet. For a brief instant, I considered running. I was in heels, yes, and I had very little practice running in them, but I had excellent balance, and anyway, I could always kick them off before I went. The slits in the dress would make for easy movement, and I'd noted every turn Lennox had taken in order to get here.

I could find my way out.

So why wasn't I running?

Lennox was closing the curtains from where we'd come in, and when he turned back toward me, his golden eyes were molten with raw anger and his mouth was the sharpest and cruelest I'd ever seen it.

"You fucked up coming here with Rhys, darling," he said, taking a step toward me. "You weren't his to bring."

"I keep *telling you*, I'm not anybody's."

Another step. "But that's not true, is it? I already own

you. I have for years."

I shivered at his words. Because I hated them . . . or because they were true, I didn't know. I just know they made me feel like he already branded his initials on some tender, vital organ in me. Like my heart.

Why did he captivate me so much? Why did I smile when he carried me, why didn't I run away when I had the chance?

Was it that mouth? Those unnaturally beautiful eyes? The cruelty?

The challenge?

I didn't understand it, and I hated things I didn't understand. Dad always said it would be my biggest weakness in criminal justice: my hunt for the bigger reason, the *why* of it all.

Sins very rarely have an interesting motive, he'd told me once. *Lust, greed, ambition. Everything gets boiled down to something predictable in the end.*

"Why?" I asked Lennox now, knowing that I wouldn't get a satisfying answer but needing to ask anyway. "Why this? Why us? Why did you decide I was yours? Why did you ever even notice me?"

He was in the middle of taking another step forward, and I could see my question surprised him a little. A faint line appeared between his brows. "I noticed you because you're you," he said, as if it were an indelibly obvious answer. "But as for being mine . . . well, I decided that once I heard your name."

"My name? But—"

"That's when I learned you were Nathan Lauder's daughter."

"Why—"

But I stopped myself, because I already knew why that

mattered, didn't I? After three years of thinking it *couldn't* be the reason, here it had been all along, plain as day. Obvious to anyone with eyes.

Obvious to anyone who hadn't blindly trusted her father's lies.

My next words came out slowly, reluctantly dragged from somewhere deep in my throat. "Years ago, my dad told me he was only barely involved with your father's case, but's that's not true, is it? He finally told me this week. He was the one who made the arrest. He was the one who investigated your father."

I couldn't read Lennox's face or voice now; it was as if everything in him had gone flat. Dead. "Investigated is a kind word, Sloane. A very kind word."

"And what—I'm some sort of revenge plan? Because your dad was a criminal and my dad was a cop? I thought you *wanted* your father in prison—I know Aurora does—so how can you blame my father for putting him there? How can you blame *me*? Want *revenge* against me?"

A muscle jumped in his jaw, and he opened his mouth—and then closed it again. As if he'd changed his mind about what he was about to say.

Instead, he took another step forward. He was close enough to reach out and touch me now, though he didn't. Not yet.

It was strange, the disappointment I felt right then. All this time, I'd thought I'd somehow earned Lennox's hatred on my own. I thought we'd become mortal enemies because of some marrow-deep connection . . . some fated gravity between us.

But no.

The bullying, the torment, the stolen kisses . . . it was all about a years-old grudge. Despite what I'd believed—what

I'd foolishly *chosen* to believe—it was about my father all along. Not about me at all.

I was completely irrelevant.

"It doesn't matter how it started," Lennox finally said. "We're still going to finish it."

I looked up at him, feeling dull and teary. But I did everything I could to blink the tears back. He hadn't made me cry in four years, and I wasn't going to give him the satisfaction now.

I had to go. I needed space away from him, from us, from this toxic bloom that was our fascination with each other.

"There's no finish for us, Lennox. I don't know what this is—" the words left me in a choked breath "—but it's over now. Goodbye."

I made to step around him, but his hand shot out to grab mine and his eyes shifted then, going from winter sun to blazing summer light. "Don't go," he said, and there was something wild in his voice, something that wasn't cold or cruel at all. "Please. Don't go yet."

I looked down at where he held me. He wasn't holding my arm or my wrist. He wasn't gripping me with any real strength. Not because he didn't care if I left—I could practically feel him vibrating with how much he cared—but because he was *asking*.

For the first time, ever, Lennox Lincoln-Ward was asking for something.

"We both know you can fight me," he continued, bending his knees a little so he could catch my gaze. "We both know you can fend me off, beat me down, kill me if you have to. So stay, Sloane. Don't go. You know I can't really hurt you."

"You should know," I tell him, pulling my arm free and

glaring, "that there are more ways to hurt a person than only with their body."

"Then hurt me for every time I hurt you. Kick me when I sneer. Punch me when I taunt. I don't care, *just stay.*"

Misery shimmered through me like waves over hot asphalt. "I don't want to kick you or punch you, Lennox. All I've ever wanted is for you to leave me alone."

The wildness was still in his face and voice when he reached for me again. "I won't, I won't leave you alone, not ever—"

His fingers made contact with my wrist and something snapped in me. Something that was more than anger, something that was worse than embarrassment.

Hurt.

The outside edge of my free hand came down hard on his wrist, loosening his grip, and then I shoved him back, hard enough to make him stagger a step or two backwards. It felt so good that I did it again, and again, shoving and shoving him until he was practically in the fire pit. Shoving him until my body was hot with something other than hurt, until my hand was fisted in the lapel of his tuxedo, and my nipples were hard enough to bead against the silk of my dress.

"Do it until you feel better," he said, his voice ragged and his breaths coming fast. "Hurt me as much as you want."

"I'd have to hurt you for a thousand years to make up for all the things you've done to me," I whispered, and his eyes were so gold right then, and his mouth was so gorgeous, and the fire gleamed all along those sharp cheekbones and that perfect jaw, and I hated him, I hated him, *I hated him*—

This time it was me seeking his mouth. This time it was

me yanking him down to my lips and kissing him like I'd die if I didn't. Like the only way I could breathe was against his mouth, and the only air I could drag into my lungs was the air we breathed between desperate, hungry kisses.

CHAPTER ELEVEN
Sloane

IT WAS HIS turn to shove now, and I was pushed right onto my back, like he really was a Viking intent on pillaging me. Except I didn't fall onto the ground, I fell onto a pile of luxurious cushions and blankets, and he was no Viking, but all prince, with his ten-thousand-dollar tuxedo and his white-gold hair falling into his eyes as he crawled over me.

"Go ahead," he breathed, "hurt me. Stop me. We both know you can."

I could. I could have him off me in a heartbeat. I could have him cupping his testicles and weeping. I could have him blinded and screaming.

But instead, I threaded my fingers into the white silk of his hair and pulled him down to my mouth again.

His kiss was as hot as his heart was cold, and when his mouth opened over mine, a moan worked its way free from my throat. There was nothing like his kisses, nothing at all, nothing like that tongue slipping past my lips and stroking against my own. Nothing like the way he searched and plundered my mouth, seeking out all my secrets and all my lies.

An exquisite heat knotted between my legs, directly tied

to the fluttering in my stomach and the ache in my breasts, and I parted my thighs, my hands finding his hips and pulling him closer. There was no argument from him, and the moment his tuxedo-clad erection pressed against my needy core, we both groaned.

Still he kissed me, still his mouth made me his own, but now he propped himself on one hand as his other hand slid up my leg. One of the dress's slits had opened around my thigh, and so my leg was completely bare and exposed to the chill of the night. The contrast between the cold air and his warm hand was enough to start my stomach fluttering all over again.

And then his hand moved between us, using the slit for its inevitable purpose.

"A thong," he murmured. "Have you ever worn a thong before, Sloane?"

His fingers traced around the edges of the fabric as he talked. As thongs went, it wasn't meant to be sexy. It was a seamless thing meant to hug my body and prevent any lines from showing through the dress. It was functional and direct. Like me.

But when Lennox touched it, he made it feel like it was woven of the naughtiest lace and the purest sin. His fingers were shaking, and his pupils were so blown that his eyes were no longer gold, but black, with only a gilded ring around the outside.

His breathing was harsh. Ragged. Like this was the sexiest thing he could have ever imagined.

This is definitely the sexiest thing I could have ever imagined, with the possible exception of watching him jerk off in his sleep.

"No," I managed to say. "I've never worn one before."

"It's wet here," he said, the back of his knuckles brushing over my seam. I bit back a moan. "So wet. Did you feel naughty wearing this? Did you feel naughty knowing I'd inevitably see it?"

"Yes," I admitted. "*Yes.*"

He tugged at the fabric, causing it to press and pull against my swollen flesh. This time, I couldn't hold back the helpless noise I made.

"I want it off," he growled, his fingers now curling around one side of it. "I want you completely bare for me."

It didn't even occur to me to argue. Why would it have? I wanted less between us too, I wanted *nothing* between me and his touch. I helped him pull the thong off, and I didn't even mind when he tucked them into the pocket of his tuxedo pants, as if he planned on keeping them. And then he kissed me fiercely, almost like a reward, and I was lost. Lost to his drugging kisses, lost to the feel of his hand roaming everywhere—cupping a breast, searching out a nipple, sliding to my hip and the slit in my dress and rubbing me until I was arching and gasping.

"Um, why are you—" His voice cracked. "Have you had a Brazilian?"

I groaned. "Oh my god, Serafina insisted when we did spa day. Can you imagine?"

He coughed a laugh. "Sort of. But I like it."

I bit his bottom lip. "Okay, it feels kind of amazing, actually. Your fingers on my bare skin."

"Who are you telling?" he growled.

I couldn't answer, I couldn't even think, because he was doing something to my clit that rendered all thoughts null and void. All I could do was lift my hips and pant.

"Every time," he breathed between kisses, his hand lifting from my pussy to his fly. "Every time we do this, I get you there, and then you leave me so fucking hard up for it,

Sloane. And I can't stand it. I spend hours tossing myself off after, and it's still not enough. I'm still miserable for days and days, and it kills me, it kills me."

My hands were everywhere too, unbuttoning his jacket and sliding up his stomach and pulling at his bow tie. "I'm miserable for days after too," I confessed. "You make me come, and then I want more and more, and it takes everything I have not to find you and beg you for it."

"Is that so, darling? All you've ever had to do was ask."

"Liar."

"I never lie about what's important. You belong to *me*. If this virgin cunt needs to come, then I'll be the one seeing to it. No one else. Not Rhys. Not anyone. Is that fucking clear?"

His bow tie was finally undone, hanging from his collar and tickling my throat. "Still jealous of Rhys?" I asked.

A scowl curved his mouth. "Yes, I'm still bloody jealous. I don't like it when other people touch my things."

My heart twisted a little as I remembered why he'd claimed me as his thing—not because he wanted me, but because he resented my father—but the feeling was quickly overridden by his fingers between my legs again. Then his knuckles. Brushing oh-so-gently against my naked skin.

"And I'm your thing?" I asked, arching against his touch.

"My pretty, broken thing."

"I'm not broken yet," I reminded him, although the point seemed rather academic as I was currently panting underneath him with my panties in his pocket.

The scowl turned into a vicious smile. "You will be."

And then I realized what the brushing of his knuckles was: he'd been freeing himself from his tuxedo pants. And now he impatiently shoved the rest of my skirt out of the way so he could wedge his erection against my pussy as he leaned in to kiss me again.

We looked like a mess, a complete and decadent mess. Me with my gown up to my hips, him with his tuxedo still on but his bow tie unknotted and dangling.

And the way we *felt*—well, that was beyond decadent. The hot, velvety skin of his thick length pressed against me, the combination of silk and expensive wool tangled everywhere, his firm lips dragging over my mouth and jaw and throat.

He moved down to my breast, sucking my nipple through the silk bodice, and then back up to my mouth. Every time I moved, his swollen cock rubbed against my clit, sending bursts of pleasure rocketing through my core and sizzling all over my body.

"You're so fucking wet," he said, rocking against me. His thick inches spread me apart when he moved like that, made it so I got him even wetter. "You get so fucking wet when we fight, my darling. You get so fucking wet when I tell you all the ways you belong to me."

"I—don't belong—to—you—" The words came out as moans, as sighs, and we both knew them to be false. At the very least, they were false right now, as I was chasing his hips with mine, as I was kneading my clit against the erection he'd freed from his tuxedo.

And then it happened. We were tangled and arching and his teeth were scraping along my jaw, and suddenly the blunt, wide crown was pressed to my wet opening.

"Oh," I murmured, the different pressure sending frissons of need into my belly and thighs.

And at the same time, he muttered, "Christ, fucking Christ."

We didn't move for a moment, both of us absorbing the

fact that his flesh was touching mine—*there*—the flared tip of his cock nudging against my hole. One thrust and he'd be inside me. Fucking my virginity away.

He lifted his head, his silky hair tumbling in his eyes, and stared down at me. His eyes were hooded, his lips swollen from kissing. "Let me," he said. "Let me."

He was trembling. His entire body was shaking. If I'd ever doubted that he wanted to have sex with me, then there were no doubts, not anymore. He was about to fly apart at the seams with how much he needed to shove himself inside me and fuck.

I was shaking too. My entire body screamed for this, for him; my thighs ached with the effort it took not to wrap around his hips and have him spread me open.

"You don't have a condom," I whispered foggily, trying to think. "We should have a condom."

"I'm clean," he said, dropping his forehead to mine. His breath was warm against my lips. "I'm clean. And we know you are. Are you on birth control?"

I shook my head under his.

He let out a ragged curse. "Ahh, fuck me, Sloane, the things I'm thinking right now . . ."

I moved my hips a little, swiveling on the head of his dick and shivering at how good it felt. "What things?"

"Fucked-up things. Filthy things."

"Like what?"

I could feel the tops of his thighs against the inside of my own, and I could feel how they flexed ever so slightly, pushing his crown just a little deeper. I gasped.

"Like I want to come inside you anyway," he murmured, kissing the side of my jaw and then nipping at my ear. "Like I want to pump you so full that you're leaking me down the inside of your thigh for the rest of the night."

Another flex of his hips, a tad bit deeper. He was still only barely inside me, but it was enough to pinch, enough to make me squirm with something that could have been pain or could have been pleasure, I wasn't sure which.

"I could fuck a baby into you," he purred into my ear. "I could keep you here all night, coming inside you over and over again. I could drag you back to my room at Pembroke and fuck you night after night until you were pregnant."

This shouldn't have been hot. I shouldn't have been squirming even more at his fucked-up words. But I was. I was.

His hand came down between us, and he spread it wide over my stomach. "You like that, darling? You like how hot it makes me to think about fucking you without a condom?"

"I shouldn't," I said, which wasn't an answer, and he knew it.

I could feel his smirk as he took my hand and guided it down between us, directing my fingertips to trace the place where he was notched against me.

"That's the head," he said, as my fingers found the ridged crest at the top. "Now, here, circle me, just like that. You feel that throbbing? You feel how it jerks sometimes? That's for you. That's because I'm aching to sink deep inside you and fuck."

I shivered. I was aching for that too. "Really?"

His cock jolted in my hand, swelling even more. "Yes," he ground out.

"As revenge against my father?"

"Sure," he said. There was something evasive in his tone. "That's what it is."

I shouldn't have wanted him to go inside me bare—I had too much planned for my life to risk pregnancy—but something about it, about him claiming me in such a horribly primal way . . .

Well, it did make me wet. Something he felt, because he grunted, "I can feel you getting slicker, darling."

"I can't help it," I said, wanting *so badly* to have more of him inside me. "You mess with my head. You mess with everything. I hate you so much, but your cock feels so good—"

"Brilliant, because it's the only cock you're ever getting," he vowed. To underscore his words, he pushed his crown all the way in.

"*Lennox,*" I moaned. He was wide, so wide, invading my channel. He was maybe only an inch deep, but I felt him everywhere, my thighs and my belly and even in my chest.

"Shit," he mumbled, pressing his forehead to mine again. "I can't go any farther. That's your hymen stopping me."

He flexed his hips a little, moving back out and then again, as if to test the barrier. He was shivering, like he had a fever, and his forehead was burning hot against mine.

"I'm owed this, Sloane. I've been owed this for years. Your virgin pussy around my cock. Let me break your hymen, baby, please. Please. Please."

He was begging now. Wild. Like he'd been every other time we'd fooled around—a bully and a prince brought utterly low by me, by the mere *idea* of fucking me.

It's revenge to him.

He doesn't care about you.

But I was so aroused, so frantic. Desperate for more and more and more. And even if I knew it was a lie, it felt like power to have him like this, to have him begging for something that I could so easily deny him.

God, it felt even better than power. It felt like its own kind of revenge, its own fucked-up victory.

Maybe that was what it would always be between us.

One of us pushing until the other broke.

"You can, but only if you make me come first—"

The words hadn't even finished leaving my mouth before his thumb found my clit, expertly circling and rubbing and pressing. "I could spend every waking minute making you come, Sloane. It's the only time you smile, did you know that? The only time I get to see your smile is when you're limp and shuddering from an orgasm I just gave you."

My head was thrashing on the pillow—I knew my hair was going to be ruined and I didn't even care. It felt so good, so unimaginably good to have him working my clit with his cock inside me. With the thrilling potential that he could sink all the way in at any moment.

The climax was abrupt, sharp, wonderful. I dug my fingers into his hair and pulled him down to me as my orgasm broke against his talented touch, around the tip of his cock. I gasped into his ear as my cunt fluttered and fluttered and fluttered.

"Sloane," he rasped, and that was all. "Sloane."

He pushed against my hole and lifted his head to look down between us. I looked too, seeing the crude joining of him to me, seeing his thick erection pressing into me.

"I can feel you coming," he said in a tattered voice. "I can feel—it's so tight, Sloane. God, and knowing that I am the one who made you come—"

The climax was still rippling through me, but I wanted more, I wanted to fuck, I wanted Lennox to be the only thing that existed tonight. Him and his rough sex and the fire next to us and the sea roaring in the distance.

"Fuck me, Lennox," I pleaded. "I want it to be you. I want you to be the first—"

"I'm going to be the *only*," he growled, and slid his arms

underneath me.

I realized what he was doing; he was gathering me close, he was anchoring me so he could plunge in as hard as he needed, so he could shove past my virginity and fuck my whole pussy. There was the hard pulse of my orgasm still clamoring through me, there was the brutal pressure of his cock just barely wedged inside, and there was the feel of wool and silk tangled together, and then there was the smell of flowers and metal and the sound of the ocean—

And then I heard Lennox's name. Not from my lips, or from his, but from outside the temple folly, in the maze.

"Lennox?" a girl's voice called. "Lennox, are you in there?"

Chapter Twelve

Lennox

WE BOTH FROZE, looking at each other in a kind of lust-drunk panic. The kind of panic that says *maybe no one will notice us, maybe we can keep going, because we'll die if we can't keep going.*

At the very least, *I* would die. My erection gave a hard throb against her, arguing with me.

You're about to be all the way inside of Sloane Lauder's pussy, my cock shouted at me. *Nothing gets in the way of that.*

But then the voice called my name again, and we both recognized it at the same time.

Aurora. My twin and one of Sloane's best friends.

"Fuck," I said, but I didn't move. "Darling, I—"

"We have to get up," Sloane whispered.

"This isn't over," I said, in mortal agony. I propped myself on an elbow and looked down at the stern, beautiful face that haunted my dreams. "This is the furthest thing from over, Sloane."

"Okay, fine, it's not over—now get up or she'll see—"

I somehow managed to pull my cock free. How, I don't know, because it was the tightest, wettest thing I'd ever felt in my life. And it was virgin too, totally untouched except by me. As if she really had been waiting for me. As if I really had been owed her all these years.

Fuck. I'd been tossing off to this since the day I met her; my singular goal of making her life a living hell had somehow fused with the necessity of fucking her. And that had somehow fused with a possessiveness I couldn't explain even to myself.

She was mine. All fucking mine.

I wincingly closed up my tuxedo pants around my erection as Sloane attempted to rearrange her dress and hair. She held out her hand with her eyebrow raised.

"Panties, please."

I smirked at her. "It's cute that you think I'd even consider giving them back."

That earned me a typical Sloane scowl.

"Lennox?" I heard Aurora call again. Now that my dick was back in my pants, I could hear the warble in my twin's voice.

Concern battled with my initial irritation at being interrupted. Aurora liked crying about as much as I did—which was to say, not at all. We hadn't cried when Dad was arrested or when our mother's humiliation was smeared all over the tabloids. We hadn't cried when we were sent off to boarding school.

We both had too much of that stupid Lincoln-Ward pride.

I helped Sloane to her feet—without asking her, by the way; I merely scooped her up and then set her down on her heels, which earned me another Sloane scowl. And then I pushed through the curtains separating the inside of the folly from the rest of the maze.

Aurora stood in front of the folly, shivering in her tiny, strapless gown. Her skin was covered in goosebumps, and her mascara was running down her cheeks and dripping off her jaw.

"Bloody hell, Rory, are you alright?" I asked, coming down the temple steps as fast as I could, Sloane right behind me. I shrugged out of my jacket and flung it over her shoulders, pulling it tight around her. "What the hell were you thinking coming outside like this? You'll freeze."

She sniffled. And then threw herself against my chest and started sobbing.

I held her tight, smoothing my hand over her back while I met Sloane's confused stare. That made two of us who were utterly lost as to what was happening.

"Did someone hurt you?" I asked, already growing angry at the thought. Aurora and I sparred plenty, but no one fucking hurt my twin, *no one*.

Aurora nodded tearfully against my chest, and I gently pushed her away from me, just enough so I could study her face and arms. If I saw any bruises, any scrapes, so help me God—

But there was nothing that I could see. Just her swollen lips and mussed hair.

"What happened?" I asked again, as softly as I could.

Her chin was dimpling, and I could see she had to swallow once or twice before she could force the words out. "Phineas," she whispered. "Phineas happened."

Phineas, that *fucking* playboy arsehole, I was going to kill him. I understood equal opportunity hatred very well—just look at Sloane and me—but whatever this was had crossed the goddamn line. Pleasant images of smashing his face with my fist danced in my mind, and given the way Sloane's scowl had curved into a darkly gleeful smile, I had to think she was imagining much the same thing.

"Let's get you inside," I said to my twin. "I know a

place."

✧   ✧   ✧

TWENTY MINUTES LATER, we were in the Huntington kitchens, and I was getting a glass of water for my sister and a bottle of whiskey for myself.

I say kitchens *plural*, because the Huntington Mansion is old enough to have required hordes of servants and cooks back in the time before electric ranges and dishwashers, and so the kitchens are actually a cluster of rooms beneath the house, each room with a different purpose. There're pantries and larders and butteries and sculleries, and we were currently in an unused-for-decades scullery, close enough to the main kitchen that we could faintly hear the catering staff chattering and clattering dishes, but far enough away that we were hidden well out of view.

"How did you know this was here?" Sloane asked as I walked in with the water and whiskey. The water I handed Aurora, and the whiskey I unstoppered and took a swig of before I handed it to Sloane.

I expected her to fight me on it; I'd never seen her drink, not even once, but to my surprise, she grabbed the bottle by the neck and took a few healthy swallows.

"Rhys showed it to me," I said, taking a seat next to my sister. Sloane had found Aurora a blanket, and one of the reasons I'd chosen the scullery was because it had an old, clunky radiator that still worked, but Aurora was still shivering. I took the whiskey from Sloane and gave it to my twin. "Here, this will warm you up."

Aurora accepted it, her eyes hooded as she took several long drinks. Between the drama and the cold and getting warm again, I had the feeling she'd be asleep soon.

"Rhys knows where his scullery is?" Sloane sounded doubtful.

"More like he knows all the spots in his house where he can fuck someone without getting caught," I said, and then narrowed my eyes. "He might have tried to bring you down here, you know."

"He might have," Sloane agreed.

Jealousy rose in my blood again, so violent and sharp that I wanted to smash something. "And would you have gone with him?"

Aurora was watching our exchange with the glazed listlessness of the almost-asleep. For her sake, I managed to keep myself from roaring and pounding my chest at the thought of Rhys touching what was mine.

It was Sloane's turn to narrow her eyes now. "Maybe."

"You're never going anywhere with him again," I said coldly. "If you go anywhere else like this, I'll be the one to take you."

Sloane's mouth tightened, but she didn't reply, turning away to smooth Aurora's messy hair with her hand instead. My sister sighed and then slid down to the floor, curling into a ball next to Sloane, her eyes already closing.

"What did he do, Rory?" Sloane asked softly, arranging my tuxedo jacket so it was a kind of pillow for her friend.

"What he always does," Aurora whispered. "He makes me think he cares, and I start to believe that he really does. And then I find him with his dick wet."

Sloane's free hand curled into a fist, but she didn't say anything. She merely kept stroking Aurora's hair, and within a few minutes, Aurora's soft snores filled the scullery. My sister was finally asleep.

Sloane got carefully to her feet, the slits in her dress showing off her leanly muscled legs as she did. Despite my sleeping sister only a few feet away, my cock surged to attention. I wanted to spend hours exploring those incredible legs of Sloane's. Tracing every muscle with my tongue.

"What are you doing?" I asked Sloane as she started opening drawers and cabinets at the far end of the scullery.

"Looking for knives," was the succinct answer I received.

"Er. Knives?"

Sloane turned and fixed me with a look that both made my cock hard as granite and also terrified the fuck out of me. *This* was the girl that made me finger her while she held her forearm to my throat. "Have you ever heard of a Colombian necktie?" she asked calmly.

"I—what?"

"I'm going to cut Phin's throat and then pull his lying, manwhore tongue through it."

I considered for a moment. Phin was my friend, but a Colombian necktie was about what he deserved after making my sister cry. "I'll help," I said. "Actually, I'll do it while you hold him down."

She glared at the empty cabinet in front of her, and then she slammed it shut with a bang. "I don't have time to teach you how to cut someone's throat, Lennox."

But there was something like a smile on her face when she turned to face me.

"Come here," I said from the floor, not sure what I was doing, but unable to stop. "Sloane, come here."

She hesitated for a moment, and then she walked over to me. I reached up and pulled her by the wrists so that she was straddling my lap. Next to us, Aurora continued to snore.

"What are you doing?" Sloane asked. "More to the point, what am I doing? I need to go kill Phineas."

"We'll kill him later," I murmured, looking up at her. It

wasn't very bright in the scullery, because the only light came in from the doorway, and the shadows made her so very lovely. Almost like she was meant to be in them always. They turned her eyes dark and glossy, like mistletoe leaves in midwinter, and they set off her sharp jaw and her elegant cheekbones. They even traced her plush pout of a mouth—a sliver of shadow lingering under her full lower lip, a curl of shadow in the dip of her cupid's bow.

I extended my hand and traced her lips myself, all the places where they curved and dipped. And then I pushed my finger past her lips and groaned in surprise when she sucked it. And then groaned again when she bit it.

Fuck, I was so hard.

I dropped my hands and ran them up her thighs— exposed by the slits in her dress—and then gripped her hips and pulled her firmly onto my lap, so that her cunt was against my erection.

"Oh," she said, her eyelids hooding as she felt me against her. She gave an experimental little rock against me and then shivered. "Okay," she whispered. "Okay, yes, we can kill Phineas later."

I let out a strangled laugh and then yanked her down to my mouth, kissing her like we were still alone in the folly. Kissing her like I still had her mounted.

Breaking our kiss, she looked over at Aurora, as if to reassure herself that Aurora was asleep still, and then she reached between us, hiking up her gown and fumbling for the fastenings of my trousers. I hissed the moment her fingers found me, throbbing into the cool air.

"This isn't because I care about you," my shadow-kissed tormenter said. "But fair's fair, and you've made me come so many times . . ."

I looked down at where she gripped me, her strong

fingers wrapped around my shaft, the tuxedo and her silk gown rumpled between us, and then my head dropped back.

"Fuck," I mumbled. "*Fuuuck.*"

She moved her grip up and then down, slowly, as if testing it. Without moving my head, I looked at her. "Have you ever tossed someone off before?"

She shook her head. "Am I doing it wrong?" She moved her hand again, her fingers so strong and tight, and my toes curled in my patent leather Oxfords.

"No," I managed, my breath hitching. "Not wrong at all."

She gave me more strokes, a little tentative, but plenty tight, and my balls drew up close to my body, ready to release. It was almost embarrassing how little it was taking to get me there, but in my defense, this had been almost four years in the making. Four years of jerking off in my room alone.

And then she did something that will undoubtedly lead to four *more* years of jerking off. She let go of me and then shifted forward, until her bare cunt was on top of my dick, and started *moving*. Fisting her hands in my shirt and rocking over me, like she was giving me a handjob still, but with her pussy instead of her hands, and oh my god, oh my bloody god—

"You're so wet," I breathed, finding her hips and moving her over me harder, faster. "So wet. More. Fuck, give me more."

She widened her thighs and buried her face in my neck, letting me work her cunt over my erection, and it was so wet, so hot, and all I had to do was flex my hips just the right way and I could be inside her . . .

"Darling," I said in a choked murmur, "my sweet nothing, I'm going to come. I'm going to get you wet with it if you don't move."

"Do it, Lennox," she whispered against my throat. "Come all over me. I want to feel it on me."

That's all it took. I arched up, my thighs tense, my stomach rock-hard, and then for the first time, I came with Sloane Lauder. I came against her, *on* her, my cock throbbing jet after jet of hot fluid underneath her slick, wet cunt. I came and it spattered onto her, onto my dress shirt, making everything between us wetter and wetter. And every time she slid over me, I could feel the place where she opened. I could feel how close I was to heaven, and the knowledge made me come even harder.

I *would* be there. Soon. So fucking soon.

Sloane was mine, and tonight had proved it.

She gave a few small shudders against me as my pulses stilled and then slumped against my chest. I realized she'd been able to wring out an orgasm for herself too. I wrapped my arms around her and held her tight against me. Not because I wanted to be affectionate, obviously not.

Just . . . it felt better like this. My arms around her, her breath on my neck, our bodies still warm and wet and pressed together under her skirt.

"Seeing you with Aurora tonight . . . you're different than I thought you were," she murmured after a moment.

I ran my nose through her hair. Fuck, she smelled good. Like honeysuckle. Who knew the girl made entirely of knives and glares would smell like honeysuckle? "How am I different?" I asked idly.

"I don't know," she answered after a minute. "I guess I thought you were selfish, you know? Greedy."

Greedy. The word punched through me like a cannonball.

"Greedy," I repeated flatly. "Why would you think

that?"

She tried to sit up a little, and I let her. I wanted to see her face. "Why did you think I was selfish? Greedy?" I pushed. "Because of my father? Because your father told you that's what you should think of me?"

My voice was rising now, echoing off the walls of the scullery, but I didn't care. I didn't fucking care. It didn't matter what I did or who I did it for—it didn't matter how many years passed—I was always going to be my *fucking father* to the rest of the world.

Sloane regarded me warily. "You're extrapolating," she said in that quiet, clipped way of hers. "I never said any of that."

"You didn't fucking have to," I growled. "Get off me. Get off me right now."

A wounded look flashed over her face, and then it was gone before I could process what it really was or what it meant. She climbed off me and rose gracefully to her feet, adjusting her dress and checking on Aurora before walking to the door.

"Stay here with her," she said. "And then after she's awake, feel free to go fuck yourself."

CHAPTER THIRTEEN

Sloane

MY HEAD SPUN.

How had everything gone so terribly wrong? How had I gone from writhing underneath Lennox in the maze—writhing on *top* of him in the scullery—to trying not to cry in Sera's limo on the way back to Pembroke?

Sera was wrapped in a cashmere blanket, dozing on her seat, and I was pretending to myself that I didn't have streaks of Lennox's orgasm painted on the inside of my thighs. I was pretending that I didn't want to curl into a ball and sob forever.

Everything in my world was upside down. But there were some simple facts.

First, I'd watched Lennox Lincoln-Ward masturbate . . . to me.

Secondly, I'd stolen information from him.

Third, Lennox proved in front of *everyone* that he had a thing for me.

And finally, I'd come with Rhys to the gala event. And then, I'd made out with aforementioned Lennox, nearly banging him in the gardens and then riding him in the scullery like a seasoned seductress.

Who the hell was I? None of this was my life. I was hardly a femme fatale.

But tonight you are.

The worst part of this whole damn thing was a part of me liked him. Or at the very least, was drawn to him. I couldn't fight the attraction. There was no more walking around pretending that I didn't orient myself around him, even if it was for express avoidance. Even if I could tell myself that I was around him for my own protection, so I could watch him better. It was a lie. I *wanted* to be around him.

I *wanted* his attention. I'd been pulled to Lennox like a magnet since the first moment we met.

I could still feel his lips on mine. The way his tongue delved into my mouth. His hands on my body. His lips on the tips of my breasts. The low growl he'd made as he'd pushed inside me still reverberated in my ears, making my body and skin hum with awareness, and arousal, and adrenaline.

I wanted Lennox Lincoln-Ward.

For once in my life, I felt like I was important to someone. I'd felt beautiful. Like someone saw me. The *real* me. Someone thought I was beautiful and stunning. Someone thought I mattered.

Yes, we'd been interrupted, but then there had been a deeper shift. As we'd worked to take care of Aurora, there had been this connection between us. As if we could actually like each other. Like we could speak and get along. Maybe we were just at the tipping point where hate and distress turned into something else. And then, that sweet, sweet friction as I'd worked my slick heat over him, making him come . . . all over the both of us.

Then I'd said the wrong thing. And there had been the

disgust in his eyes, the hatred in his voice, the anger on his cruelly beautiful face.

Because your father told you that's what you should think of me?

I'd wanted to bite back at him, to yell, to seethe. I hated that Lennox's fascination with me began and ended with my father. I hated that the moment he was wounded, he assumed it was my father doing the wounding through me.

My father had nothing to do with me!

Your father has everything to do with you. Your father arrested his.

Your father asked you to spy on him.

And Lennox still doesn't know.

I winced just thinking about it, because I *had* done what my father asked. Not necessarily blindly, but I had done what I was told to do. And I hadn't asked any questions. I hadn't wondered if maybe I shouldn't have been doing it. Or why it felt icky. I'd done it. But now, as Lennox's words rang in my head, I couldn't help but wonder what piece I wasn't seeing, because there had to be more to the story. Yes, my father had lied about his involvement, but even knowing that now . . . there *had* to be more than my father simply investigating Lennox's.

Investigated is a kind word, Sloane. A very kind word.

I was used to seeing the pieces and making them fit the puzzle. And all puzzles eventually made sense. You just had to find out where your thread was, how to pull it correctly, and I still couldn't quite figure it out.

When we got back to Pembroke, it was late enough that the lights in the dining hall were on as the cooks began to work on the Sunday morning pastries. Sera stumbled sleepily into the en suite and started a shower I knew would last until dawn, and I got a single text message from Keaton—

not Lennox notably—that Aurora was spending the night at the Huntington mansion with everyone else and would be back at the dorms tomorrow. Keaton promised to keep Phin away from her, and as pissed as I was at Lennox, I trusted him and Keaton to protect Aurora. Lennox obviously cared for her deeply, maybe more than he even cared for himself.

I zipped out of my dress, relieved to be able to breathe in a full gulp of air for the first time in several hours. But after I scrubbed my face clean, peeled off the lashes that Sera had made me wear and scooped my hair back into my usual tiny little ponytail, I stared at myself in the mirror. The same green eyes, fair skin, and completely unremarkable face stared back at me.

It was as if that hidden fairy princess that I had felt like tonight hadn't existed. Without the adornments and without the gaze of the fairy prince, I was just plain old Sloane again.

I checked the clock. It was close to five. Which meant my father would be awake, getting ready for his morning run while he glanced through any new APBs that came out while he was asleep. I picked up the phone and made a call, even though I wasn't entirely sure what I was going to ask for.

"Sweetheart?"

"Hey, Dad."

"Sloane, the sun hasn't even risen, what are you doing up?"

I fidgeted with the hem of my t-shirt. Part of my Sloane uniform was a t-shirt and boy shorts to bed. Hair pulled back. Nothing sexy or beautiful. "I have a question. And I need you to be honest with me."

"Sure. I'm always honest with you."

A brief shot of anger hit my blood, followed by hurt.

How quickly he seemed to forget that he'd lied to me. He'd lied to me and while he hadn't known that Lennox was torturing me, he'd inadvertently made everything worse by not giving me all the facts.

"The Lincoln-Ward case . . ." I started, and then paused, not knowing how to phrase the question I wanted to ask.

There was a moment of silence, and then a long sigh. "Sloane, is this what you really want to talk about? It was a complicated case. I worked on it. That's all."

"Yes, it's what I want to talk about!" The hiss of Sera's shower through the en suite door mimicked the blood rushing through my ears. "You asked me to pull information on Lennox—don't you think I deserve to know why? Don't you think I deserve some context? Some background?"

I knew he'd agree. I had a point. If he could ask me to spy on Lennox, then he could tell me what I needed to know.

"All right," Dad said, sounding suddenly very tired. "What do you want to know?"

"Just—more. I guess. More than what you've told me."

A heavy exhale. "It's not a pleasant story."

"I know it's not," I replied. "Ponzi scheme stories rarely are."

"I meant it's not a very pleasant story about *me*," Dad clarified. "I meant what I said to you last week. I'm not— I'm not proud of this chapter in my life. I just want you to know that before I begin."

I didn't know what to say to that.

Investigated is a kind word.

What had my father done?

"So their father, Boris Lincoln-Ward," Dad started.

"Billionaire Ponzi scheme guy."

"Exactly. When he got caught, he was quick to argue the

charges until we leveraged him for someone even bigger. He was part of a Ponzi scheme, as you know, but he was also connected to a woman who had thwarted Europol for nearly a decade. She not only swindled rich men out of their money, but the people they worked for, and companies as well. Up until Boris, she had walked away with over ten million dollars. She used different aliases and was hard to track. When we caught Boris, he was already going to go to jail for a long time. Word was that he had hidden billions of his own money away, and not all of it was recovered. But he was willing to work with us on a deal. Less time. He was only going to do fifteen years, instead of the thirty many of the complainants called for. His children's trusts weren't to be touched. In exchange, he gave us the woman."

"Okay," I said, still not seeing why this would have been worse than any other criminal investigation. "So he traded away an associate?"

"Her name was Graciella de Marco," Dad said. "She's basically an international thief. As best we can imagine, but with access to the kind of people and money most of us only dream about. Her mother was a minor heiress of a Greek shipping tycoon who made bad investments, lost all his money. Her family was destitute. Not much was known about her after her family had lost everything. Either way, she wanted to go back to living a bountiful life, thus the criminal escapades. She'd been on the scene for a decade. Finding rich men, not just getting them to fall in love with her and allowing her to live the lavish lifestyle, but to invest in things that she suggested. Invest in her 'friends', invest in businesses she would talk up to them. Businesses that didn't actually exist. Before we caught her, she was able to take off with a lot of money. Most of it American. She was the bureau's white whale for over a decade. So when Boris offered to give her up—well. It was two birds with one stone, in a way. Except . . ."

He trailed off, clearly hesitant to say what he needed to say next.

"Except?" I prompted.

"You have to understand, once I had my teeth in Boris, I wasn't about to let him go. I was tenacious, and it took two years of my life to pin him down and nail him for what he was doing. Men like him are slippery—so slippery—and they rely on charm and camouflage to get by, and it was the same with Graciella. After years of watching the both of them slip through the net time and time again, I had to make sure. I had to make sure that everyone would know their names. I had to make sure not only that they were caught, but that if they got away, the world would still know every terrible, criminal thing they did. So instead of bringing them in quietly, like we'd arranged with Boris, I arranged for something more . . . visible."

"Visible?"

"Graciella wasn't just an associate of Boris's, she was his mistress. He thought he'd have one last liaison with her before he betrayed her to us, and that's when I arrested them. I tipped off the press as well, so that it was as much of a spectacle as I could make it. And it worked—both Boris and Graciella had their sins aired out for the world to see. If they ever get out of prison, there will be no more victims left for them, no more slipping away into the shadows."

"Dad, that's not visible. That's *lurid*."

A heavy noise of agreement. "I hadn't factored in the human cost, I suppose. With Boris's wife being a princess, it attracted for more, um, intense speculation than I could have foreseen. It embarrassed Lennox's mother, the entire royal family, and dragged their good name through the mud.

It must have been quite devastating for the children."

I thought back to that letter I'd found. The one that talked about *Vater*.

None of this still explained who Nicholas was or why Lennox had been writing to him.

But it did explain something else.

"So this is why Lennox hates you," I said in a dull voice. *This is why Lennox hates me because of you.* "Not merely the arrest, but the humiliation you caused doing it."

My father sighed. "I recognize that his children probably see me like a monster. I was the one who encouraged Boris to make the deal because I wanted de Marco too. I arranged the public arrest, and I embarrassed their mother. Embarrassed *them*."

Embarrassed them.

I got it now. I understood why it was more than his dad being a criminal and my dad being a cop.

It was because of my father that their mother was humiliated. That everyone in the world—including an eighth-grade Sloane—knew what their father had done and whom he'd been fucking while he did it.

With my mother gone, and Dad working ninety-nine percent of the time, it was sometimes easier for me to stay for summer sessions at boarding school, but I remembered seeing the coverage even in my school dorm. It had dominated the news media for months. It was sordid.

People had lost their entire life savings. And maybe the investors could be written off as greedy, but what made it worse was that their workers, their staff, all the innocent people around them . . . they'd lost everything too. And to cause that much pain while you were gallivanting around the Med with a gorgeous woman who wasn't your delicate, princess wife . . .

No wonder the media ate it up.

No wonder Lennox was so scarred by it.

Why did you think I was greedy? Because of my father?

"So you had me looking into Lennox because what, you think he's doing the same thing his dad did?"

"No, nothing like that. But there are suspicious deposits and withdrawals in his accounts. And we couldn't touch his trust because the grandparents are the trustees. Their parents, of course, have put money into it, but their trusts were off limits. All we can do is monitor their banking activity. It's always been my theory that Lincoln-Ward wasn't entirely honest. All his money isn't gone. My guess is he's squirreled some away. Once he serves the reduced sentence of fifteen years, he would need something to come back and live on. I theorized that he's found a way to access it and that it's going through his son's trust to launder it. Make it clean money so when he gets out of jail, Lennox can give him the cash. Then he can start over."

My stomach roiled. "Dad, I'm not sure—"

"Look," he interrupted me. "I know he's your classmate, possibly your friend, but it's entirely plausible. I mean, you *know* it's possible. You're too smart not to see that. That's why you agreed to investigate."

Jesus Christ. I *had* agreed to investigate. But I still hadn't given Dad everything. And I didn't know how to walk that back now because Lennox was right. I had believed exactly what my father told me. Without any question. I was just like him.

But worst of all, any hope that I would once again be that fairy princess I was the night of the gala—or be seen as beautiful by anyone—died. That dream turned to ash in my palms.

Because now that I understood . . . now that I knew

why Lennox hated my father, why Lennox was so angry . . . I knew there was no way we could ever be together.

Because beyond anything else, Lennox Lincoln-Ward was proud. Haughty.

An arrest he could have eventually forgiven—but a public disgrace? Deep and visible shame?

He could never forget that, never forgive it. And if he found out that I'd been looking through his things, helping my father ensure his could never, ever reclaim any scrap of wealth or dignity . . .

I shivered with misery.

If he found out . . . it would be all over then.

Chapter Fourteen

Lennox

I RETURNED TO campus the next morning with a hungover Aurora. After I settled her in her room, I made sure she drank enough water and took enough aspirin for her to feel better after a long nap, and then I went back to my room. I'd just toed off my Oxfords when a big fist pounded on my door.

"It's unlocked, you pillock," I yelled as it swung open to reveal the broad shoulders of Keaton Constantine.

"I know you didn't forget about the Hellfire meeting tonight," he said, as I threw myself back on my bed with a groan.

I covered my face with a pillow. "Fuck."

"Yeah," he said in sympathy.

"They want us in dinner dress?"

"You know they do."

I swore again, dropping the pillow to the side and blinking up at my ceiling. I was wrecked from last night. I felt like I was walking through a knee-high marsh, every step exhausting and bitter.

My brain was still whirling, and it refused to give me peace.

"Fine," I mumbled. "I'll get ready."

Keaton made a noise of assent, like he'd had no doubt all along, and then he left to go get ready himself.

✧ ✧ ✧

THE HELLFIRE CLUB was founded in 1871 to do what most clubs back then were meant to do—forge alliances and consolidate power. The first Hellfire Club members at Pembroke were the sons of robber barons and senators, and through the friendships they forged at school, and through the equally connected peers they invited in, they went on to find their own wealth and power too. And so on and so forth, each previous generation of Hellfire members nurturing the next—opening doors, making introductions— until *that* generation could help too. It was a web of green paper and cigar smoke stretching back a century and a half, and it was an invitation that would have been foolish to refuse.

Yes, I was a prince, but my father was also a disgraced, imprisoned billionaire. I didn't have the luxury of rejecting a foothold like this, even if it came tied with incredibly annoying strings. Like the occasional dinner in the city. Like being examined by Hellfire alumni like we were livestock at a meat market.

And while it was undoubtedly annoying, I'd grown up around this kind of secretive, self-important pomp and circumstance. I knew how to play their game better than they did. It had been invented by my forefathers, after all.

The cars came for us at noon, and we ducked dutifully inside—Keaton hustling me into a car with him and Owen before I could get within fifteen feet of Phineas.

Or *fucking* Rhys.

November wind buffeted us in our tuxedos and dress coats before we could escape into the warmth of the car. I welcomed the wintry chill. The cold reminded me that I was still alive, even though I felt like I was dead inside.

What the hell was wrong with me?

You know what's wrong with you.

Sloane. Fucking Sloane.

I flung myself back into the leather seat and closed my eyes before Keaton and Owen could try to talk to me. I was in no mood for chitchat, not after last night. Not after all the ways the night had gone all fucked up.

First, Rhys had had his goddamn hands all over Sloane.

Second of all, she looked like she was into it.

Third of all, she'd looked like something out of an ethereal dream, all that vibrant blue-green gossamer. The bodice of her dress, the deep vee. Her lips stained pink, and plump, and glistening, and so god damn soft. And why for fuck's sake had she tasted so good?

Her eyes, everything about her had been amplified. Enhanced. She looked like a fairy. All of her sparkled. All of her shimmered. All of her shined. And despite her slender frame, that dress had shoved her tits under her chin somehow, giving her enough cleavage to make my stupid mouth water.

And then all I could think about was Rhys putting his hands on her. And I'd snapped.

Way to go, Neanderthal.

I had literally picked her up over my shoulder and dragged her out of there.

Let's not forget the crazy shit in the garden.

Motherfucker. I'd been about to stick my dick inside her. Okay technically *had* stuck my dick inside her . . . just the tip though. That didn't count, did it? I couldn't lie.

That's where we'd been going. We'd been about to shag in the garden. I could still feel her sweet tightness around the tip of my dick.

Just the tip, motherfucker. Like a moron.

I knew better. Hell, I'd never had sex without a condom. *Ever.* I wasn't that dumb. There were a few lessons my mother had imparted quite well on me. Like don't knock anyone up. Don't be an idiot. Do not leave illegitimate children to be accounted for later.

But still, with Sloane, I was ready and more than damn willing to slide home . . . bare. To feel her heat, to have her velvet slickness mold around me and make me her bitch.

I'd been riding on the edge of dangerous arousal. But then Aurora had come in. Drunk and sobbing and distraught. How in the world had I been able to pull back?

You were a saint, that's what it is.

But then everything had changed, and I had fucking relearned who Sloane really was. My destruction . . . wrapped in a tight-arsed package that was difficult to ignore. She was so casual about it all when her father had *ruined* my family's life.

I'm some sort of revenge plan?

She'd been angry, furious, pushing and shoving me until somehow we ended up on those soft cushions with me between her legs.

I'd have to hurt you for a thousand years to make up for all the things you've done to me, she'd hissed—but what about me? What about all the things her family had done to me?

How can you even want her?

Well, that was a problem with my cock. Motherfucker didn't listen. It was all his fault.

Even as I tried to nap my way down to Manhattan, the damn thing twitched in my pants. He was thinking about how soft she was. How damn near perfect she felt. My brain conjured up that feeling of her slick wet heat and sent a buzz up my spine that nearly snapped my head clean off. Right from the base of my spine straight to the top of my neck. It was such a jolt that I thought I was going to die. And die in heaven, no less.

But then that high had all come crashing down.

Goddamn Sloane.

The drive ended up being uneventful and boring. Owen tapped through emails on his iPad—his family ran Montgomery Media, a group focused mostly on magazines and apps, and his parents treated him like a baby COO—and Keaton watched rugby footage on his phone with a scowl on his all-American face. I was grateful for the silence though, because I couldn't handle all the feelings vibrating up my spine, and I was terrified that if I opened my mouth to make polite conversation, something ugly and vulnerable would come tumbling out.

Like my fury at Rhys. My extra fury at Phin for making Aurora cry.

My fury at Sloane.

My hunger for Sloane.

The strange dagger of pain between my ribs whenever I thought of the look Sloane gave me last night before she left. As if *I'd* been the arsehole.

Had I been?

My mind circled back to Phin and how much I'd like to smash his teeth in for hurting my twin. Yes, that was a safe anger, a safe feeling. Much safer than thinking about Sloane.

I let the anger fill me all through the drive there, pooling in my gut like oil ready to burn. I'd find Phin at the dinner and then throw him out the window, right onto Fifth goddamn Avenue.

"Thank fuck," Keaton groaned, stretching his giant body as the car rolled to a stop in front of a narrow but ornately trimmed mansion squashed between two equally ornate apartment buildings. Gas lamps flickered on sconces outside the wide, old door, and the huge windows glowed with the kind of light that only came from rooms paneled in wood and upholstered in leather and velvet. A stone lion guarded either side of the stairs leading up to the black-lacquered door, their claws anchored in flames and their mouths parted in toothy snarls.

It looked every inch a nineteenth century industrialist's house, opulence built on the backs of the poor, and for over one hundred years, it had been a den of old money and even older sins.

Hellfire House.

Keaton got out first, and Owen followed, not looking up from his iPad as he did. Owen had grown up among the moneyed bustle of Manhattan, and so he was as unimpressed by Gilded Age mansions as I was by castles back home.

Keaton himself only gave the building a brief, appraising glance. I knew he was only a member because it was expected of him and not because he wanted to follow in his brother Winston's footsteps and become a captain of industry or whatever it was Winston Constantine did with his time. In fact, I'd bet my family's private Austrian ski chalet that the moment Keaton graduated from Pembroke, he'd be gone from this world altogether. Off playing rugby and fucking his girlfriend. Not clinking port glasses and comparing big game hunting trips.

We were greeted at the door by staff who took our coats and escorted us to the drawing room, where a large fire crackled in a stone fireplace and servers circulated with aperitifs. A few older Hellfire alumni were in here, but most were still cloistered somewhere else, probably attempting to seal a few more corrupt deals before dinner officially began.

Keaton turned to face me as we were walking inside. "Don't do anything stupid tonight. Even my Constantine hands might be tied if you attack a Yates."

"I'll do whatever the fuck I want," I muttered.

"Whatever happened with Aurora last summer broke him, man."

"So that gives him the right to make her cry?" I demanded, but I didn't waste any more breath on Keaton, because we were in the room now and I could see *him*.

Phin.

Fucking Phin, just sitting by the fireplace with a lazy smile and his hair all over the place. Drink in fucking hand, like he didn't have a care in the world aside from drinking and finding his next lay.

"You fucking wanker," I seethed, striding over to him and yanking him to his feet by the lapels of his tuxedo jacket. I was aware of the interested stares of the other men in the room, and just as aware when they went back to their conversations, as if used to pre-dinner drinks erupting into violence. "I should kill you right now for what you did to my sister."

Phin's smile faded, but he didn't shove me off him, he didn't try to wrestle free. He only glared at me over the collar of his jacket. "You know, no one ever asks what Aurora did to *me*," he said. "And I'll have you know that last night, she was the one to stop things between us. *She* was the one to walk away, not me. Yes, I found someone else after, but only because she made it clear she was done with me."

"I don't believe you," I said.

"Well, believe this—do you really think Aurora would have let me live if I'd promised her something and then

331

ended up inside someone else?"

I loosened my grip.

"She walked away first," Phin continued. "If she hadn't, she would have shoved me into a meat grinder, and you know it."

I let go of his tuxedo. He was right. Aurora had been devastated last night, but if Phineas had *truly* screwed her over, she would have killed him first. *Then* cried about it.

"And it's not my fault I had to take care of the blue balls your sister gave me," Phin muttered, and I grabbed his lapels again.

"If you talk about my sister one more time, I will throw you into this fire and not think twice. I fucking mean it."

"Boys," Owen said in a bored, cold tone, coming up to us and leaning against the side of the fireplace. "Can we not with the murdering before dinner? I haven't eaten yet, and bailing one of you out of jail is certain to put me off my appetite."

I let go. Reluctantly.

Rhys sauntered over to our little scene, clapping slowly. As if Phin and I had just put on a show for him.

I leveled a look at him. "You don't want to start with me, Rhys. Not after the shit you pulled this weekend."

"Oh, is that right? It was nice to see you finally get off your ass, by the way."

I blinked at him. "If you know what's good for you, mate, you'll shut it."

Rhys chuckled. "No need to get touchy with me. I did you a goddamn favor."

I scowled at him. "What the hell do you mean?"

"Well, I knew you weren't ever going to fucking do anything about Sloane unless you were pushed. And now I've pushed you. You're welcome."

I glowered at him, taking a step in his direction. But Owen was quick and inserted himself between us. "Not worth it. Dinner, remember?"

Phineas's chuckle was low, as if he lived to see what was going to go down. He also probably wouldn't mind seeing my face beaten and bloodied after I just threatened to hurl him into the fire. Tosser.

Keaton merely rolled his eyes. "You two have done this already. Let it go."

I glared at our de facto leader. "You hear that bullshit he's spewing?"

"Rhys, you're a dick," Keaton said in the beleaguered tone of a parent with squabbling children. "We love you, dude, but seriously, stop being a gaping dickhole." Keaton looked at me and threw his hands up to say, "Satisfied now?"

No, I was not goddamn satisfied.

Rhys shrugged. "She's no longer of interest to me anyway."

Say what? He'd put me through the wringer and now he was bored? "What the fuck do you mean? You did all of this just to tick me off?"

Rhys gave me a level stare, and a chill ran through my body because it was as if, for once, the shield that he used as a barrier to ever having to feel any emotion came down for just one moment, and his eyes were clear. "You wanted her. You acted like you didn't, but you did. It was apparent to everyone here. And hopefully, it's apparent to you now. You were never going to take any step besides just torturing her, which I'm a fan of. But it was boring. I wanted to see if I could make you do something. And you did. Congratulations."

I swiped Owen's hand off my chest. "Relax, I'm not going to hit him."

Owen's smirk was cold. "So you say. But your emotions are running rampant. Lock them down. We're Hellfire. We're all mates here."

I growled at him. "Some mate."

Rhys grinned at me. "You know, I can always go and kiss her again."

I started toward him, and this time Keaton stepped in front of me then shook his head. "That's enough."

"Fine." But then, I dug deep for the one thing I knew would rattle Rhys. "You know what? It's not really going to work out with Sloane. Irreconcilable differences. Instead of her, you know who is well fit for me? Serafina. I danced with her last night. I'm pretty sure you saw."

Just like that, the walls went right back up around Rhys, and he lifted a brow. He didn't say anything, so I pushed further. "God, that arse. You haven't lived until you've palmed that perfect piece of an arse. She's so slender but has curves just where they matter. A simple squeeze could take you to heaven." I gave Rhys an evil grin, and I could see his lip curl as he scowled at me.

"Stay the fuck away from Serafina."

I laughed then. "Why should I? She is very interested in me."

Rhys started towards me, but Keaton stood in front of him. Thanks to rugby, Keaton was massive. Even Rhys didn't want that kind of fight. "I warned you because we're friends. You put your hands on Serafina, I will end you."

Keaton rolled his eyes. "You two are ridiculous. Rhys, you might be the worst."

"The thing with Serafina and me, it's private."

Keaton shrugged. "Yeah, well, you're both dicks." He turned to me. "Better figure out your shit with Sloane."

I rolled my shoulders. "Like I said, irreconcilable differences."

Rhys threw up his hands. "Jesus Christ, for a fucking smart guy, you're an idiot. Whatever issues you've got with her, she's under your skin. There's no way you're letting her go."

Owen clapped me on my shoulder. "He has a point. You've been obsessed with Sloane since she got here. I don't understand it. Is she worth this messy shit? Is any girl? Whatever irreconcilable difference this is, maybe you should find a way to reconcile that because we have all seen it. You literally carried her out of there over your shoulder. I hate to agree with him, but Rhys is right."

Rhys settled into a chair and leaned back into it. "I'm always right. Just none of you are smart enough to agree with me."

I watched my friends. They had a point. Sloane was like a promise, a pact, a vow, signed with our blood. She was mine to torment. Or maybe I had it wrong. She was my tormentor. I couldn't shake my feelings for her off no matter how hard I tried. And I needed to figure out just what I was going to do about it. My dick chimed in with a, 'Oh, she's mine. If you can't get her for me, I'll be taking the reins.'

Sloane was in my blood. There was no purging her from my system. I hated that Rhys was right. He was just so goddamn smug about it all. I had nearly kicked him in the arse. Sloane is the key, though, to sorting myself out.

But would we even be able to get past everything? Was that even a possibility for us?

The real question is, can you get over what her father did to yours?

The question dogged me through dinner and through the interminable drinks after. Ostensibly tonight's meeting was so we could discuss nominations—each year's outgoing seniors nominated freshmen to replace them in the club—but it was a farce, and we all knew it. The incoming Hellfire members had already been decided years ago. Probably at fucking birth.

If you had a house in Bishop's Landing or an uncle or a godfather who'd been in the club, then you were in. Letting the current members pretend to choose was the most token of gestures.

So I tuned out the nomination talk, and the inevitable turn of the conversation toward the initiation ceremony that would happen at the end of the year, and I thought of Sloane. Of her hateful father, of the dark months that followed my father's arrest when paps crowded outside our house trying to catch glimpses of Boris's betrayed wife.

When even after our retreat to Liechtenstein, the internet teemed with the worst kind of rumors and gossip, and my mother used to cry alone in the dark of the library, hoping no one would notice.

But inevitably my traitorous mind drifted back to Sloane herself. To her full mouth and perceptive, green gaze. To the watchful, careful way she held herself, like a knife waiting patiently inside its sheath.

To the way her mouth parted in something almost like wonder when she came.

To the way she *smiled* when she came.

For the first time in four years, I had no idea what I wanted. And it terrified the shit out of me.

Chapter Fifteen
Sloane

SERAFINA FOUND ME curled up in a ball on my bed when she came in from brushing her teeth. She'd slept in until the November day was bright and silver outside our window, but I'd barely slept at all, kicking off my blankets and tossing all over and generally just being miserable. And now it was nighttime again and I'd done nothing with my day except brood and sulk like a goddamned girl. I mean, I *was* a goddamned girl, but still. I hated it.

I couldn't stop seeing Lennox's face in the scullery shadows from the night before.

Why did you think I was selfish? Greedy?

Get the fuck off me.

"Oh my god, do your feet hurt as much as mine do? I don't care how pretty those Jimmy Choo's were, they were *not* worth it. Also, I was talking to Nika Monroe from Croft Wells, I guess some girl got attacked at a party two nights ago, but she managed to fight the guy off. Scary as hell, right? Can you imagine if something like that happened here—" She cut herself off as her gaze slid over me.

"Hey." She approached the bed and eased herself onto it, tucking her feet under her body and settling in next to me. "What's the matter?"

"I don't know," I whispered.

She laughed. "Um, I highly doubt that you don't know what's going on."

"Well, as it turns out it's not really going to work with Lennox."

Concern etched itself onto her face. "What are you talking about? The way he picked you up and tossed you over his shoulder, god that was so hot. Tell me why it's not going to work. That's ridiculous."

I shook my head. "It's just not."

Sera rolled her eyes. "Whoever this is, are you done whining yet? Bring Sloane back. My badass friend who thinks anything can be done with a switch blade and some hot glue."

I did love my switch blade, and hot glue could fix anything but—not this.

"I'm not in the mood, Sera."

She frowned and patted my knee. "What in the world is going on?"

"I realized that everything I'm doing is futile."

Sera grabbed hold of my knee and rubbed. "All right, spill it. Tell me everything. And if we're going to go kill someone, at least let me change into something chic but comfy. I don't want to get blood on my favorite bathrobe."

I laughed and then broke into a sob.

Her eyes went wide. "Hey, now you're really freaking me out. What's going on?"

God it was so weak, but I couldn't help the sob. "It's just never going to happen. And I just, I don't know why, but it hurts. It was so much better when I didn't let myself feel anything."

"Lennox is an idiot, Sloane. He's clearly all about you.

He was willing to fight Rhys to have you. And let's be clear, he's the lucky one."

"Well, doesn't matter," I said around a sniffle. "He doesn't see it that way now."

She blinked slowly once, then twice. "I'm going to kill him."

"It's not even his fault. He has a right to be mad, sort of. Okay, so after he picked me up like the stupid caveman that he is, everything was going great. We were in the maze, he was kissing me, and it was amazing, and I've never felt like it before. Just beautiful and sexy, and just . . . hell, it was . . . incredible."

Sera was quiet, and she just kept patting my knee as we talked. So, I walked her through everything. How much I wanted him. How much I'd been willing to give him. And how close I had come to giving it to him. Then Aurora, and then his subsequent blow up, which ended with the conversation with my father. The revelation of what he'd really done to the Lincoln-Wards all those years ago.

When I was done, Sera stared at me. "Jesus Christ. When you go big, you go *big*. Also, let's call my concierge doctor and get you on the pill. I don't care how hot all that 'I want to fuck you bare' shit is. There's no need to be careless." She paused. "It is really hot though."

"I don't even know what I was thinking," I mumbled. "It just felt so good, and I could smell him, and he smelled like metal and flowers, and I couldn't even breathe for how much I wanted him to do it. You know?"

"I'm not sure I do," Sera said softly, but there was a line between her brows as she looked away from me to the floor. As if she was thinking about someone else, someone who wasn't here right now.

I had an idea of who it might be. "And let's be clear, so

that there's no confusion with us," I added. "You and I both know Rhys was only kissing me to make you jealous."

Sera shuddered, looking back to me with a face that was all pretty haughtiness once again. "First of all, we're not talking about Rhys. Second of all, *hardly*. Third of all, the only Hellfire Club idiot I care about right now is Lennox and what he's done to you."

"But you see, it's not even his fault. I'm not only revenge, Sera, I'm *deserved* revenge. He's right to want that revenge, he's utterly right to hate my family for what we've done to his. If I were in his shoes, I might have already killed him by now."

Sera lifted a brow. "You are kind of prone to murder though."

No lies detected.

"Right? I wouldn't ask any questions, so how can I expect him to ask questions? How could I expect him to give me the benefit of the doubt?"

She nodded sagely. "Well, honey, the thing is, do you like him?"

I wiped my nose with the back of my hand, only mildly grossed out when snot came back and met me. "I didn't think I did. But then he was kissing me and it just—god, it felt good. And much different than when Rhys kissed me."

"What did you feel when Rhys kissed you?"

I shrugged. "I don't know. Like, it was nice. Even fun, I guess. But I don't know. When Lennox kisses me, it's like I've been lit on fire on the inside, you know?"

Sera grinned at me. "You like him. That's good. I'm surprised I have to be the one to tell you this, but direct is always better. No dancing around. You've done that enough. Has it worked for you?"

I frowned at that.

"Yeah, so maybe you don't do that anymore. Maybe you should open up with him. If this was me, you would be telling me to just deal with it. No pussy-footing around, not be afraid of it, just deal."

I leveled my gaze on her. "So is this the time we talk about Rhys or not?"

Serafina wrinkled her nose and then pursed her lips as if she'd smelled something gross.

"I told you, we are *not* talking about him. Besides, could you imagine addressing anything with him head on? He's impossible to talk to. Ever tried having a conversation with a flat-out dick?"

I nodded sagely. "I still have a point." Because while Rhys deigned to toy with me, I had known I was only a mere substitute for Sera. The two of them had been in the same boarding schools since the lower grades. I couldn't explain it, but they had this *thing*. "Fine, I appreciate your advice, but Lennox is not going to listen to me."

"Maybe he will. You won't know unless you try. And my friend Sloane isn't a coward. My friend Sloane deals with things no matter what may come."

I gave her a weak smile. "Thank you."

"Anytime. You are my rock. If I see you distressed over a guy, then I know you must really like him. Even if you can't get through to him, that's okay. Because you're awesome. And if he isn't going to see that, that's his loss. You're beautiful, and there's a sweet core in there. I don't know where it is, but it's in there."

I coughed a laugh. "Don't tell anyone."

"*Moi*? Never."

She pushed to her feet then. "Now, can you help me get the rest of this double-stick tape off from last night? The left side wouldn't come off in the shower, and now I'm regretting all my fashion choices."

I grinned up at her. "But you looked awesome though."

"Thank you very much. Beauty before comfort, I always say."

She turned away from me, sliding her robe off to her waist. I started picking at the edge of the tape on her ribs, tutting at her whenever she flinched or fussed.

"Why don't you maybe go knock on Lennox's door?" she suggested as I got hold of the tape and peeled. "Aurora said they had one of their stupid Hellfire meetings in the city today, but I bet they're back by now."

I frowned. "Then I don't want to bother—"

Sera lifted a brow and pursed her lip, making me feel like I was a six-year-old who just spilled nail polish over her fancy dress. "Are you really going to make excuses?"

Was I?

Was I going to spend the rest of my life like I did today, tossing in bed and replaying every moment I spent with Lennox?

No. No fucking way.

And maybe this is the time to fix what you've done.

I thought of the letter in my safe right now, throbbing at the edge of my consciousness like Poe's telltale heart.

I sighed. "Actually, good point. Here." I'd gotten the tape to the edge of her breast, where she could reach it to pull off the rest. I definitely didn't want to be around when she had to pull it off certain sensitive parts of her skin; I wasn't sure my ears could handle the storm she was sure to swear up.

I grabbed my hoodie, and while she wandered into the en suite to see to the nipple-tape situation, I quietly opened my safe and pulled out the letter, tucking it into my hoodie pocket.

"Have fun," Sera said, poking her head out from the bathroom. "Don't do anything I wouldn't do. I mean, there's not much I wouldn't do, so that gives you a lot to do."

I snorted a laugh. "I'm not going to do anything."

"If you say so."

I pushed out of the room and moved down the hall towards the common balcony. The way the upstairs dorms were set up was that at the end of each hall, there were staircases leading down and up. There was a door to a balcony that was common for both sides. Boys and girls. But to get from one side of the hall to the other, you had to go downstairs and then go up the other stairs on the other side. And the doors at the top of the stairs were closed as it was past 10 p.m., and you had to have the keypad code to enter.

This was to keep the boys and girls on opposite sides. It was changed daily and communicated to the dorm mother and father. But of course, I had my own code. It was called *Sloane can climb buildings like Jason Bourne.*

Next to the door to the balcony, there was a window. As I opened it, I quietly glanced around for anybody coming along, then eased myself out onto the sill which was only six inches wide. Luckily, the lip on the boys' side ran all the way around like a ledge coming up the sides of the building. It wasn't uncommon to see the boys sitting in their open windows, straddling their windowsills on the lip that went around. I eased along it as quickly as I dared. I knew the hedges below would catch my fall if I did misstep. But it would still be unpleasant. And I'd likely get several thorns up my ass.

When I reached Lennox's room, I peered inside before opening the window. The room was dark and quiet—maybe he hadn't come back from the city yet. Disappointment mingled with relief: it was better that he wasn't here, surely, so that I could put the letter back.

But I wanted to see him again. Even after our fight, even knowing how he'd look at me, how he hated me for what my father had done . . .

I wanted to see him.

Stuffing the feeling down, I used my student ID to lift the window hook from its eye, and I eased into his room. I was certain he would have his security team with him in the city, but I was less certain that there wouldn't still be someone here in the dorm. And while they didn't have any cameras in his room—no one needed to see how often the prince jerked off, after all—they could still be patrolling the corridors. I kept myself quiet as I lowered myself to the floor.

The letter I'd stolen from him burned a hole in my pocket.

You're just going to put it back and then you're going to leave.

But when I tiptoed back over to his laptop and pulled the letter out of my pocket, a deep rumbly voice said from behind me. "What the fuck are you doing here?"

Alarm and lust blurred together, but at least my brain was one step ahead. I jammed the letter under the stack of papers before I whipped around. "Um, hi."

Lennox sat up groggily, clearly in the middle of a nap. He was shirtless. The silvery light coming through the window cast shadows of the ripples of muscles along his chest and his belly. Obviously, he was ripped. Hell, the night I caught him stroking himself, he had been shirtless. But I'd been far too preoccupied with what his hand had been doing.

"Um, sorry. I—I should . . ." I tried to think of a good

explanation as to why I was there that didn't involve me obsessing about him all day *or* the pilfered letter. "I don't have your number, and I wanted to talk to you. And I'm sorry. I shouldn't have snuck in here. It's sort of a bad habit."

His brows popped. "You call sneaking into a guy's room a bad habit?"

His voice was still sleepy, but amused too. Like last night hadn't even happened.

I rolled my shoulders. "I'm sorry. I'll go."

"Wait."

I turned to him as I got to the window. "No, it's fine. I'll just go back to where I came from."

"Jesus Christ, Sloane. Stop. Where are you going?"

"I'm sorry. I just—I felt bad about what happened in the scullery, and I wanted to apologize. I didn't think you'd be asleep already."

"I'm not anymore. I had a strange dream."

I swallowed hard. "Oh, okay. Right. You had a dream. So, anyway, I'll be going."

His chuckle was slow, and the sound made my belly weak. I wanted to run but forced myself to be brave. "Um, sorry about last night. About the greedy thing. I didn't mean any of it."

He sighed. Then he frowned. "I think part of me knows you didn't mean it. I don't know why I was such a dick about it. I'm sorry."

My brows lifted. "You're apologizing to me?"

He nodded slowly. "Yeah, I think . . ." He scrubbed his fingertips through his sleep-tousled hair. "Everything about you, everything about how you make me feel, has been so tangled up and twisted inside me, and it fucks me up, Sloane. It fucks me right up. And then I was feeling a little vulnerable considering what we'd gotten up to in the garden."

I blinked at him. Did he just say he was vulnerable?

He tilted his head at me. "I wish I knew what you were thinking right now," he murmured. "Sometimes I feel so fucking transparent around you, and you're . . ."

"Not transparent at all?" I suggested, and he smiled a little.

"Right."

It was the way I'd been made—the way I'd thought I wanted to be. But right now it felt awful; it felt like there were walls between us that could never be torn down, that couldn't even be tunneled through. I could viscerally feel the presence of the letter I'd just hidden, viscerally *feel* my deception thrumming in the room.

Maybe it was a good thing I wasn't so transparent after all.

"I should go, Lennox."

"Do you have to get back?" he asked. "Or could you stay so we could talk?"

"You're not going to have, like, security burst in here and arrest me, are you?"

A smile—sharp and charming—tilted at his mouth. "They know when to leave me alone. They did when we were in the maze, didn't they? Now stay. Stay with me."

I meant to say no—but somehow I found myself nodding and heading for the chair at his desk. Maybe I could hide my feelings from him, but I couldn't from myself.

I wanted to stay. I wanted to stay with my beautiful bully for hours and hours and hours.

Lennox chuckled low before snatching his sheets back. I could not help but stare as he pushed to his full height. My gaze lingered at every single fine muscle in front of me. He was built lean. Like a swimmer. Nice broad shoulders, tapered waist into boxer briefs. And wow, that looked like one hell of an erection.

Not that you care, because you don't care about erections. You care about . . . what the hell do you care about again?

I couldn't remember. My synapses were fried by looking at him. He walked over and took my hand. Something burned in his golden eyes—a desperate hunger that matched the one burning inside me right now.

"Come on," he whispered. "We don't have to do anything. I could just hold you."

I parted my lips to tell him that even holding me was a bad idea, but he pre-empted me.

"Just for a minute," he said in a husky voice. "Let me feel you against me for just a minute."

Lust shook me hard. "Just for a minute?"

"Or longer, if you like," he said roughly. "Unless I scared you in the maze last night."

Scared? More like infected me with a miserable desire nothing could ever shake.

I shook my head. "No. I liked it. It felt good, and I felt wanted, and . . . I felt pretty."

He raised a hand to my face and tucked my hair behind my ears, a gesture both gentle and possessive at the same time. "Don't you know that you're always pretty?"

I tucked my head down. "No, I know what I look like. I'm not like—"

"Do you? I don't think you do. Or at least you don't see clearly."

"But—"

He inclined his head towards the bed. "Come on, Sloane. I'm cold and I know you are too."

He eased into the bed and backed all the way up into

the wall, making plenty of room for me to climb in. Most of the beds in the dorms were twins, but his was a full one, because of course it was, because he was a fucking prince and he got whatever he wanted.

And he wanted me right now.

Need was lacing the blood in my veins, and my chest was a mess of tight, swirling feelings. It made me want to run away, how he made me feel, and protect my heart before he could hurt it. But I was also no chicken shit. I swallowed hard and then climbed in next to him.

I rolled onto my back, and he propped himself up on his elbow and watched me. "So, sneaking into a guy's room is a habit?"

"Only when duty calls."

"Ah. You mean your little detective inspector business."

"It's not a business," I corrected, looking up into his painfully pretty face. "I help people who need it. That's it."

"As long as you're not crawling into anybody's bed but mine," he said, and there was a rough edge to his voice. *Jealousy.*

"Would you care if I did?"

"You know I would."

We looked at each other for a long moment, neither of us speaking, neither of us even breathing. It felt like we were poised on the knife's edge of something.

"What were you really doing in here?" he asked quietly.

I hesitated and then spoke the truth. Or part of it at least. "I wanted to see you. After last night . . . I wanted to apologize. It wasn't my intention to hurt you, and I know with what happened between our fathers that you might think . . ." I trailed off. I wasn't sure what I could say next that wouldn't make everything worse.

He closed his eyes. When he opened them again, the

gold irises burned with too many emotions to name. "I don't want to talk about it," he said, the words curt.

I winced, but I nodded. I understood.

"Can I ask you something?"

"Yes."

"Do you really like Rhys?"

I laughed at the unexpected conversation. "No. I mean, sure he's good-looking and all that, but it just didn't feel—I don't know, real? I figured he was running some kind of weird Rhys experiment."

"But you let him kiss you."

"Yeah. I mean, it's not like I have a mile-long line of guys begging to try and go out with me. It was flattering. And once I realized it kind of annoyed you, I wanted to do it again."

His jaw unhinged. "What? Sloane. You played me."

I shrugged. "Well, I didn't really play you. I like seeing you being a little jealous."

He nodded. "Noted."

As we laid there on his bed, we talked . . . really talked, I wondered why I instinctively avoided him for so long.

But one touch of his fingers on my cheek, to my shoulders and my elbow, and my head swam. It was intoxicating. And I wanted more.

"Hey, Sloane?"

"Yes, Lennox."

"Can I kiss you?"

I knew it was dangerous because we were in his room, and there was no way Aurora was going to come bursting in this time. No way she could accidentally save me from giving this boy more of my heart like she did last night.

But still, I nodded. "Yes."

CHAPTER SIXTEEN

Lennox

I THOUGHT I was dreaming at first. I full-on thought I'd woken up and my dream had manifested into reality. But no, she was here. In my bed. And she was talking to me. Considering what I'd said to her earlier, I didn't expect that. But here she was, still willing to talk to me after I'd been a jackarse.

I can fix that.

I leaned forward. I just wanted to be close to her. In no way did I mean for the kiss to go further than that.

But she made this soft exhale as I kissed her. Just a gentle brush of the lips, and then my brain somehow lost the battle with my dick, so I couldn't exactly focus.

Instead of lying there stiffly with her hands clasped over her belly, her hands loosened. One rose up to my face, just as I cradled hers in my hands. And then I gently licked across the seam of her lips, and she gasped, letting me in.

I sort of lost rational thought after that. She smelled like honeysuckle and something a little minty fresh. I'd meant for it to just be a kiss. I'd meant it to be soft—a sort of apology.

Instead, she gasped, and made this soft little whimpering

sound at the back of her throat and well, I got a little carried away.

It wasn't my fault. She was just so damn soft.

Her skin was like satin. And everything about her was a mystery.

If I was being honest, Sloane wasn't the first girl who'd ever crawled into my bed. But she was the only one I'd ever wanted to. She thought she wasn't beautiful, but that was so not true. To me, she was stunning. Those eyes, her mouth, even the secrets of her body. Ninety-nine point nine percent of the time, she dressed like wearing a skirt was something she had to be forced into doing, but it didn't matter what she wore, because everything on her looked like it was made to be worn by her. Like it was made to show off her sharp edges and subtle curves.

Another moan from Sloane, and my ricocheting thoughts refocused on her.

Before I knew what was happening, Sloane molded her body to mine. And her tongue met me stroke for stroke. It was her who deepened the kiss. And it was me who lost control. I couldn't help but fall. Fall so deep into the abyss that I never wanted to come back out again. My skin buzzed as my dick got hard. All I could think of was her. How she felt. How she smelled. Her strong voice when she spoke. The secret smile when I caught one. Those vibrant green eyes of hers, as they always regarded me with stark honesty. God, I could fall for her.

You already have, you prat. Welcome to the party.

When Sloane molded her body against mine, I knew the right thing was to stop this. Nothing was sorted between us. I was still reasonably certain that I could never forgive what her father had done to my family, and I was still reasonably certain that she could never forgive me for what I'd done to *her.*

But somehow that didn't affect my craving to make her mine. It didn't temper at all the hot, tormenting need I had for her.

I didn't mean to roll on top of her. It wasn't planned exactly. But then, when my hips were nestled between her thighs, and she'd widened her stance, making room for me, I groaned. The head of my dick peeked out of the top of my boxers, and Jesus Christ, I rocked my hips against her. Ever so slightly. Her hips lifted to meet mine, and I swallowed the moan on her tongue.

The tingling in my balls was like a loud clanging bell, jolting me awake, making me want to do the things I had sworn not to do only a few hours ago. At least, in here, I had condoms in my nightstand. But fuck, I already felt woozy. I knew exactly what she felt like around the head of my dick. I knew that she'd be soft, and hot, and satin. And God, she was so wet.

I rolled my hips again, and Sloane met me with each one. Sliding my hands up over her hips, I bracketed her narrow ribs and then slid my hands farther up. The gentle curve of her breasts fit my whole hand, and I stopped breathing. "Jesus Christ, Sloane."

"Lennox."

Her voice was husky, warm. Aroused. I wanted to keep her in this space forever. When my thumb rolled over her nipple, she groaned and her hips swiveled. Then it was my turn to groan. Fuck, I was hard. All I wanted to do was shove my fucking boxers down, pull down the ridiculous pajama pants that she had on and take us back to where we were the night before in the maze.

She wriggled out of them for me, and then her hoodie, so it was just her in boy shorts and a tank top with no bra. I could viscerally recall how it felt to have the tip of my dick coated in her juices; I wanted to be back there. The slide of my dick against her clit had me groaning, even with the fabric of our underthings between us.

Fuck, if I kept this up, I was going to come inside my boxers. Or worse, all over her . . . again. And she wasn't some hook up. This was not some random situation. This was Sloane. She'd been under my skin from the moment she showed up at the school. And I was tired of staying away from her. But if I wanted to keep her, I needed to take it slow.

"Oh my god, Lennox."

With a growl, I rolled to the side, bringing her with me, pressing our lips together again.

She pulled back and tore her lips from mine. "Is something wrong?"

I kissed her gently again. "No. Nothing is wrong." I stroked my other thumb over her cheek, even as my palm gave her breast a squeeze. "I want you more than I've ever wanted anything, but I'm trying to take it slow."

She frowned at that. "Did I ask you to take it slow?"

I chuckled. "No, you did not. But for once in my life, I'm trying not to be a dick."

She lifted a brow then. "Wow, this is a hell of a time to start that."

I chuckled softly. "I know, right? Look at me, great in conscience and feelings, and all kinds of shit." I kissed her again. Long, and slow, and deep. With a whimper, she rocked her hips against my thigh, and I understood. She was keyed up too. She needed this just as much as I did.

With my thumb teasing over her nipple, she arched into my body. My other hand slid from her face, down the soft skin of her slender arms, over her hip. And then at the hem of her boy shorts, I paused. I made sure that she met my gaze. "Can I touch you?"

With short breathy pants, she nodded. "Yes."

"If there's something you don't like, tell me, okay?"

She nodded vehemently, and then I let my fingers dip under the elastic of her boy shorts. Her hips were slender. I could easily trace the V-line of her hipbone. She parted her legs for me, and my fingers slid over her bare lips before finding her wet core. I bit back the string of curses as I paused.

Sloane wriggled her hips and stared at me with wide eyes. "W-why are you stopping?"

I swallowed hard. *Holy fuck.*

I squeezed my eyes shut. She felt incredible. "I'm stopping because you feel really good."

I slid my fingers gently in and out and then back up to her lips to tease her clit.

She continued to bite her lip, and I wanted that pleasure, so I leaned forward and nipped her. "You're so soft. I could do this all day."

I slid one finger inside her, and then a second. I cupped my hand just a little bit so the heel of my palm would rub her clit. And then, I slid in and out, and in and out, my other hand still covering her breast, teasing her nipple, kissing her softly. She kept arching into me, wanting more. Begging for more from me.

My body was screaming. My dick was so hard it might explode. I honestly thought it would. Was that possible? I certainly didn't want to find out, but if I wanted her, I had to show that I could be more than just that guy that used to torture her. Her hand clutched my shoulder. "Lennox, oh my god, I—"

I knew what was happening. I used my thumb, slid it

through her wetness, and then rubbed at her clit ever so gently as I dipped inside her, back and forth, back and forth. Then on a low moan I planted my lips on her, drinking in the sounds of her coming apart over my fingers. Convulse and tighten. Convulse and tighten.

Her hips undulated against my fingers, and her walls squeezed me tight.

Jesus Christ, Sloane Lauder's coming was a hell of a thing to watch. And I wanted to spend my life watching it again and again.

I eased my fingers from her and pulled her even closer to me. "You are so beautiful."

Her face went pink again, and she ducked her head as if she was going to deny it, but she said nothing. After a long moment, her frown returned.

"But what about you?"

"I will take care of me later. This is about you. And I want you to stay here for a little bit, if you want."

"I can't sleep here. Hellfire boys might be immune to dorm checks, but I'm not."

"I know. But can I just hold you for a minute?"

She nodded. And as I wrapped my arms around her, I knew that for as long as she was in my arms, I'd sleep well.

CHAPTER SEVENTEEN

Sloane

THE THING ABOUT good intentions is they never quite go how you planned.

I'd meant to leave Lennox's room.

The problem was, once he wrapped himself around me and held me tight, and tucked me into his shoulder, I had fallen asleep. Like the dead. And then at some point in the middle of the night, I'd woken up to the hard erection poking me in the ass.

And there had been snuggling and nuzzling and more kissing, and more fingers. His mouth sucking at my nipples, and I'd come again. And that was some time around four. I had wanted to touch him. I had wanted to explore and play, but he wouldn't let me.

In the dark, he'd whispered to me how beautiful he thought I was, how badly he wanted me. He'd whispered apologies for being such a dick, which I was entirely here for. He'd apologized with his kisses and his soft touches. And we'd fallen asleep . . . again.

So when the sun streaked in at six, I knew it was too late. There was no way to easily sneak out. When I jerked up in bed, he stirred, trying to drag me back to bed. His hand was already poised to slide back between my legs to its new home. "Lennox, we can't. I have to go."

He frowned and whispered groggily. "We have time, don't we?"

I lifted my head and stared at the clock. "It's 6:05."

He snapped to attention then, whipping around to glower at the clock. "Fuck. I didn't mean for you to stay all night."

"I know."

In a flurry of arms and muscles and a very sexy expanse of bare male chest, he helped me find, then put on my discarded clothes. When he grabbed my hoodie off the floor, helping me into it, he frowned. "Do we try and sneak you out the door?"

I shook my head. "The prefects do the checks at six-thirty. There might be some walking around already."

He cursed and glanced at the window. "There's no way I'm letting you go back out there."

"I have to. I can't go out the door."

"Well, what if you stay in here till seven?"

"What, and casually walk out? Everyone will know I spent the night in here."

He lifted a brow. "Does that matter?"

I tilted my chin up and met his gaze so he could see that I meant what I was saying. "No, not at all. I just don't want you to get in trouble. My record is clean, not a single mark. Yours however . . ." I let my voice trail off. He was a senior and a Hellfire Club member, so likely it wouldn't be too bad a punishment. But he'd had more than a few disciplinary marks. Mostly for drinking and insubordination towards prefects and teachers. A mark like this could get him suspended. Or worse, go on his transcripts for colleges.

He nodded slowly. "Well, I can't let you climb out the

window."

"We have no choice, Lennox. It's how I came in yesterday. It's safe."

His brow only furrowed deeper. "It's dangerous."

What was wrong with him? "How do you think I got in here yesterday?"

"Sloane," he pleaded.

"Lennox." I mimicked him.

"Why are you so damn stubborn?"

"Why are *you* so stubborn?" This was the only way, and he knew it, so why was he fighting me?

"Christ, you could fall."

"Trust me, this is far less dangerous than when I've done it before. At least I can see my feet on the ledge this time."

He massaged the bridge of his nose. "Please don't tell me that."

I frowned. Nobody worried about me. No one. Not ever. I wasn't sure how I felt about his worry. "Relax. If anyone sees me out there, they'll just assume it's just me being weird. Or at the very least, me trying to assassinate you. No one will ever think that I'm actually *sneaking* out of your room after spending the night with you. And I'm good at climbing and sneaking. Promise."

He swallowed hard, then licked his lips as his gaze fell to my mouth. "Actually, maybe we should change that."

I lifted my brows. "What? Which part?" Then I zipped my hoodie tight.

He cleared his throat, and a faint blush crept up his neck. "Yeah. Look, obviously we uh, like spending time with each other."

I grinned. "Obviously."

"So, I mean, I don't want to make a big deal or whatever, but shouldn't we just do it the conventional way? The hell I care if anyone knows you spent the night with me? Let the prefects dock me points. Fuck them. Besides, Keaton would fix it if they tried."

I blinked. He wanted this in the open. Where everyone could see.

He didn't know me well enough to know that not wanting to hide me was probably the number one way to my heart. "Okay," I said softly.

The furrow eased then. "Excellent. Meet me at the big tree at one."

I thought a moment. "After history?"

"Yes."

I gave him a slow nod.

A smile opened up his face. His eerie eyes glittered with pleasure. "I'll see you then."

I grinned. "Right. So I'm going to go now."

He nodded slowly. "Yeah, you should do that."

I laughed. "You should let me go, so I can go."

"Right. I'm going to let you go out there. Where it's dangerous, or I could kiss you and keep kissing you until it's 8:30 and all the prefects are already off to class. No one would notice."

He was tempting me. "Except, I have class at eight."

He groaned. "I want to kiss you more."

"I want you to kiss me more too. But I gotta go."

I stood on my tiptoes and tilted my head up. He was so much taller than me. I kissed his chin at first, and then he laughed and tilted his lips down towards mine. It was only when his tongue was in my mouth that I realized I probably had morning breath. Why was his so damn minty?

I pulled away. "Oh my god, my breath."

He laughed. "I might have cheated. I have one of those Listerine breath strip things."

"What, and you didn't offer me one?" I turn to the window.

"You could just walk out the door," Lennox said, his voice tight. "If we're going public anyway."

"I'm not risking running into the prefects," I informed him. "It may be all right for you, Mr. Hellfire, but I can't have disciplinary shit on my transcript before I'm accepted to Georgetown. Not to mention, your disciplinaries are so long, this one might actually affect you."

"Dammit, Sloane—"

I was already standing and finding my handholds. I could feel Lennox's gaze as I tiptoed over the ledge all the way to the balcony and hopped down.

Only then did I feel him breathe.

After hopping the ledge to go back to the girls' side, I turned back to him and gave him a saucy smile and then winked. He just rolled his eyes and shook his head. When I sauntered into my room, Sera was sitting on her bed, cross-legged, fully dressed for class and waiting for me. "Oh my god, you are so late."

"I'm not. I have plenty of time to shower and get ready for class."

"Yeah, I know you do. But that's not the point. You're so late for me, because I have a seven o'clock seminar, and I need to be able to hear all the juicy details first. Did you bone?"

My face flushed. Sera jumped up off her bed. "Oh my god, you did."

I shook my head. "No, no. But I mean, we did kiss and *stuff*."

Sera's eyes went round. "Oh my god, 'and stuff'? You need to tell me everything." She frowned as she studied her watch. "God, I hate you. I only have ten minutes to get down the stairs and then eat, and then run to the seminar. But when I get back this afternoon, you and me, we're doing a full deconstruction. Do you get me?"

I laughed. "Yeah, I get you."

I watched my best friend prance out of our room. I could only laugh. I had never in my life snuck in before. This is a whole new experience, and I loved every moment of it.

✧　✧　✧

AT ONE O'CLOCK, my palms were sweating. I had no idea what any of this meant. Were we together now? All morning my stomach was tied in knots. I was barely able to eat. I'd seen him a few times in the hallways, and he would give me this wide grin whenever he saw me. A couple of times he winked. We had history together, right before the lunch hour, and he took his usual seat, which was far behind me in the back. I could feel his gaze on me the entire time.

When that final bell rang to free us, we walked through the doorway together. It was packed and crowded as we all were trying to hurry up and get out to our respective lunch meetings and study groups. His pinky found mine for the briefest hair of a second, and he leaned close. "I have something to do, so I can't have lunch with you. But I'll see you at one, yeah?"

My skin heated, and I flushed. I was convinced everybody could tell. I was convinced everybody must know. But everyone around us acted completely normal. As if Lennox hadn't just been holding my hand. Or that I hadn't just spent the entire night in his bed. This was crazy.

So, as I marched towards the big tree in the center of the campus, my stomach knotted even more. I'd had lunch with

Serafina and Aurora, and Serafina had showed amazing levels of restraint in not forcing me to talk. I think she gathered that I didn't quite want to tell Aurora yet. Lennox was her brother. It was complicated, and I didn't really know what was happening. I knew that when we got back this afternoon though, I'd have to tell her everything.

There was a part of me that was worried none of this was real, and that I'd imagined it all. But there he was, sitting on a blanket, underneath the big tree, looking as if he owned the damned thing. He had on a rumpled blazer, hair looking perfectly windblown. It wasn't fair that he looked so good.

When I approached, he smiled and then stood up, deftly coming towards me. I was hyper aware of how everyone might see whatever we might do, but then he smiled. And I promptly stopped giving a rat's ass. "Hey."

He grinned at me. "Hey to you too. How was lunch?"

"Good. You know, just the girls."

He grinned. "Did Serafina grill you?"

I shook my head. "Nope. I didn't really know what I could tell Aurora and what I couldn't."

He laughed. "You can tell Aurora. I told her first thing this morning."

"Wow, she didn't even say a word."

"Well, she was waiting for you to tell her."

I groaned. "Now she's wondering why I didn't tell her. Great. We should have coordinated."

He laughed. "She's my twin sister. Basically, as soon as the dorms were open to each side, she was knocking at my door wanting to know what the hell I'd been doing last night."

Heat suffused my skin. "Excellent."

"Look, I didn't go into detail. But I did tell her I was

with you."

"Right. Okay." How was I going to navigate this?

"Relax, she was really happy."

I would be infinitely more comfortable with a battle plan. "Lennox. We should have—" I paused when I noticed him staring at me. "Why are you looking at me like that?"

He grinned. "I'm going to kiss you now."

I swallowed hard. "Ohhh-kay."

"You're okay with that, right?"

I nodded. Except, I was freaking out because what if in the harsh light of day I didn't measure up or something? *Stop overthinking this.* Squaring my shoulders, I said, "Yup, go ahead. Do your worst."

"I'll have you know that it's my best. Just so we're clear."

"If you say so."

"I *do* say so," he said with a low chuckle.

"Let's do it."

He walked up to me, slow and sure, and then leaned down with a smile before his lips met mine. "Just so you know, from our peripheral vision, everyone is staring."

Heat lit my cheeks, but I wasn't going to be deterred. I tilted my chin up and kissed him back. When he pulled away, he took my hand and gestured towards the blanket. "I got you something."

My cheeks were still enflamed, and I tried not to look around to see who might have noticed, because frankly, I didn't really care what they thought for the most part. "You got me a present? You didn't have to."

He laughed. "I know I didn't have to, but I wanted to. That's the point."

I ducked my head. I didn't have the heart to tell him that usually the things most guys got girls, I was not into at all. He pulled out a box that looked about the size of something like a necklace, and I was worried. I didn't like necklaces. They interfered too much. They were easy to catch on things. But if he gave me a necklace, I would wear that necklace every damn day.

His laugh was low. "Don't look so worried. Just open it."

I plastered a wide smile on my face, hoping that just this once I could lie. And lie well, because I didn't want his feelings hurt. Nonetheless, I opened the box. And then my heart skipped. "Oh my god."

He grinned. "Do you like it?"

I grinned so wide my cheeks started to hurt, and he stared at me. "Do you have any idea what you look like when you smile?"

I tried to control it, but there was no stopping that grin. "No."

"You have the most amazing dimple. It's really cute. You look adorable. And stunning, and beautiful, and you know what, I'm glad you don't smile more often. Otherwise, somebody else would have noticed. This way, I can keep you all to myself."

"You're ridiculous, but thank you." Nestled in the velvet of the box, was an ornate switch blade. When I lifted it, I tested it on my finger. Perfectly balanced. Outstanding craftsmanship. And on the hilt of it was what looked like a fairy. "This is amazing. Thank you."

"You are welcome. Now, I did get this information that a lot of couples carve their names into this tree, so we're going to carve our names on it."

"I had no idea you were so cheesy."

He grinned. "Just call me cheese master. Now, hand it over. Let the man get to work."

I frowned at him as he took the knife. He was holding it wrong. He was going to hurt himself. I watched him as he found a patch on the bark and started to try to etch. I was worried with the way he was using it. I gently put my hand on his shoulder and said, "Why don't you hand it over?"

"No, I can do this."

I laughed. "No, I know you can. I'm just saying that maybe you let someone who handles a knife regularly do this."

He looked at his etching and frowned. And then he nodded. "Yeah, good point."

With a grin, I took the knife from him, and then resumed what he'd started to carve. I etched our initials onto the side of the tree, and then I stepped back and smiled.

He whistled low. "Well, I'm glad I let you do that because what I was doing was not going to work."

I glanced up at him. "Thank you for this. I didn't—" How the hell did I explain to him that I never thought I'd be *that* girl. To have someone like this. Someone who made me feel fluttery and light. Who saw me for who I really was. There was too much to say, so instead, I said, "This is the best day."

I switched the knife again and placed it back in its box and into my backpack. Lennox pulled me to him as we sat under the tree, then pulled out earphones for the both of us. "So, why don't you explain to me about why the hell you used to kiss Rhys?"

I laughed. "Haven't we been over this? It's really been eating at you, hasn't it? Are you worried that I've been crawling through Rhys's bedroom window too?"

He smirked. "I know for a fact you would never sneak into Rhys's room. You don't trust him. Unless, of course, you're holding onto his throat. You don't trust him as far as you can throw him."

I shook my head. "You'd be right about that."

The smirk softened into something happier. Warmer. "So I know I'm the one you trust," he said quietly. "Which for me is the best of all."

I could barely look at him when he was smiling like that. "Why do you see me so clearly?" I whispered.

The answer seemed to be easy for him.

"I've always seen you clearly, Sloane Lauder."

CHAPTER EIGHTEEN
Sloane

THE WEEK WAS like a dream. A dream I'd never dared to have, because I'd hate myself for wanting it. Wanting the boy who'd made my life hell since ninth grade.

But he was so much more than that, wasn't he? He was so much more than his sharp edges—he was full of love for his sister, he was a loyal friend, he was obsessed with making my body limp with pleasure.

He was obsessed with my smile.

Every night I snuck into his dorm room, and every night we kissed until we couldn't breathe, until the only thing we could do was touch and touch and touch, until we were both shivery and sated.

The first night we did this, I thought maybe we'd finally have sex, that maybe we'd finish what we'd started in the maze. But when we were kissing in his bed, and I asked him if he had a condom, he'd stared down at me with his gorgeous golden eyes and said simply, "Not yet."

"What do you mean, not yet?" I'd whined, taking his hand and pushing it into my panties so he could feel how wet I was. "I want it now."

"But I want it perfect," he'd insisted. "You deserve

better than a bloody dorm bed, Sloane. Give me some credit. Besides, if all this pussy needs is to come, then I know something that might help . . ."

And then he'd disappeared beneath the blankets, all gold eyes and wicked grins, and then I was too distracted to protest about anything.

So yes, the week was a dream. Of his hot kisses and greedy touches, of walking together through the halls, of knowing our initials were carved into the school tree, of being *his*.

But it was a dream threaded through with a nightmare—because between every kiss, between every lick of his tongue or slide of his fingers—the truth lurked.

I'd spied on him. For the one person Lennox could never forgive.

I'd spied and stolen, and even if I hadn't given the letter over to my father, I'd still given him everything else. I'd still *taken* the letter when I had no right to, and I still hadn't told Lennox that I did.

I'd still treated Lennox like he was his father, when his father was all he'd ever tried *not* to be.

"EARTH TO SLOANE," Colston Constantine said. I looked up from where I'd been staring at my wrapped hands. I needed to unwrap them, I needed to shower and pretend to go to bed so I could sneak into Lennox's room, but my father had texted an hour ago and it was all I could think about.

> **Dad:** lmk if you see anything new from our friend. from our original friend too.

He wanted more on Lennox. More on Colston too, although I didn't know how many ways I could tell my father Colston was no more involved with trafficked antiquities than he was involved with competitive pie eating.

I still wanted to catch criminals when I was older, I still wanted this life, but god, I didn't want to investigate my friends. My boyfriend.

I wanted even less to lie to my boyfriend, which was what I was doing every day I didn't confess.

"I'm here," I said to Colston, offering him a weak smile. "Just thinking."

"Well, I'm always here if you want to talk," he offered hopefully, his eyes dropping to my mouth.

"I don't talk," I reminded him, unwinding my hand wraps.

"I know," he said with a swallow, his eyes still on my mouth. "But, uh, if you wanted to. I could be there. Listen. Shoulder to cry on and all that."

I wound the hand wraps into neat bundles and fixed him with a look. "Do I look like the type of girl who needs a shoulder to cry on?"

"Well, no. But maybe you're the type of girl who needs someone who'd help her bury a body? I could do that too. The Constantines aren't always as up-and-up as they claim to be, you know. I could maybe help destroy some evidence for you?"

That did make me smile again. "Maybe you do know me after all, Colston." I tossed my hand wraps in my bag and stood. "And thank you. It's just parent problems."

And Lennox problems.

"I definitely know all about those," Colston said. "Anytime you need me, Sloane. I'm serious."

"Same to you," I said with a nod. And then I went back

to my dorm to shower.

That night passed as they all have—with Lennox licking my pussy until I came against his mouth and then me passing out in his arms—but the next day did *not* pass as it should have. I emerged from my last class to find Lennox leaning against the wall opposite my classroom door, a smug, evil smile on his face.

"You're coming with me, my sweet, vicious darling. We have plans."

✧　✧　✧

LENNOX WAS A prince.

I forgot that sometimes, when it was just us in his bed, just his fingers inside me and his raunchy murmurs in my ear; I forgot that he had the kind of money and influence someone like me would never fully understand.

And so when I followed Lennox outside—thinking he'd planned another autumn picnic for me or something—I was led not to the lawn or the woods, but to his family's waiting Maybach, where a bag of my things had already been stashed in the trunk and my coat was waiting on the seat, folded neater than any coat should be.

"It's all arranged with the school," Lennox had said as he'd handed me into the car. "They think you're visiting your father."

"What do you mean? What's been arranged?"

"You're mine for the weekend, Sloane Lauder." He'd given me a look that sent goosebumps popping all down my arms and legs. "All mine."

And so now here we were in New York City, in a hotel so expensive and glamorous that of course it belonged to the Constantine family. We were whisked through a soaring,

Beaux Arts lobby by a private butler, who also saw us up to our room and shepherded in a lavish dinner served on embarrassingly fine china before he left us to eat and explore.

"Come eat," Lennox said as I wandered over to the window nearest the food-laden table. "I promise it's not fairy food, you won't be bound to me forever if you eat it."

He almost sounded sad about that when he said it, but when I turned to look at him, there was only his usual mocking smile, the one that looked so unfairly good on him.

"Sloane," he prompted after I turned back to the window. "Come."

"I can see Central Park from here," I said to him. "And so much of the city too. And these rooms . . ."

I pivoted on my heel as I gestured to the sumptuous suite around us. It was done up in dark wood floors and soft gray walls, hung with silk brocades and upholstered in leathers and velvets. Beyond the dining room, a four-poster bed waited in a bedroom the size of some apartments. It was in the very center of the room, like an altar of fluffy pillows and Egyptian cotton.

"Why are we here, Lennox? Why did you bring me here?"

He got up from his chair and prowled over to me, his smile fading into something darker. Hungrier.

"Guess."

You deserve better than a bloody dorm bed, Sloane.

"We're going to have sex here," I said, not as a question, but as a statement.

"Yes, we are," Lennox replied, sliding his hands over my hips and down my legs. I was still in my Pembroke skirt, and so he was able to ruck up the fabric and grab handfuls of my ass, squeezing the flesh there until I gasped and dropped my head on his shoulder.

He kneaded my bottom as he whispered in my ear. "Always with these sensible knickers, my little virgin. It's like you know how much they fucking turn me on. Because you don't mean to get me hard, do you? You don't mean to make me crazy. But just *seeing* you makes me crazy. And now that I know how soft this pussy is, how wet it gets for me, I can't even think when you're around. I can't even think when you're *not* around. My mind is just filled with you and when I can see you again. When I can touch your cunt again."

He moved from kneading my ass to pushing his fingers down the front of my panties. I slumped in his arms as he found the swollen bud of my clit and started rubbing.

"So yes, darling girl, we are going to have sex tonight, and tomorrow night. I'm going to make you as crazy as you make me. I'm going to make you as obsessed with me as I am with you, so that you can't think, can't breathe, can't even *exist* because wanting me is that excruciating."

His clever fingers moved down even farther, and he nudged my boots apart with his handmade Italian brogues to spread my legs.

"Fuck, you're so wet," he groaned, pushing his fingers inside me. "How are you already so wet?"

I bit his neck in response, right above his uniform shirt collar, and he groaned again.

"Forget the food," he breathed. "I have to fuck you now. Tell me you're ready. Tell me you want it."

I grabbed his hand and pushed his fingers deeper. "I want it." God help me, I wanted it. Even though we'd hated each other. Even though I'd spied on him. Even though I was pretty sure I was falling in love with him and it might be the worst mistake of my life.

I wanted it.

I lifted my face for a kiss, and he obliged me immediately, his lips firm and hot on mine, wasting no time before they demanded I part for his tongue. And then he stroked inside my mouth with it, kissing me like I belonged to him, kissing me like he'd caught me and now he would claim his prize.

And when I opened my eyes as we kissed, I saw that his were already open, heavy-lidded and sultry, like a lion watching his next meal.

Lust kicked me in the clit; my belly was a bottomless well of want. All I wanted was him, was his erection deep inside me. I wanted him to fuck me so hard it felt like fighting. I wanted us to tear each other apart until we were both sated and wet and spent.

"Lennox," I murmured, moving my mouth to his jaw, to his throat. "I don't want to wait." My hands went to his belt; they were shaking as I tried to work it open, that's how needy I was. "Right now, let's do it right now. Right now, please—"

He was half-laughing, half-groaning as I finally managed to get his belt open. "Let's at least go to the bed—you deserve—"

"We've nearly fucked on a rugby field and in a maze and in a cold-ass *scullery*, I'm not a princess or a shrinking violet. Goddammit, Lennox, just put me out of my misery."

His cock jumped in my hands as I freed it from his uniform trousers, and pre-come was already beading at the tip. "I think you've got it wrong who's been more miserable," he growled and then he spun me around. "Hands on the fucking window, Sloane. Stick that pretty arse out. Present yourself for me."

I obeyed, letting out a shuddering breath as he flipped my skirt up over my ass and tugged my panties down to the floor. I heard the tear of a condom, and a low, ragged breath as he rolled it over his length, and then his fingers were back at my slit again, smearing my wetness all over.

"It should be like this," he said hoarsely, fitting his wide crown to my narrow opening. "It should be exactly like this. In our uniforms. Dirty and urgent. Just like I've been stroking myself thinking about for years."

My head dropped forward against the cool glass of the window. "If I'd known . . ."

"We would have both failed out of Pembroke, wouldn't we? We would have never left our rooms. We would have been fucking every chance we got."

"We still hated each other then," I pointed out, my breath hitching as he pushed the head of his cock inside me.

"That would have made it all the more fun," he purred, giving me a small stroke. Just that plush crown going in and out. "Think of the scratches you would have left on me. Think of the handprints I would have left on your tight little bottom."

I was barely breathing now. "Lennox . . ."

He kept going with his magnificently dirty words, giving me another toe-curling nudge of his thick cock. "Think of how you would have pinned my wrists to the floor and took what you wanted until I couldn't give you any more. Think of how fun it would have been to have me between your legs and not know if I was going to tongue-fuck you or bite you or both."

"Are you saying that we're not going to do that now?"

"You want me to fuck you like I hate you? Because I'll happily oblige, my cruel temptress. I may not hate you, but you can bet everything you own that I still hate how much I want you."

I lifted my head enough to look over my shoulder at

him. He'd taken off his uniform blazer when we got to the room, so it was just him in his shirt and uniform tie, with the sleeves rolled up and the tie loosened. His white-blond hair fell onto his forehead, and his sharp, beautiful features looked sharper than ever in the low, ambient light of the hotel room.

"I hate how much I want you too," I admitted in a whisper. "It's a weakness."

"Then it will be a weakness we share."

And for some reason, that felt like the most romantic thing he could have said. He wasn't promising me forever, he wasn't promising me eternal devotion. He was telling me that we would suffer this sickness for each other together. That we were both in this, and that we would try to survive it together instead of separately.

And if my traitorous heart ached for more—if my mind warned me that I was in real danger of loving Lennox Lincoln-Ward—then I ignored them. I would take Lennox with a blindfold and my ears stopped up, that's how much I needed him with me and in me.

He leaned forward, not to kiss me, but to bite the back of my neck. "I'm there, Sloane, can you feel it? I can feel it. Right fucking there." He nudged his hips a little to prove his point, showing me exactly where the resistance was just inside my channel. "I'm the first man inside you. The first you'll ever have. Almost like you saved yourself for me. Almost like you knew you were supposed to."

"Oh, is that right?" I challenged, but my breathless squirming belied my words.

"Yes, that's right. You were mine from the moment I saw you. I would have killed anyone who touched you, who got to know what your cunt felt like before I did. Who got to know exactly how you liked to be rubbed . . ." His fingers followed his words, finding my sensitive spot at the top of my seam, and caressing it expertly, sending tremors all down my legs.

"Lennox," I murmured. "Please . . ."

"Breathe in, sweetheart," he said, and I breathed in. At that moment he bit my neck again right as his hips punched up—right past my virginity.

The pain from his bite was the perfect distraction from the pain between my legs, but I cried out all the same, crumpling against the window as Lennox bottomed out inside me.

I was used to pain—both the pain of being struck in sparring and the sore muscles that came from sparring—but this was something different. Something deeper and sharper. But there was no escaping it, no recoiling away, because I was still impaled on him, I was still caught between his lean but powerful frame and the window.

He kissed my neck and stroked my hip under my skirt. "Stay still, my little sprite, and I'll make it better." His fingers resumed their strumming on my clit, sending confusing signals of pleasure to compete with the pain of his invasion, and then he started talking, and my body melted at his words.

"You're so fucking tight, Sloane, just like I knew you would be. So narrow you can barely take me, can you? And it feels so good in here, it feels so hot all around my cock, I don't think I can ever leave. I don't think I can ever stop fucking you. I want my entire life to be fucking you . . ."

Abruptly, and I didn't know how because his thick erection between my legs was still taking my breath away, I came against his fingers. My knees buckled and my entire body shook as I screamed out his name against the glass.

And that seemed to be the last straw for his control. All

of a sudden he was gone, no longer inside me, and then I was being scooped up and carried into the bedroom.

"I feel like a princess," I said dazedly as he placed me on the giant fairy tale bed.

"Well, I *am* a prince," he said, yanking off his tie and unbuttoning his shirt. "Just say the word if you need me to make things more princess-y."

I watched him strip off his shirt, revealing etched muscles and a line of golden hair arrowing down from his navel. I parted my legs and raised up my skirt so he could see my wet cunt as he undressed, and his gold eyes practically scorched me into ash.

"On second thought, I've been told I have more of a *fairy assassin who fucks* vibe," I said as he crawled onto the bed. His wet, latex-covered cock jutted lewdly from his uniform pants as he did. He was like having my own personal pornography.

"I'll take the fucking literally," Lennox said, covering my body with his own and then entering me with one rough thrust.

I arched against him, running my hands up his back, grabbing at his shoulders and arms. He braced himself on his hands and stared down at me with a raw animalism that took my breath away. All that muscle, all that power, all that unfiltered will—all of it was bent towards fucking me. To claiming me. As if this was the inevitable outcome after all these years, and the insane thing was that I welcomed it, I wanted it, I was claiming him right back. Scratching his back like he said I would, writhing underneath him as my second orgasm built and built.

And as I panted his name and shivered through my climax, as he gave me several deep, bed-rattling thrusts as his own orgasm tore through him, I decided I didn't want to know if this was still revenge for him. I didn't want to know if part of him still hated me, if all of him still hated my father, if I was the tawdry means to a bitter end. I didn't want to know, because somehow, against my better judgement, I'd fallen for him. I'd fallen in love.

Fuck me.

Chapter Nineteen

Lennox

I NEVER SLEPT better than when a well-pleasured Sloane Lauder was snuggled in my arms. There was something about someone so strong, someone so fierce and yet so remote, trusting you enough to sleep in your embrace. And that it was *this* girl, the one I'd known was mine since the moment I saw her . . .

Well. It made my cock hard and my chest feel strange. The usual Sloane problem.

I woke her up that morning with slow, wet kisses between her legs, knowing she was sore and would need to be eased into more fucking. But there *would* be more fucking, if she'd let me. Whatever tender feelings were growing for Sloane were still indelibly tied to my need to possess her, for her to belong to me, and *those* feelings were indelibly tied to my cock.

And after she came, we ate a leisurely breakfast and then went for a walk around Central Park to enjoy the last of the leaves. And when we came back, I had a surprise all ready for her.

"Oh, Lennox," I heard her say as she walked into the bedroom and then caught sight of the bathtub in the doorway beyond. "Jesus, I'm so cold and that looks so good right now."

I was smiling as I came up behind her. Steam curled off the surface of the bath I'd arranged for us while we were gone. Champagne chilled nearby, and fresh rose petals drifted on top of the water, subtly scenting the air. "That's the idea, darling."

Sloane turned and gave me a look like I'd just moved a mountain for her. "You did this?"

"What better way to warm up after a bracing stroll in the cold autumn air?"

She nearly smiled, catching her lower lip with her teeth just in time to stop it. "You shouldn't have."

I was obsessed with her smile, obsessed with seeing it as much as possible. "On that, dear ferocious one, we shall have to disagree," I said as I pulled her lower lip free of her teeth with my thumb. "Now, let's get you naked."

An arched eyebrow. "Ah, so there's an ulterior motive."

"You doubted that there was?" I asked as I unwound her scarf and unbuttoned her coat. I tossed both on the bed, and then started on her clothes—a black turtleneck and leggings, along with her boots—and she let me undress her with a small sigh.

"I guess I don't mind. If you didn't have an ulterior motive for this afternoon, then I would have."

"That's what I like to hear."

Once I had her naked, I took my time looking at her. At her small, high breasts, at her flat stomach and narrow hips. Her arms were sculpted with elegant curves of muscle, as were her thighs and calves, and between those firm thighs was a triangle of dark, silky curls that I knew would smell like honeysuckle if I buried my nose in them like I did this morning.

"Fuck, you're gorgeous," I murmured, already hard against the placket of my trousers.

She blushed. "Thanks."

"I mean it, Sloane. Feel me."

She reached out and wrapped her strong, slender fingers around me through my trousers, and we both made a noise. I'd never been this horny, never needed to fuck *so goddamn much*, but with Sloane, I felt insatiable, like an animal in rut. I needed to fuck her more than I needed my next meal or swallow of air.

"Get in the bath," I breathed. "Wait for me with your legs open."

She squeezed me—hard. "I'm not an obedient girl," she murmured. "But luckily for you, I also happen to want to wait for you in the bath with my legs open."

And then she sauntered off, her firm arse swaying hypnotically as she did.

I undressed in record time, flinging my clothes everywhere, and striding into the bathroom to find her not only with her legs open, but with her fingers in between her thighs, petting herself.

"Bleeding Christ," I choked, staggering to the edge of the bathtub. "Are you trying to kill me?"

She laughed—and there! There was that fucking smile! Lighting up her entire fucking face like the sun. Just seeing it made me want to fall to my knees and worship her forever, but I settled for a long, urgent kiss that left her gasping and then climbing into the water behind her. I hauled her into my lap, so that my hard cock nestled against her arse, and then I helped her lean back against my chest, so that her head rested on my shoulder and I could see all the way down her front, from her wet breasts to her parted thighs.

I found a tightly pointed nipple and started teasing it

under the water. "Are you warmed up yet?"

"Not yet," Sloane murmured. "I think you'll have to help."

"Hmm, like this?" I covered her tits with my hands and plumped them, kneaded them, until she was breathing hard in my lap. "Does that help?"

"Yes," she said. "Oh god, yes. Oh, Lennox." She took my hand from her breast and molded it over her hot mound. Her seam was slick with more than water, and I played there, running my fingertips back and forth.

"You're amazing, you're so good at that, I love when you touch me," she was confessing, all in a dreamy, lustful chatter. "I wish you could kiss me forever; I wish I lived in your bed; I wish I'd known you earlier."

"We've known each other for years," I said, biting her earlobe as I circled her clit with my fingers.

"*Really* known you. Known how loyal you are and perceptive you are. How smart and thoughtful and kind. Known how much I would lo—"

She stiffened in my arms, cutting herself off, and suddenly my heart was pounding against my chest, as if it was trying to crack my rib cage open and slither out to meet her. As if my life depended on what she was about say.

"Sloane?" I said hoarsely. "Known how much you would what?"

She hesitated. "How much I would like you," she finally said, and it felt like my heart had fallen flat out of my body and gone down the bathtub drain, that's how disappointed I was. That's how much I wanted her to have said something else. Another word.

She tried to change the subject, I could tell. "I started birth control at the beginning of this week," she said. "Just in case. And I trust you, Lennox, I trust that you're clean."

She had my complete attention then. "Are you saying you'll let me inside without a condom?"

"Yeah," she said, wriggling her bottom against me. "I am."

My cock jerked so hard against her that she laughed again, but I was past laughter, past everything but hunger and need. I lifted her higher against my chest and then reached under her to fist myself. "Right now, Sloane. Right fucking now. Work yourself down on me," I said. "Make it so I'm splitting you open."

I'd fucked so many girls before now, but fucking Sloane was ruining me for anyone else. Because watching her slender, athletic frame arch and shiver and flex as she slowly impaled herself on my thick cock made me realize I only wanted to fuck strong girls. Lethal girls. Girls who could choke me out as soon as make me come. It was something about those sleek muscles maybe, or about that deadly grace as she moved. About knowing she was strong enough to take everything I had to give her—which was a lot. Which was so much it scared even me.

And then there was the fact that my cock was entering her tight hole without anything between my skin and hers. I'd never fucked raw before, and feeling the silky clasp directly on my dick was excruciating, pure hellish bliss. I needed to come right away, I needed to pump her full of my seed so she could finally *see*, finally *feel*, how she'd destroyed me and made me her thrall. Maybe I was a prince on paper, but I would be a pauper for Sloane and her tight, velvet cunt in a heartbeat.

She finally took all of me, her tight backside flush against my lap as her thighs spread on the outside of my mine. And then she leaned back against me as I started playing with her tits again, breathing hard, because the effort of not coming right away was almost too much.

"You feel like every dream I've ever had," she murmured up to me, raising her chest up to my roaming hands. "Like every fantasy I ever wanted."

"God, you are so fucking sweet when I'm inside you," I groaned, squeezing her tits and biting at her neck. "Ride me, Sloane. Use that little assassin's body of yours and make yourself come on me."

She did. God, she did, her thighs and her arse flexing deliciously as she sat up and started screwing me, started moving in small figure eights. Water dripped off the slick, flat muscles of her back and trailed down the furrow of her spine, and right below the water, I could see the twin dimples at the small of her back, dimples made for my thumbs as I wrapped my hands around her hips.

She looked back at me over her shoulder, and her green eyes were filled with more than lust, more than need. They were filled with that word she hadn't been able to say, the word I wanted her so desperately to say. And I knew then as she started to come, her eyes still on mine, that I'd been lying to myself since the maze. Since long before the maze.

This wasn't revenge.

This was something scarier and more dangerous to us both. And when my stomach tensed and my balls tightened and I started throbbing my climax into her pussy, I knew what it was. Because I trusted her. I *liked* her. I wanted her in my life not just now, but after Pembroke, after college. Forever.

She was mine, I'd known that for four years, but now I knew the truth.

I was hers.

I loved her.

CHAPTER TWENTY

Lennox

I WAS A sap. It was all right. I knew it.

Coming back from the city, and I still couldn't let go of Sloane's hand. Even at her door, when she opened it and turned around with a smile on her face, all I wanted to do was keep holding her hand, stand there, and just be with her.

You've gone soft, mate.

"This is me." There was a smile in her eyes as they danced.

"I guess it is."

She inclined her head back towards the open doorway. "Well, I'm going to go in now."

But still she made no move to step inside. No move to take her hand from mine. I leaned against the wall, next to the door jamb. "I really don't want to let you go."

Her lips twitched. "I really don't want to be let go."

I knew she had things to do. On the way back she'd mentioned her economics exam she needed to prep for. *Don't be that bloke. Let her go so she can be great.* I leaned forward and pressed a soft kiss to her lips. "Are you okay though?"

The smile that touched her lips was shy. "Yeah, I'm okay. I mean, I'm sore in places I didn't know I *could* be sore, but it's a good sore."

I shook my head. "Oh, Sloane, what am I going to do with you?"

"What? I'm just saying."

What she was saying was good for my ego, but I still didn't let her go. "So what are the chances that you might want to sneak into my room again? I mean, at another time, obviously, when you are not quite so sore. And after you've studied." God, I was an arsehole. She'd just told me she was sore. I'd kept her naked basically all weekend.

Not to mention, she might want a break from me. She might be tired of me already.

She laughed but pulled her hand free of mine. "Well, I have some homework to do, and I need to make headway on econ, but maybe when I'm done, if you don't have any homework to do, we can 'not do' homework, together." Her smile was sly.

And just like that she gave me hope. "Sounds like a date." I kissed her again. This time I lingered, savoring every flavor on her lips, because I knew it would have to tide me over until I could see her again.

Which would be in probably several hours. God, several hours without her.

Get it together.

I could do this. I wasn't a complete pussy. I was, however, a bloke with a girlfriend now. So that was new. I pressed one more kiss to her lips, and then I let her go. I already felt cold and sought her out again and gave her another. One that held more promise, but then promptly let her go. This was becoming a problem. "Oh my god, why can't I stay away from you?"

"Why don't I want you to?"

"Sloane, you're killing me. Okay, let's take care of business, okay? I'll see you after."

"I'll text you when I'm done," she promised. "And then I will head over there."

"It's a date."

I forced myself to walk away. And as it was, I walked briskly. Down the hall, down the stairs, across the landing, up the other set of stairs through the boys' corridor, and then down the hall to my room. It was the only way. Otherwise, I was going to stay, or ask her to come study in my room. If she did that, there is no way in hell she would ever get anything done. Nor I.

Once I got to my room, I grabbed my laptop from my desk and plopped on the bed to get something done. But a stack of papers fell with it. With a groan, I knelt to pick them up, leaving my gaze eye level with my desk.

I frowned when I saw the fateful letter just sitting there.

That was not where I'd left it before. I never left that out. It—and everything like it—always went into the file cabinet. Christ, *especially* this one.

This one was a letter to Nicholas. After all, he was my little brother, my father's love child with Graciella, currently being raised by his grandparents in Cyprus. I wouldn't have just left this out for anyone to find. And then an unpleasant memory surfaced.

One with Sloane, when I'd caught her in my room, standing *right next* to my desk.

No, mate, don't jump to conclusions, steady on.

The problem was, even as my brain tried to work out any viable reason she would have to be snooping, I couldn't come up with one, so I sent her a quick text.

Lennox: I changed my mind. Can you come here for a minute?

The little dots jumped and her reply was quick.

Sloane: I still have econ to study for . . .

Lennox: I promise, I'll be quick.

Sloane: I feel like I've heard these words before. It can't be quick.

Despite my current mood, my cock twitched. Because she was right. I couldn't be quick.

Lennox: It's important.

Sloane: I'll be right there.

She arrived in less than three minutes. Concern was written on her face. "What's the matter?"

The letter burnt a hole in my hand. I knew I had to ask her. In my body, in my soul, I felt like I already knew the answer, but I needed her to tell me. "This letter, have you read it?"

Her face, that beautiful elf-like face with the delicate features and her beautiful eyes, told me everything I needed to know about the truth in that moment. But I still needed her words. I needed to complete the process of her breaking my heart.

"I can explain," she whispered.

I blinked at her and then sank down on my bed. "You can bloody *explain*?"

Sloane ran a hand through her soft chin-length hair. "Look, I know. It was a huge breach of trust and downright pathetic of me, but you should know that when I took it, our relationship was nothing yet. We hated each other. And my father, he'd asked for some information, I didn't know what to do then. I couldn't refuse him, so I did it. Now that I know you, and now that we've—"

I put a hand up to stop her talking. "Your *father*?"

She paled. "Lennox, I'm so sorry."

Sorry.

She had torn through my tender, fledgling trust of her, she had searched through my life without seeking any context, she had found the one thing in here that I'd poured the most of my heart into and planned to deliver it to my father . . . and she was *sorry*.

You know fucking what?

I was sorry too.

"Even if I could accept that you didn't know me before when you came into my room and read something that wasn't yours, before you pretended to care about me, the fact that you're trying to suggest you did it for your father makes me not want to believe a word you've said."

She started to shake. "Lennox, I *do* care about you. I didn't then. Admittedly, we were on opposite sides."

"And what about after?"

"I just—I'm sorry."

Her words were ineffectual, because how could you just say sorry? How could you just overlook the pain and think it could be okay. Sorry didn't even begin to cut it. "Your father. You know what your father did to my family. You know, and you still broke in here to spy for him." My voice stayed low, stayed cold.

Even though everything inside me felt shredded and raw and hot.

She started to stutter. "I—look, I know. I didn't expect these feelings. And I thought you hated me. And that's no excuse. I wanted to tell you. Especially after I knew you, I wished I hadn't done it. I wish I had just told him no, but he knew the one thing that would get me to give in to his request, so I did it. But I want you to know that even though I broke your trust, I didn't tell him about that letter. I just gave him the information on the computer."

I couldn't breathe. In the place where my heart had been, something mangled and pulpy gave a sharp, sudden lurch. "My computer?"

She swallowed hard. "I know I messed up."

"What did your father want? It must've been something big for you to offer your virginity to me for it, right? So what was he after?"

She shivered at my cruel words, and I hated myself for caring, I hated myself for even noticing. She'd done this. She'd done this to us.

Not me.

Sloane swallowed, and I could see her doing the math if she should tell me the truth or not.

I sighed and made it sound bored, the way I usually do. The way I pretended with other people, people who didn't know me and never would. "Let me just make this simple for you. There's nothing you can say that would make me care about you ever again, so you might as well tell me the truth. What would make you do this to me . . . to us?"

Her beautiful face went from a flushed pink to stark chalk. "I guess there were some murmurings that your father had left accounts unreported and the government is still trying to recover those. Yours and Aurora's accounts were untouchable, because you were minors, and you had trusts which were given by your grandparents. My father thought that maybe you and your trust could lead them to the money, or maybe you had access to the accounts that your dad had left behind. He wanted me to do research and see if

I could find it."

"So your father asked you to fuck me and get access to my accounts?"

She flinched as if I'd slapped her. "No. He didn't. He asked me for information before I fell for you. Up until two weeks ago, I thought you hated me. Besides, I would never do that. Us getting together had nothing to do with my father."

Was she daft? "You can see how I don't believe you, right?"

Tears shimmered in her gaze, and I almost relented. I wanted to forgive her.

I wanted to pull her into my arms and tell her that while I was angry, I couldn't give her up.

I also wanted to throttle her, legitimately watch as the light went out of her eyes. It was better if I didn't touch her.

"I know, Lennox. I'm really sorry. I just—I did it because it was my father. He's all I have . . . all I've had for so long, and all I'd ever wanted was to be like him. But not anymore, and if I could go back in time, I would."

"Well, too bad there's no such thing as a time machine. At least I know what I'm dealing with now. You can go."

She reached for me. "But Lennox—"

I forced my face into a mask, wiped it blank of any pain that I felt, because then she would *see* too much. "I said you can fucking go. I have nothing to say to you. We're done. You know what, I was bothered by that idea of you and Rhys because he would have ruined you. But as it turned out you're just like him. You're a devil in disguise. You deserve someone like that."

She stepped toward me. "Lennox. I just—"

For a moment, I let the mask drop. Just enough that she could see my anger, every sharp blade of it. So she could see exactly what I thought of her fucking lies, her fucked-up excuses.

"What part of *leave* didn't you understand?"

It didn't matter that every part of my soul was on fire. It didn't matter that I just wanted to hold her and believe her explanations. None of that mattered, because she cut me deeper than my father ever could.

Or hers.

"Lennox, I didn't tell him about who you were writing to. I didn't tell him about the letter."

"I don't believe you. Now get out."

I marched to the door, yanked it open, and waited for her to go through it. I was done. Done caring. Done obsessing over her. I was just done.

CHAPTER TWENTY-ONE

Sloane

THIS WAS MY fault. I knew it was my fault. What I hadn't expected was quite this level of pain.

What, you weren't ever going to tell him?

Maybe I hadn't planned on telling him. What the hell did that say about me? I'd allowed myself to get so caught up in Lennox Lincoln-Ward wanting *me* that I forgot the simple basic tenet of being me. I believed in truth and justice, and I had wronged him.

There was no point in crying about it. No point wallowing in the pain like I had been for the last week. I had made my own bed. I had done this to myself.

Of course he no longer trusted me. Of course he no longer wanted to be with me. It was the predictable result and consequence of my own actions.

You are an idiot. Did you really think this would last?

Why hadn't I asked my father for more information? Why hadn't I simply said no to the old man?

At the end of the day, I was responsible. Even though I should not have been participating in missions. And more importantly, it had felt wrong at the time, and I'd still done it because my father had asked me to. I'd still done it because I wanted to impress him so badly that I was willing to forget who I was.

I wasn't above stealing something from a room. I wasn't above giving someone their comeuppance. I wasn't above a little revenge. Hell, I thrived on it, had built my reputation here at Pembroke on it, but I was always, always honest. And I hadn't been honest with Lennox. I had hurt him, however unintentionally.

This was the outcome. An outcome I'd created for myself.

Serafina stepped into the room, clearly surprised to find me not curled up in a ball as I had been most of the week. Sure, I'd gone to classes. But outside of those classes, and doing the bare minimum I had to for school, I hadn't done much else other than lie in bed and cry.

I just hadn't thought it could hurt so much. That feeling of disappointing someone. That feeling of someone no longer wanting you. That loneliness I'd felt since my mother died, it was nothing compared to now. Nothing compared to the rejection I'd felt from someone I cared about.

He didn't reject you. He simply walked away from a damaging situation . . .

Lennox had been the only person besides Sera, Aurora, and Tannith to really see me and care about me as a whole, and I'd ruined that. I had hurt him. No wonder he'd rejected me. But while I might not be able to fix us, while he might never forgive me, at the very least, I could make it right.

I could get my father off his tail, to stop investigating him and his family. If my father wanted information on the Lincoln-Wards, he was, A, going to have to get it himself, or B, going to have to let me go. Lennox and Aurora, they hadn't done anything wrong. They were just boarding-school kids—the ones parents pawned off to the Ivy League pipeline as soon as they could hold a pencil—like I was. And if the agency couldn't see that, then did I really want to go to work for people like that?

"Okay, so you look like maybe you'll be eating today?"

I gave Serafina a wan smile. "I have eaten, and I showered. And I've been to class. Happy now, Mom?"

She lifted a brow. "As my grandmamma used to say, don't sass me." Her words dripped with an added southern drawl. Her grandmother on her father's side of the family had come from New Orleans. The old battle-axe held up a damn long time. And Sera had spent quite a few summers with her before she passed. So every now and again, she had these random southern utterances intertwined with her van Doren cultured inflections.

"Sorry, I didn't mean to sass you, Mama Sera, I'm just saying, I've done all the things you always ask about. Showered. Ate. Class. Homework."

"Oh, well I see you're feeling better."

"Not really. But it's possibly time for me to stop wallowing. I messed up, but now I have to deal with it head on."

"I know, babes. But how are you going to fix it though?"

"That letter I stole along with the files on Lennox's computer, I'm going to use it to show my father that Lennox isn't working for his dad. I want to show him that Lennox is a good person. If he can see that, maybe he'll stop the witch hunt."

Sera folded her arms as she plopped onto her bed. "Do you think that will work?"

I shrugged. "I don't know. I did a lot of damage. And maybe he shouldn't ever trust me again. I might not be able to fix us, fix what I did, but I can get my dad off his tail. At the very least, I can do that."

She levelled her gaze on me. "Sloane, can I say something?"

I sighed. "What?"

"Know that this is coming from a place of love. And I love you a lot."

"Stop sugar coating and just tell me."

"Honey, are you in love?"

I blinked at her. "I don't understand the question."

With a soft laugh, she shook her head. "Right, I get you. Of course, you don't. It's just, yeah, you messed up. Everyone messes up. And I know you, your whole thing about honesty and forthrightness. You will do everything in your power to correct it. You just have that *crusade* look about your face. Like you cannot sleep until you fix it. And honey, that's a love kind of thing. The way you've been carrying on with this not sleeping, not eating zombie version of Sloane. Hell, as far as I know, bad guys could have broken in here this week and you would have let them."

I rolled my eyes. "I would not. I would have snapped out of it to kick ass, then gone back to bed."

She laughed then. "Okay, probably. But my point is, it's okay if you love him. And if you're going to talk to him, maybe you start with that."

I frowned. "I honestly don't even know if he'll accept that. I tried to, but he wouldn't give me a chance. And honestly I didn't deserve one. I really messed up. Really, really, really messed up. So maybe I deserve this. And the least I can do is put it right. This isn't about love."

"Uh huh. Well you said you were sorry. But sometimes, you have to go deep within the apology to show someone that you really, really care about them, more than just you're sorry for hurting them. But that because you care so much, it never would be intentional. And he doesn't know that. He thinks you're the same Sloane who has always loathed and despised him."

I frowned. "I never loathed or despised him. *He* has always been the one who loathed and despised me. He was just a guy I stayed away from. The guy whose radar I tried to stay off of. But somehow he was always there, always messing with me."

Sera rolled her eyes. "And why do you think that was?"

I shrugged. "I don't know."

"Sloane! Lennox Lincoln-Ward has loved you since the moment he saw you. He, just like every other idiotic male mammal of our species, had no idea how to say that. And so, he pulled your pigtails and tortured you. Because he's a man, he couldn't just say, 'Hey, you've given me pants feelings. I don't want pants feelings when I think about you because maybe you're not what I pictured for myself. But still, *pants feelings*.'"

I choked in a laugh. "Oh my god, did you just say pants feelings?"

She nodded. "Yep, pants feelings. Because, accurate."

"Yeah okay. I'll start with pants feelings."

She laughed. "Or you could say, 'I love you and I'm sorry.'"

I mulled over what she said. She had a point. If I told him how I felt instead of just saying 'I'm sorry. It's hard to explain,' he might be willing to listen.

I stared at my laptop then. At the very least, maybe if I apologized better and got my father off his back, at least he wouldn't hate me so much.

"You may have a point there, Sera."

"What? Me have a point? Honey, do I have to remind you, I'm never wrong?"

I laughed. An actual genuine laugh for the first time in a

week.

"Hey, one chuckle, I'll take it. Better than the grunts and head nods I've gotten all week."

As Sera got busy doing homework and tapping away on her computer, I was closing up my research. I finally found the address that Lennox had been writing that letter to. I thought it was in reference to the lawyer or something, but it wasn't. The address I found was for a little boy about seven years old, living with an elderly couple in Cyprus. They were Graciella de Marco's parents, but despite them having the same dark hair and olive skin as Graciella, the school picture of Nicholas I found showed a little boy with white blond hair and bright gold eyes.

Lennox hadn't been writing to a lawyer. He'd been writing to a little boy. A little boy, who like him, had lost his father. Lennox was his only protection from the world.

That little boy was Lennox's half-brother.

CHAPTER TWENTY-TWO

Lennox

"**Y**OU WOULD THINK after you're finally getting laid by the girl you've been obsessed with since you got here, you'd be in *much* better spirits. But no, you're still in a shit mood. Maybe I should have fucked her first. Tested the roads. I wouldn't have fucked it up."

I pushed away from the ledge along the roof on top of the dorms—a spot we came up to when the weather was decent—and walked towards my friend. I was going to kill Rhys tonight. Throw him right off. I gave zero shits.

But Owen and Keaton were there, and even Phineas made a move to stop us. And Phineas was a shit starter. He loved to watch and see if things would actually come to blows. But after the last time, I think he saw that we were really going to kill each other if allowed.

Rhys fought against Phin's hold. "No, let me go. He wants to pop me, and he thinks he can. He's welcome to give it a go. It's not my fault he's a pussy. I'd primed the girl for him. I'm the world's best wingman, brought him the girl he's been mooning over for ages. *Ages*, mind you. And I let him have her. But he fucked it up. And she's a fantastic kisser."

"You don't know what the hell you're talking about," I ground out.

Owen kept his arms wrapped around me. "Keaton, Phin, get him the fuck out of here. This isn't helping right now."

I thought Rhys was going to fight the command, but Keaton was already approaching him with crossed arms and a grumpy expression. Rhys could fight all he wanted, but when Keaton said it's time to go, it was time to go. And there was no fighting him. The fucker was too big.

On our way back downstairs, Owen pinned me with a glare. "Seriously, what the hell is wrong with you?"

I grumbled. "Nothing."

"Look, I get it. You and Sloane had some kind of dust up, but you've been in this mood for over a week. Time to snap out of it. If you don't like her anymore, great, fine, you don't like her. But this has to stop. You almost threw Phin *into a fire* last week. And with Rhys, you'd both end up bloody if this shit goes on for much longer."

Just Rhys's reminder that I could no longer feel her lips on mine sent a pang of pain through my body. She'd betrayed me. The one person who I'd given my full trust to. How was I supposed to forget that? And why did it hurt so bad? I'd thought I'd insulated myself from it all, but Sloane had cut me deep.

Owen sighed as he took the spot next to me. "Look, I get it. You got beef with her old man. And him trying to spy on you and getting her to do it, that was fucked. But your beef is not with her. It's with the old guy. You're mad at the wrong person. You should be mad at *your* old man because he was the one who actually fucked up. He made a mess of your family. Not her father, not her. Your father. Sure, her old man was tenacious. Went after yours with everything.

But her father didn't actually do anything wrong. He was doing his job. Her old man, I'm sorry to say, put a criminal behind bars. And that criminal happens to be related to you. It sucks. Utter bullshit. But he's the one who hurt you. You're punishing the wrong people."

My brain felt like it had been put through the blender. Like I was walking on a tightrope of emotions and if I took one misstep, my soul was going to go through a meat grinder.

I hated him. I hated them all.

Are you sure about that?

The pain was too close to the surface. All my defenses, my ability to push the pain down. Sloane had chipped that all away, and now I was one raw nerve. The words tumbled out even before I was aware of talking. "He was a prick," I mumbled. "Lied. Cheated. Charmed us and bribed us with gifts and games and hugs whenever he felt us slipping from his grip. And that was just at home. Outside the home . . . he ruined people's lives and still . . ." I blinked away the stinging in my eyes. "I can't let it go."

Owen sighed. "Look, parents are complicated and shit. And it's okay if you're mad at him. But be mad at *him*. Be mad at the person who actually brought you this situation. Her father had a job to do. He did it. Did your family get hurt in the process? Absolutely. And it sucks. But again, he was doing his job. And that's not on *her*. And the Sloane I know wouldn't have just left you hanging out to dry."

"The Sloane I know wouldn't do that either. But she did, didn't she?"

"Because her father asked her to. He's her dad, man."

"She still chose him over me."

Owen's chuckle was harsh. "So, you're telling me that even if your old man called from prison, asked a favor, there isn't some small part of you that would be tempted to do it? It's your father, you idiot."

I ground my teeth together. "Whose side are you on anyway?"

"Yours, man. Always yours. But when you're fucking up, it's my job to tell you that. We're more than Hellfire Club, more than just a couple of dudes that went to school together. You are my best mate."

"I didn't mess up anything. She snuck into my room, *stole* information from me, and gave it to her father."

"Yes, but maybe ask her why. Any idiot who knows her knows how badly she wants to work with him. He's all she's got."

"She had me." Those three words slashed a gaping wound over my heart.

Owen shrugged. "Did you tell her that?"

I opened my mouth to argue, but then that little nagging voice from the inside needled me.

You didn't tell her how you felt. You shagged her until you both couldn't walk. But you never once told her how you actually felt.

Not true. I'd given her the knife. She must know.

I didn't realize I'd said it out loud until Owen laughed. "Dude, she's a girl. Girls need the words."

"And you're such an expert?" I muttered.

The smile slid off Owen's face. "I know enough. At the very least, I know when something important is about to slip through your fingers."

"That's not my fucking fault, Owen. She chose her father over me."

"Don't you know her? That essay in English that first year, talking about a significant moment in your life, when she talked about when her mom died of cancer, leaving her just with the old man. I'm not really in for the feelings things, but that got me right in the heart area. When she talked about how her father was all she had left, and she would do anything to make him happy. Do you remember?"

I swallowed hard. I did remember. Not that I wanted to.

"Right. So if you remember, you can see how she would have done this. And she feels terrible. You're punishing her for something your father ultimately did. That's not cool. She can't go back in time and tell your father not to steal billions from a bunch of unsuspecting people. She can't go back in time to tell him not to have a mistress. She can't go back in time and undo all the layers of pain your dad caused. She can't go back in time and make her father not do his job. You're mad at the wrong person, man. Or maybe you could be mad at Rhys because he's a dick, but don't be mad at Sloane. That'll only hurt you."

"I don't need a therapy session."

Owen scoffed. "As if you could afford my rates. Look, idiot, you can choose to actually have what you want and see that you're fucking this up, or you can continue on this path and let it eat you. Your choice."

"Didn't she have a choice when she decided to spy on me for her father?"

"Yeah, she did. But that choice was between someone she cares about and someone she refers to as the only person that she has left. Was that even a choice?"

I was pretty certain I hated Owen in that moment. I hated him for being right about this. Sloane's father had asked her to do something, and even I knew she would do anything to make her father proud. Anything.

Fucking hell.

I hated it when Owen was right.

CHAPTER TWENTY-THREE

Lennox

EVERYTHING INSIDE MY chest and my stomach still felt like it was in a blender, but there was something else now. I wouldn't dare call it hope, but it was *almost* like hope. Maybe it was even better. Maybe it was understanding.

Maybe it was forgiveness.

I tried her room and found only a glaring Serafina, who'd briskly informed me, "I'm not a secretary for idiot boys who fuck everything up," when I asked where Sloane was, and went back to painting her toenails before I could figure out a reply that wouldn't further irritate her. I tried the library, the gym, the track, everywhere Sloane would normally be, until the memory came to me of her strong fingers curled expertly over of the handle of the knife I gave her, and then I knew.

I ran straight for the tree, thankful that at least it was warm enough for the grass to be dry and unfrozen, and slowed down at the far end of the quad once I saw her. She was sitting like I'd never seen her sit, not once, with her legs tucked to her chest and her head resting on her knees. Her hand was outstretched, idly tracing our initials where they'd been carved into the wood, and she looked so small and forlorn and sad that I wanted to rip something apart, I wanted to make something bleed.

Except that it was *my* fault she looked so forlorn and sad. It was my fault she was alone and curled up in a tiny ball. My fierce Sloane and what had I done? I'd dulled her sharp edges. I'd dimmed her burning glow.

All because I'd been blinded by my need for revenge, by my fury at her father. When really my fury was all about my own father. God, I'd been so colossally stupid.

I came up behind her, slow and quiet, trying to think of what I should say. Trying to think of the words I needed to make things right before she knew I was there.

But before I could even speak, she said, "Nicholas is your brother."

I shouldn't have been surprised that she knew I was there, she was the daughter of a former spy, but I still was. And I was impressed.

"How did you find out?" I asked, coming to sit in front of her.

"The address on the letter was a solid lead. It didn't take long to piece everything together once I realized Nicholas was only seven years old. And of course, there were the contents of the letter itself. I finally translated it. You want to meet him someday, but in the meantime, you're giving him all your money."

I shook my head. "Not all. I set up a small trust fund for him, and the rest of my trust fund is going into new, smaller funds to help the children of the people my father defrauded."

She was still gazing at the tree, her head turned away, but I could see the quick flutter of her eyelashes as she blinked. "Oh. The transactions. The lawyer."

"It's not strictly legal, you see," I explained. "The trust fund is designed to *hold* money, not for it to be split up and sent all over. My lawyer and I had to be very creative to make it happen, but I had no other option, Sloane. The alternative was just letting the wound my father made in the world fester, and I couldn't live with myself that way. He'd already humiliated my mom, gutted our family . . . the least I could do was try to help the other families he'd humiliated and gutted, you see."

She finally turned her head to look at me. She looked miserable, her green eyes dark and open. "God, Lennox, I'm so stupid. It was all to help people, wasn't it? All that money you were moving around, it was to make things right."

"I want to make things right with *you*," I told her softly. "I was so angry about the breach of trust that I didn't stop to ask myself why you might not have trusted me. I was so angry at being treated like my father that I didn't ask myself if I'd partially brought it on myself. I spent so long making myself the bad guy—*your* bad guy—that I hardly deserved the right to be aghast when you treated me like a villain."

"I talked to my father. About Nicholas. I told him that it seemed that the money was going towards your brother and not toward anything shady, and he agreed. And when I tell him about the other people you're helping . . . well, he's already backed off. And he'll stay backed off."

"I know," I said. And then I put my hand over hers where it still rested above our initials. What I was about to say next was so hard to say and yet when I said it, it felt so good I could cry. "I trust you, Sloane."

"How can you?" she asked thickly. "After what I've done?"

The answer was so easy. "Because I love you."

A tear spilled out of each moss-green eye, twin tracks

running down her face.

I leaned forward to kiss them. And then I kissed her. Gently, without demanding anything, until she could speak again.

"I love you, Lennox," she whispered, "and I'm so sorry, so incredibly sorry. I shouldn't have invaded your privacy. I shouldn't have taken anything. I shouldn't have hid it from you after. We spent so long being enemies, so long in this fucked-up game of chess with each other, that when the game changed and we became something more, I didn't know what to do. I didn't know how to change with it."

"Me either," I told her. "But we can start now, can't we? Start our new game?" I flatten my hand over hers, pushing her palm against our initials hard enough that I knew she could feel them against her skin. "Because if the alternative is being without my violent little sweetheart, I don't think I can handle it."

Even though tears still spilled from underneath those long lashes, a smile tugged briefly at the corner of her mouth. "I'm not that violent."

"You dry-fucked me on the rugby field after tackling me and mounting me. You choked me while you did it."

The edge of her mouth tugged upward again. "You brought that on yourself."

"Then let me bring more of it on myself. I've spent the last four years making you miserable, so I think it's only fair that you torment *me* for the next four years. Maybe for a handful of decades on top of that, just to make extra sure I've paid my debt to you."

"And how should I torment you?" she asked.

"Well, the dry-fucking was nice," I said, and she giggled a little. She'd uncurled enough that I could pull her into my lap, and so I did, guiding her lithe legs to wrap around my hips. She was all lean muscle and black boots and soft lips. Her eyes were the color of my entire world. And the minute her core rested against my semi-erect cock, we both sucked in our breath. My shaft quickly grew hard as granite underneath her and she started rocking against it.

"Dry-fucking is all well and good, but I think the best revenge would be something a little more intense," she said, reaching between us. When I realized what she was doing, I groaned.

"Darling, people might see."

"My skirt will cover it."

"But—" It was too late. She had me out of my trousers, and she had her knickers tugged to the side, and then she was spearing her soft cunt with my erection, wiggling and squirming her way down to the root.

"Bloody Nora," I swore, dropping my head forward onto her shoulder. "How are you even tighter than I remember?"

"Does that mean that I'm succeeding in tormenting you?" she asked coyly, moving her hips in such a way that her heavenly pussy caressed my entire length. My testicles drew up tight, and already a knot of urgent tension was pulsing at the base of my spine. I was about to come.

"God," I rasped. "Yes."

"Good," she purred, her tears drying, her nipples visibly hard even through her uniform jumper. "I have a lot of torment to pay you back for."

"Please," I groaned. "Torment me forever. Make my life agony. As long as you're in it, I'll suffer anything. I'll give you anything. My mouth, my cock, my fingers."

"What about your heart?" she asked, stilling her movement in my lap to look into my face.

"My vicious darling, it's yours," I said, flattening her

hand over my chest like I'd flattened it over our initials earlier. "It's been yours for four years. Since the moment I first heard your name."

And that glorious smile of hers bloomed across her face like a flower finally facing the sun. "Then I suppose I better take good care of it."

"I don't care if you stomp on it, as long as you know it's yours."

"And how long is it mine for?" she asked as she started to come.

I held her shuddering and pulsing in my lap, savoring each and every flutter of her body before I followed her over the edge. What started in hate, in revenge, in lust, was now the one good thing in my life that I would never, ever let go of. Even if it was still dirty as fuck.

But that was how we liked it.

"How does forever sound?"

EPILOGUE

Sloane

"**I** S IT COLD?" Lennox murmured evilly in my ear as he gave me a slow, deep thrust. "It looks a little cold."

"Fuck you," I gasped, my naked breasts pressed to his dorm window. Outside was a blizzard—a real New England blizzard that was flinging snow and ice everywhere—and behind me was a very delicious, very naked prince, using my pussy. All while my nipples ached with a wonderful agony I couldn't decide if I loved or hated.

The lights were off, so no one would be able to see us, especially not with the storm, but there was something exciting about being in front of the window. Of knowing anyone could look up and see Sloane Lauder, the pierced and booted badass, getting railed by her former bully and loving it.

"I thought *I* was supposed to be tormenting you," I managed to say.

"Oh but you are," he breathed. "Do you know what torment it is to have this silky pussy around me? What suffering it is to see my cock sliding in and out of your tight little hole? The affliction of knowing your nipples are rock hard? And don't forget your clit against my fingers right

410

now—it's so swollen and ripe, and that's just pure pain to feel, my lovely. Pure pain knowing you're about to come all over me."

"Lennox, after I come, I want . . ." I cleared my throat. I could be brave. After all, I'd climbed dorm room walls for him. I'd risked my heart for him. I could say this thing I wanted. "I want you to fuck me somewhere else."

"Somewhere else? You don't want the window anymore?"

I gave him a look over my shoulder. "No, your highness. Somewhere *else*."

"Oh," he said, his beautiful face going blank with shock. "*Oh*."

His cock throbbed inside my cunt; it clearly was on board.

"I know you have lube, and I want to try. I want—" I was shy about saying this too, but I made myself because it was important that he know. "I want you to have been everywhere. I want my entire body to know you. To have felt you everywhere."

He stilled, his head dropping onto my shoulder. I realized he was catching his breath, as if the idea of fucking my ass was too much and he was having troubling existing just knowing it was going to happen.

"Darling," he finally said. "Are you sure? We don't have to do this. If this is you trying to prove that you're some kind of sex assassin, then I already know that—"

"I'm sure," I said softly. "I want to do everything. And I know you'll make me feel good." Even when he thought he hated me, he still made me feel good. Like it's part of his genetic makeup, wired right into his very brain, that he has to make Sloane Lauder orgasm as many times a day as possible.

Lennox didn't answer me, only resumed his rough thrusts from earlier, and his exquisite handling of my clit. And within seconds, I was coming, keening, rocking back against him and arching against the cold glass at the same time. He let me use his erection as long as I needed, and it was only until I slumped back into his arms that he pulled free and carried me to the bed, where he settled me on my side.

I was still limp and boneless from my climax when I heard the click of the lube bottle and felt the cool slickness smeared over my tight entrance. He was generous with it, coating me inside and out, and then sliding a finger inside to make sure I was completely ready.

And when he decided I was, he knelt behind my ass while I stayed on my side, and he pressed the flared crown of his cock to my slick rim. "I've never done this," he confessed to me with a sheepish smile. "I guess that makes me a kind of virgin."

I smiled back, and I could see him melt. He always melted for my smile.

"I hear the first time hurts," I teased him. "Are you sure you're ready?"

"No," he said, but he pushed forward anyway.

The invasion was intense, scorching, like nothing I'd ever experienced. It *felt* obscene, utterly filthy, and even though I didn't know if I could come again, I felt the stirrings deep in my belly of another orgasm as he slowly wedged his cock deep inside my tightest hole.

"I—" His entire body was trembling as he pushed all the way in. The snowy light from outside made his hair silver and his eyes an unearthly platinum. His cheeks and jaw were as sharp as his gorgeous mouth was swollen from kissing, and the look on his face as he looked down at me. . . Like his entire life had been formed by fate for the sole purpose of meeting me and fucking me.

"Fuck. So . . . good. Tight. Fuuuuuck me. So tight."

I dropped my hand between my legs and rubbed myself, climaxing abruptly and hard, and even though he hadn't even moved, Lennox followed me over, the slick heat of my ass too much to stand. Every muscle in his stomach and thighs tensed, and then his cock jerked hard inside me, over and over again, flooding me with his come.

And then after several long, breathless, urgent pulses, we both went still.

He looked down at his erection still gloved in my body and then up to my face.

"Marry me," he said, and I laughed.

He didn't laugh though. He pulled free, took us both to the en suite shower for a quick clean, and then he put me in bed and climbed in. He pulled me into his chest. "I'm not having a laugh, Sloane. Marry me."

I tilted my head back to look at him. "We're not even done with Pembroke yet," I said, thinking he must still be joking somehow. "We're way too young."

"Then we wait until we're not too young. But I said forever, Sloane, and I meant it. I need you to know that I meant it."

I stared up into his perfect face. My former tormentor, the sole source of my misery for years. I loved him so much it hurt.

"Yes," I said.

His arms tightened around me, but his face didn't change. "Say it again."

"*Yes*, Prince Lennox."

He swore and his mouth came down over mine, his tongue in my mouth and his cock already stiffening against my belly again.

"But we have to wait to actually marry until after college."

"Fine," he said in the way of someone prepared to argue the point at a later date.

"And we can't tell anyone we're engaged until we graduate Pembroke."

He sighed against my mouth. "*Fine.* But I'll be reminding you every day. Every hour. You are mine, my sweet, fierce darling, and I'm keeping you."

"I'm keeping you first." I smiled against our kiss, and he swore again, rolling me onto my back and crawling over me, sliding into my still-slick body with no resistance.

"That fucking smile will be the end of me," he grunted, starting to rut. "But never stop. It's the way I want to go."

"Killed by my smile?"

"Tormented to death by it."

And then for the rest of the night, there were no more words. Only the best kinds of torments.

And smiles.

BRUTAL BLUEBLOOD

BECKER GRAY

Chapter One

Tanith

Summer before Senior Year—Ibiza

I DIDN'T BELONG here.

Below me, the Mediterranean stretched out to the horizon, a dark mirror reflecting the lights of the other yachts and party boats in the harbor. Behind me, Ibiza Town reared up in a rocky clutch of white buildings and twinkling lights. The pale tower of the town's medieval cathedral pierced the velvety night while tourists crowded into confetti-strewn clubs nearby. Music pulsed into the air, punctuated with laughter and shouts, and the warm evening smelled like salt and spilled champagne.

And I, Tanith Bradford, did *not* belong here.

I turned and surveyed what I could see of Serafina van Doren's yacht. Above me was the pool deck—crowded with lithe, inebriated bodies—and below me was the club deck, thrumming with music and flashing with lights.

The deck I'd escaped to was a little quieter, a little tamer, but only barely. Couples and throuples were snuggled into giant chairs and canopied beds, giggling and kissing and *more* than kissing. Every few seconds, a wet, shrieking partygoer went streaking down the massive inflatable slide off the top of the yacht, catapulting into the warm water below and emerging with a victorious yell. These were people so rich and worldly that a summer in Ibiza was nothing to them. These were people so beautiful they were influencers by default.

And here I was, the scholarship student, the plain girl, the poor girl from a nothing family.

Nobody.

Which was perfectly fine—I'd never needed to be somebody at Pembroke Prep, the elite boarding school I attended. I had plans for my *real* life, life after school, where I'd not only make my name as New York City's resident literary tastemaker at *Gotham Girl*, but I'd help new writers, photographers, and illustrators make their names too. I'd be part of the literati, just as I'd dreamed of being since I had been a girl and learned what publishers and editors did for a living.

I just had to survive one more year at Pembroke Prep. One more year of scraping every last possible networking opportunity and CV enhancer from Pembroke's vaunted halls. One more year, and then I'd be on to Columbia University and the beginning of my career.

And so, there was only one more year of being hopelessly, stupidly, perversely in love with Owen Montgomery.

Maybe even less if I accepted the Everston Fellowship offer sitting in my inbox right now. It was a fantastic opportunity—maybe even a once-in-a-lifetime opportunity—but it was so far away, on the West Coast, over two thousand miles away from the city I truly wanted to live in. And if I were being honest with myself, it felt strange to think about being so far away from my friends and family. Sussex County, New Jersey, wasn't exactly a short drive to Pembroke Prep in Vermont, but at least it could still be *driven*. If I were in LA, my noisy but affectionate family would be out of reach for an entire semester.

More importantly, I would miss my friends. And despite the elitist climate of Pembroke, I did have amazing friends.

Serafina, queen of the school and whose family owned the yacht I was standing on; Aurora Lincoln-Ward, a literal princess; and Sloane Lauder, boot-wearing badass extraordinaire. They were why I let Sera convince me to come to Ibiza this summer . . . even though Sloane couldn't come, and it would just be me reading in the shade while Sera and Aurora sunned themselves on her yacht. And partied. And pretended they weren't flirting with the Hellfire boys here.

Ah, the Hellfire Club. A not-so-secret club of the richest and cruelest boys at school. The absolute worst part about going to Pembroke Prep.

Also, the prettiest part of Pembroke Prep.

Especially Owen Montgomery.

Stop. Don't. You're smarter than that.

Which was exactly why I should say yes to the Everston offer. It would get me away from a certain Hellfire boy, juice up my CV, and, really, it was only a few months away from my friends and family. I could do anything for a few months, right?

I looked into the bright pink cocktail I was holding and decided to take a sip, wincing as it went down. It was strong, too strong, but maybe that was what I was going to need if I were going to successfully make it through this trip without thinking about Owen Montgomery again. And his dark blue eyes, and his full, pouty mouth—a mouth like the statue of a Greek god might have. And his cheekbones, and his hair, which was like BBC period drama hair, and his hands, strong and elegant at the same time . . .

I took another drink, a much bigger one this time, and

when I lowered my glass, I saw someone standing at the far edge of the deck, their back against the railing and arms crossed over their chest.

Dark eyes gleamed in the Mediterranean night. They were gleaming at me.

I tried to catch my breath. I shouldn't have been surprised; of course Owen was here along with the other Hellfire Club soon-to-be seniors: Keaton Constantine, Lennox Lincoln-Ward, Phineas Yates, and Rhys Huntington.

But to *see* Owen right now, with the sultry breeze toying with his perfect hair, with the ancient hills of Ibiza behind him, with the mingled light of the moon and the raucous party reflected in his eyes—

I realized I was staring and pivoted away, keeping my eyes fixed on the sea below, taking a performatively casual sip of my pink cocktail. I'd spent the last three years honing my theatrical skills around Owen Montgomery: pretending I didn't notice him, pretending I didn't hear his cultured, British accent icing up the hallways, pretending I didn't smell the subtle notes of his Dior cologne whenever he sat in front of me in class.

Citrus and spice, if you were curious.

It was hard to pretend because not noticing him was impossible. But it was necessary to pretend, and I hated myself for noticing him, impossible or not.

I was smart, ambitious—I had *plans*. And I'd read enough self-care Instagram captions to know having a crush on the wealthier-than-God asshole never ended well. No matter how sexy his sneer could be. No matter how tempting his cool aloofness was.

I took another oh-so-casual drink.

Maybe he was already gone.

Maybe he'd gone back in to find his friends—or a beautiful girl. While Owen was less of a capital-F fuckboy than Phineas, I was still painfully aware that he rarely spent a night alone. And if the rumors were to be believed, all those cold, Mr. Darcy-like manners of his disappeared the moment the lights went off. (Or stayed on, according to certain legends about how he spent his study hours in the library.)

And there were plenty of beautiful girls here tonight. The kind of girls who effortlessly flaunted bikinis more expensive than my entire wardrobe put together. The kind of girls who wore top-tier contacts and didn't have to worry about their glasses misting if they stood too close to the pool.

I adjusted said glasses now and decided to check and see if the coast was clear when I heard a low voice at my side.

"Not dancing?"

My stomach was nothing but flutters when I slowly turned my head to see Owen Montgomery next to me, one dark eyebrow lifted into a perfect, cool arch. It was the kind of gesture that layered curiosity with disdain, observation with judgment. Owen wasn't the kind of person to give away his regard—or even his interest—for nothing.

It was one of the reasons I'd found him so fascinating these last few years. Nearly every other boy at Pembroke was an open book—utterly obvious, utterly transparent. But not Owen. While he was the most scrupulously dressed, even now on vacation, and possibly the best behaved of the Hellfire boys in the most technical sense of the word, he was a complete mystery.

Unknowable and impossible to thaw.

In fact, the only emotion I've ever seen from him was icy boredom. Which was exactly what I saw in his dark eyes as I turned to face him fully.

"I danced earlier," I said, trying to sound like I didn't care he was here talking to me. That he'd sought me out after three years of having class together, of having social circles that often overlapped, when he'd never done so before now.

What if all that time I thought he hadn't noticed me, he had?

What if he's been wanting to talk to me . . . what if he'd merely been waiting for the right moment?

No. No, I had to stop. I was better than going all flushed and giggly because a Hellfire boy had sought me out.

I forced my voice into something unaffected and indifferent. "I notice you're not dancing, either, even though I think there are a lot of girls who would be happy if you did."

The eyebrow stayed arched, and something pulled at the corner of his mouth. "So, you've been paying attention to what girls think of me, is that it?" His voice was still low, nearly intimate now, the kind of voice I had to lean in to hear over the music.

"No," I said, finishing the last of my cocktail. "I'd simply noticed there are more girls than boys dancing here tonight. It would be polite to help even out the ratio."

"I'm nothing if not polite," he said dryly. "But I don't enjoy dancing. Or . . ." He gestured to the club deck, where bodies writhed and rubbed and sweated. I could practically smell the spilled alcohol and body odor from here. "Whatever that is."

"No, you don't seem like you would," I murmured. Unlike the other boys who were wearing swim trunks and glow-in-the-dark necklaces, Owen was dressed in boat shoes, cuffed trousers, and a button-down shirt with the sleeves rolled up to expose his forearms.

He looked chic, sharp, grown. Like someone who'd

already graduated from high school games and was ready for other, bigger ones. Ones much colder and darker.

"I haven't seen you around the van Doren yacht," he said. His gaze raked me over from head to toe, no doubt cataloging my lack of yacht wear. I was in a T-shirt that said, "Bury Me Next to My TBR," a pair of cutoffs, and tennis shoes that were still dusty from my earlier tour of the cathedral and nearby Punic necropolis. My ash-blond hair was in a braid that had started tidily enough but was now all messy and windswept from a day of sightseeing. I had no makeup on, and without my usual ensemble of serious black clothing, I felt like my glasses looked, well, *nerdy.* And not in the cool, NYC, arty way like they usually did.

I adjusted them self-consciously, my cheeks burning as I mentally compared myself to all the Instagram-ready girls on the yacht. But when I glanced back up to Owen's face, I saw something that surprised me.

Heat.

He was looking at me like I'd personally lit him on fire.

"I've been around," I managed to answer. It was the truth—I could only afford to come to Ibiza because Sera's family owned both the plane that brought us here and the yacht we were staying on.

"No, I don't think you have," he said softly. "I would have remembered."

I couldn't breathe for the way he looked at me then. Like I was the only person he'd ever seen in his life. Like I was the only thing that had ever stirred his interest.

"I was in the town today," I said, mesmerized by that look. God, to see him looking at me like that now when I'd spent so long hiding how I felt . . .

The eyebrow drew up again. "In the *town*? During the *day*?"

Most visitors our age only hit the town after sundown and spent their days sleeping off the mistakes of the nights before.

"I wanted to see the architecture and the history," I explained. "Did you know that the goddess of Ibiza is named Tanit? And that's the origin of my name? I had no idea *Tanith* came from the name of an ancient Carthaginian deity."

"I don't know," he said, his lower lip tucked behind his teeth for the barest instant before he released it. "I could believe you take after a goddess."

I laughed, but I was blushing too. "Stop. Tanit wasn't even *that* kind of goddess. She liked human sacrifice."

"Well, I can think of a few humans on this yacht that might be sacrifice material," he said, flicking his eyes over to a group of people currently whooping and screeching on their way up to the rooftop pool. "But perhaps I should start with something smaller. How about another drink?"

Another pink drink did sound good, but I was already breaking enough rules tonight. While I didn't normally participate in the "we're too rich to have consequences" parties at Pembroke—since I *wasn't* actually too rich to have consequences—something about being on a yacht in Europe made me feel like I wasn't in the real world at all. Like I could taste just for a night what my classmates tasted so carelessly all the time.

But there were some of my own rules I'd never break.

"I don't accept drinks I haven't watched being made," I said, a little apologetically. "But I appreciate the offer."

I expected this to ruffle him—another eyebrow lift, at least. But instead, I got an amused pull at the corner of his mouth.

"That's probably for the best, especially here," he said,

his gaze going back to the clump of screeching people. "What if I brought you something sealed? Would that be an acceptable offering for a goddess?"

I blushed again. Goddammit, I needed to be stronger than this. But still I said, "Maybe."

With another pull of his mouth, he disappeared into the fray, and within only a few minutes, returned with an entire tray of things, including a glass, a second glass full of ice, and two full-sized bottles of liquor, both unopened.

"I meant, like, a beer or something," I said, watching as he commandeered a nearby table and set the tray down. "I don't need an entire bottle of gin."

"Nobody does, except maybe Winston Churchill," Owen said crisply. "I'm making you a fresh cocktail."

With efficient, graceful movements, he had the apple brandy and gin measured out, along with a splash of grenadine, and was shaking the mixture with ice. Even for Pembroke Prep—a school of playboys and princesses and parties famous for their indulgence—this was a level of sophistication I'd never seen before. Certainly not from another eighteen-year-old.

The surprise on my face earned me a wry look. "If I'm going to make an offering to a goddess, I'm going to do it right," he murmured.

And then he poured the bright pink cocktail into the clean glass with impossible neatness—no flourishes, no showing off. Simply the expertise of a gentleman used to making real drinks.

He held the glass out to me. "Here. A Pink Lady. Minus the egg whites—they didn't have them at the bar." A subtle hint of disapproval curved his lips. Clearly, a well-stocked bar for an Ibiza boat party and a well-stocked bar for Owen Montgomery were two different things.

After accepting the glass, I took a sip, hesitantly at first, and then another one as the deliciously dry flavor revealed itself. "This is really good. Better than the first drink, even."

He nodded, his eyes on my mouth as he watched me drink. "It's an old Prohibition cocktail. Not too sweet, not too cloying."

"Thank you," I said, and meant it. "I don't think anyone's ever gone out of their way to make something like this for me before."

"Ever?" Owen asked, genuine surprise coloring his tone. "In your *life*? What about your family?"

"I have a big family," I explained. "Four sisters, and my mother takes up as much emotional energy as four more sisters. It's very crowded. At home, I mean. So, there's not a lot of special treatment going around. It's more like survival of the fittest."

He seemed to absorb that, his brows pulling together. After a minute, he said quietly, "I don't get much special treatment either."

Being so much quieter and more restrained than the other Hellfire boys, I didn't know a lot about his family life or background the same way I knew about Lennox's or Keaton's, but I did know he came from money and comfort, and so it would be easy to dismiss his despondency. So easy to say, "Aw, poor little rich boy," and write his words off as a symptom of affluenza or whatever it was called. But there was something about the way he'd said it—low and clipped—that belied a much deeper feeling than the words themselves indicated. And when I searched his face, I caught a glimpse of something fleeting under all that cool control. A glimpse of something beyond the famous Ice King.

"I'm sorry," I replied, meaning it.

He shook his head. "It's fine; it's fine. I don't know why

I said that, actually."

And he did seem a little confused, like he truly didn't know why he said it. Like he wasn't used to sharing anything about himself at all.

He changed the subject then. "Is this your first summer in Ibiza?"

I took another sip, licking my lips after. His eyes followed the movement, darkening as my tongue traced over my lower lip. A flicker of heat curled somewhere low in my belly.

"What gave it away?" I asked, trying not to betray how much my body responded to his presence. "The sightseeing? The T-shirt and jean shorts?"

He reached out slowly, like he was giving me time to back away or tell him no. I did neither, and then he carefully brushed a knuckle over the curve of my cheek. "You're a little burnt," he said. *Burnt,* not *burned*—that inflection of a British accent again. "It makes me think you didn't realize how sunny it would be here."

"I'm also flushed from my drinks," I countered, even though he was right. I had actually caught a little too much sun today while on my walking tour. "Maybe that's why my cheeks are pink."

Something glittered in his eyes then, a cool darkness that made me feel bright and hot everywhere. "Is that the only reason you're flushed, Tanith?"

I looked down at my drink, pretending nonchalance when all I felt was panic. Panic that he could see the horrible, embarrassing truth. That I was flushed because of him, because he'd been making me flush for years before tonight. That hearing him say my name after all this time was more wonderful than I can bear.

"Yes," I lied. "Of course it is."

"Hmm," he said. "What do you think of going somewhere a little quieter?"

My first instinct was a deep flush of excitement; my second was wariness. I might have been secretly in love with Owen, but that didn't mean I wanted to be a notch on a bedpost.

He must have seen some of that wariness on my face because the corner of his mouth lifted. "Here on the deck," he clarified. "Just someplace less loud."

Oh, who was I kidding? Tonight was my night without consequences, right? Why not do exactly what I wanted, which was to go with Owen and listen to that seductive accent some more?

I nodded, and the other corner of his mouth lifted too. A firm hand came up to my elbow; with gentle but unyielding pressure, he guided me to the farthest edge of the deck, where there was nothing but railing and warm, open sea. The music and laughter still reached us here, but it was fainter now. I could actually hear the wash of the waves against the yacht's hull.

"There now," he said. "Much better."

"Much better for what?"

"For hearing you admit the truth," he said, pressing those full, sculpted lips together in something like mock disapproval. "You were lying to me back there. About the flushing."

I almost lied again—actually, I very nearly considered hurling myself over the balcony and swimming to shore—because any option seemed better than admitting the awful, humiliating truth that he affected me.

But when our eyes met, I couldn't lie. He was studying me with a gaze so avid and so penetrating that I felt rooted to the spot.

I felt *seen*.

And after three years of being invisible, being seen felt incredible. I liked it far too much. Even if a Hellfire boy, heartless and cruel, was doing the seeing.

I couldn't say what came over me then. It wasn't bravery and it wasn't recklessness, or at least it wasn't only those things. It was partly lust, maybe, and partly the pink drinks tickling through my veins. It was partly that once, just once, I wanted to believe I could have my own fairy tale, my own Mr. Darcy jumping into a lake about his feelings for me. I wanted to believe my life wouldn't merely be reading about love and desire but experiencing those things for myself.

With him.

The oldest story there was.

I wanted to fall in love.

I wanted him to fall with me.

"You're right," I whispered. "I did lie."

It was a good thing I'd only ever seen Owen bored before because Owen *victorious*—Owen triumphant—was stunning. A wide smile cut across his perfect features, and his eyes danced with something more than reflected lights. And the slow swallow of his throat, like he couldn't believe his luck, was like a tiger who'd just woken up to find his prey already wriggling under his paw.

He caught his lower lip between his teeth. "I thought that might be the case." The words came out pleased and a little rough. "Am *I* making you flush, Tanith?"

In for a penny . . .

"Yes," I admitted, and then my blush burned even hotter. There was something thrilling about this, about skating along the edge of vulnerability and desire. About the potential currently searing the air between us.

His smile returned, but he didn't respond—not at first.

His eyes seared a trail down to my mouth, and then to where the worn T-shirt stretched over my breasts, and then down to my legs. When his gaze met mine again, it wasn't only hot and victorious, but determined. He seemed to have made up his mind, and I wondered what he'd made it up about.

About me? About having me?

For the night?

For the summer?

Longer?

"What are you thinking right now?" he asked in a husky voice. "I can see so many things in those big, blue eyes, but I don't know what they are."

I was a little surprised. I'd thought he was about to feed me a line, something irresistible and smooth, something like what I assumed he'd fed to scores of girls before me. But his question, his honest admission that he couldn't read me, was far more powerful than any pickup line.

My pulse kicked up as I summoned the courage to be honest too. "I was thinking you could make me flush some more."

"Oh?" His voice was still very controlled, still so very cool, but his gaze was beyond hungry now, beyond avid. It was existential almost, like his next breath depended on what I said next. "And how should I do that?"

"You could kiss me."

CHAPTER TWO

Owen

I'D PLANNED ON spending the night drinking alone at the villa Rhys's parents had rented for us, drowning my bad mood in sangria and hierbas while I stared out at the sea and cursed whoever had beaten me out for the Everston Fellowship. But Phin and Keaton had been unbearably annoying until I'd finally agreed to come out. Phin because the idea of spending a night silent and alone was utterly alien to him; Keaton because he wanted another cool head nearby if Phin or Rhys got into trouble, which happened often enough to be a real consideration.

So, I'd allowed myself to be dragged out to the yacht, but I'd kept myself away from the crush of the party. Serafina van Doren was an old friend of mine and I liked her a lot, but I had no patience for these kinds of things, even when she was the hostess. What usually started as an invite-only event turned into an "I know someone with an invite"-only event, which meant a party this big was crowded with a mix of socialites, social climbers, and random drunk people who'd somehow piggybacked in with a group of friends. And all of them seemed in a race to drink the most, screw around the most, and post the most on social media about doing those things, no matter how ridiculous they looked doing it. No matter how in bad taste it all seemed.

I liked drinking and sex as much as the next trust fund kid, but I preferred my pleasures less tawdry, I supposed. More rarefied. Perhaps because I was the responsible brother, the invisible but dependable son, and responsibility had been drilled into me from birth—or perhaps because I'd inherited my mother's distaste for anything common or gauche.

Either way, I had no interest in dancing in a sweaty crush of people or drinking badly mixed drinks while looking for someone to grind against. I still planned to stare at the sea and fume inwardly about the lost fellowship.

It would've helped me become even more of an asset to my mother's company, given me a change of pace and scenery—*something* to shake up a life that had become nothing but an endless parade of too-easy schoolwork, my mother's impossible expectations, and friends too preoccupied with money or girls to see the bigger picture. The bigger world we were all going to inherit one day.

Instead, I'd been wait-listed.

Wait-listed!

I'd never been wait-listed for anything in my life. It irritated me, but it made me curious too. Who was smart enough, creative enough, *ambitious* enough to muscle me out of a spot that I should have gotten just by virtue of who my mother was? Who?

And then I saw her standing by the railing, and everything else fled my mind. The fellowship, my bad mood, everything.

The only thing left was her.

She was standing alone as the breeze toyed with tendrils of hair that had escaped from a simple french braid, wearing cutoffs that showed off her long legs and a worn T-shirt that hugged the lithe curves of her breasts and waist. Unlike the people running up to the slide or dancing on the deck below, she was quiet, pensive. The gaze behind those big glasses was keen but curiously, not haughty. Sharp but not biting. As if she saw everything for what it really was and had no interest in it because she was preoccupied with deeper, more interesting thoughts.

I found, with some surprise, that I wanted to know those thoughts for myself.

And that *mouth*. Plump and pretty and sometimes catching gossamer strands of her hair as they fluttered in the gentle wind, it was settled into a soft line that was neither pouting nor self-pitying, only thoughtful.

She was simply apart. Apart from the immature games the other guests were playing, apart from the shallow, transparent hungers of the people around her. Apart from the teeming, glow-stick-y fray of the party. She looked innocent and wise all at the same time, and for the first time since I'd dragged myself to Ibiza, my blood ran hot. There was something about her that was almost familiar, but I suspected the almost-familiarity was because she was temptation incarnate. Not only gorgeous but interesting too. A riddle for me to solve.

I wanted to kiss that plump, pretty mouth. I wanted to twist my hands into the thin fabric of her T-shirt and yank her close to me. I wanted to see if I could make that thoughtful expression turn into one of interest. Desire.

Fellowship forgotten since the first time I'd heard I'd been wait-listed, I'd uncrossed my arms and strode over to make her acquaintance.

✧   ✧   ✧

TWENTY MINUTES LATER, I was slowly pushing Tanith against the railing, my arms on either side of her hips, lowering my mouth so it hovered over hers.

But I didn't kiss her. Not yet.

She smelled like the sun and fresh paper, and she looked too good to be real, all full, bitable lips and inquisitive eyes behind her big glasses. I could hardly believe my luck in finding such an angel here tonight—or perhaps she wasn't an angel at all, but a goddess set apart from the rest of us.

Tanith. Of course I'd learn her name at the same time I'd learned about a goddess.

"I could kiss you," I murmured down to her. "And then what would happen?"

Even this close, even in the flickering, half-light coming from the rest of the yacht, I could see her fair but sunburnt cheeks go even pinker.

She swallowed. "I could kiss you back."

A zip of triumph joined the lust simmering in my veins. I gave her a small smile. "And then what after that?"

She pulled her lip between her teeth. I felt that small gesture like I would feel a hand down my trousers.

"I don't know," she said after a minute of thinking. "I've only had one kiss. A boy back in eighth grade. The rest of my experience comes from reading Stucky."

"What's a Stucky?" I asked.

A smile curved those perfect lips, and I felt warm all over, like I was lying out on a beach under the Spanish sun. "Fan fiction. Steve Rogers and Bucky Barnes—but I read lots of different ships—there's one with Steve and Sam Wilson called—" I leaned down even closer, enough that I could feel the warmth of her exhales as she began breathing faster. "Freebird."

"Is that so?" I murmured, feeling an answering smile on

my own lips. Never, and I mean *never*, had anyone responded with fan fiction explanations when I'd been trying to seduce them into a kiss. I loved it.

"And when Steve and Sam and Bucky are all together—" She was blinking fast, her face lifted to mine. "All Caps," she finished in a pant as I brushed my nose against hers. As I moved my hands to the dip of her waist.

"Well, I don't know how All Caps does it," I told her, still smiling. "But maybe I could show you what can happen after a kiss."

I wanted nothing more than to slant my mouth over hers *right now*, to fit my lips against hers and kiss until the sun broke over the sea, but I forced myself to pull back a little, to be still. To let her steer this.

Tanith blinked up at me, her bottom lip between her teeth once more, as if she were thinking. Considering. Again, I had the sense that she was familiar somehow, that I'd seen this very same expression before . . .

I shook my head to clear away the feeling. No, I would have remembered this girl if we'd met before. There was no way I would have met her and then forgotten someone so different, so apart from this world that I belonged to but despised at the same time.

Then before I could react, she'd released her lip from her teeth and pushed up to her toes to press her mouth against mine.

For a moment, neither of us moved. Or breathed. It was only lips against lips. Only my hands on her waist and my feet on either side of hers and the breeze blowing her hair against my cheeks.

I'd never breathe again if it meant I could stay here forever.

Then I curled my hands into her T-shirt, pulling her

tight to me as I parted my lips and moved them against hers.

"Open for me," I breathed. She obeyed, parting her lips so I could lick inside her mouth. I grunted my approval the moment I tasted her, the mingled taste of berry-flavored lip balm and the drink I'd just mixed for her, and she let my flickering tongue coax her into a deeper kiss, deeper and deeper, until she was panting and pressing her body back against mine.

Fuck, she could kiss. I didn't know what was in that fan fiction she read, she knew to answer each stroke of my tongue with one of her own, to clutch me tighter when I dragged my mouth over to the corner of hers and down to her jaw and neck, inhaling her delicious scent. And her hips were so restless against my own that I reached down to find one of her thighs and pulled it up to my hip so she could alleviate her restlessness and grind against me if she wanted.

Apparently, she did want. The moment she arched and felt the long, thick ridge of my erection, she gave a shuddering moan against my mouth and arched even harder. I could hardly stand it—the silk of her mouth, the needy press of her body against the neediest part of mine.

"Your pussy is so hot," I mumbled into her mouth. "I can feel it through your little cutoffs."

"Oh my God," she breathed, kissing me harder. "You feel so good—this feels so good—"

She moved even faster against me, and I wondered if I could make her come just like this. Just by dry fucking her against the railing. God, even the thought had me close to blowing, and suddenly I knew this wouldn't be enough. This kiss, this night, wouldn't be enough. It couldn't be. Not with this girl. I needed more.

"Where will you be after tonight?" I asked between nibbles of her lower lip.

"Here," she said, sounding dazed. "On the boat with Sera."

With Serafina van Doren? How strange. I thought I knew most of Sera's friends. "Do your families know each other?" I asked, moving my mouth down to her neck and sucked on the sensitive skin there. A primal satisfaction surged through me as her hips moved more eagerly against mine.

"No—" Her breath hitched as I bit gently at her throat.

"When do you go home?"

It took her a moment to answer. "A day and a half."

I swore, my gut clenching with panic at the thought of not seeing her again. "That's not enough time," I said darkly. "I want days and days with you available to me." I pressed my mouth again to hers, my hand seizing the sweet curve of her backside, our hips mating below as our mouths mated above.

"Maybe," she said, and I could feel that smile curving against my lips again, "you'd be available to *me*."

I laughed and kissed her harder. I slid my hand from her waist to her stomach, and she layered her own hand over mine and guided it up to her breast. It was firm and warm, and already I could feel the hard berry of her nipple against my palm. All I wanted was to take her back to my room at the villa and suck on her breasts for hours.

I needed those hours. I needed more than hours, actually. I needed days and weeks and months.

"Where do you go to school?" I asked. "I need to see you again. I need to have you again."

Her breathing slowed, her body slowing too. For some reason, the panic clenched me harder.

What if she didn't want to see me again?

"Please tell me I can see you after Ibiza," I said, giving

her another hard, searing kiss. "I have to see you after the summer. I can travel, I can come to you, just please . . ."

She went still in my arms. When she spoke next, her voice was wooden. Distant.

"I go to Pembroke. We've gone to the same school for the last three years."

I pulled back to stare down at her. "Really?" That must have been why she'd seemed so familiar to me, but how could I have missed her? This goddess of a girl who wore T-shirts to yacht parties and read fan fiction and kissed like it was her last night alive? Where had she been hiding all this time?

"Huh," I said, trying to figure it out.

She pressed her hands to my chest, and it was instinct that had me putting my hands on top of hers. "Tanith—"

"You only knew my name because I said it first," she realized, pushing at my chest. "God, I'm so stupid."

Displeasure rolled through me as she pulled her hands free from my touch. "Where are you trying to go?"

"Away from *you*. To be alone."

"*Why*? What did I say?"

"Nothing," she said, venom overflowing in her tone. "You said nothing for the last three years. You literally had no idea who I was even though we've gone to school together forever. Jesus Christ."

The panic bled back into my displeasure then, and I reached for her. "Don't leave. Don't walk away from this. Who cares about the last three years? I want you now—"

"It's too late, asshole," she said, but then before I could say anything more, a fresh crowd of people burst onto our deck, shouting and laughing. I heard Sera's tinkling laugh, like a delicate bell, and Phin's boyish chuckle. Tanith and I both turned at the sound of our friends, both instinctively putting space between us.

It burned—like my body had already decided it should be pressed against hers. Always.

Sera was walking toward the slide with the group, laughing. The yacht lights gleamed along her dark brown skin and caught along the delicate necklace strung at her throat, and her long, shapely legs stuck out beneath a navy blazer that she must have borrowed off one of the boat staff since when I'd seen her earlier tonight, she'd been showing off her latest Fendi swimsuit and nothing else. I assumed she'd gotten chilled on one of the inside decks; God knew most of our friendship was her stealing my sweaters or coats when she was cold. Sera hated cold the way most people hated bugs or Nickelback, with an impatient disgust.

Not that I could remember what being chilled felt like after spending the last ten minutes making out with Tanith.

I saw Rhys, tall, pale, and dark haired, moving past Sera and the group with a scotch in hand and a cold expression on his face. He was dangerous in the way that fairy kings were dangerous in old fairy tales. Or the way vampires were in classic horror novels. Beautiful and hungry.

And every once in a while, I caught him looking at Sera like . . . like I don't know. Like he wanted to drain her dry.

But tonight, like every other night I'd known him, he seemed content to hang back in the shadows and watch everything with glittering black eyes.

"What a party!" an obnoxious voice boomed from the direction of the stairs, and then a boy I didn't recognize, his fair skin sunburnt and his blond hair slicked back, stumbled into Sera and spilled his drink all over the blazer and the front of her new swimsuit. She slowly looked up from the stain, and I was already feeling pity for this guy, because *one did not fuck with Sera's swimsuits*, when the idiot opened his mouth.

"Hey, can you get me another?" he asked her, shoving the now-empty cup into her chest. "There's a tip in it for you if you can hurry up with it."

The group stilled. At the edge of the crowd, Rhys's dark eyes locked on Sera, missing nothing.

"Excuse me?" Sera asked calmly.

"You're boat staff, right?" the idiot asked. "I spilled my drink."

The calm surrounding Sera didn't diminish, but the temperature on the deck still plummeted about thirty degrees. Sera deliberately dropped the empty cup to the deck, and then stepped closer to the boy.

"This. Is. My. Boat. Dickhead," she said. "And you're currently invited to get the fuck off it."

"Whoa, no need to get touchy," the idiot protested. "I just thought—"

I was already stepping forward to deal with this pillock, but Rhys beat me to it.

"And why did you just *think*?" he cut in coldly, stepping through the crowd.

Although Rhys was taller and stronger than this guy, that wasn't what made the guy step back as Rhys approached. No, even from where Tanith and I stood, I could see the murder in Rhys's face.

"Maybe you saw a girl with brown skin, and even though she was in a designer bikini, even though she was holding a drink of her own and talking with people who were obviously her friends, you thought there was no other way she could be on this yacht other than as the staff?"

"I—" The boy was flushed now, defensive. "That's not what happened."

"Seems like it was," Rhys countered softly, and now the

boy was backing up, right to the railing.

"It was a mistake," the guy said. "For fuck's sake she's wearing a staff jacket. She didn't have to go and be such a bitch about it—"

That was the last thing he said before Rhys's fist connected with his face and he toppled over the railing and fell into the sea.

"Rhys—!" Sera started, but Rhys looked back to her with a glare so sharp and hot it nearly made *me* take a step back and I'd known him for years.

"Don't get any ideas, princess," he sneered.

"Ideas," she echoed.

"He was killing the vibe, that's all. You know I'd saw my own hand off before I'd go out of my way to help you."

Sera's mouth slammed shut, and fury sparked in her eyes. "Then don't *fucking* bother next time. I can take care of myself."

"You'd better," Rhys said ominously. "Because I won't be there to."

And then he stalked off, his knuckles bleeding. He didn't even look over the railing to make sure the guy he'd punched had managed to break the surface and swim to shore.

"Shit," I muttered, stepping toward the railing to make sure the arsehole wasn't drowning, and then remembered Tanith and I were in the middle of something.

Fuck, it sucked being the responsible one. "Don't move," I told Tanith. "We're not done here."

"Sure thing," my blond goddess said flatly.

I gave her a quelling look and then jogged down the deck stairs to the swimming deck and ladder on the stern. The knobhead was already heaving himself up wetly onto the deck. A fat lip had started swelling on his face with a trickle of blood oozing from the corner of his mouth, but he wasn't missing any teeth or permanently fucked up in any other way. That was more than what most people who crossed Rhys could say.

"Okay, mate, back to the shore with you," I said, hauling him off to the small tender to be ferried back to Ibiza Town. He didn't protest, just cast me a sullen look every now and again, which didn't bother me in the least. I'd spent most of my life getting my older brother, Felix, out of his own messes, after all. If sullen looks still had the power to wound me, I'd be dead a million times over.

The guy now deposited in the tender and the tender pilot pulling away, I took the stairs up to the main deck two at a time, eager to find Tanith and fix whatever had gone wrong. She would understand, once I told her it didn't matter that we went to the same school. Once I explained it would be ideal, actually, perfect, because then we could see each other as much as we wanted. I could kiss her senseless every afternoon after classes, maybe even sneak her into my room . . .

But when I got to the deck, she was gone. So was Sera, though, and their other partner in crime, Aurora, and even though it made me want to howl at the moon, I also understood why she wouldn't want to be on the deck any longer and why her friends would be with her. Sera was my friend, too, and I wanted her to be okay.

It didn't matter anyway. Tanith could hide from me all she wanted here in Ibiza, but come the start of the fall semester at Pembroke, there'd be no place to hide.

I'd find her, apologize for not knowing who she was, and then we could finish what we started.

✧   ✧   ✧

EXCEPT, FOUR WEEKS later as summer ended and we all moved back into our rooms at Pembroke, Tanith was nowhere to be found. She wasn't with Sera or Aurora; she wasn't in the cafeteria or any classes or hiding in the library. It wasn't until a week after school started, when my obsessive desperation had gnawed my pride down to nothing, that I broke down and asked Sera where Tanith was.

She wasn't at Pembroke, and she wouldn't be coming back until the end of the semester. I'd lost my chance, not only that night on the yacht, but for the first half of our senior year too.

And even worse? The fellowship I'd been wait-listed for?

It had gone to Tanith. She'd deprived me of herself and of the fellowship I'd wanted in one fell swoop, and I couldn't decide if I were furious . . . or more fascinated by her than ever.

CHAPTER THREE

Tanith

Beginning of Winter Break

WHY HAD I said yes?

This felt like a mistake. But to be fair, it was really hard to say no to Serafina.

I'd spent the last semester doing the Everston Fellowship for digital journalism in LA. I'd had to do my classes remotely, which had been a challenge and the schedule had been grueling, but I was so happy I'd done it.

But now I was back at Pembroke Prep, and an offhand summer promise to spend the winter holidays with Sera was coming due.

I mean, why did she even care? Mom was working during the holidays and my sisters were each spending the holidays with boyfriends or friends, so it hadn't made sense to go home. I still didn't understand why I couldn't just stay on campus. I could unpack, reacclimate. Relax, read. *Big* plans.

But, oh no. I was headed to New York with Sera and the wild bunch. Kill me now.

The one silver lining. I'd managed to wrangle myself an interview with Preston Media. Fresh off my fellowship, my name should be at the top of the heap. Elizabeth Preston was my idol. I would do anything to be able to learn from her.

Or, for once in your life, you can have a little fun. Kiss someone under the mistletoe.

I scanned my gaze around at the sea of gray and navy and woven across the dark oak of the school's front foyer like a living tapestry. Who was I kidding? For that to happen, I might actually have to talk to someone voluntarily. The chances of that were nil.

As usual, Serafina didn't do anything small. Nothing at all. Which was okay, I guess, if you liked that sort of ostentatious, wild-party thing. But wow, her Rolls-Royce limo had pulled up with a driver in uniform, and it was hard not to slide her a side eye. Sera was normally so down to earth. It was hard to remember she was of *those* van Dorens. The New York van Dorens who'd outlived, outmoneyed, and outsocieted so many of the original Four Hundred families in New York. Old Money with a capital *O* and a capital *M*.

A prickle of awareness made the hairs on the back of my neck stand at attention like little saluting soldiers. Surreptitiously, I glanced around to see who was watching me, but I didn't have to look far.

Instinctively, I knew. Knew whose gaze singed the tops of my shoulders under layers of fabric. Knew who made me want to clamp my legs together.

All it had taken was one swipe of his tongue on mine and the moment had been indelibly seared into my brain. I couldn't count how often during the last several months I'd thought of last summer. The yacht, the kiss. The way one little groan had made me feel like I was a goddess. The way his erection had nudged at me, making me ready to beg.

And then, I'd learned the truth. I'd been the only one

seeing him for who he really was. He had never seen me. Hell, he'd thought I was some random friend of Sera's.

All that time I'd been pining after him, I'd been invisible.

Asshole.

I'd been hoping to avoid him for a little bit longer at least.

Because you're a chickenshit.

I was totally a chickenshit, but also, I wanted my bearings before getting caught up in him.

My gaze tracked and searched until I saw them. The Hellfire Club. The *cool* kids—boys only, of course.

They were the ones having a great time. Usually, I was busy studying while everyone else was having fun. Us scholarship students didn't get any breaks. Pembroke Prep was expensive. So, I didn't want to screw up. My scholarship depended on keeping my grades up and staying out of trouble. Which meant, apart from that one night in Ibiza, no parties, no boys, no fun.

Certainly, no boys like Owen Montgomery who would almost certainly ruin my soul.

I didn't give a damn about him.

"Oh my God, Tanith, there you are. Why are you all doom and gloom?"

I dragged my gaze from Owen's long, lean, dark-haired frame and told myself he wasn't as cute as I remembered. Because these were the lies we told ourselves to help us remember to stay away from assholes.

"I'm not doom and gloom. I'm just having a breath of fresh air before we head out."

"Are you so excited?" Sera grabbed my arm and squeezed. She wasn't usually effusive or particularly demonstrative, but she loved nothing more than commanding her court and fixing problems. And I was the problem du jour.

"Nice ride."

She rolled her eyes. "Ostentatious is the word you're looking for. My father is ridiculous. But ridiculous parental unit or not, I'm really glad you're here. No friend of mine spends the holidays in the dorms." She wrapped an arm around me.

"Thank you for inviting me, but I would have been fine."

Sera shook her head, her dark, springy curls giving a little light bounce. Sera had changed for the long drive and she was in winter white, which gleamed against her dark brown skin. Her long white peacoat was lined with matching fur. Only she could look that good in all white.

All around us, the boys snuck surreptitious glances at her. That was what happened around Serafina. Most guys almost always took a second look to admire her beauty. Girls too. She oozed van Doren power and coolness.

"Okay, Tanith, promise me you'll chill. This is supposed to be fun. All work and no play make Tanith a very exhausted girl. And you've been gone all semester. Now is the time for fun. Please tell me you at least understand the concept of fun."

"I'm fun," I muttered, only half insulted. "I know what fun is. It usually involves a book."

She laughed. "Now, listen, I love books as much as the next person, but we have to deviate sometimes and turn to other pursuits for fun."

I lifted a brow. I knew the van Doren library was extensive because of Sera. She might have been gorgeous, but she wasn't an airhead. The van Doren library had been one of her projects, giving under resourced youths access to her family's library. It came complete with researchers to help them work for the best scholarships at the best schools in the country.

"Okay, I got you. I swear, I'm trying to have fun."

"Ugh, this isn't meant to make you feel bad. I just want to make sure you know you're welcome. And I missed you."

I wanted to bite my tongue out. Here Sera was showing feelings and I was distracted. I gave her my full attention. "I'm sorry. I'm trying, honestly. I just . . . I feel a little out of place."

"Is this the part where I remind you that you feel out of place because of you and not because anyone's making you feel that way?"

"Yeah, probably. It's a good reminder." It was hard when you knew you didn't belong.

She laughed. "Look, there are boys here. And you're already getting some attention."

I pursed my lips. "Not interested." I refused to repeat the Owen debacle.

She tracked over to where I had been looking and rolled her eyes hard. "Montgomery wouldn't know hot ass if it stripped down in front of him. He's a robot. The Ice King. Now that you're back, we're going to get you a hot sexy boyfriend who's not a robot."

I'd broken down and told the girls what happened with Owen when I'd told them I wasn't returning for the semester. Sera had been ready to murder him. "I'd settle for one who realized we've been at the same school for three years."

"He's such an ass."

"That he is."

She laughed. "Come on, you're not a stick in the mud. I've seen you have fun. Like that one time we Christmas wrapped Constantine in his dorm room. That was fun."

I laughed, thinking back to it. I'd been a first year then. Oof, we'd gotten in a lot of trouble. The Constantines had been pissed when they'd come to pick up their baby boy Keaton for winter break and he'd been wrapped into his room. That was when I'd re-adopted this path of the straight and narrow. Sera could get away with that kind of stuff. But I could *not*.

I shrugged. "You know I can't be up to no good like that anymore."

The stunning Aurora Lincoln-Ward came striding over with her hair spilling over her shoulders in dark, inky waves. "Are you two ready for some winter fun? I hear there's ice-skating in our future."

My stomach pitched. I'd been skating before. I wasn't particularly good.

But we are trying to have fun.

I could handle a little ice-skating.

"Why do you look so pale, Tanith?"

I forced myself to smile and fake it because truth be told, this was supposed to be fun. And I *was* ruining it with my anxiety. Not taking full advantage of the opportunity to spend some time with my friends, to not think about school or the future aside from the one teensy internship interview I'd lined up. My mother always told me to grasp every opportunity that came my way with both hands.

Instead, I was sulking and afraid. And that wasn't me.

I pasted on a fake smile. I'd read in *Gotham Girl* once that even a fake smile can trick your brain into thinking you're happy. "I'm ready for all the fun!"

As we watched the boys laughing and throwing snow-balls at a howling Lennox, I rolled my eyes because God, could they be any more of the prep school, rich-boy vibe?

Except, my gaze landed back on Owen, I couldn't seem to drag my eyes away from him.

Sera sighed. "I see you looking at him."

I snapped my gaze away from Owen to my best friend. "I am not." Lies. "He's staring at me. Bet you he's trying to figure out where he remembers me from. Such a jackass."

Sera shrugged. "You know what, I agree with that. He is maximum dickage, and not in a fun, I-watch-smutty-dramedies kind of way."

I choked back a laugh. "I couldn't agree more."

The boys turned around, still laughing, and Owen's gaze met mine. I meant to look away. Honestly, I did. Except I couldn't. We were like the magnets we studied in class; no matter how hard you pulled them, they always wanted to be together. Suddenly, his brows furrowed, and he scowled like I had done something to him.

I glanced around. Sera and Aurora were now busy chatting about something and they hadn't even noticed. I frowned and glanced back. He was still staring at me, still frowning.

And clearly, Owen Montgomery was still very much a dick.

CHAPTER FOUR

Owen

FUCK ME, SHE was back.

I could hear the girls chatting and the one voice above all with its sweet melodic tone.

She was fucking back.

My skin instantly went tight and itchy all over. I stilled and told myself not to turn around. My bloody body didn't listen, as if pulled into compliance by the sound of her laugh alone. I turned toward it to see Tanith Bradford sweep a lock of hair over her ear.

It was like my body seized. Fucking Tanith. The flavor of her berry lip balm hit me hard as the memories of Ibiza assailed me. She'd tasted like nothing else I'd ever tasted in my life. And in those few moments with her, I'd been about as reckless as I'd ever let myself become.

What the hell was she doing back? Why didn't she just go home since it was the end of the semester? Why come back to Pembroke at all?

I'd adjusted to her not being here. Hell, I'd even gotten over the fact she'd slid into a fellowship that should have been mine.

If I could go back in time, I would say something different. The moment I'd not recognized her had ruined everything.

Like the twat that I am.

I'd made plans to apologize when we were back on campus after the summer. Not that I was ever wrong, but she seemed to need the apology.

But she hadn't been here. She'd been in LA doing the Everston Fellowship. The same one I'd gone for. Without telling my mother. Only one student was accepted, and thousands applied.

She'd gotten it. I'd been second.

Bloody second. I was second to nobody. *Ever.*

But yet she went, and you didn't.

My mother had been displeased, to say the least. Displeased I'd applied without telling her so she could pull the requisite strings. Displeased that I'd failed. Displeased all around.

She was smiling now. Fuck, I felt like I was under siege. My heart was beating too fast, and my mouth was too dry. And fucking hell, I couldn't activate my bloody body to move. Scratch that—my cock had glorious ideas on what we should be doing right now.

Dirty. Filthy, raunchy ideas that culminated with her pressed against the stone wall on the way to the gardens, her skirt lifted, and my cock buried inside.

Fuck.

The girl who'd taken my fellowship wore simple studs in her ears. No makeup. Freckles dusted just over her nose. Her eyes were a deep-sea blue I'd gotten lost in once.

God, I was a fucking mess. I needed to get my shit together. So she was back. So what? I didn't want to be *anything* with this girl. She was cute enough. But I'd decided in the months since Ibiza that she wasn't my type. Not at all.

I preferred girls who were a little wilder, who weren't going to take quite so much work. Girls who weren't looking for me to stick around. I had plans. And Tanith looked like she was one of those "stick around" girls.

She is cute, if you like that naughty book-girl thing, and you don't.

No, I did not.

I liked my girls—I don't know—different. Or at least not my competition, perhaps. In the months since I'd learned she'd nabbed the Everston, I'd done some investigating. Tanith was inching her way to magazine fame—fame that was mine by birthright. She'd not only written for the paper and the school literary mag, but she'd even had something published in the *New Yorker*. I was begrudgingly impressed, but still, that made her all wrong for me to date.

And besides, she was a scholarship case, which meant I had to be aware I was prime property for a social climber looking to better their connections through dating me.

You're also a prick.

No lies detected there.

But despite the fact she wasn't my type, and a relationship was out of the question, I couldn't deny she haunted my thoughts constantly. Haunted my body, even. For the last four months, I'd been seared alive with the need to finish what we'd started in Ibiza. Even if only to prove to myself that I could get this brainy, T-shirt-wearing, fan fiction–reading girl out of my system.

I watched as she pushed her glasses up over the bridge of her nose and then pressed her lips together into a mild purse as Lennox grabbed his girlfriend, Sloane, and dipped her, practically mauling her in front of everyone. Sloane took one kiss, then easily evaded him and did something with her arm that nearly had Lennox on his ass. He laughed and reached for her to kiss her again, which she finally allowed with a secretive smile. This was their weird, violent version of foreplay, I guessed.

I never pictured the two of them together. But if I were being honest, they'd circled each other since we'd all arrived at Pembroke like a couple of caged lions. Sometimes, I worried about Lennox's safety. Sloane was an odd duck, being the daughter of a legitimate spy and all. If you crossed her, you might wake up missing your nuts—if you woke up at all. But he loved her, which I still found odd because it wasn't an emotion I understood easily.

You loved your parents; you loved your mates. But hell, my mates were dropping like flies, wanting to lock things down with these girls in bloody *high school* that they barely knew. The girls were nice enough. But really? That forever shit?

Don't worry, that won't be you.

Damn straight, it wouldn't be. I would have Tanith because I could. And then she'd be out of my system, and I could go back to normal. Back to my pre-Ibiza, pre-Tanith-ruined self.

My gaze skipped back over to Tanith. Her lips made the perfect cupid's bow. They looked pouty and soft as hell and were completely unadorned. I kept staring at her lips and realized that was the last thing that would help with the problem in my jeans.

Meanwhile, Serafina watched our friends like they were her royal court, laughing at their antics. She was the unspoken queen of them all, or rather of us all. She had a full itinerary for this trip, and she was in charge. An itinerary *and* a guest list.

Sera was bringing Sloane and Aurora and . . . Tanith.

Which meant I would have my chance to finish what

we'd started in Ibiza even sooner than I'd thought. *But*, I had to get myself under control first. I'd get to the city and then figure everything out.

I forced myself to turn around. Nothing good would come from watching Tanith. However, my dick begged to differ. It twitched as if to say, "Me, I could come."

Jesus.

I did a mental checklist of all of my mates.

Keaton had already headed to the airport to pick up his girlfriend, Iris, who was coming in from France. He'd meet us in the city later. Rhys was riding with me, and I'd seen him outside downstairs lounging insolently, waiting for the limousine. Lennox was going with Sloane because she was going with Sera, so he was already accounted for, which left bloody Phineas. God-fucking-Phin.

Was he wasted? Again? This heartbroken-over-Aurora shit had to stop.

I didn't understand having some emotional response to a bird. I'd allow some concessions for it, though. But this was going too far. These days, we were more likely to find Phin plastered than sober.

I took the dark mahogany stairs of the boys' dormitory two at a time, weaving my way through the underclassmen who looked vaguely shell shocked and confused. Many of them were going back home for the first time since coming to Pembroke and were desperate for a sense of the familiar.

I mentally did my scan of the blokes to see if any of them made good Hellfire candidates. I had until the end of January to finalize my pick for my replacement. If I were being honest, I hadn't really given the nomination much thought. I'd had my hands full with school and losing that fellowship, scrambling for something else to pad out my CV. And hell, the family business. But I'd have to pick soon.

Luckily—or unluckily, depending on how you looked at it—such things were carefully controlled by the Hellfire Club alumni. While, in theory, I would choose my replacement, in practice I knew the alumni had a very short list they wanted me to pick from.

The dim dormitory halls with their dark, stained wood had light streaking in through the stained-glass windows, giving the dorm a strangely churchlike feel. Ironic, that, when I was heading to the room of the biggest sinner I knew.

When I reached Phin's room, I knocked on his door loud enough to get his attention. When there was no answer, I tried the knob. When that didn't work, I pulled my lockpick kit out of the back of my jeans.

My internal judgment meter started flashing, but I muttered to myself. "Don't judge me."

Last summer, we'd learned how to pick locks from an actual thief Rhys knew. God, to be young, rich, and bored. I hadn't wanted to learn, but fuck, it certainly came in handy this time as the lock released.

I should have been worried about what I was walking in on, but I'd seen Phin's bare arse more times than I cared to, and naked girls with my mates happened more than I liked. But, thankfully, with all the torrid drama between Aurora and Phin. He did keep shagging anything and everything that looked like her, though. Or what she used to look like before she went full maneater and dyed her white-blonde hair a midnight black.

When he didn't budge. I calmly went into the bathroom, grabbed a glass, filled it with cold water from the faucet, and then calmly marched back into the main room. I tugged back his blankets, and then I poured the water on his lap.

That did the trick. He jumped out of bed. "Fuck! Jesus Christ!" He scowled at me. "Why would you do that?"

"Because it's nearly fucking eleven, mate. We're trying to get to the city. You're the last one not up yet. Let's go."

He mumbled something under his breath that sounded like, "Time-keeping German asshole."

"I'm not fucking German; I'm half-British. You're thinking of Lennox. And he's half-British, too, anyway. Move your arse."

"Look, I'll just hire a fucking car. I'll meet you guys there."

As he tried to tug the blanket back up, not giving a fuck that he was wet, I shoved him back.

"Listen, you little twat, we've had to put up with your bullshit long enough. It's time to get yourself cleaned up. I don't care who you fuck. Fuck anyone. Fuck a lot of people. But get your shite together. We all agreed we're going to New York for this holiday, so I need you out of fucking bed, dressed, packed, and ready to roll, or I let Rhys come and wake you up. And then whatever he does to you, I don't want to know about."

Phin's eyes went wide, and he paled. "You wouldn't fucking do that."

"Rhys is part devil and gives no fucks about anything. You know that. If you don't move your arse, he'll be the one to come to get you. You prefer me, I promise."

Phin growled at me but stood. "Are you happy now, *mate*? I'm up."

"Brilliant. Now, can we move on? I get it. Aurora's got you twisted or whatever. I don't understand why, because she's just a girl and there are a million other girls who would love to jump into bed with a Yates heir. So you need to get yourself together, do you hear me?"

He scowled but still pushed himself out of bed. "*Fine. Better?*"

I crossed my arms and leaned back against his desk. "Yeah."

He lifted a brow. "Are you going to wait for me?"

"Not because I have nothing fucking better to do, but because I want to make sure that we leave on time. Let me guess; you didn't pack?"

Phin just grinned.

"I will fucking end you. Move your arse."

"Yeah, yeah, yeah. Give me fifteen minutes. If I'm not down there completely packed and showered and dressed, *Dad*, you can send the devil on his way."

"Deal."

I let myself out and slammed the door after me. Sometimes I wasn't sure why I put up with the lot of them. My fucking mates, the Hellfire Club.

We'd all been tapped as freshers by the seniors that year. The chosen ones. It was standard secret society stuff, but graduates were senators and princes and titans of industry. We were a small but mighty group, and the streets were paved with gold for us.

Once we'd been tapped, we'd been untouchable. Whatever we wanted, we got. The world was our oyster.

I jogged down the stairs, all the way down to the first floor. I found Rhys talking to an all-too-familiar face.

"Felix?"

My brother grinned at me, the cold making red splotches in his pale cheeks. "What's up, baby brother?"

I gritted my teeth. "Fucking Felix." I might be the younger one, but I was forever looking after him. With him was his best mate, Chad. Just seeing his tousled blond hair made me frown. I hated Chad. He brought out the worst in my brother.

I gave the wanker a nod. He gave me a cheeky grin back, his chalky face even splotchier than my brother's. *Fucker.*

"You know, it's weird you never look happy to see me," Felix pointed out.

I drew in a deep, calming breath. It didn't work. I wasn't calm. "That's because wherever you show up, chaos reigns." I ran my hands through my hair. It was true. You named it; Felix got into it. He was, as my mother always said, a beautiful disaster. It was like he couldn't help raining hell onto the world.

"What are you doing here? We're headed to the city."

"Yeah, Mum sent me here to fetch you, sort of. She said you'll have to take me and Chad to the airport to fly for Vail. Probably to make sure I actually get on the plane and don't stay home in New York to ruin her holidays."

I schooled my face. Felix and Mum had the kind of rows that made me want to be adopted out of my own fucking family. He pushed her buttons on purpose and she hated he wouldn't fall in line. It was so like Felix to just fuck off to a ski resort over the holiday break, but it was probably for the best. Things would be calmer.

"Fair enough."

I frowned at my brother because he was looking in the direction of the girls, primarily the queen. Was he checking out Sera? He'd never looked at her before, even though we lived so close to each other on the Upper East Side and had also gone to the same elementary school, so he'd known her forever. Why was he staring now?

He's not looking at Sera, you dipshit.

My gut clenched and my gaze flickered back when I realized Sera and Sloane had skipped down the stairs and were climbing into her Rolls. Tanith was still fiddling with her backpack and checking her phone.

I looked back to Felix and scowled. "What are you staring at, Felix?"

He shrugged. "Were the girls always this fit when I was here?"

Why did he have to be here? Why couldn't he have gone to Vail already? "She's just average if you ask me."

Lies. I shoved down the emotion I couldn't quite name.

"Are we all ready?" I heard someone ask.

I glanced up the stairs to see Phin jogging down with his backpack slung over his shoulder. "See? Showered. Packed."

"Did you even look before you shoved anything into your bag? And is it clean?"

Phin's grin was a quick flash. "As if I need to answer that. Anything I'll need, I'll just buy."

I rolled my eyes at him. "Let's go."

At the bottom, Sera waved me over. "Okay, so you know the plan, right? Once we get home, everyone unpacks, unloads, and then we are headed for ice-skating. Are you guys all set? We'll meet at Central Park. Text for any delays. I know how Phin likes to preen."

The corner of my lips quirked. "Yes, you know how Phin likes to preen, but really? Must we go skating? It's not really my thing."

She lifted a delicate dark brow. Even in her displeasure, she was beautiful. Why had I never dated her again?

You like your balls attached to you and not in anyone else's possession.

Well, that wasn't really fair. Sera wasn't a ballbuster. But she was tough. Not the kind of girl you fucked around with. And since that was the only kind of girl I was interested in, she was firmly in love-her-like-a-sister territory.

Besides, Rhys would have had my head. He might claim

not to want her, but if anyone dared touch her, he'd murder them.

"Yes, I have the agenda. If I didn't love your organization, I'd find you really annoying."

Her smile was sweet, and it completely transformed her face. On any day, Serafina van Doren was stunning. Honestly. Dark skin that I'd never seen with a single blemish. Big, wild curls. One time when we were first years, a teacher tried to make her straighten it, or pull it back, or something. I don't think the old geezer had ever recovered from what Serafina had told him.

She'd gone on and on about the glory of Africa being in her hair and how his comment showed his racist and colonialist ideals. Honestly, the old bloke nearly cried. I'd thought she was amazing. And when she smiled, you completely understood why Serafina van Doren got just about anything she wanted.

If I ever thought about settling down or being with someone, it would be someone like her. Not her, exactly, because God, it really would be like dating my sister. Our families had done so much together that I knew Sera better than any other girl in the school. And she was bossy. Neither one of us was going to give up control of anything anytime. It'd be chaos if we dated, and I didn't want to tangle with the queen even on the best day.

I gave Sera my most *we've been friends for years* look. "Must I go?"

"Yes, you must. It is what it is. Deal with it."

Felix sauntered over. "What's this about ice-skating?"

Sera gave him a warm smile. "Felix. How are you?"

"Can't complain. Let me take you out, Sera."

"When I suddenly start dating fuckboys, I'll give you a call."

Felix moaned and placed a hand over his heart dramatically. "You'd wound me if it wasn't true. I am a fuckboy. I don't mind, though. Who's your friend?"

Sera lifted a brow. "Tanith? She's not for you."

I agreed wholeheartedly, grabbing his arm. "Let's go, Felix."

My brother shook me off. "Oh, come on, she's cute. I do love blondes."

Sera wrinkled a brow. "Weren't you just declaring eternal love for me just a second ago?"

My brother grinned. "Hey, you'd look great as a blonde."

"Why go blond when I'm a hundred percent perfect just the way that I am?" Sera countered.

That shut Felix up, because what could he say? She was Serafina van Doren, after all. And, well, I had to agree with her.

I didn't have a thing for blondes, but my eyes still skittered over to Tanith.

I attempted to drag my brother away, but he tried to catch Tanith's attention by waving vigorously at her and then flashing her a smile. My gaze went back to her. She smiled back. I scowled again. I did not like my brother smiling at her.

It was nothing. Ignore her. You don't need the distraction.

It was true. I didn't need the distraction. Certainly not from a girl like her.

✧   ✧   ✧

ONCE WE WERE in the city and back at mine, everyone had been assigned a room. A flurry of texts later, we were meeting with Sloan, Lennox's permanent hip attachment, and the rest of the gang at the ice-skating rink in Central Park.

It was a cold night. Cold enough that my peacoat, jumper, and sheepskin gloves weren't enough to ward it off.

The girls were teetering on their skates, and Sera was directing everyone with her usual efficiency. Even Rhys was listening to her. Or rather, more like Rhys was staring at her like she was a steak, and he hadn't eaten in a month. I wasn't sure if he were listening as he wore the kind of expression that said he either wanted to fuck her or kill her. I wasn't sure which. And it wasn't my business. Besides, Sera could take care of herself.

I, on the other hand, planned to stay on the sidelines. No way was I going skating.

Unsurprisingly, my idiot brother decided to stay with us, announcing Vail was dull in comparison with the delights to be found here. Worst of it all, Chad agreed, so they would be around for the holidays after all. Mum was going to have a strop on when she found out, but I decided that wasn't my problem. I wasn't going to start my holidays by cleaning up yet another Felix mess.

My brother and Chad skated out on the rink and were flirting with the girls. In particular, Tanith. My gut clenched watching Felix skate around her as she bit down on her lower lip with sheer concentration, like she was trying hard not to fall. That was odd because winters at Pembroke afforded plenty of ice-skating opportunities, and apparently, she'd been at Pembroke all this time. So why didn't she know how to skate?

I didn't even know what possessed me to do it, but I marched over to the rentals. I hadn't brought my own because I truly hadn't planned on skating, but I asked for size thirteens and then put them on with quick efficiency.

As I reached the group, I skated behind Tanith and my brother. Felix was in flying form. His usual form. Laying it on thick.

Tanith still had that deer-in-headlights look on her face. And then Felix did what I expected him to do—cause chaos. He executed a spin right in front of her. Unfortunately, he nearly crashed into her as he spun, and she struggled to stay upright as she scrambled to get out of the way.

I could see her losing her balance. Then just like that, one skate slipped from under her. As she tipped backward, I slid right into position and caught her under my arms, lifting her with an *oof*.

Her gaze snapped to mine, wide and alarmed. "Oh my God, I'm so sorry. I'm not a very good skater. I still can't believe Sera talked me into this."

"Then what are you doing out here if you're not very good?"

"Well, I didn't want to be left out. And I promised Sera I would try and have fun."

As she spoke, my gaze stayed on her lips. She was saying words, words I understood. Words that made perfect sense. But still, I couldn't help but stare. It took me several moments to realize she was staring back at me.

"What?"

"Um, can you put me down now?"

My brow furrowed, and then I skated over to the side and eased her down onto her feet. "There. All good to go. I suggest you hold on."

"Yeah, but if I hold on, I'll never learn."

"We've all been skating so many times at school, why don't you know how to skate?"

She shrugged. "I'm usually studying, so I never come."

I squinted as I tried to remember her being there. But I

still couldn't remember seeing her anywhere at Pembroke before the yacht.

"Well, clearly you missed out."

She frowned at me. "Well, not everyone has the same easy access and opportunity. So, I guess I'll figure it out on my own. If you'll excuse me."

Fuck. I said something to irritate her, and I didn't have the patience to try and figure out what it was. "Wait, I'll help you."

I put my arm out, and she resolutely ignored me as she skated past. "No, I don't need your help."

"Obviously, you do."

I took her elbow and she whipped around, this time staying on her feet. "I told you, I don't need your help."

The fire in her blue eyes had my attention flipping to her lips again. And despite myself, despite everything I had told myself, blood rushed straight to my cock every time I looked at her. She smelled good. That same fresh paper scent, but also sweet somehow. And her breath was minty, as if she'd been sucking a candy cane.

And those lips . . . Jesus, those lips. I knew how good she tasted. I'd give anything to taste them again.

What the hell? No. That was the last thing I wanted. I wasn't going to *give* her anything. She'd come to me. Right?

I released her quickly, recognizing my brain was going foggy, and I was on the verge of doing something dumb, like leaning forward and kissing her. I didn't know this girl. I didn't know what she wanted from me, and as a Montgomery, it was a guarantee she would want something from me. The riddle was how to scratch my Tanith-itch without giving it to her.

But my blood ran hot. Too hot. I could practically feel her in my nerve endings.

She forced me to release her elbow. "You can let go. I'm fine."

"You're not fine. Why don't you just listen? Okay, look, how about I help you get to the group, and you skate with Sera?"

She snorted a laugh. "Do I look like any old skater to you?"

Despite myself, I chuckled. "Good point. She's pretty good."

"Yeah. Don't worry; just get me with the group, I'll sort it out. Sloane looks like she's uncomfortable, too, but she's more athletic than I am. Also, she's got Lennox to land on."

I could hear myself saying the words, feel my mouth forming them even as my brain knew it was a bad idea. "I'll stay with you. You could fall on me if you need to."

"Oh, so you do know what gallantry is."

I wrinkled my nose. Manners were for gentlemen, but gallantry was for fools. "Of course, I know what it is. I just find it a waste of time."

She blinked once, then twice, and then burst out a laugh. "Oh, gallant and charming. Wow, be still my heart."

I knew she was teasing me, and I knew I should be irritated, but I had other problems to contend with. Problems that were going to be difficult to hide if I kept staring at her mouth, wondering if it tasted as good as it had on the yacht.

I eased up on my speed to let some space grow between me and Tanith. Once I settled her with the group, I hung back. Then my brother caught up to me. "Isn't this fun?" he asked, looking ahead to the group.

Chad had already skated ahead and was now talking to Sloane and Tanith. I watched him warily. He definitely couldn't be trusted. If he started flirting with Tanith, I'd have to—

Have to what? You still don't even really know this girl.

I might not know her, but I knew Chad shouldn't be anywhere near her. Felix leaned in. "I saw you talking to her. Come on, how much are you willing to bet I can bang her?"

I normally didn't give my brother any thought if I could help it, but in this moment, I gave him all of my sharp focus. "What?"

"The blonde. How much would you bet I can bang her? The quiet ones are always wild in bed."

"If you touch her, brother or not, I'll fuck you up." And then I skated ahead to join the girls.

Felix wasn't going to do what he did to most girls to her, which was use them, destroy them, and then walk away unscathed. I might not know her, but I knew Tanith wasn't that kind of girl.

And God help me, I'd be damned if I let him anywhere near her.

CHAPTER FIVE

Tanith

AS THE DOORS closed on the group of potential magazine interns who'd all been interviewed with me, and the elevator began to sink toward the lobby of the Preston Media building, I knew I was going to throw up. The residual post-interview nerves were twisting my stomach, speeding my pulse.

What the hell had possessed me to schedule a job interview the week before Christmas again?

You were thinking it was handy that you were going into the city with Sera anyway.

Being with her had made things so much easier. No figuring out a train ticket, no begging for a ride to said train. No worrying about if or how I would have to spend the night in the city.

All things I would have managed, but they would have cost money. Money I needed to save every penny of, so I'd erred on the side of fortuitous opportunity and booked this interview.

I had no idea how well I'd done. There was a secret inner part of me that was internally twerking. In my head, I was cool and sexy and had rhythm. I knew the reality of that would look a lot like a twitchy giraffe.

The other, more realistic side of my brain was worried.

Internships didn't get much better than the Preston Media internship. It came with transportation and a stipend, and after the internship was over, priority consideration for employment at *Gotham Girl,* or its parent magazine, *Gotham.*

Supposedly, Ms. Preston really put the interns through their paces. She demanded the best and only took the best. I knew she'd seen a lot of candidates. How many others looked just like me on paper?

She wanted to turn out actual journalists, so that meant keeping the interns eighteen and older on call at all hours, which I could handle. I could absolutely handle that.

God, I wanted this so bad. I'd been prepping for weeks, even while I was on the Everston Fellowship. Sometimes I wished I could be like every other teenager. Like one of my friends thinking of dances and parties and bonfires in the woods. But if I didn't make this work, that was it. No money for a fancy college besides what scholarships I could gather up, and since my mom made just enough to push us over the income threshold to be considered for any of the free tuition programs, I would be on the hook for anything the scholarships didn't cover. Sure, I could take out a ton of loans, but I'd have to go to a state school, and while that was fine, I'd always dreamed of Columbia.

It was *all* I'd dreamed about.

So, I had to hustle. It was my only option.

If I were being objective, my first round had gone well. It had taken several hours. Of course, Sera had dressed me for the part: a mauve pencil skirt, silky gray blouse that made my eyes pop. I looked like an adult instead of like a teenager who was on the brink of desperation.

I had other possibilities for internships, but they were more like local Sussex County papers, and those were the last thing I wanted. I wanted to work at an ambitious media company. I wanted to work for my favorite magazine.

As the elevator slowed, my stomach flipped one last time as the journey ended with one final, gentle spring. And then we stopped. The crowd of uber-slick, New York-savvy modern girls in the car with me went still as they waited for the doors to open. I knew in my bones that even if I got this internship, I still wouldn't be able to shake who I was at the core of it.

An outsider.

I was lucky to attend Pembroke. From the moment I'd stepped onto the campus as a first year, I'd known the other students weren't my people.

Well, aside from my friends. Friends like Sera.

Sera was different. She gave not a single hoot who I was or where I came from, just who I was as a person. She was an *actual* friend. And then she'd tucked me under her wing and nestled me close. Even when I didn't want to be nestled. Even when I'd wanted to be on my own and free. And by free, I meant in my room, closed away, studying.

But no, Sera never let that happen. She insisted I was in her crew, and so occasionally, she would force me out. If I were being honest, I was glad she did.

I strolled past my internship competition with a determined stride. Once I opened the heavy doors into the glinting glass world of Manhattan, I blinked furiously as I dug into my coat pocket for my sunglasses.

I'd only ever been to New York one other time in the summer. I still wasn't used to the crowds and the noise. But God, the constant honking of horns, the clash of people . . . there was a part of me exhilarated by it. I just needed a minute to let it all sink in and ease away the quick flash of anxiety and hint of fear I had at being in such a busy, unfamiliar place, and then I would be okay.

When my hands clasped around my sunglasses, I was going to take a step forward, but instead, I walked into a wall of wool-covered muscle. Wool-covered muscle that smelled like Dior's Ambre Nuit. I knew that scent well. My manager at the high-end boutique I'd worked in over the summer wore it all the time. She'd claimed it was her boyfriend's and reminded her of him.

I couldn't blame her—I loved the scent.

I was momentarily stunned by the impact as my body went completely still. It was only when I felt the strong grasp around my waist and was wrapped in warmth that I gathered my senses.

Then I was being gently steadied by big, careful hands.

This all happened in a matter of seconds. Or years. Either way, I was so disoriented that all I could do was hang tight. I looked up. But that was probably a mistake because I started stuttering and tried to back away, almost falling again because my foot slipped on a scatter of rock salt.

"Whoa, easy there. All right?"

I coughed. "Shit. Oh God, this is embarrassing."

"We have to stop meeting like this," Owen said in his silken, British-accented baritone.

Butterflies fluttered in my belly. The total opposite of post-interview nerves. Why was his voice so deep? Jesus. He was in high school, but he had a *man's* voice, the kind you read about in romance novels. Or the kind you heard when you watched movies and the gorgeous male lead opened his mouth and caused the panties to start dropping. Like Clive Owen.

All I could do was blink. What happened to pretending

we were unaffected?

He pulled me around the side of the building. Though it was bitterly cold even with the bright sunshine, it was even colder in the shadow of the building.

"Um, yeah, sorry. I was looking for my sunglasses and then I didn't look where I was going and obviously I ran into you. Again, I'm sorry about that."

Stop talking, Tanith, just stop.

Owen Montgomery was the epitome of gorgeous, above-it-all aloofness today with his expressionless mouth and his inky-dark hair curling onto his brow. He didn't need me blabbering on and on. I hated that he made me so nervous.

You don't have time for this. No crushes, no drama, no mess.

Oh, and he was an asshole who hadn't known I'd even existed for years and years until Ibiza.

That was my mantra. Except, how many times had I thought about Owen's kiss while I'd been away?

And sure, maybe I'd had a fantasy or two hundred about him since the ice-skating rink two days ago, but I knew better. He was unattainable.

Not that I was trying to *attain* him.

I put my hands over his to push them off, but then stopped. Even under tailored leather gloves, they were warm enough to feel good against my own bare hands. "Um, okay, I think I'm good."

His lips quirked and he stared down at me, his blue eyes keen, missing nothing. I felt like he was completely, fully inspecting me. "Are you sure? You seem off-kilter."

"Yes, I probably shouldn't try to do two things at once."

"Okay, if you say so." He released me. Instantly, I missed his warmth because the bite of the wind chased inside my coat. Well, the coat Sera had lent me, to be precise. A scarlet-red coat made of thin wool. If I had been paying attention, I would have closed it by now. But I hadn't.

I felt Owen's gaze sweep over me. He wasn't shy about it either. He openly assessed me. "I'm sorry. I shouldn't stare. I'm just trying to figure out whatever it is about you that has you falling all the time."

I lifted a brow. "It's only happened twice, but I'll also have you know that a distracted mind is a great sign of intelligence."

Stop talking, Tanith.

"Is it now? I wouldn't be inclined to believe you, but I've seen some of your writing for the school newspaper. And that junior editorial you did in the *New Yorker*."

The breath swooshed out of my lungs. He'd read my articles? "Uh, you read my articles?"

"Because I was curious about the girl who beat me out for the Everston Fellowship."

My eyes bulged. "Oh, I—you tried for the Everston?"

His smile was slow. It started on one side of his face, and as if one cheek had to convince the other to do the same. The other one slid up slowly with it, too, showing off a brilliant grin that had my heart breaking the rhythm of its normal, everyday beat into a rapid gallop. Jesus Christ. Owen Montgomery should smile all the time, or none of the time, because if he always smiled like that, no one at school would get anything done. Women all over the world would be dropping panties.

"I did. But I suppose the better woman won."

"Sure. I guess you finally figured out we went to school together."

It came out brusquer than I'd meant it to, and we both winced.

Why didn't I know how to talk around him? Didn't know how to make my brain cells work. Of course he didn't want to talk about that particular horrible moment.

That you should have gotten over by now.

He bit his lip and seemed to come to a decision. Whatever it was made him square his shoulders and lift his chin, like a conqueror sighting his next conquest. "Come on, where are you headed?"

Where was I headed? That should have been an easy question to answer, but I had no idea how because my brain went on fucking vacation the minute he looked at me like that. "Oh, sorry. Yeah, no, I think I'm headed back to Sera's."

"On foot?"

At some point, the clouds had rolled in and a light snow had started to fall, cementing my decision to enjoy the city in its most magical season. "Well, I mean, it's Christmas in the city and I've never been here for Christmas, so you know, see more sites, explore a little."

He rolled his eyes as if he knew me. "Shopping."

As if. Me, shopping? I'd gotten Sera a small thank-you gift for letting me stay with her, a simple bracelet. But it was the extent of the cash I had. No, shopping was not really my thing. I would have loved it to be my thing. To do nothing but spend days rolling through the streets and going into boutique after boutique trying to find just the right item. But honestly, even if I had the money, I would be bored within the hour.

"I'm not a shopper," I explained shortly.

This seemed to surprise him, but he quickly pivoted. "Well then, why don't we go around for a bit? Sightsee on your way back to Sera's?"

I should say no. I *needed* to say no. I'd left Pembroke

because I didn't want to have anything to do with Owen, so it made no sense to spend any time with him voluntarily. None at all.

Except I *did* need to go back to Sera's, and I *had* wanted to sightsee a little anyway, and then there was the way Owen looked in his peacoat and scarf right now, with his dark eyelashes catching the occasional flurry and his lower lip tucked expectantly between his teeth . . .

It was a lost cause and had been since the moment I'd collided with him and smelled his peppery, citrus scent.

I nodded in agreement. "That would be okay."

"Brilliant."

As Owen led me back toward Preston Media, I couldn't help but notice the way the girls poured out of the building, smiling and waving at him. He gave them all a nod, but his attention stayed on me. It was flattering, and I was immediately irritated with myself for being flattered. He'd literally been unaware of my existence for years. I shouldn't feel butterflies just because he was looking at me while he spoke to me.

As we walked away from the building, he asked, "So were you coming from Preston Media?"

The way he asked—curious, a little reserved—set me on my guard a little. If he'd gone for the Everston, did that mean he also wanted to work in magazine publishing? Did that mean he could be my competition in the future too?

I answered as vaguely as I could, "Just a short meeting. It wasn't a big deal."

He looked at me, and I could tell he wanted to ask more, so I cut him off. "What about you?" I asked. "Were you heading into the building?"

His answer was as vague as mine. "No, I was just in the area." He seemed to want to change the subject because he jumped to another topic entirely. "So, how come you never hang out with us?"

What? "I hang out with Sera and the girls," I said defensively.

No, you don't. Only when Sera makes you.

"I'm glad she dragged you on this trip, then."

"Sera has made it her mission to get me to have fun. I'm not, but you know it's hard to say no to her."

"Yeah, that's Sera. Been like that since we were little."

"Oh yeah. That's right. You do live nearby."

He nodded. "Practically across the street. Once when we were four, at the playground with our nannies, I grabbed a handful of sand, lifted her hair, and put the sand all in it."

I stopped, mouth agape. "Oh my God, no. You were a little asshole."

"I was an arsehole, all right. Thank you for noticing."

I snorted a laugh, and there was that grin again. "I didn't know never to touch a Black girl's hair. I was four. But Sera just very calmly turned to me and scowled. You know that face she makes when someone's about to be eviscerated? Then she had this very sweet voice—I still remember it like it was yesterday—and promised that every day she saw me for the next five years, she was going to put sand in my hair."

"That sounds like a little Sera."

"It does, doesn't it? That cool, calm, 'I am absolutely the queen of my universe.' And you know what, she actually did. Every day when we went to the park after that, for a solid week, there was Sera waiting for me with sand in her hand. Once or twice, I tried to run; that was worse. That was much worse."

I laughed and laughed. Why was this so easy right now? To talk to him? To be with him?

Maybe it was because this was the first time we'd ever talked—*really* talked, since blurting out MCU fan fiction factoids right before a kiss didn't really count—and I was seeing glimpses beneath the frozen surface of the Ice King.

"And then, well, she heard one day that we were moving back to England, so she told me that the days of sand would have to end. But when I returned, she would find some new way to torture me. I told her she'd never catch me."

"Oh my God. Let me guess, she actually caught you?"

He nodded. "God, I can still see Sera chasing me around the playground, hand full of sand, and me crying the whole time."

"Something tells me that you don't cry."

"Well, I was four, what do you want? But still, it was a manly cry."

I giggled. Actually giggled. Like a cliché schoolgirl. *Jesus.*

At the busy crosswalk, we both halted. As the New York taxis flew by, one of them hit a puddle. Without even blinking, Owen wrapped an arm around my waist, lifted me out of the way, and shielded me with his body. Once again, my heart didn't know how to take the contact. I blinked in surprise at him. "Jesus, do you have a knight-in-shining-armor complex or something?"

He didn't grin then. Just stared at my mouth. "No, actually. I'm not really for saving people."

"But still, you saved me three times now. I feel like I owe you."

He released me immediately. "You owe me nothing. It's simply the right thing to do."

I watched him for a moment. "That's you, isn't it? Mr. Do-the-Right-Thing."

He shrugged. "Possibly. Though I think that's more a function of being told so many times what the right thing to do is. I know exactly how I'm supposed to behave in every situation. But is that merely etiquette muscle memory or actually feeling the urge to do the right thing, you know?"

"What? Does Owen Montgomery have the urge to be a rebel?"

His gaze flickered over me again, and then slowly focused on my lips. "You have no idea."

Despite the wind blistering so hard it was chapping my nose and lips, my whole body flushed hot and warm. I started to sweat. Finally, the light changed again, and we were crossing the street. I spotted a hot chocolate stand on the corner, and God, how my mouth watered. I literally would kill for one, but it would be better to wait until I got to Sera's. I didn't really have the money to spend on it anyway.

As we walked by, my lips twitched involuntarily and my stomach grumbled, which was not helpful. I wanted it to stop immediately.

"Should I buy us some hot chocolate?"

I stopped and glanced up at him, irritated I had to crane my neck to look into his eyes. "What?"

"A hot chocolate? Do you want one?"

I *did* want one, but why did he want to buy it for me? "I can get my own." It looked like I would be spending money today.

"Don't be stubborn." I could practically see his shoulders widening and setting in place as he crossed his arms. "I'm buying you a hot chocolate. Besides, your stomach grumbled. You're clearly hungry. Why won't you let me do it?"

"Because I don't *need* you to do it."

He tipped his head back. "Look, you're just being obstinate now. Clearly you want one."

"I do, but like I said, I can get one myself. I was actually looking forward to getting one at Sera's where it will be warm inside, and I could sit by the fire."

"You can still enjoy it by the fire, but let me get it for you."

"Screw you. I can pay for my own, you know?"

I could only *barely* pay for it, but he didn't need to know that.

His brows lifted. "I wasn't suggesting that you couldn't. It's just that you seem like you wanted one, and the right thing to do is—"

I shook my head. "Oh, of course, the right thing to do is offer to buy the charity case some hot chocolate." I was losing it. I could hear myself losing it. But I couldn't stop.

He sighed. "Why are you being like this? I thought we were having fun."

"I'm being like this because I know you know I'm the scholarship kid. I'm not the kind of girl who goes shopping on a whim. I'm not the kind of girl who doesn't plan out all her expenses. I'm not the kind of girl you're used to. But that doesn't mean I can't take care of myself. It doesn't mean that I can't get the things that I need for myself. Matter of fact—"

I didn't get to finish. Not because I'd lost my train of thought, not because I'd had no idea what to say, not even because he'd tried to talk over me. I lost my train of thought because Owen Montgomery dragged me close and shut me up.

With his lips.

They were firm, but soft. Soft like satin as they glided over mine. When his tongue peeked out to lick over mine, everything fell away. He groaned low as my lips parted on instinct. My heart rumbled in my chest. One of his hands slid into my hair, fisting it gently and angling my head just so. Then he deepened the kiss.

It was no longer a firm surprise but a claiming plunder. As his tongue explored my mouth, I shuddered. The sheer impact of it sliding over mine, his lips against mine, was an infusion of heat like I'd never felt before. I was going to melt, right here in the middle of Manhattan with all these people bustling around us. I was going to melt.

He moaned again, his hand tightening once more on my hair, and then he released me. Not quite a shove, but more of a deliberate separation of our bodies. He blinked at me. I blinked at him. Neither one of us seemed to know what the hell to say.

"I'm sorry," he said, in what was likely an automatic response.

For heaven's sake, he was *apologizing*? Fucking apologizing?

"You're apologizing for kissing me? Or for not letting me finish talking? Or because I'm so disgusting to you, you can't believe that you kissed me? Which is it?"

He opened his mouth, and then shut it again. "Forget it."

"Wow, you are such a dick. Not just because you kissed me without asking my permission, or interrupted me when I was talking, but because you apologized with an 'I don't know what came over me,' as if you weren't in your right mind. Do you know how insulting that is?"

His usually sharp blue eyes were unfocused. His pupils were wide and dilated, and he just stared, not saying a word.

I stepped back as far as I could. "You know what? Don't talk to me. Just leave me alone."

He didn't try to stop me. He didn't try to say anything. I knew I was being sensitive. I knew, even as I walked, that he'd been kind to offer me a hot chocolate. But I didn't want him to want to do the right thing. I wanted him to share a hot chocolate with me because he was nice and not because he felt sorry for me. I certainly didn't want him kissing me because he felt sorry for me.

If Owen were going to kiss me, I want him to do it because he wanted to. Because he couldn't think of any other thing he'd rather do. But that was a pipe dream. And while Manhattan during Christmas seemed like a fairy-tale land, in reality, I wasn't even remotely close to a world where Owen Montgomery would truly want me.

CHAPTER SIX

Tanith

THE VAN DOREN mansion was one of those venerable testaments to Old New York City glamor—all aged brick and tall windows outside, plenty of marble floors and sweeping staircases inside. And tonight, all that glamor was dripping with the best Christmas cheer money could buy.

Garlands and lights and candles. Christmas trees in every corner, their branches glinting with hand-blown glass ornaments and winking with real candles. Servers circulating with champagne and spiked nog, and the strains of classical Christmas music filtering up the stairs, mixing with the sounds of society small talk and polite laughter.

Then there was me, hiding in a corner, clutching a champagne flute and tugging on the hem of the dress Sera had made me wear, wishing I could tug at the thong underneath too. She'd insisted that it was the kind of dress that needed discreet underwear, but I was usually a boy shorts kind of girl. It was weird, feeling like I was more naked than usual under my dress.

Anyway, the van Doren Christmas Eve party was like the yacht in Ibiza all over again, only this time with a string quartet rather than an obnoxious DJ. Better booze, at least, since in Sera's world, anyone old enough not to need a nanny was served at a party. But tonight, I had more than my usual out-of-placeness making me hide.

Tonight, I was hiding from Owen.

I'd seen him downstairs, from safely across the van Doren ballroom (yes, a literal ballroom), wearing a suit so sharp it could cut glass. His hair had been swept over his forehead, caught with tiny snowflakes, like he'd just come in from outside, and his face had been set in its familiar expression of icy boredom. Next to him was his brother and his brother's friend Chad—both handsome in that lacrosse-y sort of way. Felix already had his tie loosened and an easy grin on his face—the complete opposite of Owen who was colder than the frigid December night outside.

Oh, but his lips hadn't been cold. Not at all.

I could still feel his kiss and the sure, demanding stroke of his tongue. I could still viscerally recall the firm heat of his mouth over mine, still smell his citrus and spice cologne mingling with the scent of the city in winter—concrete and metal and the sugary scents coming from the hot chocolate stand.

I hated myself for it—for loving his kiss, for wanting more. I knew how heartless he was, I knew precisely how few fucks he gave. I knew his total knowledge of me was that I couldn't afford hot chocolate on my own and that I melted for his kisses.

And that you beat him to the fellowship.

That was interesting. As was the flare of respect in his voice when he mentioned reading my work.

But no. *No.*

I was a smart girl, and I didn't get my better-than-perfect GPA because I ignored the obvious. I'd been beneath Owen's notice for years, and I'd only caught his attention at all because he was horny and bored on a boat once. That was definitely not the foundation to anything worth building, and definitely not the way for me to drill into an early and glittering career in the world of magazines and media.

But the taste of his mouth . . .

No. I couldn't let his kisses taste better than my own goddamned pride.

So I'd fled upstairs before Owen could see me, before he could hurt me again with his superiority and his pity. Now I was standing in a room full of inebriated strangers talking about so-and-so's scandalous nanny or what's her name's coked-up son instead of with my friends, but it was a price worth paying.

Anyway, I was used to it. Even when Sera and Aurora and Sloane were with me, I preferred the outskirts of Pembroke's social scene. Everything was all so fake and *pointless*—who cared about a bonfire party when there was a whole city that never slept? Who cared about rugby games when we were months away from a world where ideas, thoughts, essays, and art were discovered and passed around faster than a leather ball?

I drained the rest of my champagne and decided to go up to my room. There would be no chance of seeing Owen in there at all, which made it the safest course of action, the smartest path. Just like the path I took this semester by accepting the fellowship that night on Sera's yacht.

Because fuck Owen Montgomery.

Fuck Owen Montgomery was my new vision statement.

Buoyed by my newfound determination, I turned and stepped into the hallway, only to run smack into Sera and Aurora who crossed their arms and arched their eyebrows at me like the party police.

"Why aren't you downstairs with us?" Aurora asked. She

was wearing her jet-black hair in an updo that set off the ivory of her skin and made her look like she was on the prowl to sexily exsanguinate someone . . . probably Phin. Though none of us actually knew what had happened between the two of them last summer, whatever had happened had been bad enough that the two were irrevocably combustible.

"Is this about Owen?" Sera asked. "Because that's deeply stupid if so. I hope you know how stupid that is. *Do* you know how stupid that is?"

"Owen Montgomery is like if the Night King in *Game of Thrones* were hot and wore designer suits," Aurora said. "He would kill you without thinking twice. With, like, an ice-knife or something."

"*Metaphorically* kill," Sera cut in. "Let's not get carried away; he's not Rhys."

"But his mother, on the other hand . . ." Both Aurora and Sera shuddered in unison.

"What about his mother?" I asked, trying to keep my voice low so no one else would hear, but it hardly mattered. The guests were too busy boozing, flirting, and networking to notice a clump of whispering teenage girls.

"She's a shark, Tanith," Sera said, giving me a *duh* look, like I should already know this. "Like a five-rows-of-teeth, no bones, wants-to-eat-surfers *shark*."

"I heard that she once made an intern cry after only twenty seconds in an elevator together," Aurora said.

"I heard she fired a personal assistant for bringing her the wrong kind of sandwich."

"She once declined an award because she found their award logo tacky."

"*And* the award committee apologized to *her* about it!"

"Wow," I murmured, but I wasn't thinking about personal assistants or award logos. I was thinking about that night months ago on the yacht. About Owen's quiet words in the dark.

I don't get much special treatment either.

"Anyway, Owen comes by it naturally," Aurora said.

"Very naturally," Sera said. "It's a shame, though, because Felix seems so normal, if a little fuckboy-ish."

"And fun! Chad is fun too."

"Hard disagree," Sera said. "Nothing good comes from a name like Chad."

"I think he's nice," Aurora protested. "Nicer than Owen, anyway."

"Rory, everyone's nicer than Owen."

Somehow, Aurora and Sera had successfully shepherded me from the sitting room while I was under the spell of their gossip, and now I was at the top of the stairs, totally against my will.

I balked, planting my feet.

"Uh-uh," I said. "I'm not going back down there."

"Why?" Aurora demanded. "Granted, you'll have to see my brother and Sloane practically having sex by the fireplace, but that's nothing new." She paused. "I mean, it's disgusting. But nothing new."

"Don't forget about Iris and Keaton," Sera added with a grin.

Aurora shook her head. "They've already left. Your grandmother walked in on them in the guest bathroom. *In flagrante delicto,* if you must know. She told them to get a room, and I guess they took her suggestion literally."

"Grandmamma is nothing if not sensible when it comes to public boinking. And look," Sera said to me, taking my hands, "it's going to be totally fine. It's not like Owen is going to kiss you under the mistletoe or something. I promise you will still live out your life Owen-kiss-free."

I wasn't sure what passed over my face then—shame or alarm—but Sera and Aurora both reacted at the same time, their mouths forming round little *O*s.

They stared at me.

"Tanith," Sera said slowly. "Is there something you're not telling us?"

Even though we were alone at the top of the stairs, I glanced around to make sure no one could hear us. "It's complicated," I finally admitted. "The kiss thing."

Two pairs of eyes—Aurora's eagle gold and Sera's shimmery dark bronze—blinked at me.

"He kissed me after my Preston interview," I said. And then I waved my hand like it was no big deal. "A short one. It wasn't anything like Ibiza."

"Wait," Aurora said. "He kissed you in *Ibiza*?"

"On *my boat*?" Sera said, sounding horrified. "He harassed you on my own fucking boat? Oh my God, I'll kill him."

"No, no, we'll have Sloane kill him, darling," Aurora said, rubbing a soothing hand over Sera's shoulder. Sera took a calming breath and nodded.

"Yes, you're right, Rory. We'll have Sloane kill him. And she'll kill him so dead that they'll never find all the pieces, not even when Keaton's family's henchmen search for them. And *then* we'll kill him a second time."

Affection warmed my blood, but as much as Sera and Aurora's loyalty meant everything to me, I didn't want them to get the wrong idea. "There wasn't any harassing," I clarified quickly. "On the yacht, I mean. I kissed him—I wanted to kiss him. A lot."

My cheeks were so hot now I was sure they were singeing the air around me.

Sera narrowed her eyes at me—a queen assessing her subject. "Does this have anything to do with your abrupt decision to spend the semester away from Pembroke?"

I considered not telling them the full truth, but they were going to yell at me for hiding the kisses anyway, so I might as well give them the whole story.

So, quickly and with as much dignity as I could muster, I recounted the whole story about what happened on the yacht instead of the much-abridged version from before, and then outside the Preston Media building two days ago.

"Okay, we definitely have to kill him now," Aurora said.

"And pour his pity-hot-chocolate all over his corpse," added Sera.

"And then sear your initials into his super-dead skin so he'll never forget who you are even in the afterlife."

I held up a hand. "I appreciate the murder talk. Truly. But murdering aside, can you understand why I don't want to go back down there?"

Sera and Aurora shared a look, and then suddenly their arms were linked with mine and I was being gently marched down the stairs.

"We are not letting Owen ruin this party for you," Sera said.

"What you need," Aurora declared, "is someone cuter than Owen to flirt with."

"No, guys, I don't flirt—"

"Not Rhys," Sera said over me as if I hadn't spoken. "He's the fucking worst."

"Same with Phineas," Aurora agreed. "And he's probably balls deep in some random girl right now anyway. What about Chad?"

"Stop it with the Chad already," Sera said, the eye roll apparent in her voice. "No one wants to put their mouth on a *Chad*."

"What? I think he's hot. And friendly. Which makes him a million times better than any Hellfire boy."

We were on the main floor of the house now, heading into the crush of the party. The air smelled like fresh evergreens, and small pretty fires burned in very old and expensive fireplaces.

"Rory," Sera said with infinite patience, "we are better than Chads. Chads grow up to be the kind of politicians that get caught in hotel rooms with two hookers and an 'eight ball' of blow. How about Felix?"

"I don't want to flirt with anyone—" I protested.

"Felix is perfect," Aurora interrupted. "He's hot and it will piss off Owen *so much*. Hey, Felix! Over here!"

Owen's brother turned, giving us a crooked grin from across the room. He said something to Chad and the other person he was talking with and made his way over to us.

With his loosened tie, rumpled hair, and lazy grin, he was beyond cute—although my mind immediately conjured up the contrasting image of Owen in his tailored suit, the fabric hugging his tightly muscled frame perfectly.

I could so easily imagine his bored stare . . . and those firm, full lips pressed together in cool displeasure . . .

"Ooh, look, there's mistletoe," Aurora murmured, nudging me so I'd see the clutch of glossy leaves and berries hanging above us.

"Rory, obviously, I'm not going to—"

"Well, hello there," Felix said as he reached us. His grin widened as he took us in, and for a moment as he looked at me, his lower lip caught between his teeth. I could feel Sera and Aurora discreetly touch each other's hands behind my back, the universal best friend code for *did you see that???* "I'm glad to see everyone survived the deadly ice-skating excursion."

Unlike Owen's eyes, which brought to mind winter oceans and glacial caves, Felix's were the color of a summer sky. Easy, open, carefree. Like he was someone who lived to have fun.

I wanted to have fun too. I didn't *want* to be the girl hung up on the cold, rich asshole. I wanted to be the future editor of *Gotham* who'd spent her youth kissing lots of fun, handsome boys. In a move Sera had taught me sophomore year, I raised my eyebrow and let the corner of my mouth curl the slightest bit.

"I'll be expecting my Olympic medal any day now," I replied.

He laughed. It was a warm sound, effortless, perfectly at home among twinkling Christmas lights and champagne. Nothing like the dark, icy liquid of Owen's voice.

"You know, I could be persuaded to tutor you," he said, all dimples and charm.

For a moment, I wondered what it would be like to date someone like him. He'd call, text, DM—reach out to me at all the right times. He wouldn't forget that I existed; he wouldn't act like I'd just stumbled out of a Dickensian orphanage. He'd kiss me and it wouldn't be the kind of kiss I'd have to spend four months running away from because it terrified me so much.

Because it terrified me how much I wanted more.

No, Felix wasn't the kind of guy who could unravel a girl, unspool her into threads of messy, tangled want. He was the kind of guy you kissed and then went about your day like normal.

There was something really tempting about that actually. Who wanted to be torn up over a boy when there were laidback, friendly guys like Felix around?

Sera and Aurora had melted away at some point, leaving me alone with Felix under the mistletoe.

Traitors.

He stepped closer, close enough that his brogues bumped against the sensible heels I was wearing. "So, what do you say?" he asked in a low voice. There were plenty of people crowding the room, but they were all clumped in tight gossiping circles, all in their own worlds. It felt strangely intimate to be murmuring together in a full room like this.

"What do I say to what?" I whispered.

"Tutoring," Felix said softly, his face coming even closer to mine. "Private lessons. You and me . . ."

The kiss, when it came, was warm and pleasant. His hand settled at my waist, the appropriate blend of seductive and considerate, and the touch of his tongue to my lips was the perfect mix of enticing and polite. This was a guy who knew what he was doing.

And it couldn't have been more different to how his brother had kissed me last summer, with his mouth hot and urgent against mine, with his fingertips digging into my thigh as he'd held me open to him.

Felix kissed me like we were playing a game together, a game with rules, a game where we'd both win. Owen had kissed me like it was a war. A war where there'd be no survivors.

Felix's hand tightened the slightest bit on my waist, and my entire body rippled with the wrongness of it. It was too practiced, too smooth. Too . . . *not Owen*.

But still, I let Felix deepen the kiss ever so slightly, his tongue slipping into my mouth. It felt like kissing Cody Collins in eighth grade all over again—totally fine, but truly underwhelming.

Even though my mouth was still melded with Felix's, my eyes fluttered open.

And they locked on Owen.

He was standing across the room, his chest heaving, his hands clenching into fists at his sides. Those cold eyes were all fire now, lava hot, like volcanic fissures opening under the ocean.

And those eyes were trained on *me*.

With a gasp, I broke away from Felix. He looked down at me with concern and a dash of annoyance, as if I'd broken the rules of the game by ending the kiss before he was ready.

"Everything okay?"

"Um, yes," I said, taking a step backward, trying to put more space between me and the seething Hellfire boy at the other end of the room. "I just need to—you know, I—I'll be right back."

Real annoyance crossed Felix's face now, something unpleasant and entitled, but I didn't care. I turned and pushed my way through the crowd, fleeing up the stairs and away from the furious Owen Montgomery.

CHAPTER SEVEN

Owen

I DID WHAT I should have done months ago, what I should have done two days ago in front of the Preston Media building.

Not let Tanith Bradford out of my fucking sight.

Yes, I'd come to some decisions since that kiss on the sidewalk. Some very important decisions.

I shouldered my way through the room and up the stairs. A hot fury thrummed through my veins, blistering the inside of my skin. For the first time in my entire life, I didn't care who saw. I didn't care how I looked as I stalked through the party; I didn't care that my usual icy control had cracked right down the middle and shattered onto the van Dorens' imported marble floor.

I only cared about finding her. Finding her and telling her exactly how it was going to be from here on out. I was tired of her running away from me.

I caught a glimpse of ash-blond hair and pale skin, and I followed her up a second flight of stairs and then a third. I could still see Felix's mouth on hers, could still see his hand on her waist—as if it weren't supposed to be *my* hand on her waist. As if it weren't supposed to be *my* mouth on hers.

Fuck.

I wanted to smash something. I wanted to hit and tear and howl. I'd finally *kissed* her again, and two days later, she was kissing my brother?

To prove a point?

To make me jealous?

Well, it's working.

I crested the top of the stairs in time to see her slip into a hallway I knew led to a rooftop balcony. I doubted anybody was up here, barely any lights were on, and I caught up to Tanith in a few quick strides, seizing her hand.

She yanked it out of my grip, spinning around to glare at me behind her cute little glasses. Her eyes practically glowed with anger in the dim hallway.

Fuck. Even her *glare* sent blood straight to my cock.

"Leave me alone, Owen."

"No."

That truly seemed to surprise her. "No?"

"You owe me some explanations," I said.

She narrowed her eyes. "About Felix? Fuck off."

I practically growled then. "About Felix and so much else. About how I couldn't find you this summer. About how I couldn't find you this *year*. About how we kissed this week and then you accused me of—I don't even know what you were accusing me of—and then stormed off."

"You know very well what I was accusing you of," she hissed. "You spent years totally ignorant of my existence, only noticing me when you had nothing better to do, and now I'm what? Your pity hookup? A toy that's suddenly interesting to you now?"

"This is your fucking fault," I said, my normally cool voice coming out rough and heated. "You think I *want* to want—"

Voices—giggling and whispering—came up the stairs, and I recognized the sound of a couple sneaking off from the party to fool around. I swung my head to see Sloane and Lennox of all fucking people at the top step, and I glowered at Lennox. I was half a heartbeat away from baring my teeth and beating my chest like an animal marking its territory.

"This hallway is taken," I snarled, and the prince smirked at me, his eyes moving over to Tanith standing in the shadows and then back again.

"Rather," he drawled, pulling a curious Sloane back down the stairs. "Maybe we can join you next time. Have fun now!"

I didn't wait for them to disappear. I grabbed Tanith's hand again and dragged her to the very end of the hallway, next to the glass-paned door that led to the roof. But I didn't take her outside. I didn't want to share her with anyone who might be out there. I didn't even want to share her with the Central Park view or with the half-hearted snow spitting from the sky.

I wanted her all to myself.

To my surprise, Tanith went pliantly enough, but once we got to the door, she pulled her hand away and crossed her arms over her chest. It plumped her tits above the low neckline of the little black dress she was wearing, and with an abrupt and almost painful stir of my body, I recalled the soft feel of her in my hand last summer. The way her breast had molded under her thin T-shirt to my touch, a perfect handful, just enough to squeeze. And the way her turgid little nipple had felt against my palm . . .

Fuck.

"You were saying . . . ?" Tanith prompted. She sounded furious, but her chest was heaving with something more than anger. Even in the dark hallway, I could see that her adorable flush was back, heating her cheeks and her chest. It made me stone hard.

It made me livid too. She'd been keeping herself and her delicious flushing hidden away from me for all this time.

"You ruined me this summer," I seethed, stepping forward. "All I could think of was you. Tasting you. Having you. And then you *left*. And now you're kissing my *brother*—"

"Who I kiss is none of your business," she countered. "None at all."

"If you needed kissing, darling, you only had to come to me." I stepped forward again, looking down at her. Her lips parted invitingly. "In the future, you *will* only come to me."

"And why would I do that?" she asked, lifting her chin.

"Because I was able to bring you to the brink of orgasm in less than two minutes on that yacht," I said fiercely. "Because I could make you melt on cold sidewalks in broad daylight this week with nothing more than a quick kiss."

"You're so fucking arrogant," she said. "You think that you're the only guy who can make me feel that way?"

"Did Felix?" I asked, jealousy searing the inside of my stomach. "Were you ready to spread your pretty legs for him?"

"Maybe," she sneered. "Maybe I was about to take him upstairs to this very spot."

"Don't provoke me."

"Or what?"

My self-control was gone—nothing more than a fucking memory. I was all instinct, all jealousy, all need. "Or I'll have to prove it to you."

"And what will you prove?"

"That you're already mine."

She was the one who moved first, rising onto her toes

and slanting her lips over mine in a fast, violent kiss.

"I'm not yours," she hissed between kisses. "I hate you."

"And I hate you," I groaned into her mouth, my hands dropping to the skirt of her dress, fisting the fabric to shove it above her waist. "But I have to have you. No girl has done this to me, ever. *Ever*, Tanith. Never broken my control. You're the first, and I hope you're fucking happy now."

"I'll be happy when you leave me alone," she gasped, parting her legs for me as I let go of her skirt with one hand and pushed it between her thighs. She bit my jaw, my neck, her hands shoving under my suit jacket, her nails scratching over the Italian cotton of my shirt. "I'll be happy when I never see you again—oh *shit*—!"

I'd found the front of her thong and slid underneath. I shuddered when I finally felt her, finally felt the pussy I'd been obsessed with since this summer. Her flesh was hot and slick for me, so fucking slick, and she was—

"Jesus, Tanith. You feel so good," I groaned, trailing my fingertips up her smooth skin. My erection surged against my fly at the feel of her, wanting *in in in.* "*Fuck.*"

"Owen," she said breathlessly. "Give me more—"

She rocked against my touch, whining in protest when I pulled away to tug down the neckline of her dress. She wasn't wearing a bra, and so I could expose a tightly budded nipple right away. Her whines turned to flat-out moans when I gave it a hard lick and then sucked on it.

"Owen," she said. "*Owen.*"

Her hands were greedy—greedier than mine even. She was clawing at my backside, at my biceps, yanking impatiently at the buttons of my shirt so she could slide her palms up my abdomen and chest. "You never did make me come when we were on the yacht," she said, biting at my throat and then sucking the skin there. "You owe me."

I left her tits, silently promising myself I'd be back, and slid my fingers between her thighs again. "All you had to do was ask," I told her, finding the wet place where her cunt opened for me. I pierced her with my fingers as gently as I could—one finger, and then another into her soft, tight sheath—all while studying her parted lips and her hooded eyes. I wanted to know what she liked. I *needed* to know.

"A-ask you to make me come?" Her voice was choked with pleasure; she seemed to love it when I pressed all the way in so I could grind my palm against her clit.

"Yes, Tanith," I said. "It's the only thing I've been able to think about for four fucking months. Making you flush until you're burning with it. Having this pussy whenever I want. Watching your eyes when I make you feel good."

I didn't know why I said the last part. It was something I could barely even admit to myself. But something about the way those aqua eyes had dilated with pleasure, about the way she'd gasped and shivered and panted on the yacht as I showed her exactly what kissing could be like . . . it'd gotten to me. I became obsessed with it, with all the tiny expressions and sounds she made as I touched her, even more obsessed with that than I was with actually getting to shag her.

More dangerous was that I was also obsessed with everything *else* about her. With her sharp, insightful writing, and her goddess namesake, and the way she laughed, even when she was being sarcastic. With the way her blond hair had caught the lights strung above the ice-skating rink, and the way she'd spent her days in Ibiza touring dusty tombs instead of drinking herself into a stupor like everyone else.

I admitted something to myself then, something I'd realized that night on the yacht but had talked myself out of believing.

She must be mine.

Had to be.

There was no way beyond scratching this itch but to have her with me, near me, against me, for as long as it took.

And she would see it too. She would see I was a fucking Montgomery, and she would be lucky to have me as her boyfriend—she would be grateful. I wouldn't merely give her as many orgasms as her body could endure; I'd give her so much else too. She'd benefit from my money and my power and my family connections.

I would make all her dreams come true.

How no other bloke at Pembroke had noticed her before now astounded me. That *I* hadn't noticed her before this summer astounded me too. Why hadn't I realized this brainy little blonde would be the one to make me crazy? Why hadn't I known I needed to get inside her until I saw her on that yacht, all pensive and alone under the starlight?

Fuck me, but I'd wasted so much time. All I could do now was not waste another goddamned second.

As if she knew where my thoughts were going, her hands dropped to my suit trousers.

I grunted and shifted to give her better access. When she unzipped me, I felt the purr of the zipper down in my fucking bone marrow.

"I want to feel you too," she whispered, almost sounding shy, and I remembered what she said on the yacht that night.

I've only had one kiss.

"You ever played with a cock before, goddess?" I murmured, capturing her lips with mine before pulling away to look down at where she was touching me. "You ever held one and felt it ache and pulse for you?"

"No, I—*oh*." The last word she said on an exhale as she

pulled the waistband of my boxer briefs down to expose my erection. The monster stretched nearly to my hip, thick and dusky with blood. The swollen crown of it was already glistening with precome, ready to fuck.

"You're shaking," she whispered, looking up at me, and I realized I was. I *was* shaking.

Shaking because of *her*.

"Are you okay?" she asked, looking concerned.

I let out a rough, breathy laugh. "Yeah, I'm okay."

"Do you—do people do this? Shake?"

"I've never . . ." I trailed off, not wanting to admit how much she affected me. But she had to know. She had to see how twisted up she made me. "Only when they're with someone that they want so much it hurts."

She licked her lips, her sea-blue eyes pinned to mine. "I don't want you to hurt," she murmured and gave me a tentative squeeze with her hand.

My knees buckled, and I slumped forward, bracing myself with one hand on the wall beside her head.

She did it again, and I was shaking so hard now I thought I might vibrate all the way apart into horny, unsatisfied dust.

"What do you want?" she asked. She was shaking now, too, breathing hard, and her free hand had gone between her legs. She was fucking touching herself while she stroked me.

I was going to have a heart attack before this was over.

"Do you want to"—she paused, taking in a deep breath—"have sex with me?"

Yes. Fuck yes.

Yes, I wanted that very much.

I wanted to fuck her into next week. I wanted to carry her back to the Montgomery townhouse, throw her on a bed, and then rut between her legs like an animal. I wanted to set her on all fours and then lick her from hole to hole—I wanted to put my tongue inside her everywhere. I wanted her to ride my face while she sucked me, and then I wanted to bend her over the bed and see how deep I could leave my come inside her. I wanted us both bruised, bitten, and marked with sucking kisses. I wanted us both with our hair tangled and smelling like each other. I wanted my seed drying in beautiful patterns on her skin.

I wanted to give her the kind of orgasms that made her ashamed after.

The moment the images entered my mind, a quiet panic followed them.

I was *never* like this. I fucked efficiently, cleanly. I didn't like marks or scents or territorial shit like coming inside a girl without a condom. I didn't want *dirty*.

I kept my sex contained. I found a girl who was willing, got her off quickly, came into a condom, and then made her leave. But *this* would not be contained. It would not be efficient or clean. I would need days and days and weeks and months with Tanith. I would need her never to leave. I would need to get messy and rough and hard.

I thought I was a gentleman—the only gentleman of the Hellfire Club. Turned out there was a beast inside the gentleman all along.

And Tanith Bradford woke it up.

I clenched my hand into a fist where it rested on the wall. "We're going to fuck, Tanith, I promise you that much," I said in a sex-harsh voice as she kept stroking me. "But I don't have a condom with me tonight."

"Isn't there—is there something else we can do?" she asked pleadingly. "I want to, I want to have you. I need to feel you—"

Lost to myself, to common sense, to everything, I was

between her legs in seconds, pulling her thong to the side and pressing my erection against her bare clit.

Skin to skin. Cock to wet, eager pussy.

I hoisted her easily up so her legs could wrap around my waist and I could grind my dick against the front of her cunt, so I could move against the ripe bud at the apex of her sex. With the first grind of my hips, she was crying out, squirming in my arms, and scratching at my shoulders.

"Owen," she breathed. "Oh my God. It feels so good."

"Soon, I'll be inside you," I vowed, rocking us together. "I'll be so deep, so big in there, and I'll never want to leave. You'll have to do everything with me inside you. Homework. Showering. Sleeping. All while I'm using this perfect cunt to fix the ache you've made."

My filthy words had her whimpering, scratching harder at my shoulders, biting at my jaw. "You'd better," she said. "You'd better, you'd better—oh my God, *Owen*—"

She went tight in my arms, her entire body as taut as a piano wire, and then finally, finally, I got to feel Tanith Bradford lose herself to an orgasm.

Her cunt was hot as fuck against the skin of my erection, and I could feel her release slicking her flesh as she cried out against my neck. Her pussy gave tiny, hungry flutters along my cock. It was so slippery between us now, and all I wanted to do was let loose all over her sex and send her back downstairs with my pleasure between her legs. But I didn't, not yet. When I eventually got to come in her pussy or on it, I wanted to savor the sight. I wanted to have her spread out on my bed so I could stare at it for hours. I didn't want it hidden under a fucking dress.

So instead, I set her down and spun her around, hitching her dress up to her waist in one smooth move. I stared down at her pert little arse, giving it an appreciative slap on one cheek.

She shivered. "I shouldn't like that."

I ignored her, wedging my slick, hard cock in the valley of her backside. I lifted the back string of her thong and put it over my cock, pressed her cheeks together around me, and started fucking. It only took a moment. Only a moment of her braced against the wall, her dress up to her waist, and my cock against her soft skin. My balls drew up tight to my body, and with a grunt and pleasure so sharp it felt like pain, I pumped my seed all over her backside, pulse after pulse of it.

I wanted it to last forever.

Fucking forever.

But after several more throbs, I was drained. My come spattered her skin like wet paint, and my cock gave a valiant surge as I took in the scene. Tanith's thick blond hair tumbling down her back, my dick against her bare arse. The curve of one well-loved tit still shoved over the neckline of her dress, the swell of it visible from over her shoulder.

And then with an unhappy sigh and a vow to myself that I would have her again soon—for good, this time—I used the pocket square from my suit to wipe her clean.

"Thank you for helping," she mumbled, turning and fixing her tits and the bodice of her dress.

"Of course," I said, tucking the square into my pocket. "There're a lot of ways I can help you, Tanith."

She blinked up at me. "Excuse me?"

I stepped forward, thinking I'd kiss her again, but she dodged me, her pretty mouth pulling into a frown.

"There's a lot I can offer someone in your position," I said. "As a Montgomery. Normally, I'd be dating someone from a better background, but I think it's clear that's not an option here. I have to have you. And that means you can luckily reap the rewards of my interest."

Something flashed in her eyes then, too fast for me to read, and she said, "I think you should go."

I frowned. "Why?"

"Because," she said tightly, "I am not going to be your charity case with benefits."

"That's not what I said—"

Footsteps came crashing up the stairs, and I turned in exasperation to see Lennox. His lips were swollen, and several bites stood out fresh and livid on his neck. Despite that, he didn't look happy at all. He looked annoyed as hell.

"We got to get Phin home," Lennox said. "Rhys just found him with the mayor's daughter."

"So?" I asked, now equally annoyed. "I'm in the middle of something."

"Then take a fucking time-out! Our friend is about to get murdered by the *mayor*, and we need to get him into a car before he's a bloody corpse."

Goddamn Hellfire drama. Always fucking something.

I turned to Tanith. "Stay. I mean it this time."

"Fuck off, Montgomery," she said, but I couldn't tell if that was weariness or hatred in her voice.

It didn't matter. She wasn't leaving this house until we got some shit straight.

She was mine. And I was going to prove it.

CHAPTER EIGHT

Tanith

WHAT THE HELL had I just done?

Well, you let Owen Montgomery dry hump you against the wall at a party. So. That happened.

I scrubbed my hands over my face, refusing to go back down to the party even though staying here was obviously a bad idea. But I didn't want to go to my room and rattle around like a well-pleasured but unsettled ghost either. With a groan that nobody but me could hear, I wrenched open the balcony door and stepped out into the cold night air, which felt amazing after the hot urgency of the corridor.

I was smarter than this. I was intelligent. I *knew* things. Knew what rich boys like Owen Montgomery did with girls like me. I was just for fun. I was a distraction. I was completely expendable. I was someone he would never think about after he was finished with me.

After all, wasn't that what had happened to my mother? Wasn't that how I'd come about? Some rich prick in the city had knocked her up and promptly forgot all about her, making it impossible to find him. It'd been the ultimate ghosting.

What was wrong with me? I really needed to do better

because I did know better. It was just he'd started touching me, and . . .

And what, Tanith? He is a Hellfire boy. And you, smart as you are, are a nobody.

Hellfire boys didn't date nobodies. Hellfire boys felt nobodies up in the dark and then promptly walked away.

The admonishing didn't stop there. My brain replayed what had happened. Owen's hand on my neck and then sliding into my hair as he gripped tight. His mouth desperately seeking mine as if he couldn't *not* kiss me. As if he couldn't *not* taste me. As if he would die if he didn't get his hands on me.

It was an Owen Montgomery I didn't know. The Owen I knew was always in control. That was an Owen Montgomery so cold that ice wouldn't melt in his mouth. *Ever.* He was that guy. His mates called him the Ice King, for Christ's sake. Like he was some fantasy book character.

He was the calm, cool, dashing, debonair Hellfire type, the one least likely to do something that would incur bodily harm. But he would certainly be on hand, in case anyone needed bail money or fishing out of a river, like that time a couple of years ago with Rhys. But God help you if you expected him to *feel* anything. He didn't know what feelings were.

And you're the silly girl who just let him feel you up.

I could still feel the residual tingles of his palms on my nipples diffusing throughout me as he squeezed my breasts, and then Owen oh-so-gently rubbing his palms so my nipples hardened as he groaned into my mouth. I could still feel the length of him pulsing against my belly as I throbbed in response.

That was the problem. *The throbbing.* I could ignore the rest of it. But that constant searing, needy throb . . . Jesus

Christ. How did anyone deal with this? Was this what had happened to Iris Briggs? I'd heard she was a lot like me— quiet, studious, working her ass off.

And then Keaton Constantine had happened to her.

Now, I understood. This was how girls like me lost their heads—and their scholarships. *God, please, God, do not let this be me. I was truly smarter than this.* So what if Owen Montgomery kissed me? Made me come? So what? I could take it. It was just getting off. People did it in fan fiction once a chapter. He wasn't proposing marriage. Hell, I was pretty certain he still didn't like me given how little he thought of me.

He was just so goddamned condescending. Like he knew anything about my struggles. Knew anything about who I was. Knew anything about how hard it was for me.

He knew nothing.

"You look like you need a drink."

My head whipped around to find Felix smoking a cigarette. I made a face. "Sorry, I didn't see you around here. And no, thank you."

"That's all right. I just came up from around there." He pointed toward the corner of the house, where there was another door.

"I'll leave you be and head back inside." I knew what it was like to need your solitude.

"No. As a matter of fact, I'm glad to catch you here. Seems like you're mad about something, pretty girl."

The way he said that made my skin crawl. "I'm thinking. But thinking is really cold work right now."

"Oh, come on, I'm not a complete and total jackass. Okay, fine, I'm a little bit of a jackass. But have a drink with me anyway." He held up his glass and waved it around.

"I don't really drink that much."

"Shame. Seems like you need it."

I didn't like the implications of that at all. "It does?"

He gave me a lazy smirk. "You think I didn't notice Owen with his hands all over you?"

My stomach twisted. "What?"

"Owen. My little brother. He's jealous as hell that I kissed you first."

It was on the tip of my tongue to correct him and tell him his brother had actually gotten the first kiss from me, but I didn't. I didn't need to broadcast that, and I really, really didn't want the competition between the two of them to get worse. "Our kiss was just a mistletoe thing, right?"

He laughed. "What? You don't want me to propose?"

I furrowed my brow. "No, I'm not even sure I like you."

He chuckled low. "Well, at least you're honest. You like my brother, huh?"

My furrow only deepened. "No. I'm certain I *don't* like him."

Felix laughed even more. "Ugh, God, young love. If only I had a heart."

He passed over the glass, and I eyed it dubiously. He rolled his eyes. "Jesus."

He pulled it back and tipped the glass to his lips, wincing as he swallowed. "See, it's not like it's drugged or anything."

Had he really said that? I eyed him dubiously this time.

"You really are an innocent thing, aren't you? Normally, I eat innocent things like you for lunch. But I can tell you don't fancy me. Which is just fine. I mean, I'm confused, obviously, because you're choosing my stick-up-the-arse brother, Owen, when you could be choosing me, but whatever."

"You know what? I think this conversation is over."

He put up his hands. "Look, I already said I'm an arse-hole. I get it. But you looked like you needed someone to talk to, so I'm offering to drink with you."

"I'm not sure I *should* be talking to you."

"You know what? That's fair. No one talks to me any-way. Especially not Owen. As you see, we're nothing alike. He hates talking to me."

"Yeah, because you are a prick?"

Felix shrugged. "Yeah, I saw that one coming."

"Well, I mean, it's the truth, so . . ."

"I'm not a prick. I just don't care."

"Why? Do you like being alone?"

He frowned at me. As if no one had ever called him on his bullshit before. "Are you drinking or not, sweetheart?"

What the hell. I could relax my "watching a drink being made" rule just one time. Especially since he'd been drinking from the glass himself.

I grabbed the glass from him and tossed it back, imme-diately regretting it. "Oh God," I sputtered, coughing. "Jesus, wow. Oh my gosh. That burns."

"Yeah, it does."

I huffed and continued to cough and sputter. "Geez."

"Yeah, girl. That'll put some hair on your chest."

"Do I need hair on my chest?"

His gaze flickered down to my tight black dress. "You know what? Your tits are perfect. Don't grow hair on them." He took the glass back. "Pity Owen is the one who gets to see them. A waste, really."

God, this guy made me feel gross. "First of all, can we get off the subject of my tits?" I eyed the balcony door. "Second of all, no one is going near my body, period."

Liar.

"Third of all, why don't you just talk to your brother?

You clearly have a lot of baggage going on. Your whole family is odd."

"Let's just say that Owen and I have never gotten along."

"He's your brother, though. If this were one of my sisters, I'd try and work it out."

"You don't know the Montgomerys. Besides, Owen hates me, and he's ruined job prospects for me before."

I frowned. "Owen's a prick and he's judgmental. Proud. Thinks he knows everything. God he's so damned annoying, but I can't see him going out of his way to ruin something for you. That just doesn't even sound right. He's all about doing the right thing, or having the appearance of it, at least."

Felix's expression grew bleak as he took a step closer to me. I stepped back, the alcohol still working its way through my system, warming everything. "You don't know him like I do. He's the worst. You think you can trust him? Wait till he turns on you. Quick. Watch your back."

"I'm wondering if maybe you didn't tank your own prospects and Owen was just adjacent to your own bullshit."

Felix frowned at me. "So you're defending him? After that mauling in the hallway?"

Why *was* I defending him? I knew him to be condescending as hell, and selfish on top of it. But despite all the ways he'd pissed me off, despite his possessive, caveman vibe in the corridor, I just couldn't see him intentionally fucking someone over. Especially not a member of his own family.

"I—" I cleared my throat. "You know what? What happened in that hallway is something between me and Owen. It's none of your business. What you should care about is your relationship with your brother. And again, him going out of his way to do something to ruin you is odd in the sense that we both know Owen always does what he thinks is right. Maybe you need to check yourself and the troubles you've gotten yourself into." With that, I turned back toward the house.

Best advice you could give yourself too.

I was not going to let Owen Montgomery derail me, which meant staying the fuck away from him.

CHAPTER NINE

Owen

WITH THE HELP of Grandmamma van Doren, we hustled Phin out of there before the mayor could murder him.

"Wasn't doing anything wrong," Phin mumbled drunkenly as Lennox and I walked Phin across the street to my family's townhouse.

"Right," Lennox said, "tell that to the mayor whose daughter you just deflowered."

He opened his mouth to protest, but neither of us wanted to hear it. I was already to my front door and unlocking it, and then with him between us, we somehow maneuvered him upstairs to the guest bathroom with strict instructions to brush his teeth and *go to bed*.

"You'll be a good dad one day," Lennox said dryly as we headed back across the street to the van Doren house.

"If my future son is anything like Phin, military school will be in order. He needs to get his shit together," I muttered as we slipped inside the van Doren entrance and back into the party. Rhys and Grandmamma van Doren were currently on Operation Mayoral Calm, charming, placating, and soothing the angry politician at turns. It was surprising and kind of sweet to see Rhys working so easily with Sera's tiny but fierce grandmother, getting her and the mayor drinks, laughing at her jokes, gently flirting with her as they kept the mayor engaged long enough for us to sneak Phin out of the house. I gave him and Grandmamma an, *it's done* nod when I spotted them, and Grandmamma van Doren nodded back, a regal gesture made even more regal by the jewels dripping from her ears and neck, and set into her dark, silver-streaked hair. Rhys's eyes slid over to us in silent acknowledgment, but he quickly returned his attention to the mayor and the venerable matron at his side. When he decided to do something, he committed completely.

"Phin will never get his shit together," Lennox finally replied as we passed into the ballroom. "Because my sister will never forgive him."

"He's that gone for her?"

Lennox gave me a look that could almost be pity if the heartless fucker were capable of it. "Oh, my sweet summer child. Just wait until you know how it feels to have the woman you want slip through your fingers. It'll fuck you up worse than anything you've ever known." And with that and a quick clap to my shoulder, he was off to find Sloane, presumably to score some more bites on his neck.

I had to get back upstairs to Tanith, but I still felt out of control, like I was splitting at the seams, and I needed a drink to calm the hell down first.

What the fuck was wrong with me?

I didn't act like this. I wasn't like this. Keaton? Totally. Keaton *did* need all this shit. And of course, Lennox. Hell, even Rhys might deem someone important enough to toy with if he were bored.

But never me. I was the least likely in the Hellfire Club to paw a girl in a completely public place and make her come against a wall. Fucking hell.

My cock twitched. Again. Reminding me it had zero intention of going any-fucking-where because Tanith Bradford had *ruined* me. Of all people. Ruined me for-fucking-ever. And now it didn't matter that this wasn't me, that I never lost my self-control, I was broken with the need to have her. Keep her.

Her taste, her scent. I couldn't get her out of my god-damned head. And from the moment we'd separated in the hallway, I'd been quaking with pure fury at her nerve to destroy my perfectly constructed sanity. I'd never had this problem before. Women were to be enjoyed, then quickly discarded.

Personal attachments were messy. I loved women, but in a civilized manner. I'd take them somewhere quiet so we could be alone, where I could be in control of the situation, of the surroundings. But Tanith? Fucking hell.

Ever since that kiss on the yacht in Ibiza, she'd been messing with me. None of this felt like a sane course of action. I felt like a completely unhinged person. And of course, I couldn't exactly talk to my mates about this. What was I supposed to say: "I want to shag her so badly I can feel my skin itching with the need?"

Rhys would never let me live this down. Forget Rhys. Phin—he would eat out on this for months. I was always on him about having some fucking self-control. And the first chance I got, I nearly shagged the poor girl in the hallway.

You certainly did. Pushed up her dress, shoved aside her knickers, and ground against her until she came.

Clearly, I'd lost the plot.

At the bar, I signaled for another scotch, then ran my hands through my hair. In our world, everyone got served, and the bartender didn't look twice at me. He just nodded and started to pour.

Hell, I wasn't even sure I really liked the scotch. I preferred a really nice tequila. But goddamn, sometimes dire situations called for scotch. Fuck, this girl had me in knots and completely twisted. What was I supposed to do with this?

Go back up there and get her to understand.
Tell her you liked her.

No, that was bullshit. I wasn't going to do any such thing. And then, as if I had conjured her out of nothing, there she was, striding down the stairs with that telltale *looking for my best friend* face.

She was in a hurry. Was she telling Sera she was leaving the party and going to bed?

The tightness in my chest only increased. Where the fuck was she going? She couldn't just leave.

Before I knew what I was doing, I swigged back the dark amber liquid, then chased after her. Because I was a fool.

When I finally caught up to her, she was headed back upstairs, like she'd given up on finding Sera and decided to go to bed anyway.

"Tanith, wait."

She whirled around. "Oh my God. I am not in the mood to fight. I'm exhausted. I just want some silence for, like, two minutes, okay? I don't need you, or your awful brother in my face."

My brows snapped down, then I scowled up at the next floor. "Felix? Did he bother you?"

"No, he wasn't bothering—look, he was just being himself, okay? I want to go."

My heart started to beat so rapidly I wasn't sure I could make it stop. She wanted to go. I needed to let her go. But, fuck, I want her in my arms, and I needed to make her stay.

515

You are an idiot. This is how you get hurt.

But despite that ever-screaming warning in my head, I did the thing anyway. I had to relieve the pressure valve, or I was going to burst. "Tanith, stop, okay? Just for a second."

She sighed and fully turned, crossing her arms. She was eye to eye with me at that point. All around us, partygoers were drinking eggnog and champagne and laughing. From farther in the house, I could hear the music that had replaced the string quartet. Something grinding—a low, sexy beat. The party was moving into its later hours, with some of the more distinguished guests leaving and the younger guests taking advantage of the free booze and dark corners. I knew just how everyone would be dancing to this music too. Except, it wouldn't look like dancing. It would look like fucking while standing.

Like you wanted to do with her.

What I wanted from her was something different. Something I couldn't pinpoint. Something I couldn't put my finger on.

Something *more*.

And then, without thought, I just said it. "Look, I like you."

Her ash-blond brows shot up. "Excuse me?"

I just kept talking because I didn't want her to leave, which was ridiculous because I could see the impending disaster.

But there I was, running my hands through my hair like some kind of fool, confessing things I had no business saying. But there was no stopping my mouth now. "I like you," I repeated. "And I'm not even sure why. I mean, God, you are so fucking self-important, and you think you know everything. And that internship, the one I deserved, you got. But I can't help how I feel. Ever since Ibiza and the boat, it's like you're imprinted right here." I tapped my temple. "And I cannot make it stop. I saw you again, and now it's like that constant memory of how you feel, how you taste, and that little sound you make at the back of your throat is *always* in my head."

Her brows remained furrowed, and her gaze darted back and forth. "I don't understand what you're saying."

"I wish I fucking knew too. But at the end of the day, I like you. A lot. And I'm not even sure where the fuck this is going because it's not like we can be anything real. It's not like we're in the same circle, exactly, and my parents are going to fucking flip. And God knows you're stubborn, and you think you're better than I am. Which makes no sense because of who *I* am and who *you* are. But Jesus Christ, I just want to hold you and find out what makes you cry and obliterate it. I want you so much I feel like I'm burning alive with it."

There, I'd said that. How bad was it?

I did an internal check. My heart was still beating far too fast, like I'd run a marathon. My breath was okay, but choppy. After all, I'd pushed through the crowd to get to her because I'd been worried she'd leave. So the choppy breathing made sense.

My brain. Oh, Jesus Christ. No. Don't look at that. It's a hot bloody mess.

But I'd said it, at least. I didn't wait for months like fucking Keaton and Lennox had, playing their stupid games. My gaze searched hers, waiting for her to say something because why hadn't she said something yet?

Her brows were no longer furrowed. Instead, one of them was lifted in a delicate arch.

"Are you going to bloody say something, or leave me standing here with my heart on my sleeve?"

"Was that your heart?"

What kind of question was that? I nodded slowly. "I mean, I just told you how I feel, and you don't say anything?"

"That was how you *feel*?"

"Yes, did you not hear me? It's not that loud in here."

She huffed out a breath. "So, you think that I should be overjoyed about your confession?"

My gut twisted. The sting of rejection all too familiar, needling all my prickly pain points. *Bloody Tanith.* "You're twisting this."

"No, fuck you, Owen. What? You think because you're rich you can tell me that you like me *in spite* of yourself? You can tell me that you don't even know why you like me, and I'm not at your level, and I should be somehow *overjoyed* by this?"

I frowned. "It's not like that." How could she be mad about what I'd said?

Seconds ticked by, and very slowly my brain came online and started replaying all the words that had come out of my mouth. It was as if the process slowed down, down, down, until I took each word at its own merit.

You think you're better than I am. Which makes no sense because of who I am and who you are.

I could feel the blood drain from my face. Fuck. "That's not what I meant. That just came out wrong. I—bugger, that's not what I—"

She held up her hand. "Oh no. That's what you meant. You think I'm beneath you. You think that you're better than me. You think I should be overjoyed because you're a Montgomery, or whatever the fuck that means, and I should be happy to get the crumbs that you dole out. You think you deserved that fellowship and I didn't. And you tell me all this as you confess whatever you want to call these feelings. You're a jackass."

I snapped my head. "What?"

"You're a jackass, Owen Montgomery. I don't want you. And my family might not have the kind of money that you have, but they're all worth more than you, a hundred of you, any goddamned day. You like me in *spite* of yourself? What kind of bullshit is that? Let me make things perfectly clear for you. No, I'm not interested. Because I deserve the kind of guy who wants me because I'm awesome, who sees every one of my faults and loves me *because* of them, not in spite of them. I deserve a guy who's actually decent and will treat me like I'm a fucking princess."

With every word of hers, I flinched. "No, just listen to me. I—"

"I'm done *listening* to you, Owen Montgomery. I'm done. Yeah, you can kiss. I'll give you that. But you know what? You can hardly be the best kisser in the world. I refuse to accept it. So I'm going upstairs, calling Sera and the girls, telling them about the kind of bullshit that you just laid on me, and then I'm going to make a list of all the other boys I have always wanted to kiss at our school. And *then* I'm going to make a plan to kiss all of them because at least they won't be you."

Fury gripped me at my core. "If you think that you can—"

"What are you going to do, Owen Montgomery? *You* did this. You walked up to a girl you claim to really, really like, and then told her you liked her despite yourself. So, fuck you."

And then she marched upstairs. All I could do was stand and watch.

Turned out the appendage I was wearing on my arm was my dick, not my heart.

CHAPTER TEN

Owen

WHEN I GOT home, I stormed into my bedroom and slammed the door. Then I kicked the leg of my bed as hard as I fucking could, furious with myself and with Tanith and with *everything*.

"What the fuck, man?" a sleepy voice asked, and I blinked through the darkness to see Phin sitting up in my bed.

"Why are you in my room?" I asked, flicking on a light. Phin's dark hair was sticking up everywhere, and he was still wearing his suit trousers and his tie . . . without a shirt on.

"I thought this was the guest room." Phin yawned, looking around. "You've got nothing up on your walls, my friend. I've seen corporate reception rooms more decorated than this."

"I have books," I said tightly, walking toward the bed. "Anything else is clutter."

I liked a clean room, a nearly empty room. It helped me keep everything in its proper place, which was essential when my inbox was constantly overflowing with Preston Media work. Work my mother expected me to do since I'd one day be at the helm of the company.

Doing that work was the only time my mother remembered I was alive, so it wasn't exactly optional.

But I didn't like to think about that too hard, or I'd feel that cracking in my chest again. The same cracking feeling Tanith had achieved so fucking effortlessly tonight.

"Get out of my bed," I grumbled, grabbing Phin's wrist and pulling.

"I like it here. We can snuggle," he said. "I'm very good at it."

I didn't have a problem sharing my bed—normally. But I was in no mood for company tonight, and I was probably going to require at least two angry masturbation sessions in order to sleep anyway.

"Get *out*," I said again, trying to yank him to his feet. "I don't want to be around you or anyone else right now."

"What the fuck is your problem?" Phin asked, stubbornly staying in bed. "Are you still mad about the mayor's daughter? I didn't *know*, dude. I thought she was just some hot blonde."

Who looked exactly like Aurora did before she dyed her hair, I thought.

"It's not about the mayor's daughter, and I don't have a problem. *Get. Up.*"

"You do have a problem," Phin declared. "I can sense it on you."

"You absolutely cannot because there's not one to sense."

"You have a hickey on your neck, and you're pissed as hell," Phin observed smugly. "It's a girl, isn't it?"

I scowled. "It's not."

"It *is*. Who is it? Not Sera, because you'd already be dead."

We shared a look, both silently agreeing on that point.

Rhys might not have claimed Sera for his own, but I was reasonably certain he'd eviscerate anyone who did. And I meant that literally. He would remove someone's guts with a fishhook, horror-movie-style, and lose not a single wink of sleep over it.

Phin kept guessing. "Aurora? It's not Aurora, is it?"

He was still drunk enough that he couldn't keep the obvious pain out of his voice. Purely to put him out of his misery, I told him the truth.

"Tanith," I admitted quietly. "Tanith Bradford."

"Tanith!" he said. "God, of course. Of course it's her."

"Why *of course*?" I asked irritably. "She's the worst possible girl for me. She's poor, for one thing, and not even a 'from a good name and at least used to have money' kind of poor. Her family is nothing; her connections are nothing. I don't know what I was thinking on that yacht in Ibiza; there were so many of *our* girls there—fit as hell, and so much easier to handle. Then I somehow found myself wanting a nobody in a T-shirt and cutoffs." I shook my head. "She fucking hexed me or something. It makes no sense."

Phin stared at me, his forehead furrowed. "You didn't *say* any of that, did you? To her, I mean?"

I frowned. "Well, yes. Obviously, I had to give her some context for my insane obsession."

His brows popped. "And she took that . . . well?"

"She told me to fuck myself and that she was going to find someone new to kiss. Lots of new someones, actually."

Phin let out a bark of laughter and then clapped his hand over his mouth. "Sorry, dude, really. Sorry. But, oh my God, you are a dumbass."

I stiffened. "Fuck off, you twat."

"No, really, look. You know I'm a screwup, and you know I screwed things up with Aurora—"

"And keep screwing them up," I muttered.

He kept on talking like I hadn't spoken. "But even I can see that you messed up, bro. Like, messed up *bad*."

"How is being honest a bad thing?" I demanded.

"Because it means you *honestly* feel like she's beneath you, dickhead. Why would she want anything to do with you after that?"

Panic, slow and cold, curled in my chest. "That's not— look, when you say it like that, it sounds bad. That's not what I meant!"

"It might not be what you meant," Phin yawned, tugging his hand free from my grip and stretching back out on my pillow. "But it's what you said."

Fuck.

Fuck.

I got to my feet and started to pace. "But what was I supposed to say? That I'm glad she's nobody and poor and that I'll have to fight my parents every step of the way to date her if she doesn't want to hide?"

Phin turned to his side, burrowing into the blankets like a woodland animal burrowing into a den. Well, a woodland animal that wasn't six foot three of muscle and testosterone and bad, horny decisions.

"I don't know what you were supposed to say," he said, already sounding halfway back asleep. "But if I were you, I'd figure it out and tell her. Soon."

"She won't want to hear it," I said, the panic clawing into my throat now. I couldn't lose her. I couldn't lose *this*. She was my sickness and my cure. I had to have her.

"Then write her a letter, man, I dunno," Phin mumbled. "Bitches love getting letters."

Bitches love getting letters.

I brooded over this as Phin started snoring, like a lanky,

behemoth of a puppy. I paced and paced until my feet ached and I had to sit down at my desk. I stared at my laptop for a long time, my mind filled with the scent of her, the sounds of her, the memory of her eyes the color of a tropical sea, the feel of her wet cunt.

Her giggle when she ice-skated.

Fuuuuuck.

I buried my head in my hands for a minute, dragging in an agonized breath. If I didn't have her, I would die of this. I would fucking die.

I opened up a fresh email draft and started writing.

CHAPTER ELEVEN
Tanith

"**Y**OU GOT THE internship?" Sera squealed the day after Christmas. She, Aurora, and I were crowded on Sera's canopy bed, covered in blankets and sipping hot cocoa Rory had spiked with Baileys. Sloane had left earlier that morning to "hang out with Lennox," which obviously meant "have lots of athletic sex with Lennox." I couldn't judge her, though. After Christmas Eve, when I'd practically begged Owen to fuck me against a wall, I'd lost any right to scoff about sex.

Sometimes, you found a person who turned you into a ball of wet, aching need, and the only way to fix it was to chase that need to its inevitable conclusion.

"I got the internship," I confirmed to Sera, still stunned. I had just finished a phone call with my mom and my sisters when I'd seen the email notification pop up on my phone. They'd told us during the interview that Ms. Preston would make her choice before New Year's Eve—but still. This was a shock.

But then again, from the brisk way her assistant had interviewed me and the other candidates, I got the sense that the *Gotham Girl* team never wasted time. Even during the holidays.

My phone screen glowed up at me with the official acceptance email, and I stared down at it like a woman in a desert staring at water. Everything I'd worked for, everything I'd wanted—it was all coming to fruition.

For the next five months, I'd be spending two days a week in New York City working with Elizabeth Preston. Elizabeth Preston! At *Gotham Girl*! I didn't even care I'd be getting coffee and running copies and sitting on hold with flaky fashion designers to source clothes for photoshoots, I'd be *there*. At my favorite magazine in my favorite city living out my dream.

I'd be in the center of it all.

"There's an invitation attached," I noticed, opening it and quickly scanning the attachment. "They're inviting all the interns for a New Year's Eve dinner at Elizabeth Preston's house in the Hamptons. I'm invited to spend the night too."

Aurora's eyebrows lifted. "Spend the night?"

She and Sera exchanged a look and then looked back at me, as if I were supposed to be having a bigger reaction than I was.

But I couldn't help it; the glow of excitement in my chest was dimming a little. "I don't know if I can handle dinner and a night at Elizabeth Preston's house," I told Sera and Aurora uncertainly. "I was terrified enough just to be interviewed by the *Gotham Girl* team. She wasn't even in the room, and I was sweating through my clothes. How am I going to handle dinner? After dinner? Sleeping under her roof?"

Sera put her hands on my shoulders as Aurora slid off the bed.

"Tanith Bradford," Sera declared, "you are a badass and

a scholar. You're going to impress the hell out of Elizabeth Preston. And you're going to look amazing doing it."

"But I—"

Aurora was already inside Sera's closet, hangers scraping against the metal rods as she examined the clothes. "You need a *dress*."

"Not a gown, though," Sera called to her.

I could practically hear Aurora's eye roll from here. "I'm a literal princess, van Doren. I know what dinner and a party in the Hamptons calls for."

Sera made a face in Aurora's direction and then turned back to me.

"We're going to suit you up for battle," she promised. "By the time you ring in the New Year, you'll be Elizabeth Preston's new favorite intern."

"Okay," I whispered. I turned off my phone screen and pointedly ignored the email underneath the *Gotham Girl* one. The email I'd been ignoring for a whole day.

I didn't care what Owen Montgomery had to say to me. He was a mistake I had no intention of repeating. And anyway, I had bigger fish to fry. Fish like wowing the socks off Elizabeth Preston and ensuring my future at *Gotham Girl*.

"Tell me what I need to do."

❖   ❖   ❖

ELIZABETH PRESTON'S HAMPTONS house looked like something out of a *Gatsby* remake. A sprawling mansion of pale stone and a thousand windows, Bay House was a testament to turn-of-the-twentieth-century wealth and good taste. With the dark gleam of Mecox Bay behind it, it needed no ostentatious ornamentations, and clearly,

Elizabeth Preston agreed. There were no fountains here, no gaudy statues. Only a sweeping lawn, hunched willows and venerable oaks, and low, tasteful shrubs—a landscape that set off the pre-World War I architecture perfectly.

When the car Elizabeth had sent for me rolled to a stop, I stepped out with a quick word of thanks to the driver. A staff member greeted me at the door who insisted on taking my bag and leading me to the room I'd be staying in for the night.

The house was bustling with activity—catering staff, people carrying musical instruments, people hanging greenery and white flowers everywhere. My nerves, which had been allayed somewhat by Aurora and Sera's wardrobe and etiquette prep, came back in full force.

"Um, how large is the dinner tonight?" I asked the woman leading me down a hallway of bedrooms.

"The dinner itself is quite small," she replied briskly, stopping in front of a dark wood door and opening it for me. "Only Ms. Preston's family and the other two new interns. But the party afterward is quite large. You can expect to see most of her colleagues there. And rivals."

"Her publishing colleagues?" I asked, trying not to squeak. This was what I wanted, of course, to mingle among the literati and become part of their glamorous and rarefied world, but so soon—and with so little warning—was terrifying.

"Yes," the woman said distantly, her critical gaze running over the bedroom as if to ensure it met her standards. Seemingly satisfied, she turned to me with a nod. "This is your room. Dinner is early tonight to leave plenty of time for the party. You'll be expected in the dining room at six o'clock. Guests for the party will begin arriving at eight. You'll have breakfast tomorrow morning at ten, and then the car will return you back to the van Dorens' residence at one."

Itinerary delivered, she set my bag on the floor, gave me another crisp nod, and then left me alone in the room.

Overwhelmed and anxious, I sank onto the bed.

Maybe I wasn't ready for this. I had spent so many years believing this world—publishing, media, glossy magazines, stylish, au fait websites—was right for me. I had never considered that maybe *I* wasn't right for this world. I mean, who was I really? A girl with glasses who liked books and wearing arty, thrift-store finds. A girl who knew more about Oxford commas and Adobe InDesign than how to schmooze with strangers and network with prospects.

A nobody. Just like Owen had thought I was.

I thought of the still-unread email in my inbox and let all my conflicted anger send me to my feet. Owen *was* wrong. Not only was I somebody, even being from a semi-poor family and all, but I was going to carve out an incredible path for myself, starting tonight.

I was going to wow the hell out of Elizabeth Preston.

With a deep, determined breath, I started dressing for dinner.

✧   ✧   ✧

BAY HOUSE WAS just as tasteful inside as it was on the outside. Original wood floors and molded ceilings set the tone, and the decorations were done with an elegant but restrained hand. It looked like something, ironically enough, from a magazine. As I walked down the hallway looking for the dining room, I was acutely aware I'd never been anywhere as palatial as this. The van Doren residence was a mansion, yes, but a *city* mansion, squashed comfortably between other mansions and department stores and buildings filled with million-dollar apartments. Bay House had nothing around it but expansive lawns, and it stretched to fill them all. It was like the house was stretching all the way to the sea.

I hoped I matched the setting tonight.

Sera and Aurora had agreed I needed something glamorous but understatedly so, and we'd opted for a black maxi dress with long sleeves and a deep V neckline. I'd balked a little at showing so much skin at first, but after I'd tried it on, I'd agreed it was the one. The silk jersey material and long sleeves gave the dress an elegant, but casual feel, and my polka-dotted open-toed high heels gave a kick of playfulness to the whole affair. I wore my hair down, letting the ash-blond waves tumble over my shoulders and down my back, and I kept my makeup simple—some mascara and pink lip gloss. Then I was done. I wanted to look like I'd be at home in this world, but not like I was craving attention. After all, my job would be to keep the attention on *Gotham Girl* and Elizabeth, not to draw it to myself.

I had to ask someone hauling a crate of champagne for directions, but finally, I made it to the dining room, which was long and surprisingly cozy with a fireplace and an entire wall of windows that looked out over the bay. Snow had started falling, big flakes that meant business, and from somewhere else in the house, I could hear the strains of a string octet warming up.

"You must be Tanith Bradford," said a cool British voice as I approached the table. A tall, slender white woman was standing beside the fireplace, her hips pushed to one side and a glass of white wine nestled in her hand, the long stem hanging down like a frozen icicle. Her hair was the kind of platinum silver that was achieved by artifice, not age, and her lovely, yet stern face was unlined. She wore a white pantsuit that wouldn't look out of place on the red carpet or in a *Gotham* spread.

She was beautiful. And terrifying.

"Yes, ma'am," I said, for some reason fighting the urge to curtsey. She was a magazine editor, not a queen, for God's sake.

But she did have complete power over my future right now, and that made her queen-*like* at the very least. So I settled for offering my hand as I came close, and this seemed to please her a little. Her dark blue eyes didn't thaw, and her thin but pretty mouth didn't move. However, she did take my hand and returned my handshake with a firm one of her own, giving me a small nod after.

"Elizabeth Preston," she said, "although I imagine you already knew that. Was the drive quite bad?"

"Oh no, not at all," I said. "It was lovely. Thank you so much for offering to pick me up and take me home. It saved the van Dorens from having to send out their car."

"Don't thank me," she said coolly. "It's basic hospitality. And my assistant was given to understand that you didn't have a driver of your own."

I didn't think I was imagining the curiosity or the faint disapproval in her tone. "No, Ms. Preston. I don't."

"Where's your family from, then?"

I swallowed. "Um. New Jersey."

Her eyes moved over me appraisingly. "Your resume was impressive, Miss Bradford. The Everston Fellowship, your academic career at Pembroke. I'm willing to let your work speak for itself, but you should know that chances for girls in your position are few and far between. I trust you won't waste this one."

"No, Ms. Preston," I said, not sure how to feel about

this. Was this encouragement? Outright classism? A weird, old-money mix of both?

"I know from my son's stories that Pembroke often chooses an eclectic blend of pupils to constitute its student body—ah, there's my husband. Jasper, come meet Tanith Bradford, one of the new *Gotham Girl* interns."

Son? Husband?

I couldn't remember ever reading anything about Elizabeth Preston having a family, but then again, maybe I'd never paid close enough attention to her personal life. I'd usually been focused on her accomplishments and her sharp, witty comments in interviews.

And wait—"Your son goes to Pembroke?"

But she'd already turned away from me and was kissing her husband on the cheek.

He returned her kiss with a fond one of his own and then extended his hand for me to shake. "Pleasure to meet you, Miss Bradford," he said smoothly. He was white as well, tall, and handsome in a dad kind of way. There was something familiar about the line of his jaw and the fullness of his mouth, but I couldn't place it. "I saw your other two colleagues on my way in, so they should be here shortly."

"And the boys?" Elizabeth asked, taking a sip of wine. "Can we expect they'll grace us with their presence or are they waiting until the champagne starts pouring?"

"With Felix, you never know," Jasper said jovially. "But Owen is always punctual and present."

Felix?

Owen!

With a slow-dawning horror, I turned to the dining room's door just in time to see my enemy stroll in wearing another impeccably tailored suit and a scowl that made him look unfairly hot. He jolted to a stop when he saw me, and we stared at each other for a long moment, a thick, angry hunger stretching between us.

I thought of the unread email in my inbox.

I thought of his awful words on Christmas Eve.

I thought of his warm, drugging lips moving over mine, his mouth hot around my nipple, his muscled frame toiling to give me the most intense orgasm of my life.

"Miss Bradford, meet Owen Montgomery," Elizabeth said. "My son."

Chapter Twelve

Owen

DINNER WAS EXCRUCIATING.

The two other interns joined us before we could speak to each other, and that seemed to suit Tanith just fine. She chose a seat as far away from me as possible, and then fucking Felix ambled in—ten minutes late—and sat next to her, clearly making her uncomfortable.

She mostly ate in silence, only talking to my parents or the other interns, and so I ate in silence, too, since I had no interest in talking to anybody *but* her. And the minute my mother pushed her chair back and we were free to go, I was on my feet to get to my elusive goddess.

But as fast as I was, she was faster. By the time I left the dining room, she was already gone.

No matter. I knew she must be in the guest wing, and I had zero fucking qualms about pounding down her door.

But my father grabbed me on my way out. "Your mother expects you to help greet the guests as they come in," he said in that cool, hard *your mother's career comes before all else* voice. Unlike my mother, my father was American, but they both had a deeply inculcated sense of class, ambition, and familial duty. "Be at the front door in fifteen minutes."

I closed my eyes for a brief second, wanting to scream.

Tanith was one of my mother's interns; Tanith was *here*. There was no way I deserved this stroke of good fortune, but I didn't care. If she was here, then I had a chance, but I had to get to her first. Find her and explain to her how it was going to be.

But I also knew the rules of the game. I knew what was expected in my role.

"Yes," I said, opening my eyes. "I'll be there."

"WELL DONE," MY mother said to me nearly two hours later. Guests had mostly all arrived and had been duly shepherded into Bay House's ballroom. They were now sipping champagne and nibbling on luxurious treats from the buffet as they began their usual social ballet of flattery and gossip. "You may go mingle."

I knew that wasn't a suggestion, but my marching orders for the night. It rankled beyond measure; Felix had fucked off after only twenty minutes of greeting duty, and if I didn't go find Tanith right this fucking minute, I was going to crawl out of my skin. But there was no point in arguing with my mother. The same cold drive that guided her career decisions underpinned her parenting style. I didn't exist to her unless I was serving a purpose, and I'd rather exist to her than not, I guessed.

And anyway, there was a way around this.

"Yes, Mum," I said, kissing her cheek before I went to the ballroom. She hadn't specified how long I should mingle, and with whom, specifically, I should mingle. I'd make some polite small talk until I found a certain bespectacled blonde, and then I'd mingle very hard.

Hopefully for the rest of the night.

It took me longer than I thought it would to find her—long enough that I began to worry that she hadn't come out for the party at all and instead had holed herself up in her room to hide from me. I'd had to chat with enough editors, photographers—and worst of all—ad executives to last me a fucking lifetime. It wasn't until near eleven that I saw a glimpse of blond hair moving toward the ballroom doors.

"Excuse me," I said abruptly to the newspaper publisher I'd been charming on behalf of my mother. "I've just seen something needing my attention."

"Such a good host," he said, with enough jolliness to indicate he hadn't waited until midnight to dip into the champagne. I nodded and gave him as much of a smile as I was capable of, and then I stalked after my obsession, chasing her into the dark recesses of my house.

The noise of the party faded behind me as I strode across the large central hall outside the ballroom. There was a chance she'd gone to the guest wing, but for some reason I doubted it. I had a feeling she was escaping in a way that would allow her to make an easy reentry when it was time to ring in the New Year, and so she'd pick one of the rooms that was nearby. The library or the den, perhaps. Maybe my mother's office.

I tried the library first, equal thrums of victory and terror pulsing through me as I saw her at the far end, staring out the window to the bay. The snowy world outside filled the room with a faint, silver-white glow, and Tanith glowed along with it, her blond hair and ivory skin all agleam. When she turned to look at me, her eyes shimmered in the darkness, reflecting the firelight from the front of the room.

"Leave me alone," she said, although there was no heat in her words.

I came close behind her. I wanted nothing more than to sweep her hair from her shoulder and kiss her neck until she melted. I wanted to pin her against the glass and fingerfuck her as we both watched the snow fall silently into the sea.

I wanted her to understand that what we had between us wasn't normal, couldn't be ignored. This shit was undeniable and unfixable. Our only hope was to let it consume us and pray we survived. I wanted her to understand that I was sorry. That I knew I'd fucked up and that I was going to do better with her.

"Did you read my letter?"

She shivered as the warmth of my words moved across the shell of her ear.

"No," she said after a minute. Her voice was quiet in the dark, book-filled room.

"No?"

The snow hissed against the glass as it fell, filling the silence before she spoke. "I haven't read it yet because there's nothing you can say to make it better."

Her words sliced through me like knives, cutting clean and deep.

But she was right. There was no way to sew up the wound I'd made because the wound shouldn't exist in the first place. There was no way to justify believing someone was beneath you.

And how could I explain that I knew better anyway? That I knew she actually had earned the Everston Fellowship? That I knew she was smart and funny and talented as hell? That once I'd thought about it—*really* thought about it—I became disgusted with myself for even caring about someone's money and family? So what if my mother would hate me dating someone outside our social circle? Mum would never have to know.

Yes, Tanith was right, and no amount of chasing her into libraries could ever change that.

I leaned forward enough to press my nose into her hair and breathe her in for the last time, that faint paper-and-ink smell of hers, fresh and crisp and the tiniest bit sweet.

She froze in front of me, giving a shiver as I inhaled, and then made a soft noise when I pressed my lips to the corner of her jaw.

"Be well, Tanith," I murmured, pulling away to leave.

"Wait," she said, spinning around and grabbing my hand. "Just—just. Wait."

I stopped, looking down at our linked hands, and then up to her face. She was always beautiful. Beautiful sunburnt and beautiful with a bright red nose as she ice-skated; beautiful when she laughed with her friends and beautiful as she stared out at a lonely sea.

But she was the most beautiful like this, flushed and panting, her lips parted and her eyes sparkling. It stirred more than my eager cock; it awakened something deep in my chest as well.

"Just tonight," she said, swallowing.

I didn't follow. "What?"

"You're under my skin, Owen, and I hate it. I hate what you said, what you think about me, that I was invisible to you for years—but what I hate the most is that I can't stop *wanting you*. I see you, and I feel like—" She was breathing hard now, the flush spreading down her chest and between her breasts. I wanted to taste those flushed tits so badly my mouth was watering.

"You're under my skin," she repeated. "You're under my skin and I want to claw you out, but I can't. And so I'm just left with this—this—*need*. Like if I don't touch you, I won't be able to breathe."

When I spoke, it sounded like a croak. "That's how I've felt since this summer." I found her other hand and pressed it to my chest. "Like I'll burst into flames if I'm not tasting you. Kissing you. Fucking you."

Her eyes went half-lidded, as if my words had triggered a new wave of arousal inside her. She had to drag in a long breath to speak again. "You don't want to want me—"

"That's not true anym—"

She went on as if I hadn't said anything. "And I hate myself for wanting someone who feels that way, for wanting you when I *know better*. I've known better since we were first years! But still, here it is."

Fuck, I wished she would read my letter. "Tanith—"

"But maybe if we had tonight," she said, not looking at me now, but at the floor, "we could get it out of our systems. You don't want this, I don't want this, but maybe if we scratch the itch, it will stop."

I didn't want it to stop. "Tanith—"

"And I have to make it stop, Owen, I have to, because I can't stand it, I can't *stand it*—"

I pulled her into me, sliding a hand into her soft, thick hair and sealing my mouth over hers, stealing her words and giving her a hot, urgent kiss instead.

She made that noise again, that tiny one in the back of her throat that simply slew me, and all semblance of control fled. My discipline, my cool, my calm—it all became nothing but a raw inferno of need. Maybe I could make her see this was not something we could just work out of our systems.

"Open for me," I breathed against her mouth, licking impatiently at the seam of her lips. She parted them with a slow sigh, allowing me inside.

Her kiss was pure silk, warm and tasting faintly of berry

lip gloss. I reveled in it, groaning as I found her tongue and stroked it with mine, as I kissed her the same way I'd kiss her cunt later. My cock surged with each sweet little flicker of her tongue, my balls grew heavier and heavier with each little whimper she gave, and, somehow, we ended up near one of the oversized sofas. I pushed her onto it, crawling over her and pinning her in place with my hips, with my hands on her wrists. She squirmed wildly underneath me, her pelvis rocking up into mine, seeking friction. The hidden slit in her skirt parted around a single shapely thigh, and the heave of her chest made her tits so juicy and tempting.

"Fuck, you're a gorgeous thing," I muttered. "Can you feel how hard you make me? Do you know how hard it was to sit at the same dinner table as you, knowing how pretty you look when you come? How beautiful your skin looks with my orgasm decorating it?"

"All I know is that when you're like this, I can't fight it," she confessed, her legs wrapping around me. Her high heels dug into my back, and I loved it, fucking *loved* it. "I can fight your ice, but I can't fight your heat."

"This is more than heat," I muttered, ducking my head to suck on a nipple through her dress. It was already hard and jutting through the fabric for me. Like my dick, it was pouting to be played with. "This is pure filth, and you love it."

"God help me, I do," she murmured. "But it'll be out of my system after tonight."

Not if I have anything to say about it. I didn't say that out loud, however.

"I want to fuck you into this sofa," I growled instead. "I want to get so deep inside you that I'm part of you."

She slid her hands through my hair and yanked my face up to hers, pressing her lips to mine. "I want you to try," she said between hungry kisses. "Close the door. I don't want anything stopping this."

Fuck, neither did I. I gave her a quick, hard kiss and then pushed off the sofa, wincing a little at the jagged throbbing in my dick. I was hard enough to pound nails, my balls full and heavy, and I needed out. I needed to be unzipped and into Tanith's snug little cunt.

I closed the door and locked it for good measure, then I returned to her, shucking my suit jacket as I went. I unknotted my tie and tugged it free of my collar, and then I draped both jacket and tie carefully over a chair. I didn't want them to wrinkle in case I had to wear them again later tonight—although if I had my way, anything I'd be doing later tonight wouldn't require clothes at all.

She looked like a wet dream right now, lit only by fire-light, her silky hair spilling everywhere and her party dress falling open to reveal the lithe expanse of her upper thighs. She still wore her cute heels and her brainy glasses, but her jutting nipples and flushed chest made a lewd little liar out of her. She wasn't just a clever intern or an ambitious future editor. She was a girl who needed to come more than she needed her next breath.

She was a girl who was burning alive for me.

Tanith stroked up her thigh as I approached, her eyes tracing greedily up my body. "I want to see you," she murmured, her fingers tracing higher and higher, reaching the top of the dress's slit and pushing it up. "I want to see your cock."

Fuuuck me. "It wants that too," I grunted, unzipping my trousers. But I didn't pull myself free yet. I set to unbutton-ing my shirt first. I wanted to feel those slender hands all over my skin, tracing up my abdomen and pressing against my chest. "Show me what's between your legs, Tanith. Show me where I'm about to be."

I was expecting pretty little knickers, or another thong maybe. But she stunned me . . . giving me a saucy smile and spreading her legs to reveal her naked pussy. I froze. I couldn't breathe at the sight of it.

And when she trailed her fingers over the soft slit, I had to clench my entire body to keep from spurting into my boxer briefs.

"Bloody Christ," I rasped, stepping forward. I dropped to my knees by the sofa like a man at worship, totally entranced, utterly devoted. My cock throbbed and throbbed as I studied her perfect pussy. Bare, with a tight seam and a little pink pearl of a clit at the top.

"Wider. Show me more. The inside of it," I demanded. I didn't care that I'd never asked this of a girl before—that I'd never *needed* it like I needed it now. It didn't matter. My days of polite, efficient sex were over.

I now lived and breathed Tanith Bradford, and I would know her every secret, her every hidden place, and I would claim each one for myself.

She was as far gone as I was because she didn't argue at all. She merely nodded and bit her lip, using both hands to pet over her pretty mound. Then she reached lower and slowly spread herself open for me, revealing a furrow of pink and then a tight, glistening opening.

A guttural noise tore from my throat as she showed me the small, velvet place I was about to fuck. I'd needed to see this for months, fantasized about nothing else as I'd jerked off alone in my room at Pembroke, and still the sight of it was almost more than I could take. This was the kind of pussy that made people start wars.

"Oh, love," I said hoarsely. "I've never seen anything like this."

Her lip still caught in her teeth, she spread herself even wider, moving her legs so everything was illuminated by the low light of the fire. Her ripe berry of a clit, her slick hole, the tight rosebud of her arse underneath.

"Got to smell you," I said, and I ducked down to run the tip of my nose along her petals.

She gasped, nearly letting go of herself. "Owen, you can't—"

"Can't what?" I asked, breathing her in and then fighting off another wave of pleasure. I was dangerously close to coming before even taking my cock out, but I couldn't help it. I'd never needed a shag like this. I'd never been confronted with someone who destroyed my control like she did. I became a brute around her, for her—a ravenous animal intent on scenting and marking my mate. Claiming her and filling her with my seed.

"You can't *smell* me," she protested, clearly horrified, and my hands came up to trap hers, forcing her to keep herself spread.

"I can, Tanith, and I will. And do you know why? Because you smell like you need to be fucked. You smell sweet and earthy and like you need to come." I inhaled her again, committing the scent to memory. I wanted to start every day of the rest of my life with my face pressed to her sex.

"I do need to come," she said, panting hard. "Owen, please. I can't wait much longer."

"*You* can't wait much longer?" I replied. "I've been jerking myself raw for months because of you. Fucking my fist in the shower, fucking my pillows, using up bottle after bottle of lotion. I've been a man possessed, consumed with you."

She went still as I spoke, only shivering when I traced the slippery entrance to her channel with my thumb. "You haven't been . . . you know . . . scratching the itch with other girls?"

I looked up her silk-covered body to find those bright eyes. "I couldn't," I admitted hoarsely. "Tried once and I couldn't even stand kissing her. Her lips weren't like yours; she didn't flush like you or whimper like you; she didn't smell like opening a brand-new book. It must be you, Tanith. You broke me that night on the yacht, and now it must be you."

She swallowed, still looking down at me and breathing hard. "It's the same." She shook her head as if trying to clear it. "For me. It has to be you. But maybe this will fix us. If we do this tonight, we'll be . . . cured."

Not fucking likely, goddess.

I'd known from the first innocent brush of her lips over mine that this would take more than one night to cure. It might take years, years of nothing but this—her pretty pink cunt exposed to me and that fucking flush making her cheeks and tits all rosy for me.

But I didn't tell her that. "Keep yourself spread open," I said instead. "I need to lick you."

"Oh my God . . ." Her words trailed off as I did what I'd been needing to do since Ibiza and sank my tongue right into the hot, wet heart of her. She gasped as I laved my way up to her clit, and then nearly shrieked as I moved my way down to the tight little button below.

"Owen! You can't!"

I lifted my head to look at her, but only after treating myself to another long lick. "Oh, I can. And I will. I want to lick that hole until it's all soft and wet, until you're begging and crying for me to fuck it. Until you can't look anybody in the eye ever again because of how much you love having your little asshole serviced."

"F-f-*fuck*," she whimpered, her head falling back. "I can't *take it* when you talk like that."

"Only to you," I said, dipping my mouth for another taste of her. "Only you make me like this."

"Good," she whispered. "Good."

The side of my hip was slick from all the precome I was leaking into my boxer briefs, and I wanted to snarl with frustration against her sex because I couldn't do everything I needed to at once. I needed to eat her, fuck her, get her slick with lube, and push inside her ass. I needed to fingerfuck her cunt, mark her breasts with love bites, and watch her plush, pink mouth stretch around my erection. I needed to do *everything* with her, but I couldn't do it all at once, and it was killing me.

"I have to fuck you now," I said huskily. "But I promise to lick this pussy better the minute I'm done, okay, baby?"

"Yes," she said on an exhale. "God, yes."

She reached for me, but I was already standing, licking her greedily from my lips as I dug in my pocket for protection.

She lifted an eyebrow. "You have a condom? I thought you said you haven't been fucking anyone else since you met me."

"I haven't, and I haven't planned to," I said, pulling the foil square free and toeing off my dress shoes. "But after Christmas Eve, there is not a snowflake's chance in hell that I'll be caught without protection around you ever again."

"Even with the way we fought then?"

I gave her a quick grin. "Hope springs eternal, goddess."

She snorted, but she didn't seem that upset by it. In fact, going by the way she was already rubbing herself as she watched me pull off my trousers, she seemed pleased nothing was stopping us this time.

"I have an IUD," she said as I draped my trousers and socks over a chair. "So even if you hadn't had a condom, I mean, if you knew you were clean . . ."

I returned to her, still in my boxer briefs. The head of my cock was trapped underneath the waistband. I ran an idle hand over the plump head, watching her fingers in her pussy. "I've always used a condom, Tanith. Always. I don't want you to think that just because I've been—"

"A whore?" she supplied.

I smiled at her. "Right. I don't want you to think that just because I've been a whore, I've neglected being safe."

"No," she said, her eyes moving to my face. "You wouldn't be unsafe, would you? That's not who you are."

"I've always kept my head when it comes to sex. That's why I barely recognize myself anymore. I've never needed to fuck someone against a wall because I wanted them so badly. I've never needed to leave one of my mother's official functions so I could bury myself to the hilt in a girl and make her scream."

"I don't know whether to be flattered, frightened, or turned on," she said, a smile blooming over her face. Only someone named after a goddess could look so delighted by those options.

I hooked my thumbs into the waistband of my boxer briefs and pulled them down enough to free my swollen organ. "Maybe all three," I told her seriously, giving myself a quick, rough stroke before I tore open the packet and sheathed myself in latex. The hand between her legs moved faster and faster as her eyes seared my thick length.

"I want to break you the same way you've broken me," I growled, coming to the sofa and putting one knee on the edge, "but I'll make it feel so good while you shatter. I'll make it feel so good that you'll never want to be whole again. Show me your tits now, love. I need to see them."

She kept one hand working between her legs but used her other to obey me, tugging the neckline of her bodice to the sides so her pert breasts were exposed to the air. They were perfect, flushed curves, their peaks furled and erect, rosy-dark in the firelight. I bent my head to suckle at them as I climbed between her legs. Her free hand went to the back of my head, holding me there, forcing me to give her pleasure.

As I toyed with her peak, fluttering my tongue and then laving her, I reached down and found her fingers, which were currently sliding in and out of her slick pussy.

"Do you trust me?" I asked.

"With my body? Yes."

The unsaid part of her answer was loud and clear—she didn't trust me with anything else. Her mind or her heart or her future.

No matter. I would have it all in the end to slake this need in me, but this was a good start. I could start proving to her now that we'd need more than one night to free ourselves from this curse we'd cast on each other, and I'd begin by making her come so hard on my cock that she'd wake up tomorrow begging for me to put it inside her again.

I nodded and angled my head to kiss her. "Keep your fingers there," I said against her mouth, and then I pushed in one of my own fingers. She tensed underneath me, breathing hard. "I know it's a stretch, baby," I told her, slowly moving my finger in and out. Her cunt was slippery, and her fingers were slippery. Every time I moved my hand, I could feel her quivering response. "Want you ready to come on my cock."

"I'm ready," she said, sliding her own fingers free. "I've wanted this since the yacht. I've wanted this for years."

Years?

But then she raised her wet fingers to my mouth, distracting me like I was a dog panting after a bone, and I caught them between my lips and sucked, relishing the sweet taste of her on my tongue, all other thoughts forgotten.

She spread her legs underneath me, and the feel of my bare hips against the soft, naked skin of her thighs was like coming home. I never wanted to be anywhere but right here between her legs with her taste on my tongue. I took hold of my cock and guided the round head to her sex. We both stilled as I pushed against the wet cove waiting inside her folds.

I bent my head to brush my lips against hers. "Tell me if it hurts," I said, and then I slowly but inexorably speared her virgin body on myself.

Her fingers found my bare shoulders and she dug in, leaving marks that would almost certainly bruise, but I loved it. I loved that what she was feeling right now was pain and pleasure both because that was how she made me feel too. Like I was being burned alive but with something so wonderful that I'd rather tie myself to the stake than ever leave it behind.

"Keep going," she said, wrapping her legs around my waist. Her shoes dug into my back as I spread her, stretched her, until I was completely sunk into her soft glove of a pussy. The tight silk of her channel rippled around me every time I so much as breathed.

"You're shaking again," she observed, panting.

I was. I was shaking so hard that I felt fevered. Sick.

"It's that good," I said. Even my voice trembled now. "It's that fucking good."

She ran a hand up my chest and pressed it over my left pectoral muscle. "I can feel your heart," she murmured. "It's pounding."

"Because this is life or death, Tanith. I'm going to die if I don't get to fuck you forever. I might die even if I do. That's how good you feel." I dropped my head into her neck. "Tell me how you feel. Does it hurt? Is it too much?"

"It is too much," she said, nipping at my earlobe. "Give me more."

She *was* a fucking goddess. I withdrew a few inches and then pushed in, giving her a short stroke, and then another, sinking all the way in and then rutting with my pelvis pressed to hers so there'd be hard, grinding friction against her clit.

The first time I did this, her back arched right off the sofa; the second time, she started scratching at my shoulders.

"I want you to come on my cock so badly," I mumbled against her neck. "I want you to use me like a sex toy, like your own personal cock to ride whenever you want. I want you to own me. I want you to do with me what you will."

She made that noise again, the one at the back of her throat, the one that drove me fucking wild. I slipped my hand between us and pressed my fingers to her clit, all while I started sucking ravenously at her neck.

"I want you to do everything with me," I kept going, my erection servicing her inside while my fingers worked her needy flesh outside. "I want you to be embarrassed by how much you need to fuck me. I want you shocked by the filthy things you want me to do. I want even the mention of my name to make you flush because you want my tongue in places you can never admit, because you need to ride my dick so often that you're worried something is wrong with you."

I could feel the tension in her body ratcheting higher and higher, and the quivering of her channel around my organ was nearly unbearable now, so tight and squeezing that I had to grit my teeth so I wouldn't blow inside the condom. She had to come first, and she had to come so hard that she would be hungry for more before she'd even gone limp.

"God, the things you fucking say," she whimpered. "I can't—I can't stand it—I'm going to—"

With a sharp cry, she came underneath me, her cunt pulsing in soft, rhythmic contractions, her heels digging into my back and her nails scratching my shoulders. I kept working her clit as she orgasmed, kept kissing at her neck, and I kept her pinned hard to the cushions because she seemed to like my weight on her.

I breathed in deep to keep from ejaculating—I couldn't yet, I couldn't, I had so much more I wanted to do . . .

With a final, abrupt shudder, she went loose underneath me, her hands slowly easing their assault on my shoulders. I lifted my head to kiss her, and she kissed me back with a dazed sort of hunger.

"Good?" I purred, licking the edge of her mouth and nipping at her jaw. Then I braced myself on my hands above her, smugly surveying the deep flush all over her chest. I reached down and pushed her skirt all the way to her stomach, pleased beyond measure to see that blush stretching all the way down to her navel.

"Good," she confirmed with a belated shiver. "Better than I ever could have thought. Owen, that was—I didn't know."

"There's a lot more I can show you, my filthy little goddess," I promised, palming a tit and squeezing until her eyes fluttered.

"I know but—but just for tonight," she murmured. She looked up at me with dangerously pretty eyes. "Tonight, then we have to be done."

No.

No, that wasn't happening.

"I'm not agreeing to that, sweetheart," I said, giving her an experimental little thrust, and when her back arched again, I started fucking her cunt in earnest.

"Why?—why not?—oh God, oh God," she chanted, her hands going straight to my hair and pulling so hard I hissed. I fucking loved it.

"Because we both know we'll need more tomorrow," I growled, plunging deep as I did. "Tell me I'm wrong. Tell me that once I'm done fucking you into this sofa, you're going to stand up and walk out of here without wanting to feel my tongue in your pussy again. That you're not at least a little curious about me licking you in places you never thought of until tonight. Tell me that the next time you make yourself come, you won't be wishing it were me crawling all over you like a starving beast needing to fuck his mate."

Her flush deepened. She parted her lips to speak and then paused. "I can't say you're wrong," she said, and then gasped as I rewarded her by bearing down and toiling hard between her thighs. Churning my hips until she was moaning, whimpering, begging softly for more.

Until she was coming all over again.

This time, I made sure I could watch, bracing myself above her as I fucked her as hard as I could. Savoring the way her arousal slicked the base of my dick above the condom, relishing the sweat running down my back. Devouring the sight of my obsession coming apart underneath me.

I watched her eyelids flutter and a tiny, surprised smile grace her lips.

"*Owen.*"

That was all she said, just my name.

I couldn't hold back any longer. I was some kind of saint for lasting even this long, given her hot cunt and her sweet, flushed tits and her eyes like the same sea we kissed next to that very first time. The release landed like a cannonball in my groin, a heavy, near-fatal blow, and then exploded up the length of my cock, filling the condom with hard, thick pumps of seed. I was snarling through it, growling like an animal, still stabbing savagely at the pussy that was giving me such unbearable pleasure. My body emptied itself out for her as if the survival of the species were on the line. Every muscle in my thighs, arse, and stomach clenched and seized to squeeze every last drop of seed from my body into hers.

By the time I was done, I could barely feel my own face.

My lips tingled; my toes were numb. My heart was racing as if I'd run a marathon and then fucked a hundred women right after. When I finally went still, I saw Tanith staring up at me like she'd never seen anything more arousing in her life.

"I made you feel that," she said in wonder, almost like she was saying it to herself. She ran her fingertips over my half-numb lips and then down to my heaving chest. "That was the sexiest fucking thing I've ever seen."

"You can see more tomorrow," I said silkily, realizing now how I could lay my trap. "And if you don't want any more after then, then you can tell me tomorrow night."

Her pupils dilated, and she bit her lip. "Yes," she finally said. "I need more tomorrow. But I'll be leaving tomorrow, anyway, so I'm sure I won't need more after that."

"Mm-hmm," I said, giving her nipple a quick suck before I carefully slid free of her sex. The condom was embarrassingly full, but understandably so. Tanith could turn a monk into a serial sperm donor with that pussy. I threw the condom away and made sure to cover it up with several tissues and pieces of paper, and then walked back to the chair where I'd draped my clothes.

"In that case, I suppose we should start on tomorrow *tonight*. You know, in the interest of time."

"That seems logical," she said with a grin, adjusting her dress and hopping to her feet. She started quickly handing me clothes to put on, and I laughed.

"Excited to get back to my bedroom, are we?"

She tossed her sex-tousled hair over her shoulder and lifted an eyebrow. "I seem to recall someone promising to lick my pussy better."

Heat flooded back to my groin and I nearly dragged her back down to the sofa right then and there. "That's right, goddess."

"Well then. In the interest of time . . ."

In the interest of time, indeed. I dressed in record speed, and we slipped out of the library and ran up the stairs as the party exploded with cheers of *Happy New Year!*

CHAPTER THIRTEEN

Owen

I SPENT THE rest of the night between Tanith's legs, making up for lost time. I had months to make up for— hell, even years. She had been right there at Pembroke all that time, and I hadn't even known. If I had . . .

Fuck, if I had, then everything would be different.

At dawn, I crept back to my room, leaving her all melted and sleepy, and took a quick shower before grabbing a couple hours of sleep. I wanted to be fresh and ready to go on the offensive with Tanith before she left. My mother couldn't know we were fooling around, obviously, but there were so many places in this house where we could sneak off and hide. She would never be the wiser.

But maybe she should be the wiser?

I ignored the thought. While it didn't matter if my mother knew or not, it was easier for everyone—Tanith included—if she didn't, so there was no need to make things harder on ourselves. I wasn't that worried about it anyway.

My mother didn't matter. Proving to Tanith that we were meant to spend the months before graduation fucking constantly mattered.

But I must have done something right karmically because when I woke up and went down to breakfast, only Tanith and the two other interns were there. No parents *or* Felix in sight.

"Ms. Preston sends her apologies, but something came up at the *Gotham* offices," the housekeeper was telling the interns as I walked in. "She and Mr. Montgomery had to go into the city first thing."

"A magazine emergency on New Year's Day?" I asked doubtfully, sitting down next to Tanith and helping myself to a platter of fresh fruit. There hadn't been any Preston emails in my inbox or texts from my mother demanding my help, so it couldn't be that important. Then again, my mother wasn't much for holidays, or rest, in general.

My guess was any excuse to leave the quiet and isolation of Bay House behind and go back to the crowded energy of the city was good enough for her. And, of course, my father went with her—over twenty years of marriage hadn't made him any less besotted with her—and he hated any amount of time they were apart, no matter how short.

Normally, it was vaguely gross to me—who wanted to think about their dad constantly wanting to shag their mum? But sitting next to Tanith at the breakfast table and having to fight off the urge to tackle her to the floor and mount her was making me reconsider. Maybe my dad had the right idea following my mum around whenever she traveled.

"Where's Felix?" I asked the housekeeper, letting my fingers trail over Tanith's knee under the table. She was wearing a short gray dress with colorful tights and a long, trendy scarf. The kind of scarf I could tie her wrists together with later . . .

The housekeeper's reply interrupted my reverie. "The young Mr. Montgomery left last night during the party. It was your parents' understanding that he went back to the

Manhattan house."

Probably to spend the rest of the night—and all to-night—getting hammered with that wanker Chad. God, how I loathed that smarmy arsehole, and not only because he was a Croft Wells alum. He brought out the worst in Felix, and Felix didn't need anyone doing that. He was a twat all on his own.

But I couldn't regret that he wasn't here. If I could keep him away from Tanith for the rest of eternity, I would, along with every other male in the world.

"At least the snow means he couldn't take the helicopter," I muttered, mostly to myself, but the housekeeper gave me a commiserating grimace. Last time Felix had commandeered the helicopter, he and Chad had been totally sloshed and had demanded the pilot fly them to Boston for chowder and cannoli. The whole episode had ended with a stranded aircraft, a pilot with food poisoning, and Felix and Chad missing for a full twelve hours before they were discovered passed out in a hotel room with a live lobster in the bathtub.

The lobster had been okay, in case you were wondering.

The snow continued to fall outside as we ate, and Tanith valiantly attempted conversation with her new intern friends while I stroked the inside of her thighs under the table. The interns were eyeing the snow and checking their phones, and I had a brilliant and only slightly evil idea.

"I know you were planning on leaving this afternoon, but if the snow is going to get worse, maybe it would be better to leave for the city now?"

I adopted my best "solicitous host" face, and it seemed to work because the two other interns eagerly accepted, pushing back from the table to go pack. No doubt they'd imagined this morning as a chance to slither into my mother's good graces—she had none—and solidify their imagined lead in the competition for favorite intern—deeply foolish as my mother had no favorite interns and rarely remembered their names. They were all just more fuel for the underpaid-overqualified-employee pyre that fueled *Gotham* and *Gotham Girl*'s magazine hegemony.

Tanith started to stand after they left, but I beat her to it, sweeping her up into my arms and carrying her out of the dining room and up the stairs.

"Owen," she said, laughing a little as I kissed her. "I need to get my things together before I miss the car back to the city."

"You're not going anywhere," I told her seriously. "I'll take you back tomorrow, but today you're staying here with me."

Her mouth dropped open. "Owen, I—"

"You promised me today," I reminded her, opening the door to my room and then kicking it shut behind me as I carried her in. "And I want *all* of today. What's waiting for you back in Manhattan anyway? Is it better than being alone with me? There're no parents here, no friends to interrupt us, no dorm monitors we have to be quiet for. Nothing but us."

I pulled off the thin jumper I was wearing to underscore my point, and her eyes dropped down to my chest, her tongue licking at her lower lip as she studied my body with undisguised greed.

"You, Owen Montgomery," she said, slowly unwinding her scarf from her neck, "are smarter than you look."

✧   ✧   ✧

THE AFTERNOON BROUGHT a proper storm—thick snow, howling wind, skies as dark as night. After Tanith and I spent the bulk of the day napping and playing, I had an idea. One that she was very uncertain about.

"Owen, what if someone sees us," she whispered as we walked down to the library wing.

"We'll lock the doors once we get inside, and anyway, the staff is used to Felix fucking around all the time and they keep his secrets. Why not mine?"

"Am I a secret, then?" she asked as we opened the door to the glass-enclosed breezeway and stepped through. Snow hurled itself at the windows, but the air itself was pleasant enough since the breezeway led to the pool house, and the water was kept very warm.

"Not a secret," I said firmly, taking her by the hand to lead her on to the pool house. Even though it was nearly three in the afternoon, the storm had darkened the world to a charcoal gray, and most of the light came from the pool house, faint and golden. "It's just better if my mother doesn't know. You've met her now, so you understand. She's got very definite ideas about how things should be, and I don't want that to blow back on you."

"Are you saying—I mean, do you think it would affect my internship at *Gotham Girl*? If she found out I'd had sex with you, even if only for a day or two?"

I didn't like where her thoughts were going. "Tanith, she's not going to find out. And after break, we'll be at Pembroke, and then how will she know?"

I could hear the grumpiness in her voice as we stepped into the pool house's humid warmth. "I never agreed to anything at Pembroke. Just for today, remember?"

"Ah yes. Well, about that, Miss Bradford." I shut the door to the breezeway and then locked it, ensuring we'd be undisturbed for as long as we'd like. "I thought I'd reopen negotiations."

She was at the edge of the pool now, and I set down the leather satchel of things I'd brought next to the hot tub so I could pull her into my arms. Whatever else she was thinking, she couldn't deny her body's response to me. She shivered, her hands seeking out my biceps, my shoulders, my arse, and by the time she tilted her face to mine to demand a kiss, I felt the lusty little presses of her hips against mine.

"You want to negotiate for another tomorrow," she said. It wasn't a question.

Smart girl.

"Tomorrow . . . with an option clause of many more tomorrows," I explained after I gave her a long, searching kiss. She tasted sweet, faintly of the strawberries we'd eaten in my bed. "I can make it worth your while . . ."

She was already melting, soft and hot in my arms, whimpering between kisses and fumbling for the drawstring of my linen lounge pants.

"Say yes," I whispered against her mouth. "Give me more tomorrows, and I'll make you forget time exists in the first place."

"Bold words," she murmured, her hands finding my erection and caressing the aching length. "Can you back them up?"

"You want a demonstration, Miss Bradford? A little free trial to show you I'm good for it?"

She gave me a quick squeeze and my breath stuttered against her lips. She smirked, but I had my easy revenge by reaching under her dress and palming her naked pussy.

"I promise I am," I went on, sliding a finger through her wet petals before finding her shoulders and turning her around. "I promise I can make you forget what day it is. I can even make you forget your own name."

I unzipped her dress and unhooked her bra, leaving her

utterly naked and shivering while I shucked off my long-sleeved, waffle-weave shirt and lounge pants. Then I pulled her into the bubbling hot tub next to the pool, arranging her on my lap so I could resume kissing her right away.

"I don't know," she teased between kisses. "A hot tub seems pretty basic. Maybe I could get that from anyone with a trust fund to his name, and you know there's plenty of those guys back at school."

Even though she was only teasing me, the mere idea of her being in the same vicinity as another guy sent a bolt of cold possession spearing through me, and my hands tightened on her hard. I felt like I did last night or on Christmas Eve or on the van Doren yacht.

Fucking *feral*.

"You ready for more, goddess?" I gave her bare tit a rough squeeze. "Because I'm ready to give it to you."

She moaned into my mouth, dropping her forehead against mine. "Yes," she panted. "If it's anything as good as what we've done before, then yes."

I kept my greedy hand on her breast as I reached into the bag behind me and pulled out a waterproof toy.

"Remember what I said to you last night?" I turned it on and pushed it under the water, skating it over one nipple and then the other until she was rocking on my lap, her slippery folds rubbing deliciously over my hard organ as she did.

"Y-you said a lot of things," she managed, her breath hitching as I dragged the buzzing toy down her stomach to her navel. And then to her pretty, flushed cunt. "You said— oh God, Owen, oh *God*—"

I held the toy against her clit, savoring the pleasure moving across her face. "I said I wanted to do everything to you." I started sawing the toy back and forth—enough so she could feel the buzz at her slick entrance. "I wanted to make you embarrassed by how much you need to fuck." I pushed the vibrator farther back, and Tanith's eyes turned to saucers.

"Owen," she said uncertainly. "I . . ."

I pressed the toy right against the small rosebud of her back entrance and turned up the vibrator's intensity.

"Oh!" she gasped. "Oh, I didn't—I don't—" She was looking at me with something like panic and lust together, her lips parted in what looked like shame. Her nipples were little bullets just under the surface of the water.

"It's okay," I soothed, my voice dark and husky over the noise of the churning water. "It's just us here. No one has to know, Tanith. No one has to know what you want me to do when we're alone."

She shuddered, tossing her head like she wanted to shake it in disagreement, but she was bearing down on the toy at the same time, riding the pressure and vibrations against her little arsehole.

"It can be our secret, baby," I said, turning the vibrations higher. "How you like it when I play with you here. How you secretly want my tongue here."

"You—you said you would lick me there," she managed to say, her eyes glazed and wild as she looked down at me. She was moving in the water, rocking and rubbing her secret place over the toy. It was the hottest thing I'd ever fucking seen; it was everything I could do not to lift my hips and spray my release into the water simply from watching her.

But no. I had a plan. More tomorrows, and I would get them from her by any means, fair or foul.

Obviously, in this case, *foul* meant making her perviest little dreams come true.

"I'm going to lick you there," I promised huskily. "Until

you're begging for more."

She bit her bottom lip, her eyes on mine. "More . . . like your cock? There?"

"Yes, Tanith."

"I've seen anal in porn," she said, still rubbing herself against the toy, "but I've never thought I would want . . ."

A low groan tore from my throat at the thought of her watching porn. Of her alone in a bed with a sweet, flushing pussy and nothing but her own fingers to make it feel better.

"We're going to watch so much dirty shit together," I told her, kicking the toy up to its highest strength. She moaned and fondled her breasts, grabbing and plumping them under the water. "I want to be under the covers licking your pussy as it gets wet watching porn. I want to fuck you while you're watching your favorite videos. I want us to try everything we watch."

Her chest and cheeks were bright crimson, and her mouth was a small *o* as she panted for breath. Her eyes were as dazed as a drug addict's as she let the thrill of the toy ripple through her.

"And we can stop any time you want," I told her. "If it doesn't feel good, if it doesn't make you feel dirty enough, if you don't feel like you're going to burn alive when I'm fitting my cock into your hot little arse, then we can stop."

She shivered. "Okay. Yes. I want it. I want to try."

As her reward, I moved the toy to the front and pressed it to her clit, my other arm wrapping tight around her waist, so she had no choice but to ride it, to have it pleasure her so hard. With a hoarse, sexy wail, she fell apart on my lap, her torso curling inward on itself even as her greedy cunt kept fucking against the toy, as if to draw out the orgasm as long as humanly possible. I watched her hungrily, my cock pointing straight up like a goddamned spike, the head breaching the surface of the water between the two of us.

Luckily for me and it both, we only had to be patient a moment longer.

In a few seconds, I had a limp, dazed Tanith bent over the edge of the hot tub, her elbows on a plush towel I'd laid on the tile and her knees braced on the top of the seats. It put her arse right at mouth level for me, and I wasted no time in making good on my promises from last night. I forced her knees apart, allowed myself a heartbeat to enjoy the sight—a well-pleasured cunt, its petals swollen enough to have parted themselves to reveal the hole inside, and a firm little aperture above it like a pretty, pink star—and then I pressed my mouth to her glistening skin and began to lick. Her cunt, her cheeks, her arsehole. I glutted myself on her taste and then tongued her rear entrance until she was moaning.

And once she was softer, opening more to the invasion of my tongue, I took the lube from my bag and began anointing her entrance with it.

"Breathe," I instructed, as I penetrated her with my finger. "Breathe for me."

She sucked in a breath, her sides heaving over the nip of her waist, and then did it again.

"So obedient with my finger inside you," I murmured, pleased. "Are you ready for more?"

"Yes," she said immediately. "But slowly, please."

"I'd only ever go slow with this," I said. "I want you to feel every inch of me inside here. I want you to feel every single second of how much you'll love this."

Her head dropped between her hands as I pushed the second finger inside her. "It feels so strange," she said, sounding confused and also very, very horny. "I feel so full, but it feels so wrong, and yet I want more."

"Like this?" I asked, moving my fingers carefully in and out, a slow and decadent motion that had her hips lifting to follow me. She was all hot velvet around my fingers, a tight heaven that made my stomach clench to feel.

"*Yessss*," she hissed, rolling her head on the towel. "How do you do this to me? I'm a good girl. And I should hate you. And yet when you're with me . . ."

I could ask her the same question, but truly, I was past that now. I was past wondering why it had to be *her* and how she'd turned me into an obsessed beast when I'd only ever been a person of control. When I'd only ever wanted brief, impersonal sex, as clean and contained as possible.

But the question no longer mattered, only the answer. *She* was the answer.

I withdrew my fingers and then moved her so she was lying stomach-down on a makeshift bed of towels. I found the toy again and turned it on, and then curled her fingers over it. "Put this underneath you, right against your clit," I told her, murmuring low in her ear and then nipping at her earlobe. "You'll use it to make yourself feel good as I ride your arse. Got it?"

She nodded against her forearm, taking the toy and wedging it underneath her.

"There's a good pain and a bad pain with this," I told her, straightening and finding the bottle of lube. "The good pain is like fullness. It makes your entire body light up. The bad pain is just pain, pure and simple."

"How would you know?" she mumbled into her arm, her hips already moving as the toy tickled against her. "You've never done this."

"Who says I haven't?" I asked mischievously, dropping a kiss onto her shoulder before I straddled her legs. I rolled on a condom, slicked my erection with lube, and then added more to the now-pliant opening above her cunt. "They make many types of toys for gentlemen these days, and a boy gets awfully lonesome waiting for you."

"Fuck, you're dirty," she moaned, her eyes fluttering closed. "I want to watch you use every filthy toy you own."

It was a good thing I was behind her because I couldn't stop the smug smile that played across my lips just then. "Sounds like you're thinking about tomorrow," I purred, setting the lube bottle aside. "And lots of tomorrows."

"Don't push your luck," she panted, her hips entirely restless now. "Just fuck me already."

"God, you're bossy," I said with a laugh. "Now hold still." Uncharacteristically, she listened, and her hips went still enough for me to fist my slippery length and press the head against her entrance. The visual contrast of thick and small, my dusky cock and her ballet slipper pink pussy sent a clench of jagged need tearing through my groin. I had to suck in a deep breath to steady myself.

"The minute you need to stop, tell me," I told her. "I won't risk hurting you." I wouldn't risk hurting anyone— this kind of fucking required certain considerations and etiquette that I'd always adhered to—but there was more on the line than merely my pride in my sexual manners. *She* was on the line. All the tomorrows I needed were on the line. I had to prove to her I could give her the kind of dirty, wonderful things no other guy could.

"Okay," she murmured. "Go slow, like you did with your fingers."

"It's the only good way to do it, baby. Slow."

It took a tense second or two for the thick crown of my cock to press fully into her. Even though her pucker had been teased and pleasured into softness, it still took some effort to move past the rings of muscle, and even more effort still to keep myself from ejaculating as she panted and moaned beneath me. The noises she was making, the distant vibrations of the toy—and above all, the slippery, hot squeeze of her arse—were driving me fucking mental.

"Are you—are you shaking again?" she asked on a sharp inhale as I gave her another thick inch.

I managed to rasp out a rough, "Yeah."

"Because it feels good?"

"There're no words for how it feels," I grunted. "Tight doesn't even begin to cover it. Or hot." I pushed in a bit farther, and then stopped, panting hard. The slick inside of her was massaging me, caressing me, and the pleasure was so big and so vast, I felt it beyond my erection. I felt it everywhere: in my balls, in the pit of my stomach, in my lips, and on the soles of my feet. "It feels so good that I could die. Like this is more than any man can take."

I pushed in one more time, giving her all of me, and she made an indecipherable noise. I stilled my hips, reaching down to brush a damp strand of hair away from her temple. "Talk to me," I said, looking over her shoulder into her face. "Does it hurt?"

"It's the good pain, I think," she said, blinking fast. "It's uncomfortable, but also I think I—" She shivered underneath me, and then pleasure streaked hot and fast up the length of my organ, straight into my belly. She was moving underneath me, a small, tentative motion, but motion all the same.

She was *fucking* herself on me.

"Bloody hell," I whispered, trembling even harder now. My hands shook, my abdomen clenched, and my thighs and chest went taut against the shudders threatening to pull my body apart piece by piece.

And she kept going, kept lifting and lowering her hips,

making slow, tiny thrusts that stroked me from top to bottom. I ran a hand down her damp back in pure wonder, stroking along her spine.

"Baby," I breathed, staring down at the beautiful, brave girl in front of me. "*Baby.*"

She started moving faster now, turning the toy up as high as it would go, rocking the front of her pussy against it as her sweet arse serviced me at the back.

"It feels so full," she moaned. "And wrong. And good. And so *wrong.*"

"I know you like it wrong," I bent down to whisper in her ear. "I promise I won't tell. I promise no one will ever know that you like and need it like this."

My words stirred her even more, sending blood to her cheeks and making her whimper into her arm, and then she was like a wild thing, totally lost to me and herself and everything that wasn't the toy at her clit and the thick cock inside her. She squirmed underneath me, bucked and writhed and twisted, and I had to wrestle her down to keep my erection wedged inside her arse.

"Yes," she chanted, "yes, yes, Owen, oh my God, *yes*—"

Her squirming stopped abruptly as her climax took her in its teeth, sending heavy, hard contractions all through her body. She wailed into the towel and I gnashed my teeth above her to keep from following her over the edge because it was too much. It was too fucking much. Knowing she came with my dick *there*, came from doing something so filthy and so new, and feeling the sweet flutters of her body around myself . . .

It took her forever to come down, a long enough time that I couldn't wait any longer, and then I started fucking her hard, humping into that tight, warm place like an animal intent on nothing but release. I felt a vicious, victorious thrill as my body tightened and then began pumping an orgasm right into her willing heat. It came in hard, seizing waves, and I covered her body with my own and bit into her shoulder, snarling as pleasure racked through my body. My erection jerked and pulsed and jerked and pulsed until I was nothing but hers, hers, *hers*. Until all I was, all I ever could be, was this moment strung between the two of us. This raw, primal connection that seemed like so much more than sex, so much more than finding illicit release.

It felt like something I'd never known, but it made me want to wrap my body around her and never, ever let her go. It made me want to hold on to her forever.

"Fine." She sighed underneath me. "You win."

"And what's my prize?"

She turned her head. "Tomorrow."

I kissed the corner of her perfect mouth. "And?"

"The tomorrow after that."

"And?"

She smiled against my kiss. "Plenty more tomorrows after that."

I kissed her properly that time and pretended I didn't hear the apprehension in her voice.

I was going to make sure she had no reason to regret becoming mine. No matter what happened.

Chapter Fourteen

Tanith

*O**H MY GOD.***

I didn't think I'd ever felt like this in my life.

Mentally, I ran through the muscles in my body, cataloging every single one that ached, that twitched, that throbbed. Had I really been that person? The sexually free one screaming, "Oh my God, yes, right there," and "Again," and "More," and "Harder"?

I flushed and tucked myself deeper under the duvet, and then I shivered. The duvet smelled like Dior cologne, and sex, and *Owen*. All Owen.

An arm wrapped around my waist and pulled me up against a hard, lean body. "Just where the hell do you think you're going?"

I giggled, staying tucked under the duvet. "Good afternoon."

Owen nuzzled my hair and kissed my neck. "Good afternoon, love. Would you like a snack?"

"Um . . ." I rolled in his arms to face him. "Now that the roads are better, I probably should probably figure out what the arrangements are for getting back to the city sooner rather than later."

"That's an easy one. I'll take you back myself. Maybe we can spend the rest of day together there."

"What about your family? Don't you want to get back and spend time with them?"

He shook his head. "No. Mum, no doubt, is buried in work. Dad's likely found something to occupy himself. And as for Felix, he's probably sleeping off a bender at our Manhattan house. I have nothing to do but be with you."

I tried to tell him all the reasons I needed to leave, to give him space to realize that sharing more tomorrows was possibly an epic mistake. Chief among them was the fact I worked for his mother for the love of God. This could only end badly.

His dark navy gaze pinned on me, sending an icy shiver down my spine. "Are you running?"

I swallowed hard. "No, I'm not running exactly. Running is the wrong word for this scenario."

He didn't loosen his grip. "Okay, then, tell me what the *right* word is."

"I just—" I licked my lips. "I don't want you to regret this. I don't want you to get out of that bed and think for a moment that you don't want tomorrow after all. I'm trying not to overstay my welcome."

He nodded slowly, still not letting me go. "If I didn't want you here, you wouldn't be here. And like I said, you own me. I'm here to do with you what you will. I want as many tomorrows as I can get."

"I feel like I'd already done with you what I would before." He snorted a chuckle and I eyed him. "Was that a snort?"

"No. I'm too dignified to snort."

He did it again and then started making oinking noises as he wrapped his whole body around me and tickled. I felt so small. So petite.

Somewhere among the squealing and laughing, the tickles turned from innocent play to something naughtier. Then the thick length of him was stirring against me again. He groaned into my neck. "Jesus Christ, I cannot stay away from you. Even in my dreams, all I kept thinking about was how to have you, how I needed you with me all the time. What have you done to me?"

"I haven't done anything. I was just sitting here minding my business."

He kissed my neck softly. "Well, just sitting here minding your business while looking very cute."

"Yup, that's me." His cock nudged my opening and I hissed. "Oh my God, Owen."

"I'm sorry, love." He nuzzled the column on my neck again, then kissed me on the other side, working his way to my jaw. "I can't fucking help it. He wants inside, and you are already so soft and ready." He released one of my arms, and his hand slid over my body, palming my breasts before he leaned down to take the tip of a nipple between his teeth and scrape it gently. His hand kept traveling down until he found his way between us to my soft, slick center. He slid in two fingers and I gasped.

"Fuck. Owen."

"Uh-huh. I know you want this. If not, tell me to stop."

I lifted my hips, seeking more, practically begging him to grind on my clit. "Owen."

"What was that, love? What were you saying?"

"I was saying, 'Oh my God, please make love to me again.'"

"Oh, that's what you were saying. Well, you know, I don't think I should. You were trying to leave me."

I laughed, and then he pressed hard on my clit with his

thumb as two fingers slid into me.

I gasped again. "Jesus."

"What?" he asked with an evil grin. "I barely did anything at all."

I glowered at him. "You know exactly what you're doing."

His grin was dirty, sexy, and altogether bad boy. It told me he was the dirtiest kind of bad boy you could ever find. Then he removed his fingers and slid his cock up my wet, silky slit. "How about this?"

"Oh my God, Owen, please, yes."

"You want it inside you? Because I keep thinking that maybe you don't need to come."

I hissed. "I—"

He kept rubbing the tip of himself against me, making it difficult to think. I had an IUD. With my erratic schedules and studying, I would forget to take a pill. My mother didn't want what happened to her to happen to me. But this was . . . God, without a condom? He was . . . Oh God.

Again, he nudged himself against me, rubbing ever so gently.

"Shh, it's okay. It's just the tip. You're okay. It's just the tip, baby."

But he kept kissing my neck and now he was nipping at it. And before I knew what was happening, I lifted my hips, taking even more of him. His eyes flipped open, and a long guttural curse came out of his mouth.

"Fucking hell, Tanith."

It was still just the tip, but all of his tip was inside me now. There was no more tease. There was only me and him and this moment. He held himself perfectly still. "Oh Jesus, I was teasing. Why did you—?"

"Did you think you're only going to tease me?" I adjusted my hips, forcing him to retreat just a little bit and he groaned. "I can't—wow. We should stop. Let me get a condom." He aimed a hand at the nightstand by his bed, but then I reached between us and found him again. This time, I was in control, sliding him up over my slit in a flash. And then I nudged him against me again with my hips, tempting all of him.

With a curse, Owen dropped his forehead to mine. "Oh my God, Tanith, what are you doing?"

"I have an IUD, remember?"

He growled low. "I remember, but fuck. You were uneasy about this before since I was a bit of a whore until I met you."

"Yes, but I also know you. You are also careful. No way in hell you were having any sex without any condoms ever."

He nodded, nuzzling against my jaw with his warm lips. "And I was tested. Last summer after Ibiza."

"Oh really," I managed to murmur. I turned my face into his, nuzzling so I could look at him. "Why haven't you mentioned this earlier than now?"

He gave me a rueful look. "Because it's a little embarrassing."

"Being tested?"

He shook his head. "No. The reason why." He sighed. "It was because after Ibiza, I thought . . . well, I had assumed that . . ."

"What, that you would find me, and we'd have weekend-long sex marathons? Hope springs eternal and all that?"

He nuzzled me again. "Guilty as charged."

He was ridiculous and overconfident and—and I trusted him. I wanted this.

I squeezed myself around him and breathed out a low *yes*. Before I knew what was happening, he rolled over onto his back, and I was riding him. His hands were playing on my ass, gently stroking the sore flesh. "Are you all right here?"

I nodded and sighed because he was also so deep inside me. I couldn't breathe. I couldn't remember anything—important things like my name, what I was doing with my life. He'd stolen all of that, and I wanted him to keep taking more.

He pressed again on my back hole, opening gently, lightly, with a finger, and I whimpered. "Oh my God."

"Am I hurting you?"

"Yeah, but it feels good though."

He reached behind him, grabbing a pillow so he could prop himself up and angle himself just right to take my nipples into his mouth. He whispered around my turgid flesh, "I'd like to do it again. Not this morning, though. I think you need a break. But I'm going to play a little, okay?"

I could only nod because I was chasing bliss, sweet heavenly bliss as I rocked forward on him, his pelvic bone just hitting me right where I needed him on my clit. He was so deep inside me. One of his hands rocked my hips back and forth and the other played with my ass, and I just . . . God, this was the kind of bliss you couldn't even read about and understand without experiencing yourself. All the fan fiction in the world hadn't been enough, would never be enough.

He knew how to play my nipples. At some points, he'd slow down, and I'd feel more of a tease, which would then start a slow burn, that electrifying burn right up my spine. And he played and played until I felt ready to shoot off like a rocket.

He smirked around the taut tip. "I know what's coming."

I broke apart. He gave me no quarter, no space, no room. He just kept loving me over and over until I was coming again. This time, he reached his hand between us and took mine with it, having us both stroke my clit over and over again. I was shaking, coming again, and this time, he roared my name against my chest. "Oh, Tanith. Fuck, Tanith."

Then we were both falling over. I fell on top of him, and he rolled us to the side, holding me close, still attached, still connected to me. "Fuck, you're trying to kill me."

I shook my head. "No, I was minding my business, I swear to God."

His hands were still squeezing my ass cheeks and his finger played on my pucker. "You are okay, though, aren't you?"

His eyes were so earnest. He was worried he'd let go too much, that he'd hurt me.

I cupped his face and stroked my thumbs over his cheeks. "I'm okay. I liked it."

His dick twitched inside me again. "Jesus, we can go again. When it comes to you, I can always go. I want your arse, but I think we should probably wait for that."

I tucked my head under his chin and nodded. "But you know, we could probably still—"

On the nightstand, my phone rang. It was Sera's ringtone and I frowned. "I should probably get that. She knows I'm with you. She wouldn't be calling."

He frowned. "Ignore her."

"Owen."

He rocked his hips again and I groaned. "Jesus." At the same time, he used our juices to slide a finger into my ass and I threw my head back. "Oh my God."

"Do you still think you want to talk to her?"

Nope, I absolutely did not want to talk to Sera.

I let Owen play with me, getting lost again. The phone stopped ringing but then started right away again.

He murmured a curse against my neck. "Fuck." He removed his fingers and then slowly eased out of me; my body tried desperately to hold on to him. "Answer the phone. If she's calling and she knows you're with me, it's urgent."

I whimpered at the loss of him but rolled over and reached for the phone. I answered with a groan. "Oh my God, Sera, is someone on fire?"

"Yes. I'm sorry I ruined your shagfest or whatever, but Aurora is missing. She ditched her security and took off with Felix sometime around two this morning. She's not back yet, but the Montgomery car is here."

I sat up immediately. "What? Does she even like Felix? You know what? Never mind. Where are you?"

"I've already tried calling her a million times. I'm getting ready to head down to the foyer to grab the car keys, then maybe go look for her. See if we can find a GPS location of her phone from Phin, but also, you can't tell Lennox because he will lose his shit. Her security team is already freaking out."

I muttered a curse to myself. "Yeah, I'll find a way there. See you soon."

When I hung up, Owen's brow was furrowed. "What's the matter?"

"Aurora is missing. She went somewhere with Felix, I guess, but the Montgomery car is back and she's not, so Sera's worried. We're going to head out looking for her."

He nodded and pulled the sheets back. If I hadn't been watching him so closely, I would have missed the muscled tic in his jaw and the two extra blinks before he slid down his Owen mask of cool and calm. He was worried. Or maybe that was pissed-off reserve? "All right, let me get dressed. You hop in the shower, I'll call downstairs to pack us some food, and then we'll just—"

I shook my head. "You don't have to help. She probably just got pissed off at them and wanted to get away. I'd bet you anything she's still in the city. So we'll keep trying her phone on the way there. If we can't get her to answer, we'll find her GPS from Phin without telling him." I whirled and pointed at him. "No telling Lennox either. You hear me?"

"That's fine." Owen looked at me. "Is that all for Aurora's benefit or because you don't want people to know how we've spent the last two days?" He paused. "Or both?"

I couldn't decipher his expression, and maybe I didn't want to. "Maybe it's not a bad idea to keep things on the down low," I said slowly, even though I sort of hated the idea of it. I didn't want to be a secret, not here in New York and not back at Pembroke, but when I thought of how much pride I'd already surrendered to him . . .

Owen realized I wasn't going to answer, and something dark flashed in his eyes. "Fine. If that's what you want. But let me help you. I am good at this, you know. I've been cleaning after my mates for years, and this involves my brother, Tanith. You don't even want to know how many times I've had to clean up a Felix mess. Let me help."

"I know you're good at this. I do." I leaned forward and kissed him on the lips softly, trying to appease him. "But Aurora isn't going to want you to see whatever mess she's in. It was bad enough all of you saw the whole Phineas debacle at the Huntington Gala in November. I'll go get her."

He kissed me back but didn't relent. "Just let me help. I want to."

"And I want you to, but I'm thinking about Aurora,

okay?"

He sighed. "And I'm thinking about Felix and whatever hand he had in this. At least let me get Chef to make you some sandwiches. Take a shower. Make it fast. They'll be ready in two minutes."

I watched him for a moment, possibly seeing him for the first time. "Why are you so great?"

"I have been telling you this for weeks."

I snorted. "Oh my God. You're so impossible, you know that?"

He nodded. "Absolutely. But go on. Shower. I'll get you some food, and I'll order the helicopter, but I might be in the car with you."

"No, Owen, I got this, okay? If she's sprawled naked on a bed somewhere, she won't thank me for bringing some random Hellfire boy to play hero. Let me and Sera help our friend alone."

He sighed and rolled his eyes. "You can search for your friend on your own, but I'm coming with you to the city to talk to Felix, at least. Am I understood?"

I laughed. "Okay, yes, *Dad*."

He reached out and swatted me on the ass. "I'm certainly *not* your father."

"No, you're not." I kissed him. And then I kissed him again. I couldn't help myself and gave him one last kiss before scooting on to the bathroom, but he still managed to get another swat in. I wanted to sit in this feeling. This outright giddiness. But I'd do that later. Right now, my friend needed me.

CHAPTER FIFTEEN
Tanith

I T WAS EASIER said than done to actually *find* Aurora.

Once I had taken the Montgomery family helicopter into the city, with Owen by my side, the car from the heliport dropped me off at Sera's house. I didn't even make it up the front stairs before Sera was barreling down. "Oh, good, you're back." She gave Owen a nod and sort of glanced between the two of us but didn't say anything more about it. "My car's already waiting. Let's go."

Owen took my hand. "All right, call me if you need anything."

I nodded. "I'll see you later."

He didn't kiss me, just gave my hand two quick squeezes. It felt odd. Awkward. All I wanted him to do was wrap his arms around me and hold me close, but this had been my idea. To keep things low profile. Besides, this wasn't about me right now. This was about Aurora.

Once I was in the car with Sera, I turned to her. "What's the plan?"

"Well, the plan is there's a list of bars in Soho. I managed to talk to Felix, but—douchenozzle that he is—he can't remember who they were all with and which bars they went to."

I growled. "How many are there?"

"You don't want to know." She handed me her phone and there was quite the extensive list.

"I checked off the ones that are too swanky, so that leaves these ones. The Montgomery driver remembers dropping him somewhere in this area." She slid her finger over her phone, pointing to a map, tapping her finger on different blocks as she spoke. "So we'll start there and fan out. I sent all this to her security team, too, so they're starting here. Eventually, we'll meet in the middle."

"Has anyone told her mom?"

The look she gave me said *oh, you poor dear.*

I knew with these trust fund kids, calling their parents was a last-minute resort. But she was missing and had been for over twelve hours.

"This seems serious. Something could have happened to her. She's a princess for crying out loud."

"Yes, but nobody wants the wrath of her grandmother," Sera explained. Aurora's grandmother was the Princess of Liechtenstein and famously ferocious. "The security team won't involve the police until they're certain they can't find her on her own terms, and even if they do involve them, it might involve having to bribe people off to keep it out of the news. If we can figure out what the hell happened to her, who she was with other than Felix, we'll be in a better position. This is not the first time one of us has had a crisis. I know how to handle it."

I stared at Sera. "Wow. One day, I am going to be scared of you."

"That day should be today."

"Come on."

Three hours later, we had been to no fewer than ten

bars, at least seven of them not open yet, which meant pounding down the door until a disgruntled opening employee let us in. Only one of the bartenders had remembered seeing Aurora. But we did learn she'd been with Felix *and* Chad.

Chad had been with them. And they'd all left. Together. But Felix was back at Owen's.

Which meant she might still be with Chad. Alone.

Fuck.

We were at a dead end with no chips left to play. "Maybe we call Owen and make him press Felix for more answers? If Felix can remember?"

Serafina chewed on her fingernail. "Shit. Shit, shit."

I understood the response and reaction. Owen was the good boy. There was no way Felix was opening up to him. He'd clam up on principle . . . if he could even remember the night through his hangover.

"We have to try everything," I added.

"I know. Let me think."

Finally, when we went back to the limo. She frowned down at her phone and then pulled up a contact, crossing herself as she dialed, a resigned look on her face.

I wondered who the hell she was calling that she needed the protection of God first, but then the deep baritone that answered was more than a little familiar.

Holy hell, she'd called the devil himself.

"Listen, I don't have time for your bullshit," Sera said quickly. "But I'm out of ideas. I need someone who knows the seedy underbelly of Soho. If you were Chad, where the fuck would you have taken Aurora?"

There was a beat of silence. "Ah, my love, Serafina van Doren. Gracing the phone with that voice of yours, just this side of shrill. It's a treat, I have to tell you."

"Fuck you."

"I keep telling you, sweetheart, any time."

"And I keep telling you I'm not really in for a VD. Be serious for a moment. Aurora's missing. I need your fucking help."

His laugh was low. "Oh God, I wish I were there to see your face, that press of your lips together, as you are forced to kneel and ask me for help."

"I kneel before no one, jackal."

"Of course, ever the queen. But I bet you I could make you kneel."

"You wish."

I felt like I was watching a tennis volley back and forth and back and forth.

"And what if I got on my knees for you, Sera?" I heard him purr. "Would you like that?"

Wow. The two of them were *wow.*

"While I like the idea of you kneeling before me like the scum that you are, I'm not letting any part of you anywhere near me, so can we get to the point here? I need your help finding Aurora. Felix left her with Chad. Now I can't find either one of them and—"

"You may as well unbunch your panties and hand them over to me. I have Aurora."

For once, Sera paused. "What?"

"Yep, the Four Seasons. Penthouse Two. Don't tell Phineas or Lennox, obviously. Or her team of royal security goons."

Serafina hung up with him without saying another word and then calmly gave the driver the next set of instructions to head uptown toward the Four Seasons. Then she sat back, her lips pressed together, her hands locked.

I watched her warily. "What's wrong?"

"You heard. He has her."

"What does that mean?"

She swallowed hard. "With Rhys, it could mean fucking anything."

Twenty minutes later, we pulled up to the Four Seasons and a bellhop hurriedly opened our doors. Once we were ushered to the elevator, Sera tapped impatiently on the brass handle she held while the elevator took us up, up toward the penthouse.

"What's wrong?"

Her lip quivered. "If he fucking hurt her . . ."

"Rhys is a dick, but Lennox and Phineas are his friends. He wouldn't hurt Aurora."

The look Serafina gave me was bleak. And a little wild. "You don't know him."

She marched to the door and started banging, making a holy racket. "Open the damn door!"

Rhys swung it open. He wore a long-sleeved T-shirt with the sleeves pushed up to the elbows, exposing his forearms that were pale but well muscled. His gaze darted to me and widened just a fraction as if he were surprised I'd come with her.

Serafina was not to be deterred. "Aurora."

She shoved Rhys out of the way, but he held her with a hand on her elbow and tugged her back. "There's no need to be rude, Sera."

She glanced down at his hand. "If you do not get your hands off me, you're going to be missing a pinky."

I watched the two of them, and I knew. One of them was going to murder the other. It was the only solution.

"All I'm saying, Sera, is maybe you don't barge in here. She's in the other room."

Sera yanked her arm free. "I swear to fucking God,

Rhys, if you did something to her."

He jerked back as if she slapped him. "What?"

She jabbed a finger into his chest. "You heard me. If you hurt her, they will never find the body parts."

He grabbed her hand then, wrapping all of his around hers, capturing her. He stared down at her, fury and disgust etched all over his shockingly beautiful face. "You're really going to ask me that?"

"Yes, I am."

He shook his head. "You of all people. I may be the devil, and I've done lots to earn that title. But I would never do *this*. Hurt her? The fact that you could even think that about me. Wow. Fuck you, Serafina. She's in there. I found her walking back, coming out of Soho, trying to walk all the way uptown. No coat. No phone. No wallet. Her top was torn, skirt askew, and her shoe heel was broken. But she was determined to walk home."

Sera dragged in a shuddering breath. I stood there frozen, unable to move.

"Oh fuck."

"Yeah. Oh fuck. So, I picked her up. But she was too embarrassed to go and see you, and I was headed to Owen's. Couldn't take her there, right? So I brought her here. She's been allowed to stay in the room there down that hall, huddled in bed. I ordered her some fresh clothes. Tried to get her to eat something. But she won't. I kept her safe. That's it. I didn't do anything to her."

Sera blinked, her lashes fluttering. "Y-you saved her."

He puffed out a breath. "Even the devil can be the hero once. Just so you're aware, I have no intention of being the hero again, yeah? So you figure out what you're going to do with her, how to get her back to your place. It's not on me."

All of a sudden, the fight went out of Sera, and her body

sagged. "W-was she hurt?"

Rhys searched her face. "I don't know. She wouldn't talk to me. But I could hear her crying. I didn't want to touch her or anything, and I wasn't sure if she should shower, but she said that . . ."

Sera wrapped an arm around her middle and choked a sob. "Oh fuck."

He shook his head. "She said that he hadn't hurt her. That she fought him off, so I don't know how much of that is true or how much of that is what she wants to believe. But she won't see anyone, I can't make her, and she doesn't want comfort. She definitely doesn't want Phin or Lennox to know." He slid a glance to me. "Which means we don't tell Owen."

I'd been all for keeping Owen from seeing Aurora's business, but not telling him at all felt impossible. I threw my hands up. "Jesus, what am I supposed to do?"

"Keep your mouth shut like the rest of us," he replied in a cold voice, then turned back to Sera. "And then you called me. So, that's the whole story."

Sera reached for him with a shaking hand, but he jerked back before she could touch him.

There was some exchange happening between them. Something I couldn't understand. Then he stepped aside and waved us toward the door where Aurora was. "My work here is done. You two head on down. I'm expecting some company."

Sera turned. "Company?"

He shrugged one shoulder. "I made a call to a Morelli friend. They'll deal with the Chad situation."

Another silent exchange between them. Then Sera nodded and said something to him I never thought I would ever hear her say to him. "Thank you."

He nodded. "It'll be done by the end of the day."

Sera turned and headed down the hallway. I followed after her. "What'll be done?"

Sera's voice was low. "If he's calling who I think he's calling, he's got some very nasty men going to go after Chad. Going after him in the kind of way that her security team can't."

"After him? Like, how *after* him?"

"You don't want to know."

"Yes, I do. We should call the police."

"Do you want to call the police, or deal with your friend?"

"That's not fair."

"Rhys isn't brainless enough to have someone murdered. But they're going to beat the shit out of him for sure."

"Christ." Who the fuck were the Hellfire boys?

At the end of the hallway, we knocked on the door and Aurora called out, "Come in."

I poked my head through first before entering. "Hey, there you are. I'm looking for you."

She sat up in the bed. When she saw both of us, she sighed. "Surprised you don't have Sloane with you."

Sera sighed too. "Well, Sloane can't keep a secret from Lennox, so I figured you didn't want him up your ass. We're going to grab you and take you back to the townhouse so you can pack for school."

She frowned. "What day is it?"

I took her hand. "It's Monday; classes start on Wednesday."

She huffed. "Oh God, I've been here a whole day, then. All right. I'll get my stuff." Her voice was steady—too steady, maybe. Sera and I shared a worried look.

Sera's voice was low. "Are you going to tell us what

happened?"

Aurora shook her head. "No, I'm not."

I opened my mouth to fight her on that, but Sera took my hand and squeezed it twice, letting me know to stay quiet. Instead, Sera said, "Okay, that's your choice. But in case you do want to talk about it, just know that both of us are here."

Aurora dragged in a deep breath. "Yeah, I just want to forget the whole weekend, get back to school, and get back to normal."

As I watched her gather supplies Rhys had gotten her, I wondered if anything would ever be back to normal. I wondered what normal would even look like now. There was no un-losing Aurora, there was no un-hooking up with Owen, and soon we would all be back at Pembroke, trying to figure everything out together.

That last thought gave me a little hope, though, as we left the Four Seasons.

Together.

Owen and I were together—after everything that had happened.

I had the boy, and the internship, and my friend was safe. What more could I want?

CHAPTER SIXTEEN

Tanith

AFTER THE DEBACLE that was our hunt through New York City, we'd been back at school in Vermont for a few days, and mostly everything was back to normal. Except Aurora. She *wasn't* back to normal.

Oh, she said she was fine, walked around like nothing was wrong, but there was a haunted look in her eyes.

Also, there had been no need to keep secrets from the other Hellfire boys. The cat was already out of the bag. While the boys had all still been at the Montgomerys, Felix—forever the worst—had been going on and on about how fucked up Aurora had been and how badly she'd wanted to party with him and Chad. So now everyone knew.

God, what the fuck was wrong with him?

I'd just finished my morning classes and was charging across the massive courtyard in the snow, heading back to the dorms, when I ran into Aurora at the main doors as she was hopping down the steps toward either the kitchen or the laundry.

"Hey, didn't see you this morning for breakfast. Are you okay?"

She gave me a brief nod with a stiff-lipped determination. "Fine. I wish everyone would stop asking me that."

I winced. "I'm sorry. Probably the worst question to ask you."

She inclined her head downstairs and I followed her to where it was quieter. Most of the students were just trying to go to their rooms, to somewhere warm, so they could bemoan the frigid weather. We entered the colossal study. As she plopped into the couch, I eased my backpack down and shook off my coat. I kept my scarf on, though, because . . . well . . . it was Owen's and it smelled like him.

My belly did a little flip and I had to bite back a secret smile. I hadn't really had time to talk to my friends about any of it. Sera knew, of course, because she was nosy. But while we'd been together, everyone's focus had been on Aurora. No one else had really noticed the change between me and Owen. This was fine by me because I didn't need too many questions or to be the object of ridicule. Girls at school could be giant pains in the ass. So, for now, it wasn't exactly a secret, but we were keeping it under wraps.

I refocused my attention on Aurora. "Have you heard from Felix? Has he apologized for leaving you with Chad? Better yet, has Chad apologized?"

Has Chad encountered Rhys's "friend" yet?

Aurora shook her head. "I don't want to talk about it."

I chewed on my lip. "Aurora, I'm not going to pretend to get it. But I want you to know that you can tell me. Anytime. Even if it's five years from now, I'll be here to listen."

Aurora tossed her jet-black hair from her shoulder and looked down at her hands. "I—" She shrugged and tugged on the hem of her sweater. "It feels so silly to talk about it out loud, you know? Like so trite. The kind of thing that happens on the telly."

I nudged her shoulder with mine. "You don't have to talk about it if you don't want to. But if it helps, I don't watch much television, so it might not sound trite to me."

She snorted a laugh. "Yeah, I guess that's true. Just . . . at one point, Felix had gone to the loo and it was only me and Chad. We were at this bar, and we were playing music on the jukebox, and he was being so aggressively flirtatious, and I was trying to dodge his flirting—and it's just so cliché, you know? I can practically see a television episode playing out the same way. And okay, fine, I had a couple of drinks too. So maybe I—"

I cut her off before she could go down that path. "Stop. Having a couple of drinks doesn't give some asshole the right to put his hands all over you. Do you understand me?"

She sniffled and then nodded. "No, I know. I just . . . I kept going at it over and over in my head, you know? Like, where had I gone wrong?" She shook her head. "Fucking Phineas. I got into another fight with him, as usual, all because Felix and I had danced at the stupid New Year's party at the Yates house. Like, Phin doesn't talk to me, ever. But the moment some other guy is interested, he gets all macho, saying, 'You shouldn't be doing this,' and 'Why are you acting like this?' Like he can tell me what to do after the way he's treated me."

I sighed, wishing I could do something. But I knew even now, even before I'd left for my fellowship, that Phineas and Aurora had had a *thing*. They were in their own little *War of the Roses*, and trying to talk to them rationally about what was going on with them only put you in the crossfire.

"Okay, so Phineas is a dick, but you know that already. What else is new?"

She murmured softly. "Right? He's always an arsehole."

"Right. Phineas was an asshole. And then what happened?"

"You know, I got on my high horse about it. Like I was fucking royalty—which I am, by the way. I should be able to do whatever I want, whoever I want, whenever I want."

"Royalty or not, that's the rule. And fuck that obnoxious wankstain."

She smirked at me then. "Tanith, I didn't even think you knew any dirty words."

I smirked back. I had learned a whole bunch of new dirty words from Owen. "Well, I'm a dark horse, aren't I?"

She gave me the first real smile I'd seen from her in ages. "Yes, you are. So anyway, I was heading out, just to get away from him, and Felix suggested that we go somewhere else fun together, so I said yes. I shouldn't have, but I did."

"Okay, so, you left with Felix, but what happened? Was everything okay then?"

"Well, I thought it was just going to be me and Felix, and I trusted him because we've all known him forever. He was always around, you know? To me, Felix was safe. Then we met Chad at some dive bar in Soho."

"How well do you know Chad?"

"I don't really know much about him. Met him once or twice. He was just some bloke Felix brought around from time to time. But he knew Felix, so he was supposed to be safe."

"Were you uncomfortable in any way? Did he say anything at first?"

Aurora shook her head. "Only once Felix was out of the room. Chad saw his chance, I guess. I got away from him and managed to leave the bar. I can't believe it all started because I'd just wanted to forget Phineas for a night, you know?"

"You don't have to explain yourself to me. Not one bit.

591

I'm not judging you. Hell, I've never even been in love, so how can I even judge anyone?"

Her sharp gaze flickered to mine and pinned me perfectly still. Her eerie golden eyes refused to release me. "Right. Never been in love before, but maybe you know what that's like now."

I blinked wildly. "What?"

"You really think you can hide your relationship with Owen?"

I flushed deeply, feeling the blood rush to the surface. "No, that's not really a secret. I just like a low-profile life." God my face was so hot.

Aurora grinned then. "Look at you all shy and happy. That's his scarf, isn't it?"

I gently fingered the scarf on my shoulders and nodded. "Yeah, it's his."

Aurora nodded. "That's good, Tanith. It's really, really good. And you should be happy."

"It feels weird being happy, you know? I want to be. It's just . . . I don't know if I can trust Owen." Flashes of Bay House came back to me. Memories of his sweet kisses and dirty words. I amended my earlier statement. "Owen is great, actually. Different than I thought, I guess. I just, you know, we're in high school, and I think I might be getting too attached."

Aurora nodded. "Yeah, too attached is the problem. Because, you know, when you're too attached, then it hurts when people leave."

I winced at the bitter pain in her voice. And then she winced too. "I'm sorry. Not that Owen would. Owen is the steadiest of all the Hellfire boys, and he's nothing like Phin. He is cool, calm, and collected most of the time. And you thaw him out a little. Normally, he seems so cold. Aloof. But with you, he's finally got some fire under him, which is nice to see."

"I see what you're doing. Nice deflection."

She reached out and took my hand. "Look, I'm happy for you. And you shouldn't be worried about me."

"Well, you're my friend. So, of course, I worry."

She gave me a small nod. "In case I haven't said, you know, thanks for coming to get me or whatnot, thank you."

"Always. And I'm always here to talk more about it, if you need." I looked at her, at the lights reflected in her gold eyes, and thought of Lennox. He'd been furious when he'd found out something had happened with Chad.

"Have you talked to your brother more? Told him anything else that happened?"

She shook her head. "No. Lennox would lose his shit if he knew how bad it was. He's not rational, you know? Sloane has been great about keeping him calm and occupied and not thinking about it, but he wants to run in and protect me. And since I'm already safe right now, protecting me will just look like murdering Chad."

I cleared my throat, knowing this one was tricky. "Have you spoken to Phin?"

Her eyes went wide and she plastered her whole body into the corner of the couch. "No, I have not spoken to Phin."

"You know full well that he'd want to know if something had happened to you."

"Well, he's not going to know. He doesn't get to know what Chad tried to do. Besides, Rhys took care of him."

I sighed and nodded. "Yes, but maybe we should call the police anyway, so the consequences will be more permanent."

"You don't know Rhys. Likely the consequences *are*

permanent. And the police can't know, Tanith. If they knew, then there would always be a chance the story would leak." Aurora sighed and rubbed a thumb along her forehead. "I can't put my family through that bad press. They've already been through enough with my dad being an unmediated shitpouch. I should have never left my security behind. That was so stupid. I'd just wanted away from Phin."

"You sure you don't want Phin to know all of it?" The rest of us could see the air clearly, that the two of them were actually meant for each other. But they were fighting it. I guessed whatever heartbreak had happened two summers ago had been unforgivable, and yet they still couldn't seem to let each other go.

True to form, Aurora made a face. "He doesn't deserve to know."

"There you are."

I whipped around when I heard the deep baritone voice behind me, and my insides turned to jelly.

Aurora jumped up. "Yup, there's my cue to leave."

I looked back at her. "Hey, Aurora, we're not done yet."

She nodded. "Yes, we are." Then she scooted around with a quick nod.

"Aurora, wait . . ."

With a twirl, she gave me a wave goodbye. "I'll see you later. Oh, and, Owen, if you hurt my friend, Sloane and I will cut off your balls. Have fun." With a tight smile, she bounced out.

Owen's gaze was on mine and direct. "Is she okay?"

I shrugged. "She says yes, so clearly not."

He strode over and wrapped his arms around me, tucking me close. I automatically nuzzled into his neck. "Hi."

"Hello, beautiful. I missed you." I couldn't help but

grin. His voice went even softer as he chuckled. "I can feel you smiling against me."

"You feel nothing."

He ground his hips into me then. "Well, you're about to feel something, all right."

I giggled and then pulled back. "You're the worst."

"Well, I just want my girlfriend to know how much I missed her all day. I didn't get to hold her last night."

"No, because the dorm monitors are on a rampage. Some of the kids who stayed over break were having a good time shacking up in the dorms, so everyone's been on the lookout for infractions. Therefore, not wise."

"I'm fucking Hellfire Club. They can't touch me."

"No, not you. But they can touch me."

"Then maybe we need to make it known that you're mine."

"I think that ship has sailed. We're not being as discreet as we think we are."

He shrugged. "Fine by me. Let the whole world know." He leaned then and brushed his lips over mine.

"Does that include your mother?"

He pulled back and pressed his lips together. "Fuck. No. Okay, I see your point." He glanced back at the door. "But seriously, though, is Aurora okay?"

I shrugged. "Maybe. Maybe not. Something bad definitely happened last weekend, but she's not comfortable talking about it in detail yet."

Owen's jaw went tight. "Was Felix involved more than we thought?"

I could see the worry, the concern, the disgust in his eyes. I just wrapped my arms around him tighter. "She says it was all Chad, which matches what Rhys said when we found her. She won't tell me exactly what happened, but she looks . . . I don't know. Not okay. I can extrapolate, but . . ."

He nodded. "Phin's not talking either. He's beside himself, though. He's acting even more like a dick than usual. Fucking Chad. You know, I've always hated him. He has a way of getting my brother into these messes."

"There were messes like this before?"

His brows furrowed. "No. But you know, they've managed to run around unchecked for a long time. There was one time they went to the city, and he convinced Felix to drop acid. Felix got arrested that night and it was just so humiliating for my parents. They even had to get him to a doctor because he was tripping so bad. It was a mess."

"Jesus."

"Yeah. Then there was the other time Chad hired hookers to come to my parents' house. One of them was underage."

"Fuck."

Owen nodded. "Yeah, a real fucking mess. But Felix actually came through. He didn't mess about with her and made sure Chad didn't either. It was one of the few times I was actually proud of Felix. He took one look at her and knew she wasn't old enough to be there. He found out she was fifteen years old."

I winced. "Where the fuck were her parents? Or Chad's?"

Owen shrugged. "I don't know, but I do know that Felix got rid of the hookers, kept her behind, and waited until Mum came back from wherever she was that night. Mum sorted her, returned her to her parents or wherever the hell she was from. Probably paid her off to make sure she didn't come and point fingers, but I remember Felix was actually worried about her. So, he's not the devil; he just makes the worst choices."

"You know, he thinks you hate him."

Owen's navy-blue gaze searched mine. "When did you talk to Felix?"

"At the van Doren party. On the balcony. He thinks you hate him."

"That's absurd. I don't hate him."

"Well, maybe you tell him that. I don't know."

"Yeah, maybe one day. But anyway, I like to focus on my girlfriend, please."

I laughed. "Have you had lunch yet?"

"Well, if by lunch you mean eating *you* out? I'm all for it."

I laughed. "It's not what I meant, and you know it."

"Fine. I will also give you real food. I can have it brought to my room."

"God, you Hellfire boys, all the special treatment."

"Well, you're my girlfriend now, so you get even more special treatment."

I grabbed my backpack and Owen took it from me, slinging it over his shoulder before taking my hand. "Come on. I can't let you carry that. Also, why are there so many books in here? Jesus."

"I like to prepare for class."

"Wow, okay. We got to get you these books on a tablet because, again, Jesus."

He was so impossibly rich sometimes. "I can only get used textbooks in print form. I can't afford the new digital editions."

He frowned at that. "You shouldn't have to worry about that."

"Well, I do. And anyway, I love my textbooks, thank you very much."

He nodded, and we took the stairs silently as some students were finally starting to mill downstairs toward the kitchen. The ones with dietary restrictions always went there to grab their food as opposed to eating upstairs in the dining hall. Sure, there were gluten-free options and vegetarian options and all that, but those that had real needs and dietary restrictions always came to the kitchen. They had to be sure about food contamination.

I went in as Owen held my hand and then saw Phineas coming down the stairs. Owen gave him a nod.

A muscle in Phineas's handsome jaw pulsed.

"Mate, you talked to Aurora today? Saw her earlier in the study."

Phineas shrugged. "If Aurora wants to talk to me, I'm here. Until then, she's none of my fucking business."

He shoved past us and through the doors, letting in a gust of icy air that swooshed my skirt. I groaned. "Wow, he really hates her."

Owen shook his head. "No, the twat loves her, but he's not owning it. Doesn't even know what to do about it, so he's acting like a prick."

"Speaking of pricks, have you talked to Felix? It sounds like you need to clear the air."

He frowned, and I thought he was going to fight me about it. But instead, he said, "Yeah, maybe it's time Felix and I had a talk."

CHAPTER SEVENTEEN

Owen

I BARELY NOTICED when the car door opened, letting in the noise of New York City. Mum had sent over a feature piece she was thinking of acquiring for *Gotham,* wanting my opinion on if it fit that issue's theme or not, but half my mind was on Tanith, wondering how soon was too soon to pick her up from the *Gotham Girl* offices since my mother was leaving early today for a meeting. So when Felix opened the door and slid in, it took me a minute to tear my eyes away from my phone.

"You look like shit," I observed as the car pulled away from the hospital curb.

Felix rubbed his hands over his face and then slumped back in his seat. "I feel like shit," he mumbled. "Thanks for picking me up, by the way. I thought for sure you'd still be up in Vermont."

"I should be," I said easily. "But I pulled some Hellfire strings. Turns out all my Friday classes can be moved. *Et voilà*, I can be in the city during the weekends with Tanith."

He closed his eyes. "You really like her, then."

"Yes," I replied simply. I liked her so much it terrified me. So much that I couldn't keep my hands off her, so much that I'd snuck her into my dorm room all this week, and I was planning on sneaking her out of the van Dorens' townhouse, where she was staying on her internship days, and into my room at our Manhattan residence.

But I wasn't about to say all that to Felix.

"I was a twat to her at the van Doren party," he said after a minute. "I'm sorry, mate."

"It's not me you should apologize to."

"No, you're—you're right." He heaved a giant breath, his eyes still closed.

I turned off my phone and gave him my full attention. "How's Chad?"

"The same," Felix said tiredly. "He'll live, but it's not pretty."

Three days ago, Chad had been found behind a warehouse in Hunts Point so thoroughly worked over that the person who'd found him had thought he was dead. He'd been recovering in the hospital ever since, and Felix had been going to visit him since, apparently, Chad's parents were in Bora Bora and couldn't be bothered to come home. Since the hospital was on my way into town, I'd offered to drop him by the house before I went on to the Preston Media offices to get Tanith.

Felix's eyes stayed closed as he asked, "You don't know who did it, do you? Who hurt him?"

I could honestly tell him the truth here, because I only knew who called in the favor to have him hurt. "I don't know who hurt him. But, Felix, Aurora is an actual princess. Is it so surprising that there were consequences to him attacking her outside a bar?"

"Owen," Felix said, opening his eyes. "You must know I feel beastly about the whole thing, right? I never thought Chad would—"

I gave him a hard stare. "You never thought he would? Even after the lobster? The acid incident? *The underage sex worker?*"

He flinched.

"How could you not see that he was dangerous to the people around him?"

"I guess I thought those were mistakes. One-offs. Everyone makes mistakes sometimes, hey?" he added with a weak smile.

I shook my head. "Those weren't mistakes, Felix. Those things are who he is. And now someone else was hurt and scared because none of us would act on it."

"Don't put it on yourself," Felix said. "It wasn't your job to—"

"It's *everyone's* job," I interrupted. "It's everyone's job to watch out for monsters, Felix. And the more we make excuses for them—the more we think, *Oh, he's not that bad, and if he gets bad, someone else will do something, so I don't have to*—the more chances they have to hurt someone for real. I knew him better than most other people in our circle. I should have made him leave. I should have warned everyone what he was like."

Felix shifted uncomfortably. "No, Owen, it was my fault—"

"Oh, I am quite aware," I said coldly. "This is not me *unassigning* blame. You deserve all the misery you feel right now for leaving Aurora alone with someone you knew couldn't be trusted."

"I know," he whispered. "I know."

He looked absolutely wretched just then, and while it didn't soften my heart any, I thought of what Tanith had said, of how he thought I hated him.

I didn't hate anyone. That would require too much

601

energy.

I closed my own eyes now, the words so difficult to say they felt stuck to my tongue with glue. But I finally forced them out. "I don't hate you, by the way." The silence hung between us in this wide expanse. "Tanith told me you thought I did."

When he did speak, his reply was slow, confused. "But then why did you tell Mum I wouldn't be any good for her at Preston Media? I'm the oldest, Owen; it should be me answering her emails and giving my opinions on acquisitions and shit. Not you."

I finally opened my eyes, but I didn't look at him. I kept them trained on the window instead, watching the frozen city pass slowly by as we weaved through dense, honking traffic. "I mean this in the gentlest possible way, Felix, but I don't think you'd actually enjoy working at Preston Media as much as you think you would. You're impulsive, flaky, and selfish."

When I finally did look over at him, his expression was stricken. "Is that really what you think of me?"

"It's what *everyone* thinks of you, knobhead." I passed my hand over my face and sighed. "But you're also charming, energetic, and bold. Those are incredible traits to have in business, Felix—just not *Mum's* business. She needs someone quiet and reliable; she needs someone who doesn't care that she will always, always be the center of all the buzz and attention. She needs someone who will check his inbox every day without complaining, who doesn't mind the drudgery of spreadsheets and server crashes. I've never hated you, but I do love you enough to know that you'd die working at Preston Media, and that's only if Mum didn't kill you first."

He was staring at me, gnawing on his lip now. "I s'pose

I never thought of it like that."

Obviously not. "You're good at so many things. Once you decide to actually do them—and to quit hanging around people like Chad—you'll be unstoppable."

"You reckon?"

"Yeah, mate. I do."

He gave me another weak smile then as we pulled up to the Upper East Side house, and I gave him a small smile back before he got out of the car. It wasn't exactly an emotional symphony of brotherhood, but it was the closest we'd come in years.

THE PRESTON MEDIA building hosted the offices of all the group's many publications: travel magazines, food magazines, literary reviews, pop culture rags, and more home decorating magazines than the world needed. The *Gotham* and *Gotham Girl* offices were at the very top, and I was relieved to see they were almost completely abandoned as I stepped out of the elevator. My mother had a meeting on the other side of town, and the other staffers had clearly seen it as a chance to skate out right at 5:00 p.m. since when she was in the office, she disapproved of people leaving before she did.

The offices were empty, that was, except for one gorgeous blonde currently perched in front of a clear acrylic desk, tapping away on a laptop.

She hadn't seen me yet, and something stopped me before I reached her. Instead, I leaned against the wall separating the reception area from the office space and watched her. Watched her type, then spin to the printer, then jump up and run into another room. She came back with a stack of bound *Gotham Girl* issues and flipped through one volume, her face lighting in triumph when she found what she was looking for. She hopped up to scan it, her cute little skirt swinging around her thighs, and then plopped back down in her chair, typing again with a small smile on her face. There was a pencil holding her lush waves into a perky bun, and speaking of perky, the tight jumper she was wearing was fucking criminal. Just looking at her had my cock lengthening in my jeans.

But it was my chest that made me the most uncomfortable as I gazed at her, my chest and my throat. Everything was strangled and crushed in a way that felt oddly good.

She was *happy* here. The kind of happy people on Instagram wrote about, the kind of happy people faked for stock photos. Being here in these offices—typing and scanning and having ideas—meant something to her.

And fuck if it wasn't sexy as hell to witness.

"How's my girl?" I asked, my voice low as I strode over to her desk.

She jumped a little and then laughed. "Scared."

"Of the big, bad wolf coming your way?"

She tucked her tongue in her cheek, smiling. "Does that make me Little Red Riding Hood?"

"It depends," I said, finally reaching her and spinning her to face me. In a second's work, I had her out of her chair and sitting on her desk. "Is Little Red Riding Hood brilliant at fashion journalism and going to run her own Little Red magazine empire one day?"

She parted her thighs to let me between them, a flush already staining her cheeks as she looked up at me with dancing eyes. "Maybe."

I bent down to lick her neck, groaning slightly at the taste of her skin on my tongue. It had only been a couple of days since I'd had her, but I was half-mad from the lack. "You really love it here, don't you?"

"It's only my second week, but yes," she said happily, her hands sliding up to push my wool coat off my shoulders. "It's everything I've ever dreamed of."

I pulled back a little, draping my coat and scarf over her abandoned chair, and I took her in. The blush was in full force now, but it was arousal, not shyness. She had her legs spread so I could see what I'd thought had been thick tights were actually thigh highs.

Fuck me.

Her nipples had beaded into points under her jumper, and I could see the white cotton panties she wore under her plaid skirt. She was the wet dream version of a bookworm, and she was *mine.*

I pressed back in to kiss her, licking at her warm mouth and tasting berry lip balm and coffee. "Is it really everything you ever dreamed of?" I asked as my hands dropped to her thighs to push her skirt up to her hips. "The drudge work? The mind-numbing admin tasks?"

She laughed again, this time against my mouth so I could feel the warm puff of her chuckle as she did. It was fucking adorable. "I love every part of it," she murmured. "And I've just had the *best* idea—or rather, I've found a way to resurrect one of your mother's best ideas. I can't wait to pitch it to her."

"You'll be amazing, I'm sure," I said, my attention on her mouth, on the cotton I'd just discovered with my thumbs. I started rubbing up and down her slit, savoring each whimper she made into my mouth. "My genius girl."

"Owen," she breathed. "What if someone comes back in? What about the security cameras?"

"Back into the office on a Friday night, love? I think

we're safe." I gave her a long kiss as my hand blindly felt around her desk. "And I'll take care of the security footage after—I know the guards. Perk of growing up with my middle name on the building. Which is fortunate because I can't wait until we get back to my place to get inside you."

"Oh God," she said, panting hard. "I need it too. Yes. Okay. Here really fast, and then we'll take our time later."

She groaned as I found what I was looking for—scissors—and knelt. "Hold still, sweet thing. This will only take a second."

I felt her shiver as I carefully slid the scissors between her precious skin and her knickers. With three snips, the way to her sex was free.

"Do you want to go bare again?" I asked, and then growled with pleasure at her eager nod. I tossed the scissors on the desk as I stood and pulled my cock out of my jeans. It was so thick and full already that it nearly pushed its own way free the moment I lowered my zipper, and I wasted no time giving it what it wanted. I used one arm to scoop behind Tanith's hips and then my other hand to guide myself home. With one rough thrust, I was there, fucking this sexy nerd's cunt as hard as I needed.

Her head fell back as I rutted, papers and fine-point markers dropping to the floor as the desk shook. I pressed a thumb to her clit and rubbed the big, fast circles she liked, keeping my strokes the way she liked, too, deep and hard. She came so quickly that I didn't bother to keep the smug expression from my face, but it soon melted away as she wrapped her arms around me and pulled me down so she could suck on my neck. So she could bite and mark me, spur me into toiling harder and faster between her thighs.

The climax came with sweet violence, sharp and shivery. I chased it the whole way, my hips churning as I spilled into her soft, tight pussy, my breaths ragged and harsh. I shoved myself into her over and over again as if I could make her mine from the inside out.

As if I could make her feel the same way I felt.

Feral. Desperate.

Aching for more.

"When we get back to my house, I'm licking this pussy clean," I murmured, kissing her jaw as I pulled out.

"Maybe I'll lick *you* clean," she teased.

I nipped her neck. "No arguments from me." I tucked myself away and then helped her straighten her clothes.

"Ugh," she mumbled. "You ruined my panties, you brute."

"You liked it."

She smiled to herself and hopped off the desk. "Maybe, but now there's jizz everywhere on it—"

"Then," a horribly familiar voice said, "it's a damn good thing acrylic is easy to clean, isn't it?"

We both looked up at the same moment to see my mother standing near the entrance of the office, one perfectly sculpted eyebrow arched as she stared at us.

Shit.

"Tanith, I believe you're working a half shift tomorrow," she said, in a tone that could mean nothing good. "I'm looking forward to seeing you then."

Then she looked over to me, her face betraying nothing except weary disdain. "And, Owen, my son, I believe your trousers are still unzipped."

And with that, she left.

Chapter Eighteen

Tanith

I WAS A sweaty mess. I'd gotten dressed in a fog, only to realize I'd misbuttoned my shirt twice, only then to discover it was stained. My hair was unsalvageable. I couldn't seem to brush the bed head out of it. And I couldn't find one of my favorite flats.

It was a Saturday morning. I'd worked my school schedule so I only had classes on Mondays, Tuesdays, and Wednesdays. Thursdays and Fridays were internship days. But because of the new project I wanted to pitch, I'd signed on for some Saturday half days too.

I was regretting that now. When I arrived at my desk, there was a note with the reminder that I had to see Ms. Preston first thing.

I took my notebook, my laptop, and my tablet with me as I was ready to be fired. I knew there was hell to pay.

You have no one to blame but yourself. You really thought you could just live and be happy. You knew what you were doing.

Owen told me not to worry about it, but God, there was no way Ms. Preston was happy about this.

I knocked on her door and her "Come in" was actually

warm and friendly.

"Good morning, Ms. Preston." Her office never failed to take my breath away. It was a sprawling corner one with glass walls and a vertigo-inducing view.

One day you could have an office like this.

Not if I got fired for that shit with Owen. Honestly, how could I have been so reckless.

She looked up from the files she'd been perusing on her desk, finally noticing me. "Uh, good morning, Tanith. Close the door."

I closed it behind me, and then stiffly walked to my usual chair, but I didn't sit. "You wanted to see me this morning?"

She eyed the items in my arms but said nothing about them. "Yes, love. Why don't you have a seat?" Shakily, I did, and she didn't speak again until I was settled. She folded her fingers. "Love, I'm sure you know what I'm going to say."

I swallowed hard, squeaking out, "Yes."

Her smile was warm as her gaze searched mine. "Obviously, I know about you and Owen now."

I winced. "Ms. Preston, at first, I didn't know that he was your son. He doesn't use Preston and I just didn't know."

"Regardless, obviously, as you know, you can't keep seeing my son."

My stomach clenched. "I—um, I don't understand."

"Look, Tanith, you're great. We adore you here at Preston Media. You are bright. Honestly, you are an excellent writer, and you are going to go far. But this boy, he's *not* for you. He's a Preston and a Montgomery. He's meant for different things. And because of what he's meant for, you will always be in the shadows."

Bile started to turn in my gut, and my palms became

sweaty. "I-I don't see how my relationship with Owen has to do anything with my job. He doesn't even work here."

"My dear, after the unfortunate incident last night, I think you're smarter than that. This isn't about that, love. I know what it's like being married to a *Montgomery*. I knew what was expected of me, and I knew how difficult it would be. And even then, I was still unprepared for for how hard it was for me in his world. I don't want you going down that same path. My life was not what it should have been. It was filled with pitfalls."

"Yes, but you survived, obviously."

"I did. But it has cost me personally. I see that you're like me. And if I'd had someone to guide me when I was your age, to tell me to choose my career and not a boy, I would have done it. Jumped at the chance. And the man Owen is meant to be, you will never, ever have the spotlight. You will have to give up parts of yourself just to make him look good. And that's not for you. I am grooming you personally to be somebody great. This could be your own ticket to achieving that. Don't you want that, love?"

Why was she doing this to me? She knew how badly I wanted this. She knew what I was willing to do. Why? Why would she do this?"

"I care about Owen."

"It's not that I don't think you care about him. I know you do. Which is why you should know the kind of woman he needs. He needs someone who's going to drop everything at a moment's notice. He is a Montgomery. And I know what that means. He is also a Preston. Great things are expected of him. Things that require someone who isn't afraid of not being in the spotlight, because make no mistake, all the trappings of having a public relationship come with scrutiny. This life requires someone who doesn't need to have her own space. I've been watching you, Tanith; you insist on having a voice. And I admire that, love. It's not that I don't want you to have one. I just don't want you to have one with this boy, because it will ruin everything for you. You will not get what you deserve. And frankly, you have worked too hard. What is the point of investing time doing internships if this is what's going to happen? You deserve so much more than to be waiting at his beck and call. Don't you want that?"

"Of course, I want that. I just also want Owen."

"Forget him, my darling. I should have thought this would be easy for you. If you give him up, you get to have your dream. Don't you want your *dream*?"

I saw the devil's bargain she was asking me to make. "I do. I just—"

"Look, I'm not even angry that you lied. That you sat in front of me and pretended all along during your interview, and then you were so excited about this. I'm not even going to be upset that you neglected to mention that you had a boyfriend, which also happened to be my son. Honestly, I understand. But why don't you pick a different boy? Doesn't he have one of his friends available? What about Phineas? I mean, he is a bit of a character, but he's good looking and available, right? And if you need one that's popular, that one works. He's well liked. I know his family. I could do a setup if you like."

The bile threatened to escape now, and I swallowed convulsively to keep it down along with the rest of my feelings that I'd never expressed. "Why would you do that? Don't you care about what Owen wants?"

"I do. But he doesn't know what he wants, and the sooner you realize that, the better. Owen will always do the right thing, love. I want you to be happy. I do, honestly. I want you to have everything that you want. And I think you can have it. But maybe this isn't for you."

"Ms. Preston, truly you can't—"

"Let me be clear with you, darling, this is nonnegotiable. I like you very much. We work well together, and I think you're going to do amazing things. But if you continue down this path with my son, I can't guarantee what will happen."

I furrowed my brow. "But—"

"Don't fool yourself, darling. He will always choose his career. He will do as he's told, and you will be hurt by that. I don't want that. I want you to have some pride in what you can accomplish here and have some pride in what you do. So, don't linger and dawdle and moon over a boy. Like I said, this boy. He won't mean to, but he will break your heart. And well, let's face it, broken hearts get in the way of doing great things."

She turned her attention back to her laptop, and I wasn't sure what I was supposed to do. I couldn't stand. I couldn't talk. I couldn't move. All I wanted to do was cry. But like everything else, I squashed it down and held myself together, determined not to let anything in my way. Determined not to let out a flicker of emotion to this woman. I could do this. I wasn't going to let her control me. Bring me down. I could do this. "Is that all, ma'am?" I asked, and she turned her attention back to me.

"Oh, yes, of course, darling. Yes, that's all. Oh, and, dear?"

I swallowed hard. "Yes, Ms. Preston."

"You have a week to make your decision."

I wanted to do more than cry now. I wanted to scream and shout. I wanted to tell her that she did not control me. But she held my future in her hands, and that future meant I couldn't have Owen. That future meant I would have to give up love if I wanted it. Well, I didn't think I could do this. I didn't think I could do this.

Don't be a fool. She can ruin your career. She can make sure you'll never have a future.

Was Owen Montgomery worth it? I wanted the answer to be yes. But was I willing to risk everything I'd worked so hard for? More importantly, would Owen do the same for me?

When I reached my office on shaky legs, I eased into my seat, set my laptop and notebook and tablet down, and then texted him.

Tanith: *We have a problem.*

Maybe if we talked about it, we'd figure it out. He would know how to handle her because at the end of the day, she was his mother, and she was right. He was hers. So, if anyone knew how to handle her, he would.

Owen

THE FIRST THING I did when I met Tanith at the van Dorens was hold her. Even though she held herself stiffly. Even though she didn't say anything. I knew it was bad. I knew it was bad because she didn't give me that smile that was meant just for me. I knew it was bad because instead of fire and fun, all I had was an unyielding robot. And when she pulled back from my hold, I saw the bags around her eyes behind her glasses. She's been crying.

"Hi, love. I'm so sorry."

"What am I supposed to do, Owen?"

"I don't know. But let me just hold you for a second.

Do you want to talk about it now or when we get back to campus?"

"Campus," she murmured softly.

The long drive to Pembroke was tense and quiet. It wasn't until we were back on campus in my room, lying in my bed with her tucked in my arms, that she finally spoke.

"What am I supposed to do, Owen?" she asked once she finished telling me everything.

I sighed. I couldn't believe my mother had gone nuclear so quickly. Usually, she preferred more subtle tactics to bring me to heel. Going after Tanith was bang out of order. "Look, this is a test, love. She wants to see how committed I am to you. I'll speak to her."

She shifted in my arms. "What kind of test? That's absurd. And I don't think it's a test at all. She was very serious. I choose you or my internship. I can't have both."

"She doesn't mean it, Tanith. Besides, she can't really stop us from being together at school. And in the city, we can stay at hotels. I've seen this game a million times with Felix. She threatens, he does what he likes, she fumes. It's an old game. She's not going to fire you."

"You weren't there, Owen. She was very serious. And what happens when she finds out we're still seeing each other?" She sat up, pushing me away. "I'm not willing to sneak around."

I didn't want to diminish her feelings, but we weren't going to have to sneak. "We don't have to."

"We do. The Preston name adorns two buildings on campus. You think she doesn't have spies everywhere?"

I bit the inside of my cheek to keep from laughing. While I didn't put it past my mother to have spies, I hardly thought she was going to have someone skulking around campus trying to catch us kissing. Also, I was Hellfire Club.

There were a million ways to have a private moment where no one would ever see me. But this wasn't about that. She was scared, so I needed to do something to fix that for her. "Look, I don't want to hide either. When I want to be with you, I want to be with you. And I don't want to steal kisses. I want you in my bed, where you belong, as often as possible. Without the dorm monitors catching us, of course."

She dragged her hands through her hair and shook her head. "Owen, be serious. I need a solution before I have to go back."

"Okay, fine. We could just ignore her request."

Her eyes bulged. "What the hell do you mean ignore her?"

I shrugged. "She clearly wants a response from me. And if I don't give her one, she'll be forced to do something else."

"You're missing the point. You think she wants a response from you. I know for a fact she just wants me gone. I don't think this is about controlling you or whatever. She clearly wants to bend me to her will, and I think I have to comply."

"Bullshit. You're stronger than that. You don't have to do what she wants."

"She was very clear when she told me I needed to break up with you. That you weren't someone I could have. Hell, she even suggested I pick another boy, offering to set me up with Phineas. *Phineas.* Your *friend.* All so I would do exactly what she wants. This isn't a test. If it is a game, it's one she's playing for keeps."

I sprang out of bed then, my feet making a soft thud on the rug beneath my bed. "What the fuck?"

"Yeah, that's why I know she has zero intention for us ever being together. She's going to personally see to it. By any means necessary. To her, I'm beneath you."

Fuck. Bugger. Fuck.

My mother had gone too far now. Fucking Phineas? As if I would allow that. If she wanted to play like that, then it was war.

I forced myself to take a calming breath and sit back on the bed. When I pulled her into me, I cradled her and tucked my chin on her head. "Bullshit. You are a goddess, or hadn't you heard? You deserve to have everything you want. I know this is hard. I will take care of this. I'll make it all okay."

"I don't know if you can, Owen." She sighed. "And I don't know if I want you to. It's my work—my future—I need to be the one to decide what to do next."

"I finally have you in my life. I'm not walking away. Trust me. I'll sort it. She won't control us."

CHAPTER NINETEEN

Owen

THERE WERE TIMES in my life when I truly loathed my mother. Oh, I loved her in that sort of obligatory way that we love our parents, but there were times I *actually* loathed her.

How dare she butt into my life? As of this past August, I was a bloody adult. This was a long-standing habit of hers, deciding who I could be friends with, deciding who I could date, deciding what was best. I lived for summers when I returned to London, met my friends from around the world, had a taste of freedom I could only ever dream about.

But back in New York, ever since she'd established Preston Media here in the city, God, it was like I was being choked. And not in that fun, dirty kind of way.

I would deal with her.

The devastated look on Tanith's face hadn't gone away since we'd returned to Pembroke. Nothing I said to assure her was working. She thought she had to choose the internship or me, and she would have to make her gut-wrenching final decision in a week.

You twat. This was all my fuckup. She was hurting because of me.

All Sunday had been like that. Then Monday, she somehow managed to avoid me. There was no way I was letting that stand, though. She was mine and I was going to fix this for her.

Luckily on Tuesday, I only had one class in the morning, which gave me a chance to get into the city before the end of the workday. My mother thought she was the only game in town when it came to publishing. Preston Media was the extra fluffy cream on top of the cream of the crop. The thing was, for every industry event I'd been forced to attend with her, for every party where I'd been forced to smile, I'd made my own contacts. And if she was willing to dick with me, I was going to dick with her back.

Once I'd set my appointment, had my meeting, and pulled a few strings, I returned to campus late that night via car. I found Tanith downstairs in the study after hunting for her for over an hour.

She lifted her gaze to meet mine and I was struck by how exhausted she looked. "Oh, hi. Where've you been? I'd been looking everywhere for you."

"I had something to do in the city."

Her eyes flared. "Oh my God, your mother? She made you go all the way into the city on a Tuesday? Did she give you a . . . talk too?"

I knew what "talk" meant and there wasn't a snowball's chance in hell I was letting Tanith go. I clamped my jaw shut so I wouldn't curse; that was what I wanted to do every time I thought about my mother. About what she'd done. What she'd tried to do.

Sorry, Mum, but you don't get to do this, this time.

"No, not my mum. Something else, actually."

Her body sagged. "Oh."

"No, it's good. I've figured it out."

"What did you figure out? Did you talk to your father or something? I thought Preston was run by your mother?"

"It is. And Dad, as much as he would try to help, doesn't run the show. When Mum sets her mind about things like the running of Preston, she won't budge. He has no say, so that's the wrong tactic to take."

"Okay, then, what were you doing all day?"

I grinned at her. "Well, I sorted it because I won't give you up."

The corner of her lip twitched. I reached out and rubbed my thumb over her bottom lip, that full bottom lip, thinking of the dirty things I'd done to it and had her do to me. The blood rushed south, then I groaned as I quickly snapped my hand back. "Jesus, I can't have a serious conversation with you when you look like that."

She huffed out a small laugh. "Look like what?"

"Edible. That's the word. Edible."

She shook her head. "I'm not edible, okay? Stop keeping me in suspense. We don't want this to end, but your mother was very clear. It's either you or my job. And I just, I've worked so hard, Owen."

"I know. I know. Look, I met with a friend. My mother loathes her, but she works for *Teen Vogue*. She's a senior editor there. I've arranged for her to give you an internship."

Tanith blinked slowly. "What?"

"Yeah. I've known her for a while. She's been trying to get me to leave Preston. Offered me several jobs. And she and my mother? They had a falling out. Anyway, I told her that I wasn't available, that was going to cause the kind of war she wasn't ready for. But I had another option for her. Someone even better than I was."

I waited for it, the clapping, the squealing, the excitement that would light her eyes and the way she would look at me as if I were the most important person in her life. Someone who had saved her, someone who had fixed everything.

But that wasn't the look she was giving me. Instead, she kept doing a slow blink. Blink. Blink. Blink. "You went to *Teen Vogue* about me?"

I nodded. "It's all managed. You can even have your same schedule. She's waiting for you to call her. Once you do, it'll be all set."

"You *arranged* it? I would call this woman and I would just start an internship somewhere else?"

"Yes. My mother can't control us."

"Your mother?" Her brows furrowed as she spoke softly.

"God, she's the worst. She's always been controlling. Selected my friends, determined who I could see, who I couldn't see in a way that left me no room to grow. And if I didn't do things exactly as she wanted, there were consequences. If I ever fought back, she'd use her influence to get that person out of my life. I'm bloody sick of it. She's not going to run you off. No way. No how."

"So you called in a favor and got me a job, doing God knows what, somewhere else?"

Why didn't she look happier?

"It's publishing. I explained to her your duties, what you did for my mother. She was excited because clearly you know what you're doing. She doesn't have to train you. You can hit the ground running."

"I can hit the ground running."

She kept repeating what I said. But then, also, the tone. It was *off*. Then I really looked at her. Watched her warily. She was *unhappy*. There were no bright eyes. No secret smile just for me. There was no climbing into my lap and giving me kisses like I had envisioned.

"Are you happy?"

She shook her head slowly. "No. Oh no, I'm decidedly *not* happy."

My brows dropped down. "Why the fuck not?"

"Because you . . . after everything you said to me about everything we've been through together, about how much you cared about me, about how you can't stand to be apart from me. After all that, the one thing I needed you to do, you didn't."

I shook my head. "What's your problem?"

"*My* problem? Owen. God, how are you so brilliant but you can't see it?"

"What? You're *angry* with me?"

"Yes, Owen. I'm ticked the fuck off."

"What is your fucking problem? You should be ecstatic. We're together. You have the same exact job. Same responsibilities." I frowned at her. "Unless you don't want to be with me. Unless being with me was a ploy to get to my mother."

More slow blinking. "Wow. So now being with you is a ploy to get to your mother?"

Fuck. That was a miscalculation. "Okay. I'm sorry." I ran my hands through my hair. "I'm just frustrated, and I don't understand what the problem is. I got you what you wanted. You wanted your job and me."

"Yes. I want *my* job. The one I earned. The one I busted my ass for. Not one that you deemed would be good enough."

"It's fucking *Teen Vogue*. Do you know how many people would kill for that job? And I walked in there and got it for you."

She stood then. "That's the problem, Owen. *You* walked in there and got me a job with some chick you probably have shagged seventy-five million times."

I frowned at that. "You're jealous? Oh my God. Look, I'm sure Isabella would, but I'm not shagging her just to get back at Mum."

"Are you shagging *me* to get back at your mother?"

I pushed in my feet then, too, towering over her, glaring at this girl whom I'd just wanted to make fucking happy. Why wasn't she happy?

"Take it back."

She didn't back down, didn't step away. She was forever my goddess, unafraid. "No, I won't. Because what you should have done is gone to your mother and told her how you felt about me. Told her that her attempts to bully me to control you were not okay. What you should've done was fight for me, Owen. Instead, you slunk off into the shadows to try and squirrel me away so that maybe she wouldn't notice I was still around. God, what is wrong with you?"

"What is wrong with *me*? I'm not trying to hide you. God, you should be grateful. We get to be together. You get to do the same job that you had before."

"A job I didn't earn!"

"What, you think your fellowship and the work you've done doesn't factor into doing something for *Teen Vogue*?"

"Oh my God. What I'm telling you is that all that work that I've done earned me a job at *Preston*. I walked in there and *I* pitched *myself*. Stood on my own two feet. Looked at the job application, knew exactly that I was a fit. You walked into *Teen Vogue* and were like, 'Hey, hire my girlfriend.' And so, they did. Which tells me that no matter what, nobody would respect me for my ability."

"You're putting too much focus on that. I did you a favor."

"Wow, you really, really don't get it, do you?"

"No, I fucking don't. Seriously, I can't believe you're fighting me on this. You don't have any other options, beggars and choosers and all that. This is the next best option and you're fighting me?"

She flinched as if I'd hit her. A wash of heat hit me then, scalding all over my ice-prone nerve endings. I knew then something had gone terribly, terribly wrong and my instinct was to fix it. To get it back on even keel where I could come at it from a different way. I reached for her, and she jerked away.

"Don't touch me."

"Tanith, come on. Let's just keep talking about this and figure out where I've gone wrong."

She shook her head. "No. Not if you can't see how you hurt me, how what you just said plays into everything I've ever been told about how I should be grateful for the scraps that I get. Grateful that someone like *you* wants to date someone like *me*. You were supposed to go and fight for me. Not actually believe that you're better than me in some way and that I should be beholden and/or grateful to you for getting me another job because you're my boyfriend. I don't want *another* job, I *want* Preston. That's what I worked for. And instead of standing up to your mother, God, you did what you always do. Went around her. Hid. I should've known from the beginning when you said your mom shouldn't know about us. And I was naive for going along with you, but I see now. You weren't proud of me; you weren't proud to have me as your girlfriend or someone you cared about. I'm temporary, so you hide me. You're ashamed, when I'm the one who should be ashamed to be with you. We're done, Owen."

Shadows coiled around my heart, chasing away all the light as I stared at her. "You can't be serious."

"Oh, I'm plenty serious. I know, me, the scholarship girl, is breaking up with you, the Preston-Montgomery. I know it's a shock to your system, but since you don't actually have feelings, I'm sure you'll get over it."

She marched out of the study. I whipped around to call her back, to wait for her to turn back to tell me she didn't mean it. But instead, all I saw was her ash-blond hair bouncing in its ponytail along her back as she walked out of my life.

CHAPTER TWENTY

Tanith

M Y PHONE BUZZED again, and I threw it across the room. Sloane, without even looking up from her calculus homework, snatched it out of midair before it could hit the wall.

"You could just turn it off," she suggested mildly, her eyes still on her integrations and derivatives.

"Why should *she* have to turn it off when *he's* the problem?" Sera asked, stepping out from our en suite bathroom and bringing the stinging smell of hair dye with her. She wore plastic gloves and an apron I was certain was from a sexy French maid Halloween costume.

"Seconded," Aurora called from the toilet, which doubled as her salon chair when she needed to touch up her roots. "He should turn *his* phone off."

Sloane set her pencil down and finally lifted her eyes from her paper to me. "I have some experience with obsessed Hellfire boys," she said. "And I can tell you that he's not going to stop. You're either going to have to shut off your phone or do something that makes contacting you pointless."

"Do something like break up with him? Because I already did that!" I fussed, throwing myself back on the bed.

"We could try killing him," Sloane offered, in that way that I couldn't be sure if she meant it or not.

Sera popped out from the bathroom again, her plastic gloves covered in black goop. "I propose we crush him to death with stacks of *Gotham* magazines. And then maybe smother him with all that floppy hair of his."

"Seconded," yelled Aurora from the toilet.

I blinked up at the ceiling, both touched by their loyalty and so miserable I couldn't stand it. "I just wish I'd never known him," I whispered to no one in particular. "Never seen him, never had a crush on him. Never kissed him that night in Ibiza. Because this is so much worse than him not knowing I exist. This is him knowing me, *having* me, being with me like no one else ever has . . . and still thinking I'm beneath him. That I need his charity. That I don't know what's best for myself. That one dream is as good as another for me because I should be grateful for any crumb I get."

I realized I was crying. *Again.* I was *so fucking sick* of crying!

"I can't wipe her cheeks because of the hair dye," Sera said as she came next to the bed. "Sloane."

"No, no, I don't need anyone to wipe my tears away—"

Sloane sat down on the bed next to me, and with the seriousness of a sensei tending to a student's injury, carefully lifted my glasses and pushed the tears off my cheeks.

I relented, sniffling, because it felt good to have someone be with me while I cried. It felt good not to be alone, even if that was the only part of right now that felt good.

"He was supposed to choose me," I finally said, my voice barely audible. The tears kept coming, hot and fast. "He was supposed to choose *me*."

The bed sunk near my feet and I looked down my body to see Aurora at the end. She had a plastic cap over her hair, and Sera came back from the bathroom having peeled off the gloves that came with the home hair dye kit, although she still had the frilly apron on over her long-sleeved pajama shirt and fleece shorts.

"He's a mummy's boy," Aurora declared.

"He's *conflicted*," Sloane countered, and Aurora smacked her on her leanly muscled arm.

"Whose side are you on, Lauder?"

"It's an impossible choice, his mother or Tanith," Sera said. "And that's what he should have said to his mother. He should have gone to her and told her that she isn't allowed to give you or him any kind of ultimatum."

"Well, he *didn't* do that," Aurora said. "Ergo, he's dead to us. Right, Tanith?"

"Right," I said, without any conviction. "Right. Dead to us."

"Or just plain old dead," volunteered Sera, and Sloane agreed with a silent, watchful nod.

Later that night, as I lay in my bed and cried—quietly, so I wouldn't wake my sleeping roommate—I realized what really hurt about all this. It wasn't only that he'd thought I needed his charity, that I should be grateful for anything someone cared to toss my way. It wasn't only that he'd chosen to keep the peace with his mother instead of standing up for me.

No.

It was that he'd clearly intended to keep me a secret from her all along.

All that talk of being his, of *tomorrows*—it was all just good marketing, wasn't it? All salesmanship. He'd said whatever he had to so he could keep fucking me. He had never planned for me to be anything more than his convenient little fuckdoll. And the kicker was that when I'd been with him—when he'd been staring down at me with those deep, navy eyes and his full lips parted in lust and awe—I'd felt like so much more. I'd felt like I'd never felt before in my life: that I was brilliant and wonderful and that I deserved every dream I could think to have. *He'd* made me feel like that. And so to have him be the one to dash it all away—to show me I didn't deserve anything but scraps of a relationship, that I didn't deserve being fought for, that I didn't deserve not to be a secret . . .

It was unbearable.

And that was what Elizabeth Preston had tried to tell me, wasn't it?

He won't mean to, but he will break your heart.

She'd known exactly what was coming for me. And even though she'd been the one to light this awful fire in the first place, I found myself appreciating her honesty. If she were going to hurt me, she'd face me like a woman and do it to my face. She'd do it in the open air, with nothing to hide.

Unlike her son, who would stab someone in the back and then expect them to be grateful.

No, Elizabeth had made it very clear that to her, I was worth something. That I had every right to my ambitions, and my only mistake would be to surrender them to stay with a boy who didn't give a shit about me anyway. A boy who wanted to keep me a secret and had clearly planned on discarding me at the first opportunity.

Owen had wanted more tomorrows?

He didn't deserve a single one. All of my tomorrows would belong to *me* and no one else.

✧   ✧   ✧

I BEGGED MY counselor to let me take Wednesday off so I could go down to the city. I had to get to the Preston Media offices—and more importantly, I didn't think I could dodge

Owen for a single day more. He'd taken to hovering outside my classroom doors, to hunting for me at lunch, to banging on Sera's door whenever he thought I might be in there. Sera, Sloane, and Aurora together couldn't put him off, not until they'd threatened to call the headmaster about it.

"Tell her I just need to talk to her," he'd said through the door, his voice miserable. "Please."

"Nein," Aurora had snapped back in flawless German. "*Arsch mit ohren! Einzeller! Hosenscheisser! Kotzbrocken!*"

I'd taken French instead of German, so I had no idea what any of that meant, but given the evil smile that'd crept across Sloane's face, Aurora had really let him have it. It had been quite pleasant to witness.

But headmaster threats and German insults would only hold him off so long, and so I needed to leave Pembroke before he could get to me. Before he could remind my traitorous body how good he made it feel. Before he could coax my weak heart into believing any more of his lies. And so with the counselor's help and the van Dorens hiring me a car, I was in the city by Wednesday afternoon, striding through the blustery late January air to get to the glass-enclosed warmth of the Preston Media building.

Even though I'd already made up my mind last night about coming here, even though I'd already practiced what I was going to say, I was still chewing hard on my lip as the elevator swept me up to the *Gotham* offices.

What if Elizabeth had been lying about giving me a choice—what if she meant to separate me from Owen *and* cut me out of my internship?

Or what if she had been baiting me . . . testing me? Seeing what Owen was worth to me in some misguided attempt at maternal protection?

What if she refused to see me at all?

I was a mess by the time the elevator doors opened, but I tamped everything down—the last few days of tears, rage, and German insults—until I felt nothing but calm. Until I felt completely numb. As cold as the late winter day outside.

Just like a Preston, in fact.

I walked past reception, showing my intern's badge, and then strode into the offices. I knew there was every chance Elizabeth was at a meeting or supervising a big shoot or not in the office at all. I knew there was every chance this would not end well for me.

But that was the lesson, wasn't it? Whatever happened next, I was the only one who cared enough about me and my happiness to even try to reach for it. Yes, maybe I'd end up without the internship of my dreams; yes, maybe I'd end up accidentally burning the biggest bridge in this industry.

But if I was going to salvage any part of my life after Owen had broken my heart, then goddammit, this was going to be it.

I turned the corner to Elizabeth's glass office. Fate was with me, it seemed, because she was inside alone. When she saw me standing at her door, she gestured for me to enter.

"So," she said as I stepped in and stopped in front of her desk. "Have you made up your mind?"

Your son made it up for me, I nearly said. *He broke my heart and he'll never understand why.* It was the trouble with rich boys, really. They would never understand love the way we poor girls did—as a lifeline, as a way to be our truest selves apart from anything else. They would never understand what it meant to feel like you were *enough*. They would never know how important it was to feel that you mattered on your own.

Lesson fucking learned.

I sat down in the chair across from her. "I have."

CHAPTER TWENTY-ONE

Owen

IT DIDN'T MATTER what I did. Tanith was still not speaking to me. I'd done everything right. I'd gotten her what she wanted. An opportunity. A great one. Maybe not Preston, but still, who on earth could be mad at *Teen Vogue*? Why did it matter to her if it was Preston or not?

Was this about me?

I never smoked. I hated it. But sometimes, when I was stressed out, I came out onto the roof of the boys' dorm, and the lingering scent of tobacco soothed me. It was weird. Probably because my father had smoked a pipe for years, and it reminded me of all those times I'd tag along with my brother after him, chasing him down, wanting to be just like him. Felix smoked all the time now, like a bloody chimney. He insisted only the coolest people smoked.

Subtext, I wasn't cool. Nevertheless, the roof was where Rhys found me.

"Ah, there you are, douchebag."

I rolled my eyes. "What's your fucking problem with me now, Rhys?"

He shrugged. The collar of his coat that he had tucked up flapped slightly in the wind. "Nothing, other than you've been moping around here for the last couple of days. You're hardly any fun."

I coughed a laugh as the wind bit into my skin. "Sorry, mate, I'm not the fun one, remember?"

He sighed and rolled back on his heels. "This is some bullshit. Why do I fucking keep doing this? *I'm* not the good one." He pulled his hand out of his pocket and jabbed a finger toward me. "*You're* the good one. You or Keaton. Because, let's face it, Phineas is a degenerate. And Lennox, well, he's just whipped. It's actually sad."

"Do you have a fucking point, Rhys?"

He shrugged, and the bite of winter crawled up our spines, threatening to sap all our heat like some fuckwit Dementor. "My point is, douchebag, that you fucked up. And now we're all paying the price for it."

My brows snapped down. "What the fuck are you on about?"

He shook his head. "I hate it when you guys put me on the spot. I'm the one with the attitude. The one who can't be fucking bothered."

"You keep saying that, but you keep butting in, don't you?"

"Yeah, I'm butting in because you idiots keep fucking with my equilibrium. *Twat.* You're the one who normally says don't be a dick, but I'm witnessing you being a dick right now."

I rubbed the back of my hand over my brow. "I fucked up? What, with bloody Tanith? Since when do you care about her?"

Rhys threw both hands up and started to pace. "That's the point; I don't. But you do. You became a total fucking sap because of some chick, which I don't fucking understand. It's like the lot of you got your dicks wet, and suddenly, your brain cells stopped working."

I chuckled low with that. "Oh yeah? Should we invite van Doren here? See what that does to your brain?"

He narrowed his gaze at me. "Don't bring her up to me."

I was the one who knew. One time during our second year, some guy had been bragging he'd felt up Sera van Doren. I knew it was a bullshit lie because I knew Sera couldn't stand him. But Rhys, Rhys had proceeded to get drunk for a solid week. He and Jack Daniel's had become fast friends then. And I'd sat with him up here on this very fucking roof, listening to him rant on and on about how he didn't like her, how he didn't care, but then he'd told me how he'd really felt. That even, just once, he wanted her to look at him like he was a human being instead of some monster. When I'd asked him about it later, he'd denied ever saying those things, but he knew I knew.

"Okay, fair enough. You don't want to talk about van Doren, I don't want to talk about Tanith."

He shifted uncomfortably. "I'm a dick. The biggest dick. I know that. But you, you're not a dick. It's not natural to you. You said the wrong fucking thing when she needed you. God, it's like you fucking idiots can't see. Don't be stupid."

"Me? You're saying it's me who's being stupid? You poke at Sera at every fucking turn."

"Sera and I are a different game. Don't bring her up, Owen. You, Montgomery, you have a fucking chance. You were almost a lost cause when Tanith started to like you. Why? I don't fucking know. But there you have it. She has poor taste. Which is fine. But you, what you should have said, dumb fuck, was, 'Mum, you're a bitch. Tanith isn't quitting her job, and I'm not breaking up with her. So, deal with it.' Instead, what you said was, 'Hey, Tanith, instead of actually dealing with my interfering bitch of a mother, I got you a *different* job. It's not the one you wanted, nor is it the one that you worked your ass off for, but this fixes the problem you have without me actually having to lose anything.'"

The bottom gave out in my gut and my legs felt quite wobbly then. My first instinct was to fight back, to slap him off his bloody high horse. But it was what he said, that last bit there, that had me thinking. It was *my* fault. My mother was a great person, but she could be a killjoy sometimes. And the fact she'd caught me with my pants literally unzipped with Tanith was reason enough for her to go deep freeze and hyper controlling. To be fair to Tanith, before she'd gotten the internship and things were first starting with us, she hadn't known who my mother was. So, there was that.

I'd never thought to bring it up because it didn't matter. But Mum had been Mum. And I'd done what I had always done, fix it in the most efficient way possible. But this was about Tanith. She didn't need my efficiency. She needed my love, and I'd treated her like she was Felix. A problem to be solved. I realized to fix this now, I had to lose something too. Not just her.

Rhys was right. It was irritating that I'd fucked up. My method of fixing things had only made matters worse. Now Tanith thought I didn't love her. And she wasn't coming back unless I did something to stop it. If I didn't at least fight for Tanith, I was going to lose her.

I glowered at Rhys and he shrugged. "Eh, don't be mad at me. As you say, you're the fuckup here. God, we're goddamned Hellfire Club. We're emperors among kings. And so far, fucking Keaton, fucking Lennox, who's an actual prince, and fucking you have each taken a goddamned arrow to the heart. Weak. You might know about van Doren, but she's never taking me down. I keep her at a nice, safe distance. That weak part of me that wants her? I will manage to kill it one day. Just to save me from being common like you idiots."

I chuckled. "You know, Rhys, I see beyond you. I see you pretending to be the beast, but you're not. And I know why you're the way you are, but you're not the devil you want to be."

"Fuck you, Owen."

I grinned at that. "Yeah, mate, I love you too."

That only made him scowl. I knew better than to touch him. He might be an inch shorter than I was, and we were built the same, but he was meaner than a viper snake when he wanted to be. And any suggestion that he had feelings was enough to make him angry enough to win. I didn't feel like a broken nose or a black eye.

"Fair enough. Go on pretending you don't care. But one day, van Doren will come for you, and I just might sit back and laugh while I watch it play out."

He scowled more and then turned his back, flipping his collar back into place, and his shoulders hunched slightly. He really wasn't the devil he thought he was, but that wasn't for me to tell him. That was for him to figure out on his own. In the meantime, I knew exactly what to do to get Tanith back.

✧　✧　✧

I HADN'T BEEN able to leave school that week, and my schedule was brutal as I had several tests. But as soon as they were done, I sent for the car and headed for the city. Tanith still hadn't spoken to me. And every Thursday and Friday, she was gone, so I hadn't really seen her for over a week. Still, I searched for her in the hallways, longing to get a glimpse of that ash-blond hair and that smile that I had to work for to see.

My mother was unrelenting when it came to getting what she wanted, but I didn't care. What was she going to do to me? She needed me. I mean, of course, there was Felix. But he wasn't good legacy material. And so, I was it. And while it would be a fight, she had no choice but to give me what I wanted.

The tricky part was, I did want Preston Media. It was my legacy, and I craved it. I was good at it. Push came to shove, while I had a lot to learn, I was ready to take over one day. I could run that business and I had ideas for it. Most of the work I did was remote. I wrote some articles, but where I really thrived was on the business side. So, a few mornings a week, I was on calls with Preston Media in London going over finances and projections traffic. Making the numbers make sense gave me such a buzz.

Whenever Mum let me help on planning meetings, I flourished, so she knew of my interest and intent. But I couldn't let that thwart things because if she smelled fear, I was dead in the water.

I went directly to Preston Media, not bothering to go home first because my mother was barely there. I wouldn't catch her. I was waved in without so much as a security check because, hell, my middle name was on the damn sign outside, and I was in and out of here often enough, security knew who I was. One of the guards, Charlie, with a big round belly and a cheerful face, waved at me.

"Owen, my man, how is it going?"

"What's up, Charlie? How's it, mate?"

He gave a thumbs-up with a smile. Charlie and I once bonded because he'd been watching Premier League and I'd been waiting for Mum to finish work. He was a huge man.

"Mum is still upstairs?"

"Yeah, she hasn't come down yet."

"Thanks."

I took the private elevator all the way to the top floor, like I had done a thousand times, but none of those thousand times mattered like this time. I saw my mum in her office, no doubt grilling an assistant for having sent the wrong thing to somewhere. God help him. The bloke stared like he'd been through war, and his face was really red from the embarrassment. When he left, I knocked at her door as I leaned on the jamb. "I see nothing ever changes. How many assistants have you got this year?"

"He's tougher than he looks. He'll last."

"If you say so. How is it, Mum?"

"As happy as I am to see you, Owen, I'm a bit surprised. It's Friday, and surely you're not here to see Tanith. Don't you have something planned to get up to with your mates?"

I clenched my jaw, determined not to rise to the bait. "No. I'm here for you."

"Right. Oh, how did your paper go, by the way?"

I rolled my eyes. "Mum, school isn't the concern. It went well, though. I got an A, as expected."

She nodded her satisfaction, mirroring my same expectation. Not out of any real concern or curiosity.

"Mum, actually, I'm hoping to make this quick, but can we talk about Tanith?"

Her brows furrowed. "You're not really going to do this thing, are you, Owen?"

"Actually, I am."

"You should have told me you were seeing her. It was

very embarrassing for me not to know my son was dallying with my intern."

"What makes you think I was dallying, Mum?"

She chuckled. "Please, you're my son. I know you better than anyone else. Besides, what I saw was clear enough reason for me to do what I did. Not like you're serious about some intern of mine. Where did you even find her?"

"Mum, we go to school together."

"Yes, but she doesn't seem to be the kind of girl that you'd be interested in. She needs this internship, love. She's a scholarship kid. You can't possibly run in the same circles. Not to mention she's had a . . . different set of experiences. She might find it difficult to keep up with you and your friends."

I clamped my jaw down and then took a deep breath. "For your information, she's kicking my ass in all of our classes."

She pursed her lips then. "I know. She's very bright. I can see that. But I'm not going to tolerate you wasting precious time and getting serious with a girl like that. She's hardly even your type."

"And what is my type, Mum, since you know me so well?"

She laughed. "Oh, love, if we have to do this, all right. Fine." She sat back. "You like someone with a bit of flair, a little bit dirty, and someone disposable, because God forbid you have to get complicated and actually get emotions involved. You need your social equal who understands that sometimes you will be aloof and cold, and it's her job to pick up the slack. Tanith Bradford is not that. She'll demand more from you."

I wasn't sure what was more shocking, the fact that she understood me so well, or that she decided Tanith wasn't a possibility for me. "Yes, you're right. I picked disposable girls for a reason. And that's a bad thing, Mum. I feel so much with her. Every single day, I'm being challenged to actually express myself and not keep everything so tightly controlled." I was pouring it all out. But it was what I needed to do if I wanted Tanith back.

She chuckled. "Oh, please. That's enough. You're not seeing her anymore. She's far too bright to get caught up in that because you will dispose of her."

"Mum, please, *that's* enough. I need you to hear me out. You—you messed up with your ultimatum. You shouldn't have pushed it in the first place. Making her choose like that will never get you what you want. She will leave, and she will never come back, even though you are grooming her to be a Preston. Because while she will be grateful, she will never forget that you told her she wasn't good enough for your son."

Her brows lifted. "That is hardly what I told her. What I told her was—"

"Yes, I know what you told her. But you and I both know that you've been very controlling with my life. Since I was a child, I had to have just the right friends, go to just the right schools, do just the right things, because God help you if I turned out like Felix. But what you can't see is that Felix just has to find his own way, and you fucked him up so bad by not teaching him how to do that. What you can't see is that my control makes me a block of ice. It means that I will never have any meaningful relationships, and that's even worse. At least Felix feels something and has a sense of who he is. You messed up because Tanith will leave, and so will I. I've only ever wanted to be a Preston. But seeing that all you want to do is keep me the way that I am and not have me grow makes me realize that I need to be somewhere else."

Her eyes went wide. "You would do this? You would throw away your whole future?"

"I'm not throwing it away. I'm growing. I'd rather grow here at Preston, but it doesn't have to be here. That's up to you. You're either done interfering with my life, or I walk. And that includes Tanith, if I can even win her back, because I cocked it up. That wasn't all you. It was half me. So, I need to resolve that."

My mother pushed to her feet. "Owen, understand what you're saying here."

I gave her that smile. The cold one that said I really gave no fucks what someone thought. "You know, Mum, I've had a million girls try and force me into something. They learn very quickly, as will you. I never bluff. I don't lie. I know exactly what I want and what I don't want. Your choice. You can butt out of my life and out of Tanith's and assess her purely on her ability to do her job. Don't attempt to make it twenty times harder just because you're angry. Or you can lose us both. And, like I said, if Tanith leaves, I guarantee you, she won't come back."

She narrowed her gaze at me with the same navy-blue eyes that I had. "You're serious about this? You're serious about her?"

"Yeah. For the first time in my life, I had *the* feeling. It sat somewhere in my chest and I couldn't let it go."

Her lips twitched. "Well, I see."

"Good." I stared at her. "You're not going to fight me?"

She shook her head. "No, because I see that set of your jaw, that angle of your head. You're so much like your father. He chose me too. You have the exact look he had on his face. I know there's no budging you. So, I guess we're keeping Tanith."

"Yeah, only if she'll have me, because I fucked up."

She sighed and sat back down. "Well then, why don't you prove you're my son and do something amazing to fix it?"

"Oh, I plan to."

CHAPTER TWENTY-TWO

Tanith

THE MEETING WAS nearly over when Elizabeth closed her agenda folder and leveled her dark blue gaze at the rest of us in the room. I was sitting in the corner, taking notes on a laptop, and the senior editors were crowded around the table with Elizabeth, glossy photographs between them. They'd been discreetly answering emails and browsing restaurant menus for lunch while running through feature ideas for the August *Gotham Girl* issue, but now that Elizabeth was watching them, they all straightened up and became models of attention.

Elizabeth nodded at her executive assistant who brought up a scanned-in page from a vintage *Gotham Girl* issue. A scan I recognized because I'd just sent it to Elizabeth last week after informing her I'd chosen my publishing future over the right to call her asshole son my boyfriend. (Well, I'd said it more politely than that.)

She hadn't responded to the proposal I'd sent along with the scan yet, but now here was the scan projected onto the meeting room wall, and then there was my proposal, neatly printed and bound into slim packets that were being handed out by her assistant.

My cheeks started warming like I was sitting in front of a fire, and I could feel the answering flush creeping up my neck.

"So, Tanith sent me a very interesting idea last week," Elizabeth said, getting to her feet. "When I founded *Gotham Girl* in the nineties, one of our signature features was a section dedicated to essays written by our readers. We'd have one essay per issue, submitted with a matching photographic essay or original artwork made by the author. It was a way for young people to speak directly to other young people about the things that mattered most in their lives. We pulled the feature in the early aughts because I thought that blogging would erode the need for it. But as you can see in the proposal here, Tanith has made a compelling argument for why that's no longer the case. Why a platform as expansive and respected as *Gotham Girl*'s should be available to young people—especially those who need their voices amplified most."

Elizabeth gestured to her assistant without looking over at him, and he changed slides to a brand-new mockup of the "Speak" feature with lorem ipsum text and stock photos where the essayist's pictures would go. "I've talked it over with our art director to make sure there's a way to aesthetically and energetically match it to the contemporary iteration of *Gotham Girl,* and I think it will be a good fit. We've made it our mission in the last few years to move this magazine from more than fashion and pop culture to global issues and *culture*-culture—both criticism and commentary. Including the voices of young people writing on these themes will strengthen that vision immensely." She turned and looked at me, her gaze cool but approving. "I'm grateful to Tanith for her insight on this, and for finding an angle to make the 'Speak' feature relevant again. It's the kind of ideation and creative strategy that will earn you an editor's seat one day, Miss Bradford."

My whole face was absolutely on fire now, but in the best possible way.

I managed to squeak out a "thank you" and survive the rest of the meeting, which mostly centered around how to launch this revived feature and publicize the call for submissions. Since this was an online launch to start, we had some room to play with.

Elizabeth wanted to use the magazine's annual Valentine's Day party paired with a quickie online contest to generate buzz, with livestreamed snippets of teen contest winners reading poems and essays aloud.

Marketing *really* liked that idea, and all of us left the conference room with to-do lists as long as our arms.

As I stood to leave, Elizabeth called my name. "Miss Bradford—Tanith."

I turned to look at her. Sometimes, like now, when she exuded that haughty, icy air, she reminded me so much of her son that it physically hurt me.

I dropped my eyes to the table between us. "Yes, ma'am?"

"I meant what I said, you know," she told me. "In the meeting. This was a good idea, and it's the kind of thinking that's about making the publication stronger instead of simply gaining a byline. That's rare in ambitious young people like yourself. Hell, it's a problem I have with my own bloody senior editors sometimes. I'm impressed."

"Thank you, ma'am," I said, feeling terrified and victorious and also slightly miserable because my heart acutely aware of the price I'd paid to earn Elizabeth's praise. Even though it was a price I needed to pay for the sake of my own pride, it still hurt.

Badly.

"You know, I—" She paused, and now it was her turn to look at the table. "I wanted to say that I'm sorry. For whatever it's worth, and I know it might not be worth much now, I regret . . . interfering. Owen's father and I have a strong marriage and a deep friendship, but creating a singular vision from two powerful backgrounds wasn't easy. He was the scion of the Montgomery Media Group. I was the daughter of Prestons—their rivals from across the pond. Finding a way forward was often painful, especially when it became clear that I possessed a drive and capacity for strategy that he did not. There was a time, before he relented and allowed me to acquire the publications from Montgomery Media that I'd turned around, when I braced for divorce papers at any moment."

She lifted her eyes to mine. Briefly, the mask was completely gone, and there was only the vulnerable woman underneath, her mouth curved in unhappy memory. "I loved him," she said finally. "Even at the time, I knew he was the love of my life. And to have this impossible choice driving us apart when we already shared a life and had planned a future together—it was the most unbearable kind of pain. I wanted to spare you that."

"I think you did," I said, but she was already shaking her head.

"I should have remembered the rest of my own history. Because my husband and I *didn't* divorce. He sacrificed his legacy for my future and has never resented me for a moment. He gave me the gift of support and trust—even in our darkest hour when I was ready to believe the worst of him. I should have been ready to trust him all along . . . and I should have trusted you and Owen to make your own mistakes and find your own way forward. I shouldn't have asked what I did of you, and I hope that you'll forgive me for it."

"I do, Ms. Preston," I said, and it was the truth. It had been cruel and heavy-handed of her to force me into such a choice, but at least she had gone about it in a direct, honest sort of way. And . . .

"And you were right," I told her. The admission was painful, but it felt good too. Like a relief to speak the truth out loud. "You were right about Owen, because he did break my heart. He did care more about keeping the peace with you than understanding what I wanted or needed. It was better that it ended now than . . ."

Than what? Than after you gave yourself to him? Than after you fell in love? Because you'd already done those things anyway. It still hurt just as fucking much.

"Than later," I finished lamely.

She studied me for a long minute and then nodded. "You know yourself better than I do, Tanith. But please consider that I do not know my son as well as I thought I did, and he might be ready to prove both of us wrong. Or maybe I knew the old him. The him before you."

"Are you telling me to forgive him?"

She lifted an elegant shoulder. "I'm his mother. It's my job to see him happy."

A thousand responses crowded against my lips— irritated ones, hurt ones, pleading ones. Finally, I found the most diplomatic one. "First, you wanted me to break up with him. Now you want me to forgive him? That's very disorienting, Ms. Preston, unfair, too, and I think you know it."

She didn't seem to mind my forthrightness—indeed, she actually smiled at it. "What I want or know is irrelevant to the matter at hand. My son can be quite tenacious when he wants to be, as can you, I suspect. I only wish to invite you to consider that Owen and I are both aware of the mistakes we've made and hope to do better in the future."

"The only future I have is here at *Gotham Girl* and in this industry," I said with some finality. "There is no future with him."

✧   ✧   ✧

THE NEXT FEW weeks passed in a blur. Between schoolwork, commuting to the city, my usual intern work, judging the "Speak" contest entries, and helping plan the Valentine's Day party, I was *exhausted*. Each night, I dropped into bed and fell asleep immediately, and each morning, I woke up feeling like I could sleep for five more days and still be tired.

I needed it that way, though. Memories of Owen—of his low, accented voice; his sensual mouth; his filthy, filthy words—would filter in the moment my thoughts wandered. I'd be riding in the van Dorens' hired car down to the city and suddenly relive the brutal ecstasy we'd shared inside the pool house. I'd be waiting for a *Gotham Girl* attachment to load before I sent an email and then hear his laughter, warm and open, in the snowy, morning light of his bedroom. I'd be brushing my teeth and remember how it felt to hold hands on campus, to snuggle against his chest, to feel him stroke my hair . . .

It hadn't been real, I'd remind myself fiercely. *You were just a dirty secret he'd always planned on keeping from his family.* But a weak, awful part of me still missed it all. Still missed him.

It *hurt* loving someone who had hurt you first. It hurt more than anything in the world. So it was better to work and work and work rather than feel anything at all.

Especially since Owen had clearly taken the threats and *kotzbrockens, whatever the hell that meant,* to heart and had stopped trying to see me. He'd also stopped trying to call or text or DM, and when we saw each other in class, he kept his distance—although I could always feel the heat of his stare on me. As if he were looking at me while remembering every shocking, urgent thing we had done together. As if his hunger for me seared the very air between us.

I'd leave the classroom with shaky legs and damp panties, barely able to keep my breathing under control, barely able to keep myself from running to him, tackling him to the classroom floor, and mounting him right then and there.

He can never fix your heartache, but there are other aches he can fix . . . my traitorous body would purr to me.

But I knew I was lying to myself. Hadn't I already learned the hard way? I couldn't *just* have sex with Owen. I wished I were like Aurora and could fool around without my heart getting involved, but I couldn't.

I couldn't untangle my yearslong crush from the feel of his lips moving over my skin, from the expert press of his fingers on all my secret places. I couldn't untangle his warm, happy laughter from his moans, or the way he'd praised my writing from the way he'd rhapsodized about my pussy. They were all one and the same to me.

If I decided to scratch that itch, I'd only be condemning myself to more pain in the end.

So it was good that he kept his distance. It was what I'd *wanted*, after all—for him to leave me alone. But it felt like another goodbye too. A final one. Like he was agreeing I had no place in his world or in his heart.

Like he was agreeing it had been a mistake, after all.

CHAPTER TWENTY-THREE

Tanith

IT WAS PREDICTABLY cold and gloomy on Valentine's Day, and it matched my mood perfectly. I'd never cared I was alone on Valentine's Day before, but I *had* always indulged myself with romantic fantasies of Owen coming to find me, confessing his love for me, and kissing me senseless. Now all those fantasies were utterly poisoned. I knew the brutal blueblood behind all that floppy hair and irresistible accent. I knew he would never confess his love to me—and certainly not romantically—moreover, he would never kiss me like how I'd used to imagine it, with his hands stroking my face and his expression full of tenderness.

No, Owen kissed like he fucked. Dirty. Less *Pride and Prejudice* and more Pornhub Premium.

I knew I had a deep sickness because even now as I arrived at the Brooklyn event space—an old renovated factory we were using for *Gotham Girl's* party and the "Speak" launch—the thought sent a bolt of heat shooting between my legs.

Fuck. Would I ever be rid of wanting him?

"Tanith!" Elizabeth's executive assistant Skyler called, rushing over. He already had hectic blotches of pink in his cheeks and a look of panic in his eyes. "Thank God you're here. There's so much to do, and Elizabeth is getting here in two hours. If she sees the space like this"—he waved at the room, which currently was a debris field of stacked chairs, lost-looking catering staff, and a guy sitting on a speaker while looking at his phone—"she will *murder* us. Like Morelli-style whacking. Sleeping with the fishes. Taking a dirt nap upstate. Pushing up—"

"Got it, Skyler," I said, shucking off my coat and draping it over a nearby folding table. "Put me to work."

✧ ✧ ✧

BY THE TIME Elizabeth arrived, the venue had been transformed. The brick walls were hung with large prints of vintage "Speak" photographs; a plexiglass wall had been erected with plenty of colorful markers nearby so guests could draw pictures and write messages; and lights had been strung everywhere, giving the space a cozy, yet industrial feel. The DJ was standing by, the catering staff had trays of playfully deconstructed finger foods ready to go, and a bar was all stocked with a menu of adorable mocktails for our guests.

Of course, being Elizabeth, she merely nodded at Skyler, me, and the others, and then walked off to find her seat. But a nod from Elizabeth was like a Nobel Prize from anyone else, so we all heaved a sigh of relief and then went to our various event posts. There would be a mingling hour of music and snacks, then the "Speak" contest winners would read their entries aloud, and finally, there would be dancing until eleven, when the event would end, and we would send our guests home. I was responsible for keeping the DJ and emcee on schedule and livestreaming the contest winners, but after that, I'd be free to hide until it was time for cleanup, which I planned on doing. There was something about being around so many happy people when your heart was broken. . . . It was jarring, uncomfortable, like trying to move through a jostling crowd with an open wound.

Guests trickled in—mostly students my age but a few adults, too, local librarians and a few parents—and the music started. I was making sure everything was ready on my phone when two slender hands covered my eyes.

"Guess who?" a British voice chirped.

"She only knows one girl with a British accent," someone else said.

"If you did that to me, I'd elbow you in the solar plexus," someone else said calmly.

I spun around to see Aurora, Sera, and Sloane standing in front of me. "Guys!" I exclaimed, elated and totally confused. "What are you doing here?"

"Well, a little birdie told us—"

Sloane *did* elbow Aurora in the stomach then, and Sera cut in smoothly. "We knew how much work you put into this event and we wanted to see everything come to fruition. Plus, no one should be alone on Valentine's Day, and we were all going to be alone anyway."

"Not me," Sloane said, but then she gave me a small, evil smile. "But it's good to tease Lennox a little. I don't want him getting complacent."

"Well, whatever the reason, I'm glad you're here," I admitted, giving them all quick, tight hugs. "I was feeling a little sorry for myself."

"We knew you were too proud to ask for company," Sera said.

"Because we would be exactly the same way," added Sloane.

"Not me!" Aurora said, and then looked around. "This looks amazing, by the way."

"Thanks," I replied, leading them on to an empty table near the stage. "There're drinks and snacks, and they should be reading the entries in about fifteen minutes. I'll be livestreaming them, but then I'll be able to hang out with you for the rest of the night."

"We'll see about that," Aurora said with a wicked grin, and Sloane elbowed her again.

"We're looking forward to it," Sloane said seriously, and I left them with a reluctant smile. I wished I could sit with them, be near them, hear them arguing. It was a real palliative for a broken heart, being with my best friends. Even if it didn't cure me entirely.

Soon it was time for the winners to read their entries, and I had my phone ready and mounted on a tripod as the emcee announced them one by one to the stage. The essays were a mix of funny, heart-wrenching, and brilliant, and all the winners read them with clear, strong voices and incredible presence. By the time the last one finished, all of *Gotham Girl's* social media accounts were blowing up on my phone with people commenting and sharing posts everywhere, along with the link where young people could now submit their own "Speak" essays.

We'd done it.

I'd done it.

I hadn't really had time to appreciate it until just now, as the final winner was exiting the stage to huge applause, but I'd made this happen. This was my idea, and now it was a real thing that lived in the real world. And maybe nothing would ever feel like loving Owen felt, but this was close.

It was really fucking close.

The applause died down and the emcee leaned into the

microphone. "We have one final reading tonight, people."

We do?

I shot a look over to Skyler by the stage, but he didn't seem perturbed at all, like he'd known this was going to happen. But it hadn't been on the program, and even if it were only a five-minute reading, that was five *fewer* minutes of dancing, and was I supposed to livestream this one too—?

"In the spirit of Valentine's Day, this is a poem about love called 'One More Tomorrow,' read by Owen Montgomery."

Shock buzzed up my spine and along my nerve endings like sharp, fizzy static, rendering all my senses useless. I could barely hear, barely see, barely feel anything but an exhilarated kind of panic as Owen took the stage and strode to the microphone with his usual arrogant energy. He was wearing a thin sweater over a button-up shirt and tailored pants, an expensive watch on his wrist, and a slightly loosened tie knot visible above the neck of the sweater, as if he'd been nervously tugging at it moments before. But even with the untidy tie and his sleeves rolled up, he still looked miles and miles more mature than any other teen boy here. He looked every inch the future gentleman.

Only I knew the carnal beast that lived inside him.

My hand shook as I hit the button to go live, and it was next to impossible to breathe as I watched him search for my face in the crowd. When he found me, he offered me the same smile he gave me that first night in Ibiza. A hook to the corner of his mouth, like I'd pleased him.

It sent an automatic shiver right through me.

He held up his paper and began reading, half the audience immediately sighing at the cool melody of his accented voice.

"When I asked you for one more tomorrow,
I didn't know if that would be enough.
When I asked you for one more tomorrow,
I knew there had to be an us.

I wanted everything from you,
And I gave nothing back.
I wanted everything from you,
And I wanted you trapped.

With me.
For me.

I was wrong,
And it brought me so low.
I was wrong,
Now I've lost one more tomorrow."

The words were validating by themselves, but the way he read them—honestly, hoarsely—with despair scrawled all over his face . . .

I was crying. Silently, miserably, maybe even a little happily, I didn't know. I was so fucking mixed up. For him to be here, saying this out loud, in *public* . . .

Owen raised his gaze from his paper and found mine. "I was wrong, Tanith," he said into the microphone, his voice breaking. "I'm sorry."

And to the sound of the entire room swooning, he exited the stage.

Chapter Twenty-Four

Owen

I HAD TO get to her, I had to talk to her, but I was stopped by a phalanx of women at the stage stairs: my mother, Sera, Aurora, and Sloane.

All of them normally scared the shit out of me, but it looked like murdering me was off the table for now. My mother drew me into a sudden, fierce hug—so unlike anything she'd ever done that I had to remember it was customary to embrace in return.

"I'm proud of you," she said. "The poetry was mediocre, and you're hardly destined for laureate status, but I'm so proud that you did something to get that girl back."

"Thanks for that, Mum, and I don't have her back yet," I said, extricating myself from the hug.

"That's for damn sure," Sera jumped in. "You better go find her and finish what you started."

"Grovel," Aurora clarified. "You need to go grovel."

"Very hard," Sloane added. "Much grovel."

"And I have your permission to grovel?" I asked. I didn't need them to like me necessarily, but I wanted them to know I was sorry and that I was going to do better. I wanted them to know that from now on, Tanith was safe with me.

More than safe. I would let her shine as bright as she wanted, and I would never try to hide that shine from anyone again.

"You have our permission," Sera said regally. "But if you fuck it up again, that's on you."

"Wise words," my mother said.

Sera grinned. "I thought so too."

"Serafina, good to see you again," I heard my mother say as I started striding away as fast as possible to find my girl. "Have you ever thought of a career in publishing . . . ?"

Tanith wasn't where she'd been during the readings, and a quick scan of the room revealed she wasn't anywhere else either. I was about to panic when I saw the plexiglass wall covered in words and pictures and scribbles. A flash of blond hair moved behind it, barely visible behind the colorful graffiti.

I was done with all pride by this point. I ran right for her, coming around the wall, and skidding to a stop.

"Tanith," I said, breathing hard. "Goddess."

She turned, and it was like being kicked right in the bollocks looking at her. It nearly drove me to my knees. The pain and hope shimmering in her summer-sea eyes, the soft mouth, the flushed cheeks. She was wearing a short black dress, and the bodice was low enough that I could see how hard she was breathing too. It would take nothing to shove her skirt up to her waist, free myself, and plunge inside.

In fact, I was shaking with the need to do it. Shaking so hard that my voice came out rough and shivery.

"I'm so fucking sorry," I told her, meaning it with every ounce of my being. "I wanted to take the easy road—I wanted to have you, and I wanted to have you on my terms. And I can see what a selfish fucking thing that was now. I can see why it hurt you. Why you *should* be hurt by it. I want you back, but you have to know that if you decide to take me, I will never, ever hurt you like that again. I don't want—I don't want to hide you or to control you or for you to ever feel beneath me in any way. I just want to watch you be amazing. I want to help—but only when and how you ask for it. I want to be there, in the shadows, supporting you. Loving you."

Tears slid down her cheeks as she smiled at me.

"I'll be there loving you anyway," I said softly, approaching her slowly and reaching up to wipe a tear off her cheek before it could reach her mouth. "Even if you say no. Even if you walk away right now, which is what I deserve. I'll be there loving you anyway. Always. For every tomorrow."

Her face crumpled then, and she hid her face against my chest.

"I want to hate you," she said, crying, and then I was crying too, but I didn't care. I didn't care because I was holding her again. Even if it didn't last, even if she were about to tell me she never wanted to see me again, at least I got to feel this one last time. Her body against mine. Warm and perfect.

"You should hate me," I said. "I was a right cunt, and you know it."

She laughed through her tears, her shoulders shaking a little. "You were. And I do." She tilted her face up to mine and found my gaze. "But I don't hate you," she whispered. "I miss you and I want to be yours again. I want it to be like it should have been in the beginning—no secrets, no charity. Just us."

I lowered my face to hers, exulting when she allowed me to brush my lips over hers. "What are you saying, Tanith?" I asked her, slipping my finger under her chin so she had to keep looking at me. "What do you want?"

A small smile played over her mouth, and before she leaned in to kiss me again, I could see her flush deepen along her cheekbones. "One more tomorrow, Owen Montgomery. And if you play your cards right, maybe a few more after that."

I gave her a long, hard kiss, my tongue finding hers and laying claim, savoring her sweet and minty taste. "As many tomorrows as you want, goddess. They're all yours."

EPILOGUE

Owen

"**O**WEN!" TANITH HISSED at me. "Our parents are here!"

"They're in the auditorium," I murmured, not dissuaded in the least from my occupation. I was on my knees and lifting the hem of her graduation robe to see if she were wearing knickers. And—ah, brilliant—there were no knickers to be found. Just silky, golden curls and the tight seam of her cunt.

"But the library isn't locked, what if someone comes in—*oh*—"

"They can't see us back here," I assured her as I tickled my fingers across her soft skin. She shivered above me, her hand going to my shoulder to steady herself as I rubbed gently against her clit. "And you can't tell me that you didn't want this very thing to happen. You can't tell me that you omitted wearing knickers this morning because you *didn't* want to be fucked in your valedictorian robes."

"But not in the library—*Owen*—!"

I'd buried my face in her curls while she was talking and then given her a long lick—a wet, hard one with the flat of my tongue on the needy little berry at the top of her pussy.

Her hair had grown back, and I almost preferred it. "It won't take long," I promised, already pushing her thighs apart and giving her two thick fingers to ride while I serviced her clit. "You know how fast you come when we're doing something dirty and wrong."

She swore, but then both her hands were in my hair, and she was properly riding my face, arching against the bookshelf behind her, panting up at the ceiling.

I grinned evilly against her pussy. My dirty girl couldn't hide her dirty secrets from me. Public sex, filthy sex, rough sex—she secretly craved it all. And while I'd never thought I'd be the public, filthy, rough type of geezer, either, this girl brought out the brute in me. She made me wild and desperate and crazed until nothing mattered but touching her. Tasting her. Losing myself inside her.

It took only another minute to get her there, to feel her pussy quiver against my touch, and then I was on my feet and inside her within seconds, our robes draping around us as I plunged deep and buried myself to the hilt.

God.

Her thighs around my hips. Her hot pussy around me. Her gorgeous, flushed face right there for me to kiss.

Maybe we could find a way to stay here forever . . .

Except my Tanith was too wonderful for that, and I'd never deprive her of that moment on the stage. She'd worked so blasted hard for it.

"My genius girl," I crooned in her ear, grinding against her and savoring the feel of her wet silk massaging my cock. "My clever little valedictorian. You're going to go up on that stage full of me, aren't you? You're going to walk up there with your thighs all slick from all the filthy things you just did and you're going to give your little speech about hard work and the future and no one's going to know the things you do in the shadows with me because you just can't help yourself."

"Yes," she moaned. "*Harder.*"

"You want more, baby?" I asked, nipping at her ear. "You feel wild with how much you want it?"

"I want to make *you* lose control," she panted, her hips lifting to meet my strokes.

"You've done that since Ibiza," I replied, unwrapping her legs from my waist and setting her carefully on her feet. I spun her around, guided her hands to the bookshelves so she could brace herself there, and then I hiked up her graduation robe and guided my tip to her slit again. She was slick enough to part beautifully for me, but it was still a stretch. I could still see the obscene way my organ parted her cunt to rut inside. "You've made me wild ever since that first kiss— wild to have you as my own."

In this position, I could easily stroke her clit, which I did as my other hand greedily palmed her breast.

"And you're going to be mine for a very long time, aren't you?" I purred, knowing it wasn't fair to ask this when I had her hovering at the edge of a climax. I didn't care. Ever since I'd come so close to losing her, I knew I would do anything to keep her. Even if it meant keeping her so well-pleasured that she decided to have me around just for orgasms.

"Yes," she breathed, her body tightening around me. "A long time. Harder, Owen. I'm so close."

"My good girl needs it hard between her legs, doesn't she? She can't even make it half a day without my cock."

She moaned her assent, rocking back to meet me thrust for thrust as I worked the stiff bud at the top of her cunt. And then in only a few more seconds, she was falling over the edge again. I wanted to fuck her like this forever, with her pussy fluttering its pleasure around me, with our robes shoved up to our waists, with this raw, urgent lust coursing through my veins . . . but I couldn't. Not yet, at least.

"After graduation," I said, my voice rough and hoarse with my impending orgasm, "you're mine. Four weeks. All fucking mine."

She had a break before she started her new official part-time job as an editorial assistant at *Gotham Girl*, and I planned to take advantage of it. She'd worked her arse off for years both at Pembroke and at her fellowship and internship, and she deserved some rest and relaxation before she dove back into the hustle and bustle of publishing life. (Obviously, in this case, rest and relaxation meant *my tongue in her pussy for hours at a time*.)

"Yes," she replied in a sensual rasp. "I can't wait. I'm going to ride your face every single day."

The image had me growling, licking my lips like a hungry wolf. Then I was abruptly unloading into her, spurting my release deep into her pussy and practically snarling as I did so, grabbing her hips so I could pump even deeper. So I could claim her even more. Because when she dropped her robe and tidied up her hair, she'd go on that stage and she'd belong to the world. She'd belong to herself and to the future she'd fought so hard to make a reality.

But when we were alone, she belonged to me.

And I planned to keep it for as many tomorrows as she would let me have.

✧ ✧ ✧

Thank you for reading!

We hope you loved Owen and Tanith's scorching hot story. You can read an extended bonus epilogue for FREE right now…

www.dangerouspress.com/blueblood

And there are more books in the Hellfire Club series…

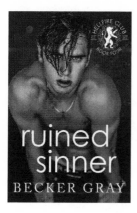

It's no secret that Aurora Lincoln-Ward hates Phineas Yates, but what most people don't know is the reason. Last summer, Phineas broke Aurora's heart in the worst way, and she promised herself then and there that she would never fall prey to the sinner of Pembroke Prep again.

But now sin is in the air.

And the Hellfire Club's number one sinner has his sights set on her…

You can find RUINED SINNER on Amazon, Barnes & Noble, Apple Books, Kobo and Google Play now.

Have you read Keaton Constantine's scorching hot book?

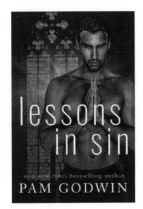

Be sure to check out LESSONS IN SIN. Keaton's youngest sister, Tinsley is in a different prep school... this one with a stern headteacher.

There's no absolution for the things I've done.

But I found a way to control my impulses.

I became a priest.

As Father Magnus Falke, I suppress my cravings. As the headteacher of a Catholic boarding school, I'm never tempted by a student.

Until Tinsley Constantine.

The bratty princess challenges my rules and awakens my dark nature. With each punishment I lash upon her, I want more. In my classroom, private rectory, and bent over my altar, I want all of her.

You can find LESSONS IN SIN on Amazon, Barnes & Noble, Apple Books, Kobo and Google Play now.

The warring Morelli and Constantine families have enough bad blood to fill an ocean, and there are told by your favorite dangerous romance authors. See what books are available now and sign up to get notified about new releases here... www.dangerouspress.com

About Midnight Dynasty

The warring Morelli and Constantine families have enough bad blood to fill an ocean, and their brand new stories will be told by your favorite dangerous romance authors.

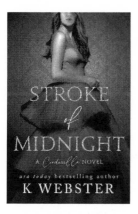

Meet Winston Constantine, the head of the Constantine family. He's used to people bowing to his will. Money can buy anything. And anyone. Including Ash Elliot, his new maid.

But love can have deadly consequences when it comes from a Constantine. At the stroke of midnight, that choice may be lost for both of them.

You can find STROKE OF MIDNIGHT on Amazon, Barnes & Noble, Apple Books, Kobo and Google Play now.

"Brilliant storytelling packed with a powerful emotional punch, it's been years since I've been so invested in a book. Erotic romance at its finest!"

– #1 New York Times bestselling author Rachel Van Dyken

"Stroke of Midnight is by far the hottest book I've read in a very long time! Winston Constantine is a dirty talking alpha who makes no apologies for going after what he wants."

– USA Today bestselling author Jenika Snow

Ready for more bad boys, more drama, and more heat? The Constantines have a resident fixer. The man they call when they need someone persuaded in a violent fashion. Ronan was danger and beauty, murder and mercy.

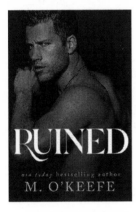

Outside a glittering party, I saw a man in the dark. I didn't know then that he was an assassin. A hit man. A mercenary. Ronan radiated danger and beauty. Mercy and mystery.

I wanted him, but I was already promised to another man. Ronan might be the one who murdered him. But two warring families want my blood. I don't know where to turn.

In a mad world of luxury and secrets, he's the only one I can trust.

You can find RUINED on Amazon, Barnes & Noble, Apple Books, Kobo and Google Play now.

> "M. O'Keefe brings her A-game in this sexy, complicated romance where you're left questioning if everything you thought was true while dying to get your hands on the next book!"
>
> – New York Times bestselling author K. Bromberg

> "Powerful, sexy, and written like a dream, RUINED is the kind of book you wish you could read forever and ever. Ronan Byrne is my new romance addic-

tion, and I'm already pining for more blue eyes and dirty deeds in the dark."

– USA Today Bestselling Author Sierra Simone

Get intimate with the Morellis in this breathtaking new series…

Leo Morelli is known as the Beast of Bishop's Landing for his cruelty. He'll get revenge on the Constantine family and make millions of dollars in the process. Even it means using an old man who dreams up wild inventions.

You can find SECRET BEAST on Amazon, Barnes & Noble, Apple Books, Kobo and Google Play now.

Haley Constantine will do anything to protect her father. Even trade her body for his life. The college student must spend thirty days with the ruthless billionaire. He'll make her earn her freedom in degrading ways, but in the end he needs her to set him free.

These series are now available for you to read! There are even more books and authors coming in the Midnight Dynasty world, so get started now…

SIGN UP FOR THE NEWSLETTER
www.dangerouspress.com

JOIN THE FACEBOOK GROUP HERE
www.dangerouspress.com/facebook

FOLLOW US ON INSTAGRAM
www.instagram.com/dangerouspress

COPYRIGHT

Made in the USA
Monee, IL
16 May 2023

33667313R00390